NEW ZEALAND FICTION
General Editor Bill Pearson

The photograph reproduced on the front cover and on these pages is an N.Z. Official Photograph printed in A. E. Byrne, *Official History of the Otago Regiment, N.Z.E.F. in the Great War 1914–18*, Dunedin 1921, and captioned 'German Prisoners carrying out Wounded'.

ROBIN HYDE

Passport to Hell

The Story of James Douglas Stark, Bomber, Fifth Reinforcement, New Zealand Expeditionary Forces

Edited and Introduced by
D. I. B. SMITH

'There is to me something profoundly affecting in large masses of men following the lead of those who do not believe in Men.'—WALT WHITMAN

AUCKLAND UNIVERSITY PRESS

First published by Hurst & Blackett 1936
Revised Edition 1937
This edition 1986

Typeset by Typocrafters Ltd
Printed in Auckland, New Zealand,
by University of Auckland Printing Services
ISBN 1 86940 009 7

Contents

Dedicated on Starkie's behalf to
The Rev. George Moreton
On mine, with gratitude,
to Dr G. M. Tothill

Introduction

Passport to Hell is the story of 8/2142 Private J. D. Stark, Fifth Reinforcements, Otago Infantry Battalion N.Z.E.F., his youth in New Zealand and his experiences in the Great War of 1914–18. He returned to New Zealand disabled and without skills and like many soldiers found enormous difficulty in adjusting to civilian life. His drift into marriage, prison, violence, and occasional labour is told in another of Robin Hyde's books *Nor the Years Condemn*.[1] He survived the outbreak of World War II, married—for the third time—a twenty-three-year-old, Peggy Christina Linton, and suffered the ironic indignity for one of his former daring, of receiving two anonymous white feathers (*Otago Daily Times*, 10 January 1940). He died in Auckland on 22 February 1942, of bilateral broncho-pneumonia with toxic myocarditis, betrayed finally by his wounded lungs. He was buried in the soldiers' section of Waikumete Cemetery by his friend the Reverend George Moreton, to whom he had asked Robin Hyde to dedicate *Passport to Hell*.

Hyde first heard of Stark through her investigative journalism on prisons for the *New Zealand Observer*. She joined the *Observer* in 1931 just after it had doubled its size, increased its price and aggressively sought more readers, believing that 'there is a place in Auckland and the provincial district for an informative, illustrated, topical weekly, presenting not so much the ordinary news of the week as the news behind the news and comments thereon'.[2] Or as Hyde put it in a letter to J. H. E. Schroder: 'We are trying more or less, to steal "Truth's" thunder without their unpleasantness: that is, to write bold & free as other papers mayn't, but certainly not to haunt divorce courts & put harassed housemaids in the headlines.' Following up this policy she 'interviewed several convicts & wrote a pungent article about Mount Eden Gaol'.[3] (*N.Z. Observer*, 9 March 1931: 'A Convict's Life in Mount Eden: Unpalatable Truths about Auckland's Prison Fortress'.) Details from this article were to find their way into

Passport to Hell[4] but as far as I know she did not hear about Stark at this point. It is interesting however to find how convincing she was in writing of prison conditions for in the same letter to Schroder she observes, 'And here was a compliment: the prison chaplain told me that the authorities spent hours hunting through the files for a convict named Robin Hyde!' When, over a year later, she came to write an article on the chaplain, George Moreton, he drew her attention to a figure immediately recognizable as 'Starkie'. Moreton had shown her letters from former prisoners requesting help:

> There is one from a gentleman whom we will call Sammy—which isn't his name. During the war, this man saved the Hon. Downie Stewart's life, pulling him out of a bombed dug-out. He was absolutely fearless, and his chest is literally tattooed with bullet wounds. In Wellington he was once concerned in an assault cause, and got the worst of it. Mr Downie Stewart sent him to a private hospital and paid for a bottle of brandy—but this unfortunately was left beside the patient's bed. Sammy revived somewhat—and when the doctor came in, he found a distinctly tipsy patient, in a cheerful frame of mind. This man sends occasional telegrams to plenipotentiaries in Wellington. 'Dear Gordon, About ten wolves at the door, waiting your O.K. for job', may be regarded as a new one on the Hon. J. G. Coates. Mr Moreton is blithely addressed as 'Young fellow me lad', or 'Dear George'. Yet this man, married now and passionately devoted to his wife and children, keeps his little home spotlessly clean, and hopes one day to pay back the 'one tin jam, 2 lbs butter, one tin baking powder' for which he now has to ask the D.P.A.[*][5]

It was not until February 1935 that Hyde returned to Starkie, this time to interview him for a book.[6] That she may have kept him in mind over those years is indicated in an undated letter to Schroder in which she describes her hopes for the book and continues: 'It was a queer true terrible story—the story of a living man . . . that simmered until written.'[7] Mid-way through March she was sufficiently confident of completing the work that she made over a half share in the royalties to Stark which he promptly assigned toward a furniture debt: being the proceeds 'from the sale of a book now being written by Miss Iris Wilkinson concerning episodes of my life as a soldier in the New Zealand

*Discharged Prisoners' Aid Society.

Expeditionary Force'.[8] On 27 March she notified Schroder of her determination: 'Am likewise going to complete a very queer sort of writing job which I've undertaken and which may be either a book or a nightmare when I've finished. It will take me about three months to finish the job I am doing.'[9] However, within a month she announced triumphantly to Schroder:

> The book that might have been a nightmare is finished. It is a nightmare, but I think it is a book—Harder, barer and more confident—It's the story of a soldier—he exists and I know him very well. His queer racial heritage—he is half Red Indian, half Spaniard—has taken him into desperate places: prisons, battles, affairs. With it all he's something of a visionary and —in physical courage—unquestionably heroic—I wrote the book because I had to write it when I heard his story, and because it's an illustration of Walt Whitman's line—'There is to me something profoundly affecting in large masses of men following the lead of those who do not believe in man.'[10]

As George Moreton remembered it, he had initiated the writing of *Passport to Hell* sometime in the winter of 1935:

> It must have been somewhere about that time that one morning, a slight woman with an interesting face and a lame leg swung into my office on a walking stick. Her name was Iris Wilkinson although, perhaps, she was better known to most people under her pen name 'Robin Hyde'. She was inconspicuous enough until she began to talk and then you instantly realized that the person sitting before you was not ordinary; the acuminated intelligence behind the sensitive face made you feel like a ponderous galleon awkwardly trying to avoid the lightning shot of a nimble frigate. I forget most of what we talked about that morning but I do know towards the end of our conversation I asked her if she would like a good story: her smile was tolerant. 'I should very much,' she replied, 'I must confess a weakness for good stories.'
>
> I leaned over and drew a package from my desk and handed it to her—it was the diary of James Douglas Stark, bomber in the Fifth Regiment, N.Z.E.F., during the Great War. I can recall the excited pursing of Iris Wilkinson's lips as she turned the pages of the document and the way she laughingly waved her stick as she left my office. And that was really the genesis of *Passport to Hell*, a book which a well-known English paper described as '. . . wild and strange as anything any warbook writer has remembered or imagined'.[11]

It is highly unlikely that Starkie kept a diary. Soldiers were officially forbidden to do so,[12] and he certainly did not have the temperament to which diary keeping is natural. But he recognized the sensational nature of his experience and hoped to make something of it. It is also probable that like other men who had performed brave acts and not been officially noticed, he wished to be recognized. As Ernest Atkins complained: 'I was recommended for a medal five times. The grievance about it all exists in my mind to this day and is the main reason for writing.'[13] In any case in 1926 Starkie was writing to Downie Stewart about his 'book': 'Downie let me know about that book of mine soon as you can because if it is jake I will finish it.'[14] Eight months later he mentions a book, again in a letter to Downie Stewart, on this occasion writing from prison: 'I have been on a book and I am just arriving in Armentiers in the Bombers with you.'[15] It is impossible to tell if this work was in the package which George Moreton handed to Robin Hyde, but she certainly possessed a very sketchy and overwritten account of a number of Stark's adventures. It is contained in a black exercise book, part of Derek Challis's collection of his mother's papers, and written in a hand quite unlike that of Robin Hyde or of Stark. Inside the left front cover is an inscription in Stark's writing: 'C. Murphy, No 1 p.1–89 inclusive 7/9/29'. The writer is clearly a novice, for he notes down 'Useful Books': 'The Commercial Side of Literature', 'Journalism for profit', and 'How to write a short story', and there are rough drafts of different material interspersed with vocabulary lists. I assume that Stark met him in prison and hoped that he would 'ghost-write' his experiences. Murphy on the other hand, hoped to break into print with Stark's story, and get out of prison. This emerges from the draft of a letter from Murphy to Stark on folio 30 of the exercise book:

> Since writing this book of yours I have decided to continue on in the business. I have always had a flair for writing and wish to utilize the time here in something of use to me when I leave. Now I wish to suggest that you let me remain the author of yours not as to any spirit of greed but that it may give me a chance to have other things published which I intend writing. Again should any money be forthcoming for your book I don't want any of it except of course at your own desire. My object is to break into *print*. With your book as a lead I shall undoubtedly have the chance of a lifetime, not only in gaining

prominence in print but as a lever to get myself out of this.
I'm absolutely alone with no influence of any description and am striving to do the best I can for myself. With my writings and stories in print I've at least a chance. Coupled with this of course I am depending on your influence with J.G. [Coates?] to get something done. Believe me Doug there is no selfish wish in my effort to shine as the author of your book that will remain a secret between you J.G. and myself. You can explain things to him and I'm sure he will understand. Nominally, the authorship and rights remain absolutely as you choose, also any acruing monetary proceeds. It is the *lead* I want.

When you leave and let me have your address I'll send from time to time such stories as I can finish. With the first book a success you ought to be able to get them accepted without trouble and incidentally collect a few quid.

On folio 19 verso, Murphy seems to have tried out his title and intended *nom de plume*: 'Dawes Bently author of Doug Stark Bomber'.[16] The interest in the Murphy manuscript lies in the fact that where the same incidents are described as in *Passport to Hell*, there are small but significant differences.[17] Robin Hyde's was not the only imagination at work; Starkie changed his story to suit his hearer. Hyde does not seem to have used the Murphy manuscript but gone straight to Stark and made notes while he talked. She also asked him to write down some of his experiences[18] but was unsatisfied with the result. When he talked, she was able to see quickly what was happening. As she explained to J. A. Lee later when commenting on *Passport to Hell*: 'I think some bits of it are pretty good—The realism is because when people talk about things they have seen and known I can see 'em like little pictures, or think I can—maybe it's only an unusually clear knack with words taking shape so quickly that it seems like a visual image—Anyhow that is how it worked with Starkie—I tried getting him to make notes—it was hopeless, no marrow in it at all. When he talked, though I havena my shorthand and the book was in no wise dictation, I seemed to get it without difficulty.'[19]

Hyde's original title for her work on Stark was 'Bronze Outlaw' and having completed it she sent it off to the agents A. and P. Watt in England who recommended it to the firm Denis Archer, who finally accepted it towards the end of 1935: 'Archers have accepted "Bronze Outlaw"—terms to come. By the way the title, which sounds like that of a Western, and is altogether vile, may be changed.'[20] Archers placed it with the publishing firm Hurst and Blackett who seem to have suggested the title *Passport to Hell* which did not altogether please Hyde as she explained in a letter to Johannes Andersen, the Alexander Turnbull Librarian: 'Hurst and Blackett are bringing out my first novel, "Passport to Hell" (I did *not* choose the title, by the way), early in March of this year, and I suppose that means it will be in New Zealand before Authors' Week. This is a book of New Zealand background except for some wartime sequences.'[21] Hurst and Blackett seem to have seen the work more as war memoir than as New Zealand novel since a great deal has been cut from the original version[22] (much of it presumably at their urging) including the last two chapters which bring Starkie back to New Zealand and underline the New Zealand moral to his life. Hyde observed to Lee that the two chapters had had to be dropped but for different reasons: 'I had two post war chapters one about Mt Eden gaol, but had to cut 'em out owing to considerations of space and libel.'[23] There is no doubt that all the cuts can be defended aesthetically; they result in a sparer, less diffuse work, with a stronger narrative line. It is also clear that the same process has gone on here as Dr Patrick Sandbrook has discerned in his study of *The Godwits Fly*,[24] namely an effort to eliminate subjective authorial intrusion, but the *result* is to focus much more vividly on Stark and his wartime experiences.

I noted above that Stark had also used his imagination in relating his life story (after all he had been polishing these accounts of his encounters for some eighteen years prior to meeting Hyde) and nowhere is this more clear than in his account of his father, which Hyde followed carefully, expanding where it seemed to her there was an opportunity to do so.[25] The result is an exotic figure: a giant full-blooded Delaware Indian from Great Bear Lake with a beautiful Spanish wife, killer of Higgins the bushranger, publican and breeder of gamecocks and race-horses. Some of this is undoubtedly true, but either Stark knew little about his father or he recreated him for Robin Hyde's benefit. These inventions were not confined to Hyde; the Murphy MS contains an account of Stark fondly leaving his parents on the way to the War when his father had been dead five years. If we are to believe the obituaries of Wyald Stark, he was a different, rather more impressive figure, a pioneer with his own claim on history.

> One of Invercargill's very earliest settlers, Mr Wyald Stark, passed away at his residence, on Thursday, in his 78th year. Deceased came to these parts in the fifties, when the present Queen's Park was covered in bush, and Dee street did not exist except as a track through thick scrub. He was born in Florida (United States), his father being an officer of the American Army, and after his death while on active service, young Stark left for England. There he remained but a short time before he was attracted to Australia by the gold fever. He put in some hard work on the diggings and, winning a considerable quantity of the precious metal, decided to try New Zealand, arriving in Southland about the year 1857. Deceased built a store in those early days on the east side of the North Road at Avenal, and . . . supplied goods to miners as far away as the Mataura district, which he waggoned all that distance. Shortly afterwards he constructed a tramway through Queen's Park, from the North Road at Avenal to Elles road, for the purpose of supplying firewood to the residents, and at a later date erected an hotel at the west side of the road, which he occupied for some years. It was known as 'The Governor Grey', and was then a small wooden building. Afterwards he re-erected a brick hotel near the site of the old one. . . .
>
> Deceased was a man of great physical strength, and his courage was exceptional. While on the Victorian diggings he demonstrated these qualities by capturing an armed bushranger named Higgins, for whom the authorities were in search . . . . Beneath his dark skin beat a kind heart, and those who knew him when he was in a position to assist others, say he was generosity personified . . . . Deceased was one of the oldest members of the St. George Lodge of Oddfellows. He leaves a widow, one daughter, and three sons, also nine grandchildren and eight great-grandchildren.[26]

The problem of fact and fiction is not an easy one; most war books contained elements of both, including the memoirs. John Galsworthy saw this in his preface to R. H. Mottram's *The Spanish Farm* where he tried to put his finger on the nature of its 'new form': 'I suppose you would call this a war book, but it is unlike any other war book that I, at least, have met with . . . . "The Spanish Farm" is not precisely a novel, and it is not altogether a chronicle . . . quite clearly the author did not mean it to be a novel, and fail; nor did he mean it to be a chronicle and fail. In other words, he was guided by mood and subject-matter into discovery of a new vehicle of expression—going straight ahead with the bold directness which guarantees originality.'[27] The finest books from World War I were *shaped*—like New Zealander Alexander Aitken's stoically elegiac *Gallipoli to the Somme*, David Jones's *In Parenthesis*, Blunden's *Undertones of War*, Manning's *Her Privates We*. Each is, as William Blissett puts it, 'both based on experience and thoroughly composed, a "thing made"'.[28] Certainly *Passport to Hell* is 'composed'; Robin Hyde is concerned to show the making of a man who can both murder a surrendering prisoner and carry a wounded comrade across no-man's land as 'gently as a kitten'. But she also wishes to claim the certainty of fact. She had to project a world in which Stark would live convincingly *and* assert, 'This book is not a work of fiction.' She relied too heavily on Stark's veracity. In one particular incident concerning his schooldays she was forced to remove the account from the 'new edition' of 1937 and wrote to the *Southland Times* with a public apology:

> I am given to understand that on page 26 of my book 'Passport to Hell' I have recounted an incident concerning which I was misled, and which may be understood to reflect unfavourably on the Gladstone School, Invercargill and on Mr Duncan McNeil, its headmaster during Starkie's period of tuition there. Starkie himself informed me—though in a perfectly humorous way, and I am sure, without intention of injuring either one of his old schools or anyone else concerned—that at the time he was such an incorrigible truant that his father on three days chained him up to the school doorstep. I accepted this and recounted it in good faith, but on Mr McNeil's statement that the occurrence never took place, had the paragraph removed from the 'serialized' version of my book, have written to the publishers to have it deleted from future editions, and finally will be glad if you will give publicity to this correction.[29]

The most powerful criticism of the factual background of the book came from one who had served like Starkie in the Otago Infantry Battalion (though he seems to have joined up some eighteen months later) and was a native of Invercargill. His name was John Tait and he wrote two letters to the *Southland Times* which annoyed Robin Hyde immensely, perhaps because she had followed Stark so closely. Tait begins:

> In the New Zealand Division there were many stories told of J. D. Stark, commonly known as 'Starkie'. Some of them were

> true, many of them distorted or exaggerated, some of them purely apocryphal; but all agreed in emphasizing his contempt of danger and discipline alike. Broadly regarded 'Passport to Hell' gives a vivid and plausible picture of a strange character. The detail, however, does not bear critical examination. The author opens her prefatory note with this sentence, 'This is not a work of fiction.' The natural presumption is that she offers her work as a record of truth in which case one would have expected her to verify such details at least as she readily could. A few minutes in a reference library would have corrected her ideas (and spelling) of Avenal, Waihopai, the time when Invercargill went 'dry' and 'the battle of the Wasr'. A few inquiries would have revealed to her the fact that two at least of the schoolmasters referred to in chapter one are still living in Invercargill, and would no doubt have been pleased to correct her picture of the boyhood of her hero; that the Magistrate she refers to by name is resident in her own city; that 'the battle of the Wasr' was fought before the Fifth Reinforcement (not 'Regiment' by the way) left New Zealand; that 'Y' Beach was separated from Anzac Cove by nine or ten miles of the Peninsula from which New Zealand and other allied troops were rigidly excluded by the Turks. But why go on? It is sufficient to say that the verity of the story could have easily been checked at many points, and Robin Hyde's palpable failure to do so has rendered her work worthless as a record of truth. The literary worth of it would in no wise have suffered had the preface run something like this: 'This book is not the product of my imagination. I have related its incidents and the circumstances under which they happened, as Starkie told them to me. To what extent he has drawn on his imagination I cannot say, but I thought them sufficiently interesting to publish.' In such case, while one might have criticized her taste in the selection of her material, her talent for vivid writing would have been fully appreciated.[30]

When Hyde replied citing J. A. Lee and Downie Stewart in her defence, Tait returned to the attack with pedantic tenacity:

> If you will permit it I should like to point out the fundamental weakness in her position as it appears to me. Let me explain that before writing my private letter I had discussed the book with many of my fellow returned soldiers and had confirmed my own belief that the book cannot be relied on as a truthful record of facts. I took particular care to give full credence only to those who had personal knowledge of the events which they

described and I checked their recollections as far as possible by reference to such records as were available to me. I do not doubt that much of the narrative is substantially true but it contains so much intrinsic evidence of the author's failure to check the facts that the whole story stands suspect. It is in this sense that I maintain that the book is worthless as a record of truth. It is clear of course that considerable portions of the narrative could be verified from independent sources only with difficulty and that in some instances corroboration is impossible. Much of it however could have been checked with comparative ease, and, had Robin Hyde made any attempt to do so, she would not I feel sure, have commenced her preface with the sentence, 'This is not a work of fiction.' The points I mentioned in my first letter were a few of those which should have led the writer to suspect the accuracy of her information. Robin Hyde dismisses them as trivial. Some of them are, perhaps, mere straws indicating the direction of the wind but the march from 'Y' Beach to Anzac Cove was a military impossibility and 'the battle of the Wasr' as described took place during the Easter of 1915 while 'Starkie' with the Fifth Reinforcements was still in camp in New Zealand. Men who were actually there have told me that the description of that event is remarkably accurate but the point is that Starkie was not there.

The reviews referred to do not, I submit, alter the position. Their laudations can properly be regarded as paying just tribute to Robin Hyde's literary talent but the writer must have assumed the narrative to be true. This applies to the two distinguished New Zealanders referred to by Robin Hyde. The period mentioned as covered by the Hon. W. D. Stewart's somewhat cautious authentication affects only some 40 pages of the book (144–183). The Hon. J. A. Lee served—I speak from memory—with the machine gun corps and would have few if any contacts with Starkie on service. He would be the first to agree that realism is a virtue in literature, or any other form of art, only when it conforms strictly with reality. I do not suggest that Robin Hyde added to or varied the facts of her story; those embellishments were there when she received it. She pleads in excuse the youth of her hero but even this will not stand. J. D. Stark was not born on July 4, 1898, as Robin Hyde believes; he was born on July 17, 1894. He was not a boy of 16 when he left this country but a young man of nearly 21.

In conclusion, I have taken every precaution which has suggested itself to me to verify the facts I have stated but unless those facts are challenged I do not propose to carry on

> a correspondence which might tend quite wrongly to suggest some animosity towards either Starkie or Robin Hyde. My protest is simply this. Let realism be truth, the whole truth if you will, but above all, nothing but the truth.[31]

The only response to such letters is the asking of those unanswerable questions, What is Realism? What is Truth? Robin Hyde's concern was for the work's effectiveness, as a portrait of Starkie and as an impression of war. She was outraged at the meanness of the attack, and replied to Tait's first letter with a long defence of the book's accuracy and a statement of her purpose as a writer:

> I trust your columns may be open to a reply to Mr John Tait's attack on my book 'Passport to Hell'.
>
> It is perfectly obvious that there may be minor (mostly very minor) inaccuracies of spelling or detail in a book written by an author who has never had opportunities to visit the scenes recorded, and whose material was gathered from a soldier (sixteen years old when he left this country) who never kept a diary. In addition, though Starkie attended several Invercargill schools before at twelve years of age, he was sent on to the Burnham Industrial School, and though I found him very far from unintelligent, his spelling does not seem to have been all it might. However, I don't think the fact that the soldier's spelling was here and there substituted for the schoolmaster's is likely to trouble many people.
>
> Starkie was unquestionably at what the soldiers called 'the battle of the Wazza', Mr John Tait 'the battle of the Wasr', and some other authorities 'the battle of the Wazir'. May I quote what your paper says in an adjoining column, reviewing another book? 'The detail is so precise, and the narrative concerned with the surrounding country all so exact, that the reader must accept it all.' If any inexactitude of mine as to date or number of contingent has confused Mr Tait, I should think that by reading the chapter he might have convinced himself of its essential reality. At all events, the fifty or more English reviews I have had of 'Passport to Hell' nowhere seem to question the book's authenticity as a broad record of war experiences—not a war history—and I suppose their staffs must contain a few men not unacquainted with Egypt, Gallipoli and France in 1914–1918.
>
> It is curious that if my book is, as Mr Tait says, 'worthless as a record of fact', the most favourable reviews and comments

> should have come from returned soldiers. In addition to personal letters, (some confirming actual incidents), the Imperial War Museum, in writing to thank me for a copy of 'Passport to Hell', which was sent on request, refers to the book as one of the most interesting New Zealand war records in its possession. Mr John A. Lee, a returned soldier of distinction, said when interviewed by The Standard that 'Passport to Hell' was the most important New Zealand war book yet published, and made special mention of its realism. As Mr Tait has chosen to question my taste (though I did not know that war was ever in good taste), I may quote a sentence of Mr Lee's: 'Some people will be shocked because Robin Hyde sends a soldier to a brothel, but will cheer when the troops swing by to their death.' Writing in the Otago Daily Times, the Hon. Downie Stewart, who for part of the war years was attached to the same battalion as Starkie, says that for this period 'the authenticity of the book is such that nobody could cavil at it', and later that 'it is hard to believe the author was not at the front'. I quote in both cases from memory, but anyone who cares to look up the reviews will find that I have in no way exaggerated. Nor do I wish to advertise my own work, but Mr Tait's suggestion that because of a few trivial errors Starkie's record and my book are practically a work of the imagination, is so unfair and untrue that it cannot be left unanswered. Does he imagine that the experienced soldiers mentioned above would be taken in by any plausibility?
>
> It is true that I could have written to Starkie's schoolmasters in order to 'correct' my view of his character, though this is the first time I have ever heard that an author is supposed to take this course. I could also have written to every policeman, warder, prison superintendent, sergeant-major, military police official, and innocent if officious bystander with whom Starkie came into conflict. But I didn't, and I would never be likely to do so. My object in writing the book was not to portray the outside world looking at Starkie, but to portray Starkie looking at the outside world. After all, that outside view, especially of any person estranged from society by lawlessness, sickness or poverty, means so little. If I have any ambition as a prose writer, it is to write from the inner centre of what people think, hope and feel, and of that Interpreter's House, those set in authority over us know curiously little, because they have no humility . . . .[32]

However, she received support over the 'Battle of the Wazza' for 'Tano Fama' wrote in, explaining that there were *two* battles of the Wazza, 'and the second one was in the early days after the arrival of the 5th Reinforcements. This is probably the one to which "Starkie" referred. In defence of Robin Hyde, may I say that far from exaggerating the exploits of this wild member of the New Zealand Expeditionary Force, there were many many vivid incidents which could be told, but were omitted by her. Is it not true that Douglas Stark carried in the Rt. Hon. Gordon Coates when he was wounded in the field of battle? I believe it was . . . .'[33] But a glance through the notes to this edition will reveal that Tait's general observations on Starkie's inventions, distortions, and slips of memory, are not inaccurate. Hyde followed Stark closely, expanding from time to time from the merest of hints but making very few changes. She darkens the portrait a little by having Starkie steal where her notes indicate he did not, and she insists on his youth throughout, even, in the first version, making him almost absurdly younger than he had claimed to be. But the charge of not checking her sources sufficiently haunted her and we find her defending herself to Eric Ramsden in similar vein over *Check to Your King*, her account of the life of Charles, Baron de Thierry. She had had neither the opportunity nor the money to travel, she argues, and thus could not consult the archives in Sydney. 'However, Charles kept copies of most of his more important documents and treasured up hoards of newspaper remarks—kindly and otherwise—and I felt at the end of my work that I understood his own point of view pretty well, which was the only thing pretended for "Check to Your King". I am not a historian, and don't want to be one. It is the individual and the mind moving behind queer, unreasonable actions which seem to me to produce a good deal of the fun of this old world; and I think that any writer has the right to interpret this as best he can . . . .'[34] Both John A. Lee and Downie Stewart were well aware that *Passport to Hell* contained a number of errors, indeed Stewart took trouble to point out some of them and to consider the question of how far *Passport* was 'a true record of the events recorded'. He concluded that for the period of his knowledge of the events 'they are told with such substantial accuracy that any minor corrections of fact would not alter the main tenor of the story'. Stewart was, moreover, conscious of the imaginative resources needed to make a person *live* in literature: 'The average normal citizen is in the habit of regarding any strange or unusual individual as what is called a "Character", and of saying that "some one ought to write him up". But people who are given to this line of thought often fail to realise what a difficult task it is to make such "characters" live in a book with such vividness that the reader feels that they are real persons and that he must have met them at some time.'[35] Robin Hyde he thought had done that most successfully. While Lee wrote to her in 1938 of 'your "Passport to Hell" which was so amazingly correct psychologically if the graphic side was out of joint occasionally; and, of course, to get the experience true and vital rather than the mere geography was the greater achievement'.[36]

Perhaps the most interesting thing about Starkie was that although a seemingly unique figure, he was also in some senses the quintessential colonial soldier. The troops from the Dominions were noted both for their magnificent fighting qualities and their casual attitude toward discipline. The two aspects were not unconnected. As Denis Winter points out the British Old Army endeavoured to turn men into cyphers, breaking them down by endless drill and repetitive burdensome trivial tasks so that they obeyed without question: 'As long as a soldier could be guaranteed to obey all orders, he could be considered "trained".'[37] The brilliant Australian general Monash knew what was appropriate for *his* men: 'very stupid comment has been made on the discipline of the Australian soldier. That was because the very purpose and conception of discipline have been misunderstood. It is after all only a means to an end, and that end is to secure the co-ordinated action among a large number of individuals for achieving a definite purpose. It does not mean obsequious homage to superiors nor servile observance of forms and customs nor a suppression of the individuality.'[38] The colonials had proportionately nine times the number of men in military prison than had the British and man for man they 'fought better, were better adapted to the longueurs of trench fighting and supplied the storm troops of the B.E.F. to the end'.[39] This is a point made nicely by Hyde's editor J. G. McLean in his review of *Passport* for the *New Zealand Observer*:

> Stark was a private from beginning to end. Anything which marked him out for promotion or a decoration was as quickly cancelled by some breach of discipline. He was one of the light-hearted roystering crew of Diggers who formed the backbone of the N.Z.E.F., who lent the sharp edge of valour to its attacks, but chafed under restraint when out of the line. There were thousands more like Starkie; not so wild and lawless, perhaps, but sharing with him a rooted distaste for formal authority as represented by brass hats, military police, and other

> martial phenomena who could stop a soldier's leave, prevent him from drinking beer when he was thirsty, and march him across the desert in seemingly unnecessary parades.[40]

In his article '*In Parenthesis* among the War Books', William Blissett outlines the two poles of war literature—the spare narrative simplicity and symbolic starkness of Henry Williamson's *Patriot's Progress* on one hand and the self-conscious *In Parenthesis* of David Jones with its extraordinary density of literary and liturgical allusions on the other.[41] Hyde's portrait of the outlaw from New Zealand is much closer to the powerful simplicity of *Patriot's Progress* though she is not unaware of that larger context of war, literature, and religion which almost overwhelms Jones. *Passport* has greater intensity and immediacy than the two other New Zealand books from World War I with which it may be compared: Aitken's *Gallipoli to the Somme* (1963) and O. E. Burton's *The Silent Division* (1935). Burton's book (which Hyde admired, terming it 'one of the greatest testimonies against war that I have read'[42]) endeavours to 'place' the almost unimaginable experience of war by providing epigraphs to each chapter (he follows Frederic Manning in this) from a whole range of war literature from Kingsley's *The Heroes* to Remarque's *All Quiet on the Western Front*. But the decision not to give names removes personalities and diminishes the necessary specificity of the work. In *Gallipoli to the Somme*, the events waited forty-seven years for publication, having been recollected through youthful notes. The result is a beautiful and humane perspective on the horrors of that campaign.

Why did Robin Hyde write *Passport to Hell*? Initially no doubt from her sense of the need for social justice. Her journalism shows her defending the Maoris at Orakei, returned servicemen, discharged prisoners, prison reform, indeed all those pushed aside, oppressed, wounded, or ignored by Society, and Starkie provides a perfect focus for these interests. In addition, as a child she had been fascinated by the War (her father was a sapper in the N.Z.E.F., 13th Reinforcements and her mother's brother was killed at Gallipoli) and wrote of having been torn apart by 'our weekly "war lessons"' and as one 'who gave to that grim uniform the unthinking hero worship which may have helped all modern men to despise all modern women'.[43] In Starkie she may have perceived her 'mask', the polar opposite, both an element of herself and an image of New Zealand. Stephen Scobie gives us an insight on the matter in his study of the documentary poem, the genre that has dominated recent Canadian writing. He notes how the authors are driven by a need for self-definition, and how in that dialectical process, they endeavour to anchor their work in the 'validity of fact' and are 'drawn towards their opposites, the images of alterity, setting between them the distances of era, country, gender, yet always recognizing in the image something of themselves, a territory that awaits discovery'.[44] Just such a need seems to have led Robin Hyde to Starkie.

A Note on the Text

IN PREPARING this edition I have used the manuscript notes (*MS Notes*) made by Robin Hyde as Starkie related his experiences, the typescript of the finished novel 'Bronze Outlaw' in the Auckland University Library (*MS B-10*), copies of the first edition in various impressions (the novel went through six impressions in 1936), and a copy of the Second Edition—the 'new edition' of 1937. I have not consulted the 'cheap edition' of 1937, nor the serialization in the *Radio Record*.[45]

A collation of the typescript and the published version reveals an enormous number of variants. Approximately seventy pages were cut from the typescript and there are between ten and thirty minor variants (spelling, punctuation, word order, substantive verbal changes) per page. Robin Hyde took considerable care over the final version of this work. The result is a much tighter, more direct, swifter narrative. Punctuation changes from the typescript show a general tendency to change semi-colons to commas and to remove commas or replace them with dashes. The most noticeable feature of the published version is the much greater use of dashes, presumably to increase narrative urgency. Unnecessary adjectives are removed, though not all the changes are simplifications; occasionally the printed version is more circuitous, in order to underline irony. The more stilted language is improved: 'Starkie elucidated' becomes 'Starkie said' or he 'effected a permanent escape' becomes he 'got away for keeps'. Very occasionally gentility requires an expression to be made less vivid: 'poor bugger' becomes 'poor blighter'. One cannot, I am afraid, tell which of the changes were at the urging of the publishers.

The differences between the first edition and the second edition are few, the most important being the change of the name of the Invercargill magistrate from Cruikshank to Sentry and the re-writing of the passage concerned with the incident at Gladstone School. Otherwise there are some minor corrections and a slightly larger number of fresh errors.

I have chosen the Second Edition as my copy text since it contains the final authorized changes. I have indicated in the notes where cuts in the typescript have occurred, with a brief summary of the material omitted. Finally, I have silently corrected such textual errors as I could readily identify.

Notes

1. Republished 1986 by New Women's Press with an introduction by Phillida Bunkle, Linda Hardy, and Jacqueline Matthews.
2. *N.Z. Observer*, 19 February 1931.
3. Letter to J. H. E. Schroder, 19 March 1931, MS Papers, 280, Schroder, folder 5, Turnbull Library.
4. See below, note for p.38 on p.220.
5. *N.Z. Observer*, 13 October 1932, 'Landlords Lock Their Doors Against the Friend of Down and Outs: The Prisoners' Aid Society's Nomadic Life'. Some of the same details appear in Moreton's account of Starkie in his biography *A Parson in Prison* by Melville Harcourt (Whitcombe & Tombs 1942), pp.222–7.
6. Notes from a brief interview with Stark in an exercise book held by Gloria Rawlinson have a date of 19 February. See Patrick Sandbrook, 'Robin Hyde: a Writer at Work', unpublished doctoral thesis, Massey University, p.99 and note p.404.
7. MS Papers, 280, Schroder, folder 6, no.84, Turnbull Library.
8. Document dated 18 March 1935 held by Mr Derek Challis.
9. MS Papers, 280, Schroder, folder 6, no.79, Turnbull Library.
10. 26 April 1935, MS Papers, 280, Schroder, folder 6, no.80, Turnbull Library. Hyde wrote 'believe in man' in this letter, but 'believe in Men' appeared on *Passport*'s title-page. I have been unable to trace the Whitman quotation.
11. Melville Harcourt, *A Parson in Prison*, pp.222–3.
12. Denis Winter, *Death's Men*, Allen Lane 1978, p.170.
13. Winter, p.190.
14. Letter to the Hon. Downie Stewart, from Wairoa Hospital, dated 27/11/26. Copy in the possession of Derek Challis.
15. Letter to the Hon. Downie Stewart from Mt Eden prison dated 4/7/27. Copy in the possession of Derek Challis.
16. The manuscript of 'Doug Stark—Bomber with Otago on the Western Front' by 'Dawes Bently' (two exercise books written in the same hand as the Murphy/Challis MS) turned up in the Turnbull Library some years ago (see *Turnbull Library Record*, vol.12, no.2, October 1979, p.121) and was drawn to my attention by Dr Patrick Sandbrook. It had been transferred from the

General Assembly Library where it had no doubt been deposited by either Gordon Coates or Downie Stewart, whom Starkie relied on to get it published: 'Now about that book Downie, can you do anything with it. If so and you think it worth while, can you sell it and help me to furnish my home for the love of Mike' (letter to Downie Stewart of 3/7/30, copy Derek Challis). And, 'Now Gordon if that book of mine would only prove a success and you could send me 50£ or 25£ for it . . .' (letter to Gordon Coates of 29/7/30, copy Derek Challis).

17. See below, notes for pp.152,160,161 on pp.235–6.
18. See below, note for p.142 on p.233.
19. Letter to John A. Lee, 9 June 1936, Auckland Public Library.
20. Letter to Schroder, 'Nov/Dec 1935', MS Papers, 280, Schroder, folder 6, no.86, Turnbull Library. See letter no.84 for A. and P. Watt's response.
21. Letter of 28 February 1936, MS Papers, 148, Andersen, 29, Turnbull Library.
22. See 'A Note on the Text', p.xxii.
23. Letter to Lee, 29 May 1936, Auckland Public Library.
24. Sandbrook, 'Robin Hyde: a Writer at Work', doctoral thesis, Massey University.
25. See below, notes for p.9 on p.216.
26. *Southland Daily News*, 5 November 1910.
27. R. H. Mottram, *The Spanish Farm* with a Preface by John Galsworthy, Penguin 1937, p.viii.
28. William Blissett, '*In Parenthesis* among the War Books', *University of Toronto Quarterly*, Spring 1973, p.283.
29. *Southland Times*, 17 October 1936.
30. *Southland Times*, 3 October 1936.
31. *Southland Times*, 17 October 1936.
32. *Southland Times*, 10 October 1936.
33. *Southland Times*, 17 October 1936; see also note for pp.75–78 on p.222.
34. Letter of 26 December 1936, MS Papers, 196, 173, Turnbull Library.
35. *Otago Daily Times*, 4 July 1936.
36. Draft of a letter 2 September 1938 with Hyde's letters to Lee, Auckland Public Library.
37. Winter, p.40.
38. Cited in Winter, pp.47–48.
39. Winter, p.49.
40. *N.Z. Observer*, 4 June 1936.
41. *University of Toronto Quarterly*, Spring 1973.
42. Unsigned review, *N.Z. Observer*, 18 July 1935.
43. N.Z. MSS 412, Auckland Public Library, ff.5, 13.
44. 'Amelia or: Who Do You Think You Are? Documentary and Identity in Canadian Literature', *Canadian Literature*, no.100, Spring 1984, p.280.
45. *N.Z. Radio Record* (Wellington), 30 October 1936–25 March 1937 (22 instalments); also in *N.Z. Sporting Life*, beginning 31 October 1936.

Acknowledgements

I AM MOST grateful to those who have helped me with this edition. Bill Pearson, who first suggested the project, has sustained me with assistance and support throughout and has provided the bibliography. Derek Challis generously allowed me access to all his mother's papers to do with *Passport to Hell*, without which I could hardly have begun. Dr Patrick Sandbrook sent me many useful references arising out of his own research on Robin Hyde. My colleague Terry Sturm assisted with some vital material on *Passport to Hell*, Sir Keith Sinclair and Trudie McNaughton tracked down some newspaper reports of Starkie's exploits, and Robin Dudding helped me cut and shape my vast and unwieldy annotations. The librarians at the Alexander Turnbull Library, the New Zealand/Pacific section of the Auckland University Library, and the New Zealand section of the Auckland Public Library could not have been more helpful or considerate.

D.I.B.S.

Author's Note

THIS book is not a work of fiction. I have related its incidents and the circumstances under which they happened, as Starkie told them to me. But after leaving the happy realms of childhood, all names in the book become completely fictitious, with the exception of those belonging to one Field Chaplain, two Generals, and two New Zealand politicians—all, oddly enough, mentioned in a complimentary way. At his own wish I have given the names of Starkie's family circle correctly, and those of the little group of friends who during the war were leagued together as 'Tent Eight'. Apart from these, I wish to emphasize the fact that in particular all names of N.C.O.s, military police, wardens, provost marshals, warders, bobbies, and women are as fabulous as those of film stars, and that any possible similarity to the names of living persons is coincidence and coincidence only.

Introduction to Starkie

I FIRST heard of Stark when a very glum welfare worker—a friend of mine—informed me that he had declared, that unless he could lawfully come by a pair of trousers he was prepared to steal them. This raised rather a pretty little point of law—whether it were best for Starkie to help himself to the main form of covering prescribed by society, and almost inevitably—he being fatally conspicuous in size and colour—be picked up by the police; or to go ahead, minus trousers or in trousers no longer fitted for the gaze of eyes polite, and thus eventually be arrested for the sort of offence which makes thoughtful parents gently remove the newspapers from the hands of growing girls. 'What's a man without his breeches?'

However Starkie resolved this affair with his conscience he was, when I first saw him at his little house in Grey's Avenue, wearing trousers. He had also an elderly and sleeveless black shirt, which made him look like a Fascist general—but a finer figure than most of them. He had no socks, no fingers on the left hand—the thumb of which was brilliantly tattooed with the legend, 'Here's the Orphan'—and an unconquerable smile. When something happened to amuse Starkie—and a good many things amused him—his black eyes lit up and sparkled, his mouth cracked open to show as many magnificent white teeth as half a life-time of combats with N.C.O.s, military police, common or garden coppers, and other heretics—all of whom he described impartially as 'The Villains'—had left him.

Apart from these marks of identification, Starkie had a little blue ring tattooed on his massive bronze chest. That was where the sniper's bullet tore through his lungs; and his Colonel, the regret in his voice strongly tempered by relief, remarked: 'Curtains, Starkie.' On each shoulder are tattooed the handsome stars of captaincy. During the War, Starkie became by degrees very tired of the manner in which his laurels wilted before the blasts of hot air emanating from those holes where gentlemen with long memories sat and brooded over crime-sheets. One honour at least, he decided, should be his beyond recall. So he spent an hour with a Maori friend, and came out pale but triumphant—the one and only tattooed captain in the whole army.

Grey's Avenue was built in Auckland City's first slow edging towards the beautiful and true. It was then known as Grey Street; and despite the fact that it was christened for the most distinguished gentleman who ever acted as Governor over the unruly Benjamin of British colonies, it was characterized by an invincible lust for the disreputable. The three-storeyed red-and-white bawdy-houses of Upper Queen Street extended into Grey Street, and mingled happily with Chinese grocery-shops, masonic clubs, and pakapoo saloons, all known to the city's then very few moral uplifters as 'Chinese Dens'. Needless to say, the little Celestials were by far the most orderly of the street's tenants. But Grey Street's reputation was well-founded.

There was really no reason why it should not have been rather a beautiful byway. So near the city that the Town Hall's posterior is thrust into its lower half, it is afflicted by neither street cars nor buses, and slopes upwards, fine and straight, garnished with a double row of half-hearted English trees whose falling leaves, in their sallow little pools, add to the general shiftlessness. But nothing could be done about it. Grey Street remained the sort of place where husbands with impunity and gusto thrash their wives—and *vice versa*—where policemen with a great deal of sound and fury, signifying probable fines of from £50 to £100 to be inflicted later in the police courts, smash in the steel doors of opium dens, and where it is possible—though very remotely—to win £60 by marking your ten characters correctly on a green sixpenny pakapoo ticket.

The name of the street was changed to Grey's Avenue, apparently in a wild hope that the more distinguished nomenclature might induce in the savage breasts of the inhabitants some dim longing after respectability. Nothing much happened. The Salvation Army took up its head-quarters on one side of the street, setting down a solid white ferro-concrete chunk of gospel truth which looked like a market-woman among whores. Adjoining this depressing building there is now a free kindergarten and a park—rather a nice little park, where the children slither down mighty chutes and wear out cotton drawers bouncing about on see-saws. But the other side of the street—the side where you will find, near the top, Starkie's little house—remains given over to the shiftless pools of dead leaves, to Chinese cafés so grimy that even University students won't eat in them, to shops that appear to be empty until after nightfall.

These empty shops of Grey's Avenue are rather intriguing. In the more prosperous days of my childhood a better pretence was kept up. They appeared as pastrycooks, confectioners, or grocers; but the curious thing was that nobody ever went in to buy pastry, confectionery, or groceries at these particular shops. There were, of course, respectable provision merchants a-plenty in the street. We were strictly forbidden to approach the street at all, and, technically, at least, remained in complete ignorance as to the existence of its masquerading shops. None the less, we were devoured by a frightful curiosity about them; and I remember one day when a party of us, all between the ages of seven and ten, invaded the confectioner's. Timidly we whispered a request for chocolates, there being in the window several dusty boxes.

The lady with the enormous white face and the stupendous bosom encased in bright pink wool leaned right over the counter, showing three teeth in a snarl.

'Yer little devils, gwan out o' this. . . . Yer know bloody well them's dummies!'

Since the War, however, professional immorality has suffered a sad decline; and the Chinese card-games, which offer the gambler that delightful something for nothing so sternly denied the lover, have taken over practically all the old haunts. By day the empty shops are shuttered and dirty. Passing by in a wet blue dusk on my way to Starkie's house, I observed that the doors of the empty shops rustled and rattled, that men slid in and out, mysterious as rats, that within, faint and warm light glittered from inner doors. The patrons of the gambling-schools leave little sentry groups on the pavement. These are part white—unshaven—and part Chinese—very discursive, in that clicking, unknown tongue. The white men look much the less attractive; but, on the other hand, there is such a derisive note in those rattling Chinese discourses. I always feel that they are mocking the gait of the passer-by, declaring in their own speech that she is bandy—or, alternatively, knock-kneed. Not that either is the regrettable truth.

A few of the shops live open to daylight and lamplight. One displays vile-looking rowelled spurs—God knows where they are used. . . . A Chinese one is as charming as an early book of Ronald Fraser's with its queer, thick porcelain spoons, its ginger-jars, its tins of water-lily shoots. A little Chinese lady lives here, much prettier than the one with whom you used to be in love when you first sipped green tea from the frail cup with the flower-faces and the absurd, dignified robes. Pass by the 'Carpenter's Arms', which is conveniently wide-windowed so that you can observe whether your husband happens to be one of the drowning flies in the one-and-sixpenny bottles of amber in the bar. Then come a few vacant sections, where mangy stray cats live out their mysterious lives of hunger, sorrow, and—as Mr Lionel Britton puts it—love. The residential area begins—little dingy houses squeezing and shouldering together, eaves touching, verandahs joining, board-fences broken down for firewood between the patches of scrubby garden where nothing ever grows.

There might meet you at the gate of Starkie's house a little girl with amber-yellow hair, very neatly combed, and the brightest of brown eyes in a face no darker than the Italian biscuit colour. This is Josie, Josephine, Flossie, or Flo, at three years old by way of being the beauty of the Stark family. Or the heir to the house of Stark, one year old and a rich cream-chocolate colour, may stagger out on his fat legs and regard you with such a sleepy smile that you will feel an astonishing desire to pick him up. His costume is like Joseph's coat, of many colours, being composed of all the bright-coloured scraps that have ever come into the house.

Within, a mellow voice says reproachfully, 'Hey, Banty! Banty!' The four little bantam hens, a rich auburn colour and with feathery trousers down their legs, quarrel bitterly for a place on Starkie's shoulders. The outlaw sits at the table, brooding over a cup of tea. He has washed the children's clothing, scrubbed the floor, induced the baby to take a nap, and once again successfully beguiled the formidable rent man—a wisp of a youth whom I privately believe to be terrified of the dusky enormous Starkie—into waiting one more week. But life is still complicated. The City

Council is down on him for keeping fowls in a city area, and can't or won't believe that the four red bantams are Starkie's brothers. The matter should be clear enough to any reasonable authority, since indirectly those bantams were the cause of one of Starkie's prison sentences. Being badly in want of manna, he stole and devoured the chickens of a neighbour. The magistrate wanted to know why he didn't eat his own fowls, and on being told that Starkie loved the bantams, took umbrage and refused the option of a fine. 'Hey, Banty. . . . Banty. . . . Hey, Flo, what'll you do if they come and take Banty away?'

This is the house where the Maori girl, Ritahia, who was respectably baptized by the Bishop of Auckland what time her future husband was arguing with snipers on Gallipoli, took down her guitar and played her little tune for the four-and-twenty members of her tribe who had quartered themselves on her, off and on, ever since her marriage to Starkie—just five minutes before he went into the next room, to find her quiet and smiling, her lips blue with the coming of a swift death. He still has Ritahia's thousand blue iris bulbs, which she brought with much pride from the country, but which refused to grow in Grey's Avenue.

This is the house which opens its doors at times, by night and by day, to curious and unexpected guests. There is an infernal creaking downstairs. This means that a man and a brother, having spent his all at the 'Carpenter's Arms', has silently stolen into Starkie's cellar and, draping ancient coal-sacks around him, prepared to sleep it off. Or in the evening a head pops round the back door, and a one-armed man solemnly proffers a large and gleaming mackerel, caught off the edge of the Auckland wharves. 'Thought you could use it for the kids, Starkie.' And he is gone again.

There is a queer link—often unseen; never, I think, unreal—between men whose closest-written chapters of life centred round about Egypt, Gallipoli, Armentières, the Somme, Ypres. Mixing with the crowd who have not shared their experience, they are dumb dogs enough. Get them together, and they begin to draw sectors on the table-cloth, to the ineffectual fury of the good women who have been optimistic and married them.

And in these storm-driven days—oh, storm-driven as much in our obscure little New Zealand as in countries that can go bankrupt with more of a splash, I assure you!—the link is stronger. The faces of the men I have seen coming and going in Starkie's house have sometimes been pale and shadowy faces. None of the owners possesses any great margin of security. They catch their suppers off the end of the wharf, they work three days a week shovelling bits of coast in the relief gangs, for whom award wages are a bright and sweet dream from a dead generation. They cadge vegetables and coal at relief depots and welfare departments, ruled over for the most part by crisp young men and old ladies who are alike in their supreme inelasticity of mind and their surprising interest in the private affairs of their fellow creatures.

Some of the shadowy faces have a furtive air. More than one wanted man has had brief respite here from the assiduities of the police—I mean, 'The Villains'—his wants ministered to by Bunny, Margaret, Norman, Josephine, and Sonny—who, ranging from the age of ten to that of one year, represent the oncoming generation of Starks. Nevertheless, once upon a time a French general kissed Starkie effusively on either cheek—to his shame—and his Colonel informed him that his V.C. recommendation had gone through—though, as he was on probation from a military prison at the time, it was highly improbable that he would ever see the colour of it. The Colonel's doubts were well-founded. Starkie took nothing home from his war but his tattooed captaincy stars, a record of nine courts martial, a total of thirty-five years' penal servitude in military sentences—all cancelled for gallantry in action—and a conviction that the world hereafter could not be too martial for his liking. He has only one ambition—to go to South America, where they have a war on all the time. It is his conviction that he would there have become a General, and I think he is right.

There was once a story of a Zulu *impi*, trapped beyond escape, and they cried: 'If we go forward, we die. If we go backward, we die. Let us go forward.'

In Starkie, in the wraith-like, unwanted, and continually humiliated men who haunt his little house from cellar upwards, I have sometimes thought to see the set faces of that *impi*. The returned soldier is a social problem in every country today. These men lived or died, as the luck had it, without getting into war novels, talking the language of the trenches, bothering very little about their own psychology, remembering horror and fear only in the loneliness of their own sleepless nights. They were neither knights nor machine soldiers. They were that most unknown of soldiers, the ordinary man.

In New Zealand they are scattered, and many of the best among them are too shabby and too harassed to attend R.S.A. ceremonials. Yet, potentially at least, the returned soldier's desperate desire to fit in again, to go *forward* and die, is one of the most valuable things remaining in our world; as the link, the friendship between scattered and shabby men who congregate around a thousand little homes like Starkie's, is one of the most honest.

1 Making of an Outlaw

WHEN the third Stark baby was born, they didn't have to travel far to wet its head; the father, Wylde Stark, having by that time come into possession of the old Governor Grey Hotel, which stands white and square in the dusty plainlands of Avenal, near Invercargill town in the far south of New Zealand. The baby, a boy, arrived with no small inconvenience to its mother and some to itself at the hour of 1.30 in the morning. Down in the parlour, Wylde Stark's guests and sympathizers had kept themselves awake to celebrate the event, a feat which called for a fair amount of refreshment. Technically, Invercargill may be a dry district; but there never yet was a time there when a man was ashamed by lack of good liquor for his friends. If the liquor consumed had really been bestowed on the baby's head instead of on their own capacious gullets, James Douglas Stark would have started life with a head like a little seal's. However, contrary to the practice of the new-born, he fell asleep almost immediately and took no interest whatever in the celebrations, which concluded only when dawn put a white finger of light to her lips and her stealthy winds said, 'Sssh!' very reproachfully to the company.

Though the same could not have been said of every man among his guests, Wylde Stark at five in the morning still looked as straight as a gun. He stalked upstairs, never touching the oak banisters with their carved Tudor roses, waved the sleepy-eyed nurse out of the way, and entered his wife's bedroom. A gas-jet still spluttered blue and sulphur-yellow above the bed, for the baby had chosen July's black midwinter for its arrival. His wife was awake, lying with her black hair and her paleness like sea-wrack against the crumpled pillows, her dark eyes watching him sombrely. He bent over the wicker cot where his second son had been bestowed, and inspected him without any show of sentiment. The baby slept on, unwhimpering. The tall man straightened himself.

A faint voice came from the pillows.

'What is he like?'

'Black as the ace of spades,' said Wylde Stark briefly; and as though that should satisfy both his own curiosity and his wife's, without another word he left the room.

Wylde Stark's description of his third child was only correct among those who divide humanity into white men, yellow men, black men. The only things black in the composition of the small James Douglas—leaving out his later dislike of the police—were his perfectly straight hair and wide, sparkling eyes. For the rest he was a very seemly bronze colour—and this was far from being a prodigy or portent, since Wylde Stark, who fathered him, was a Delaware Indian from the regions of the Great Bear Lake. How a Delaware Indian came by the name of Wylde Stark is another matter, but the affair sounds as though possibly a Kentucky Colonel had at one time or another been following the grand old Kentucky custom of playing fast and loose among the Delawares.

Another fact which remains obscure is Wylde Stark's reason for leaving the Great Bear Lake. All that is clear is that he arrived in Australia by cattle-boat, aged somewhere about thirty, and made straight as a homing-pigeon for the gold-fields. Here he enjoyed some considerable measure of success, both financial and personal. The latter rested mainly on his shooting of Higgins the outlaw, who made an ill-advised attempt to relieve the diggers of their dust. Wylde Stark's bullet bored through his stomach, and there was no more Higgins the outlaw, but only an occasion for celebration—which, although it not merely wetted but flooded the whistles of his admirers, never made the stern Red-Indian face look any the less like carved mahogany.

When Wylde Stark came to New Zealand—not, this time, by cattle-boat—he had money and prestige. He settled down in the Governor Grey Hotel, and ruled his customers with a rod of iron, while the private comforts of his establishment rested in the slender hands of his wife—a tall girl born in Madrid, and of Spanish blood. How she came to marry her husband is not to be explained. But their life in Invercargill was a queer compromise between traditions. There was no Spanish background in her children's early days except the occasional plaintive and broken spinning-thread of a song in the language that they never understood. New Zealand society having no gift of tongues, the Starks settled on English and stuck to it.

Wylde Stark was a dignified, almost an austere, figure, and physically superb. He stood six feet four-and-a-half inches high, and his wife was only six inches below him in stature—nothing at all below him in dignity. Whether their two racial prides ever fretted each other, their children had no inkling. They made common cause together in a society which could understand them very little. The colour line was much less rigid in New Zealand than it would have been in any other British dominion, but Wylde Stark was not to be satisfied with the good-humoured tolerance bestowed by the white New Zealander on his Maori brother. The Maori population in the South Island was scanty, and largely made up of slave tribes. The Maori who drifted into South Island towns smiled and lounged in the easy background of life. Wylde Stark, his straight-backed, pale-faced wife at his elbow, stalked through the psychological fences like some mahogany Moses.

Had James Douglas Stark at the age of one hour been able to appreciate the world at large, he must have admitted that his audience was worth notice. First, his enormously tall father, whose thin copper face was rendered amazing by its growth of white whiskers. Then, as the lovely moon-stone blue of dawn deepened and faded outside the windows of the Governor Grey Hotel, and the birds, awakening, showered down their many-coloured rain-drop voices from the pines, two very singular figures crept into the room and stood over him like fairies at a christening. His brother, George, at the age of nine, was perhaps not very fairylike. He showed signs already of becoming the prodigy in height that a few years would make him. Trouser-legs, cuffs, collars, suffered wretched fates on an anatomy which grew and grew. George Stark's complexion was considerably lighter than the new baby's, but his thin lips and chiselled features were his father's.

The second figure really was a fairy . . . a cousin to Rima herself, escaped from *Green Mansions* and tiptoeing here with her pointed, bronze-tinted face, her great eyes, her hair falling softly in ringlets upon narrow shoulders. Rose Stark won out of the grudging hands of destiny that loveliness which, when sometimes we see it in its lazy, unconscious moments, seems to us incredible. She was four years old and a sprite, neither Spaniard nor Indian, but a fusing of those two strange metals. Of the two hanging over the baby's cot, Rose had the lively and laughing disposition; her brother, George, was a sober gentleman who even then resolved, from his superior height and age, to take the youngster in hand.

An astrologer might tell clearly how the stars stood at 1.30 a.m. on July 4th, 1898. But this much is certain. Mars the ruby-coloured, must have been pointing his brilliant stave straight down the chimney of that room where Anita Stark lay, her hair sombre against the white pillows. And what a Mars! . . . Sometimes with the face of a giant, sometimes a large and yet inordinately active policeman, sometimes a grinning sergeant, once a slim English officer with a slimmer yet wicked cane. The shapes of war, one after another, formed and dissolved round the sleeping child's head. From under the pines, Wylde Stark's Indian game-cocks crew their insolent and brassy challenge. The morning arrived pale and repentant. But the thing was done.

. . .

There were two moments in his life—one of sheer delight, one tinged with fear and a curious satisfaction. The delightful moment arrived when his father daily commanded him to let the horses out of the stable for their morning drink at the dam. The mornings, hazy over wide yellow fields, broken only by silhouetted pines and a blue circle of the inevitable New Zealand hills far away, smelt sharply of frosty soil; little puddles in the stable-yard frozen over with ice that tasted cold and slippery like glass; horse-dung trodden into the mire and yet gentled with the smell of warm straw. He let the big working horses out first, their breath wreathing blue as tobacco-smoke around their snorting velvet nostrils. Then he attended to the racehorses, of whom he particularly worshipped Avenal Lady. She was a chestnut girl, and his first love. He took the greatest pains in sleeking her beautiful long body, with the haughty arches of her ribs and the taper of her legs into satiny white stockings. The chestnut mare, recognizing perhaps a colour as temperamental as her own, blew frosty breath into the little boy's face and beamed on him with her arch amber eye.

Avenal Lady's lines of speed and grace were all the beauty the little boy could understand. He knew a good deal about races already, his father being known as one of the lucky owners of the Canterbury Plains, and the use to which her taut muscles in their wary satin sheath could be put was perfectly plain to his five years. But there was something more about her when she stood poised, reared up like a plume of fire, like a sheaf of tawny grain. She was *triumphant* in her beauty, and that was what the little boy very badly wanted to be himself.

He wasn't supposed to be present at the cock-fighting, but the very thought of it made a salt taste like blood come on his tongue, and his small body could wriggle between the legs of the Invercargill men—some of them the toughest old sports in town. Cock-fighting, which was of course illegal, was not to be had outside the stable-yards of the Governor Grey Hotel. Wylde Stark had imported the Indian game-cocks, and a wizened little silversmith went to great trouble manufacturing and engraving their inch-long spurs of chased silver. Nothing was too good for the Stark game-cocks, and they flaunted their magnificence, strutting three feet high, great arrogant fowls, their plumage ruby and black, their feathered trousers sprayed out, absurdly like cowboy pants, around those deadly striking feet. The cock-fights were duels, usually to the death; and the little boy never found anything but excitement and joy in them until one day a cock with its eye torn out refused to die, but flapped round and round the ring, helpless among the legs of the black-trousered, red-faced males. Then he ran away.*

It should be possible for the son of a Delaware Indian to live from day to day, stolidly forgetting all except the needs and

*These game-cocks (stuffed, of course) now adorn the Dunedin Museum.

resources of the instincts. Did it come from Madrid, the shadowy faculty of being able to see again, to remember with a sometimes terrible distinctness, the strange things and the cruel ones just as they happened?

. . .

His father's face was set like a rock. He said: 'You're going to put them on, don't worry.' And James Douglas Stark—his name now contracted to the popular version, Doug—squirmed again, but didn't weep. Neither tears nor argument was the faintest use against his father. The rebel had two choices, to be trodden underfoot or to give battle. From the time when he could walk he had preferred to give battle.

Then a rope flicked out like a black snake and pulled him shrieking away from the fence to which he clung. His feet slithered, the rope scorching his waist; and yelling defiance, he was hauled to his father's feet. His brother George was then commanded to sit on his head; and the world was thus darkened while Wylde Stark put on the feet of his lassoed son his first pair of boots. When it was finished, the boy felt that the last humiliation had befallen his brown toes. He scowled, looking like an overgrown Oliver Twist, was cuffed on the head and ordered off.

On the way to school he met George Bennett, and sold his new boots for twelve marbles. They were expensive boots—but, on the other hand, George Bennett's marbles were worth talking about, being composed in equal parts of alley tors and glimmers. He was thrashed when he went home; but as he explained only that he had thrown the boots away—nothing about the trade with George Bennett—he retained possession of the marbles, and the beautiful little sparkly lights in the hearts of the glimmers when he held them up one by one to the gas-jet atoned for all else.

. . .

His father said: 'You'll stay at school all right.'

Starkie looked at him, with eyes whose limpid darkness prickled suddenly with glints of battle. For a schoolboy, those eyes could look amazingly innocent. It was hard, thought his first masters, that Starkie could play truant with all the perverse ingenuity of a dusky lamb among Bo-Peep's sheep, and then turn up with the eyes and smile of a bronze cherub. Reason, kindness, sterner methods, all fell flat. So far as could be discovered, Starkie's urge was not so much resentment against school, as a series of angel visions that slid gently into his mind at the wrong moment. He started off with the best intentions, plodding along the dusty Invercargill roads. Half-way, his genius revealed to him Starkie bird-nesting in the park. . . . Starkie with boots off and toes deliciously muddy, hauling up a whopper of an eel, an eel that all men would admire. . . . Starkie just wandering, on a road bent up like a tea-spoon in the queer, flat-lidded saucer of the plains. Normal enough for little boys, in their classrooms, to shoot up their paws, with a hoarse, 'Please, teacher, may I leave the room?' Not so normal for them to vanish, and be discovered in God's good time, trudging patiently towards the skyline. Starkie's first school fought a losing battle with the great outdoors, and Wylde Stark, after a year, removed him to another.

Invercargill was not badly supplied with schools. The first establishment having failed, there remained the Waikiwi School, the Park School, and the Marist Brothers' School—to say nothing of more expensive establishments beyond the reach of a Wylde Stark.

To each of these in succession James Douglas Stark was either led or driven. He never lasted longer than six months. There was no manner of real frightfulness about his escapades. He was simply schoolboy—large, intractable, cheerful, and unimpressionable schoolboy. Indeed, none of his schoolmasters appears to have made any real effort to impress him. One of the Victorian poets has a heart-murmur to the effect that the law of force being dead, the law of love shall prevail. This poem had not as yet travelled to Invercargill. The youngest Stark's reputation as an outlaw preceded him, and masters rolled up their sleeves in readiness. Occasionally they had a really sound excuse, as when with a length of rubber and a pen he devised a new sort of harpoon, and—the lord of the Waikiwi School having his back turned to the class while working out a useful little problem on the blackboard—let fly with this horrible weapon, penetrating the fleshy part of the schoolmaster's thigh.

At the Marist Brothers' establishment, however, the schoolmaster—an arrogant Irishman—was a deal too quick for his notorious new pupil. James Douglas Stark arrived in company with the McCarthy twins, Chris and Pete. That Chris was making hideous faces when the roll-call was uttered in deep and solemn tones was some excuse for a brown face crumpling up in a smile at the wrong time. The arrogant Irishman was at his desk in a moment. A thin but nippy little cane slashed him thrice across the knuckles. 'Now, my boy, don't laugh at the wrong time,' advised the arrogant Irishman.

As far as the Marist School was concerned, James Douglas Stark never smiled again. Five minutes later he begged permission to leave the class-room in order to attend to the demands of nature. Seven minutes, and he was legging it down the road in the direction of Thompson's Bush. Thereafter thrashings, bullying, and cajoling were all one to him. He could be dragged to the Marist fountain, but never again led to drink. Between him and the Irish nation arose an enmity not easily mended. Ten years later, when thoroughly incapacitated for war service, he applied to a then very affable British General for leave in Ireland. He was informed that he could have any other part of the British Empire he liked, but to Ireland he might not go.

The affair with the Marist teacher was the end of his schooldays. In Wylde Stark's desk accumulated a stack of neat but ineffectual summonses from the Truant Officer's legal-minded friends. Had James Douglas been born into their own family circles they would have realized the impotence of laws in coping with some important human problems. Yet out of school hours there was never anything that one could actively dislike in the long-legged, dark-eyed, eternally smiling youth, whose whistle was the most elaborate and debonair in the whole of Invercargill. Only of one person was he afraid—his elder and much larger brother, George. Wylde Stark, in thrashing his son, was restrained by an affection which seems strange in a Delaware Indian. George Stark, when thrashing his younger brother, went stolidly ahead and thought of nothing but the subject in hand. But George, though formidable, could be dodged. If bread and circuses were the ruin of old Rome, eels and circuses were young Stark's downfall. The eels—from three inches long to massive and hideous creatures as thick through as a man's forearm—were to be discovered in the brownish Waihopai River waters, or in the little creeks that wriggled like Indian scouts under the tangled sub-forests of Thompson's Bush.

The New Zealand bush world was as disorderly as himself. Supplejacks coiled and swung like great black serpents between the trees. One of his former schoolmasters had had an unforgivable trick of sending his pupils out of class to cut supplejack wands, and on their return entreating them to bend over desks—thus chastising them with their own scorpions. The bush-lawyers had trailing arms whose every leaf and twig was spined with sharp little hooks, ruthless enemies of decent homespun jackets and pants. Wild mint, flowering purple and with the cleanest of odours, grew into the rims of the little river-pools in whose mud the eels might be sought for, sometimes in the gorse-gold and sleepy warmth of a day's sunlight, sometimes with torches after nightfall, Maori fashion. The world was happy; and moreover, the problem of boots did not arise. His toes enjoyed an Arcadian existence of muddy freedom.

He was eleven years old, and Starkie to all the world except his immediate family circle, when he made his first bow to a magistrate—a benevolent gentleman by name Sentry, whose long white whiskers gave him a distinct resemblance to God the Father. Despite, or because of, that, he received the outlaw in a pained manner, made inquiries as to his school record, and ordered him six strokes with the birch. Waiting in the locked police-station—the amenities with which child delinquents are now treated not yet having commenced to trouble the waters of New Zealand law—meant an hour of sweating terror. The policeman, though sometimes alluring, is definitely a figure of dark might on the child's horizon. But dark and mighty though the theoretical policeman may have been, the little Scotch terrier who eventually arrived and commanded him to remove his breeks was a different story. The birch didn't hurt as much as his father's, let alone George's.

There is a dread age when boys and the little white knobs on telegraph-poles exercise a baleful influence over each other's destinies. This arrived, and in acute form. A magistrate grew tired, as Wylde Stark—who would otherwise have been a respected member of his little community—had already been for several years. Starkie was consigned to the care of the Burnham Industrial School intended specially for the reform of incorrigibles.

According to all the traditions of fiction, Starkie should have suffered hell among the three hundred boys in the big wooden buildings of the Industrial School, and emerged later with a smouldering hatred of society. Actually, he disliked it no worse than any of his other schools. He liked crowds; he was both too large and too energetic to be put upon by older boys. Despite his many departures from schools, he was by no means a fool, and hours in the classroom were not the long-drawn agony to him that they were to some of the poor gangling youths mentally incapable of learning even the elements of the three R's. He disliked Burnham as he disliked every other form of authority set over him, but not much worse than the other abodes of learning, and not nearly so keenly as he hated the Marist priest. He had his first taste of the cells for running away. In the first hour the experience was no worse to him than sitting in a concrete tank. Then something he didn't understand, something instinctive in his racial heritage, rose up and suffocated him. The walls seemed too narrow, and before they took him out he was beating his hands against the door.

Sometimes into the hands of a rebel fall prizes which the well-behaved can only sigh for. How many boys of twelve years old are resolved that a sailor's is the only decent life? But if Starkie had been a social asset, a turner of music pages, a hewer of mathematical tall timber and a drawer of the waters of Latinity, his fate would have been white cuffs and collar, and a pencil behind his ear. When he informed the Burnham authorities—mainly vested in the substantial person of Mr Thomas Archey—that he wanted to go to sea, there was no obstacle put in his way. Mr Archey and Wylde Stark conferred together. Starkie was carpeted and invited to give his views. He gave them, *molto con agitato*. In a week's time he was taken down and put aboard the *Kittawa*, which was, so her senior fireman confidentially informed him, the bloodiest little coal-boat on the West Coast run.

Bloody or not by nature, the *Kittawa* in her person was black, but not comely. She ran between Greymouth, Westport, Niger Bay, Lyttelton, and Wellington, taking on the soggy West Coast coal which keeps the air filled with black-diamond dust and the faces of its tenders as black as imps in hell. He got to know wild and alluring country. The West Coast is where the gold-rush hit

New Zealand over half a century ago, filling up a wilderness with its mushroom towns, forty taverns to a main street, and nothing to show for it in five years' time but raw crosses in a graveyard. Through the forests the outlaws and the native parrots, the red-plumed kakas, had swept in varying degrees of magnificence. And though the Coasters hanged or shot the outlaws when they could lay claws on them, the life in the mushroom towns wasn't precisely Sabbatarian. There was a law about wearing coloured shirts, and a man who happened to appear in a white one at any decent hostelry would be likely to have it ripped off his back, and lucky if the shirt was all he lost. The diggers' vast boots and moleskin trousers having vanished away, sign-boards swung sullen and ghostly in the phantom townships, and the coal-burrowing began, with the muscles and conservatism of a brood known there as 'the black Irish' to do the dirtiest work. The *Kittawa* plied between one coal-market and another, picking up dirty sacks, an occasional dirty passenger, and talk dirtiest of all.

His four months on the *Kittawa* were salty days for Starkie—exciting, hard-working, thoroughly alive days, and nights when he could crawl into his hammock and listen to the old hands swap yarns, chipping in whenever he felt it wouldn't mean a boot behind the ear. One or two of the crew weren't any too fond of the Kid, as he was generally called. There was a livid yellow little Greek cook, who loved him the way he loved soap and water. This feeling was not without reason, having arisen, as so many things do on a coaler, in a pan of hash. It was one of Starkie's jobs to carry the food from the cook's galley to the sailors and trimmers, who reigned in their meal-time glory over the fo'c's'le. The Greek was born dirty, and so was his hash. On a certain day occasion arose for a trimmer to say that black and all as he might be, he wasn't going to soil his inside with grub that crawled. Starkie was requested to take the hash back to the galley and ask for more. He did, and the cook sent him back again with a clout across the ear. The trimmer, when the same hash sorrowfully presented itself in the fo'c's'le, uttered a bull-like roar and commanded him to return the hash and, should the cook object, to bloody well crown him with it.

This was an errand which would have been more after Starkie's heart had he known a little less about the yellow Greek cook, who, yellow as he was, kept a knife as sharp as a razor and unpleasantly curved. But he was more afraid, on the whole, of the trimmers than of an early death. The *Kittawa* was no place for mild-mannered men, and the trimmers stalked terribly through his dreams like the sooty pictures of fiends adorning those ancient books with which his father had tried to induce some interest in Sunday school. Starkie went back to the galley.

'You, is it?' rather obviously said the little cook, but with a steel glint in his narrow eyes. The knife lay long and handy on a bench.

'Oh, God!' prayed Starkie—and lifting the pan of hash aloft, carried out the trimmer's request. He never waited to see or hear the result. The smother of the hash gave him a moment's start, and in that moment he regained the fo'c's'le and bolted between the trimmer's legs, trembling like a dog.

Thereafter he was regarded in the stokehold as a good kid, but the yellow cook watched him; and a more powerful if less uncivilized spirit of evil arose in the shape of an A.B., who appointed himself unofficial first mate of the *Kittawa*. Starkie filled the lamps, ran errands for the crew, scrubbed the decks without making the remotest impression on accumulations of coal-dust, and tended brass with polishing rags and powder until it possessed the white shine beloved in the King's Navy. The A.B. who wanted to be mate had a lot of spare time on his hands. He followed where the boy shone the brass white and speckless, then, with a grin curling back half-shaved lips from yellow teeth, he spat tobacco-juice on it.

'Sorry—my mistake,' the tormentor would murmur, and pass on his way, returning in the next five minutes to spit on another patch of brass. The man's swagger, his very legs in their baggy trousers, his smile before and after he spat, made something very odd happen to the boy's heart. It would thud horribly as he heard the footsteps of his enemy approaching, and then stop dead. He would see the shadow on the white, coarse-grained deck as the man stood over him.

'Sorry—my mistake.'

The day before they made port at Lyttelton, on his fourth month aboard the *Kittawa*, the trimmers held a wash-day and appointed Starkie washerman. He didn't mind their shirts and underpants, for by this time the casual friendliness down among the coal-dust was about the most comfortable relationship of his youth. When he had the washing fluttering on the derrick, his friend the tobacco-spitter appeared, and burst into a tirade against the appearance of washing above decks. Then the shouting stopped. Starkie knew intuitively that something worse was about to happen. He slewed round to see the man grinning at him, his lip curled like a dog's.

Starkie knew he was going to spit. He also knew that for some obscure reason this would be a calamity, and mustn't happen. He shouted: 'You spit, and I'll kill you!'

Brown tobacco-juice sprayed in a jet on the shirt he had just pegged out.

'Sorry'—said the enemy—'my mistake.'

The blow mightn't have done much damage on its own account, but the man—twenty years older than his twelve-year-old victim, and built like a gorilla—was expecting almost anything but to be hit in the wind. His footing on the upper deck by the derrick was insecure. Back he went, and before he had time to finish the curse that left his mouth as he fell, his head cracked against the lower deck. The deck-rail broke his fall, fortunately for David—and Goliath both—but the crack on the head finished his activities for the time being. He lay perfectly still, his mouth open, his arms crooked out in a curiously helpless attitude. Starkie, his heart in his mouth, stared down terrified at his first unconscious man.

Captain Pennington of the *Kittawa* was old and fat and philosophical, and he disliked men who spat on polished brass only a little less than the police who take it upon themselves to ensure the safety and happiness of the same. He had a case on his hands with the A.B.'s cracked head, and one which would have to be reported, for the man wouldn't be on his legs again in a fortnight. He summoned Starkie to his cabin.

'There's plenty of police on shore at Lyttelton,' said an unmoved and elderly voice.

Starkie replied nothing. His head was hanging; he had liked the sailoring life.

'. . . Taking an interest,' continued the voice, 'in acts of violence . . . h'm, h'm, h'm! . . . Have to report the case, my boy. Can't do that until we're in port. No wireless aboard *this* ship.'

He stressed the *this* as though the *Kittawa*'s lack of wireless communications elected her queen of the ocean wave. Maybe he was right.

'H'm!' added the voice. 'All a question of who gets ashore first.'

Pale-blue eyes stared unwaveringly into dark ones. A head, crested like a cockatoo's, nodded gently.

'That will be all, Stark,' said Captain Pennington smartly.

Starkie turned and departed from the cabin, his sea-faring days at an end. In a yellow morning the *Kittawa* docked at Lyttelton, and before the gang-plank was down Starkie was off the ship, swinging himself monkey-like along a rope. He never saw Captain Pennington again, nor his gods the trimmers, nor the little yellow cook. Once or twice he caught sight of the *Kittawa*, creeping over listless grey waters like a particularly black damned soul shifting its quarters from one circle of the inferno to another, and thought how homely the sooty flames of her hold-lamps had been in those four months.

The fear of the law, when it comes in the form of an acute attack of panic, can be a very real thing. His brief garments soaked through with rain, a twelve-year-old boy climbed the Port Hills above the grimy town of Lyttelton until his breath caught, and a stitch tore bitterly at his side. When he was satisfied that he had put distance enough between himself and the public, he flung himself down on the tawny grasses, close-beaded with the delicate drops of the drifting autumn fog, which had followed on the rainstorm's track. At first the fog, blotting out the gaunt town, the black line of its railway-cranes standing grim and dark against the sky, was a comfort to him. Law and vengeance suffered a blurring of outline. He lay in the grass, looking down on that unreal and fog-hidden town, until its lights began to prick through the veil. Their prying frightened him once again, so he dragged himself to his feet and started off over the hills which heap up brown and bare on the miles between Lyttelton and the city of Christchurch, which has drained the port of population and money, leaving Lyttelton a disconsolate hill-slope of blackened houses, inhabited only by officials who can afford to live nowhere else. There is almost no bush on these hills. Northwards they slide into fine ranch country where the roads move with the padding of thousands of dust-brown sheep.

But the whole landscape was blotted out for Starkie by fog which refused to lift. There was neither star nor lamp to be seen. He had had nothing to eat for the best part of twenty-four hours, and his swimming head made it easier to lose the way. He plodded on, as through a tenuous blue blanket. When his stiff body refused to carry him any farther he stumbled towards a solitary tree, and found with thanksgiving that it was hollow at the base. He crawled into the hollow, stripped off his dripping coat and wrapping his arms tightly round his chest, wriggled and twisted into an aching sleep.

There was only one companion when Starkie awoke in a still fog-wrapped morning—and he, with his handsome white tail and natty whiskers, was none the better for the presence of a member of the Delawares. Starkie froze stiller than the unwary rabbit, and wriggled towards him through the fern. Hands locked about the stroller's white scruff. He killed the rabbit, skinned it with a pen-knife, and looked round for firing. He had no matches, and what his forefathers might have known of the art of twirling fire-sticks was a blank to him.

He ate the rabbit raw, shivering a little, but finding the taste of its blood less repulsive than he would have expected. Now he was terribly thirsty, and sucked the long grass-stems, curling their dew-beads on the inside of his tongue. But nothing satisfied the thirst, and fog cut him off from the world. He went on his way, beating farther into the hills. Presently he came to a square and fairly deep pond and, lying on his stomach, lapped at the water like a thirsty dog. It was yellow and tasted horrible. He recognized the dying flavour of sheep-dip used not very long before, and though he wondered if what would kill sheep-ticks would also lay out a human being, he was glad. Sheep-dip meant a farm not far away. . . .

But he took the wrong direction. It was not until the third day of his flight from the *Kittawa* that he came to the wire fence which meant civilization again. By that time he could hold the fence and follow it down to the sheep-station, but no more. He had had nothing to eat since his meal from the raw rabbit, and had spent both nights in soaked clothes. It was a queer little figure, perhaps formidably tall for a boy, but childish enough in hunger and exhaustion, that stumbled into the station yard.

As the fog rolls back on a sudden from the Canterbury hills and reveals them broad-bosomed, tawny, and gracious, with the broad wings of red hawks circling grandly over them and the thin cries of sheep in the fenced-in paddocks, so for a whole week the penalties of outlawry disappeared from Starkie's horizon. The station-owner, a tall Scot with a red moustache, was of the rare breed who ask few questions, and would sooner meet a strange youth with a pat on the back than with a rebuff. Starkie was filled and refilled with steaming bowls of macaroni soup. He was rolled in blankets, hot-bathed, hair-brushed, and generally civilized; the ancient housekeeper who attended to his bodily needs keeping up a constant mutter of scolding against the fate that permitted bairns to be fair clemmed. She took him in hand as nobody else had done since his infancy. Ruthlessly and with efficiency she penetrated the bath-room where his body lay soaking in hot water, saw him cleansed and outfitted in fresh woollens of a ghastly pink, scrubbed his head, called him a great lump, and released him with a look of womanly pride.

In the evening he was entertained in a red-plushed but not unpleasant parlour by the station-owner's daughter—a dark little girl named Rita—who played for him upon an ancient upright piano, silvery trickles of tunes which seemed not at all unbeautiful to a sleepy boy, and smiled at him with bright, friendly eyes. Did the head of the house even notice that the waif from the fog was bronze instead of the appropriate blotting-paper hue? If he did he made no sign of his perception. The next week, brown boy and Scottish girl—Rita was ten years old—rode together on the bridle-paths that threaded the valley basin. Here at an earlier point of the autumn would arise the splendid russet sweep of the corn, coloured like Freya's rich hair.

A few long-horned cattle—prize stock—occupied a corner in the fortunes of the ranch; but the real power and glory of the place appertained to its ten thousand sheep—heavy-fleeced now against the winter months, a wild-eyed, moving mass of brown on road or in hawthorn-studded pasture. This green world where the boy and girl went riding was a self-contained kingdom of eminently simple habits. There were no entertainments, neither in the station-owner's house anything more elaborate than his upright piano. Hospitality and their own self-reliance were the only suggestions which the inhabitants could offer to a swifter-moving outside world. Yet I can say in faith that these people assure a certain amount of greatness for the future of any country they may live in, and that they deserve the old-fashioned term—'The salt of the earth'.

If the boy had known it, cupped within the dark hollow of these Canterbury hills was the only little patch of untroubled and happy childhood he was ever to experience. But he was as simple as he was young. Rita and her tall Scottish father had rebuilded the world for him. He had come to them a dripping waif, and they had welcomed him and treated him as a favourite. It takes very little to restore a boy's self-confidence. He decided that his crimes were not so appalling after all, and that safely enough he could head for Invercargill. His host shook a fine red-locked head.

'You could have stayed,' he said.

Parting with Rita, Starkie experienced a sudden and dreadful pang; and, as he was no longer hungry, knew that it must be love. This struck him dumb, and he could only stand awkwardly, long-legged, thin, bronze-coloured, like a little Indian without the adulterations of civilization, when she produced from her bookshelf a small blue book, its leather cover sentimentally adorned with a circlet of white violets.

'It's my birthday book,' she informed him. 'Please sign your name in it, for luck.' Grey eyes with their shy smile looked up, as if perfectly certain that luck is on the friendliest terms with all young people. He scrawled his name—J. D. Stark—opposite the date marked July 4th, and discovered an optimistic prediction in verse against his fête-day:

> Though long in the night, thy star shall shine out
> When the proudest shall fade.

He told Rita that he was coming back; he meant it, for she was the only charming and feminine thing he had known since his old infatuation for Avenal Lady. So she folded the book and safely bestowed it again, and waved good-bye to him from the door as, directed by his Scottish host, he struck out again over shining hills now altogether innocent of fog. The amiable barking and frisking of sheepdogs and the occasional breathless slither of heavy brown ewes herded down from their ambitious mountaineering accompanied him to the top of the wire fence. When he looked back, the station was a toy in a dark cup; a little house like a box; a trim, square garden; poplar trees that might have been sawn for the roof-garden of Noah's Ark.

The curious thing was that this was the only real and quite unchangeable world Starkie ever knew.

2 Good-bye Summer

TEN DAYS after he left the sheep-station in the Port Hills, Starkie arrived in Invercargill, thoroughly sick of the flavour of turnips, and with a lasting prejudice against New Zealand goods trains. He had walked to Christchurch, hunted in the long and grimy station for a goods truck labelled 'Timaru', crawled in, and promptly been shunted from one line to another until every bone in his body rattled. At Timaru he put in a day with a friend—one, Bert Smith—and then resignedly disappeared on another goods train, stowed away under tarpaulins that wouldn't be lifted until they reached Dunedin. From Dunedin southwards it was all dusty road and hard-hearted little turnips; and when he arrived in his native town somebody must have warned the inhabitants to produce no flowers by request, for no welcome from home or elsewhere greeted him. Emerging from a near-by public-house he met David Harris, and reminded him of the days of old, when Harris as an eel-hunter had made up in keenness what he had lacked in practice. This port ran up a little flag of welcome, and a day later Dave arrived with news of a job for Starkie in Dalgety's wool-store.

George Lord, young, tall, and dandified then—he was shot through the chest during the War, but in 1912 you would have predicted a gay-dog future for him—was enthusiastic about the charms of his girl, Fanny Simms. Starkie, untouched by women, scoffed. George vowed that seeing would be believing. The Simms' home was near the wool-store, its little garden stitched neatly and in bright colours of peony and Chinese slipper, like an old sampler. But Starkie had no chance to judge coolly of the charms of Fanny Simms, since over a coprosma hedge he fell in love—without stopping to consider the pros and cons—with Fanny's little sister, May.

May Simms was a lissome brunette whose little silk frocks—she ran them up herself—clung affectionately to the lines of a slim body made for tennis, dancing, and surf-boards. She was only sixteen, and wore her hair down, the brown plaits advancing and retreating in their own minuet as she swung along the street, her head up, lips and sandals and tam-o'-shanter all a defiant berry-red.

It was the custom of the country that young men and women between the ages of ten and eighteen—after which dealings between them were of a more private nature—might walk together without loss of prestige, particularly on Sundays. It was seldom, however, that a couple walked alone. The boys, half a dozen of them, wiry and brown in their open shirts and magnificent white flannels, would start off towards the bush, lingering so that the frailer limbs of femininity could catch up with them. At a bend in the road the girls would come into sight, very aloof and splendid, like a bunch of wild mares, with much tossing of heads and flashing of white teeth as they approached the loiterers. The party without difficulty would break off into pairs, each boy falling into step beside the girl he wanted. Very seldom the couples fell out of one another's sight, and the few embraces between them were rough, childish, kissing-game affairs; but there was a tacit understanding that the walkers-out were plighted to one another, and interference between them meant trouble.

May wasn't exactly the same as the Sunday-walking brigade. She would start out, if he pleased, but had a tendency to stray from the rest. She disliked other girls, and said so. She wouldn't wear gloves, though her sister's neat little paws were invariably tucked away in brown 'fabric'. May's fingers, brown and curly and strong, fascinated Starkie; so did the rest of her—the arrogant chin tipped back, the strong shield-shaped outline of her childish face, the eyes wide between the black sills of their lashes. On May's unorthodox bush-walks, of a sudden he would find himself sitting beside her; an outcast from the herd but extremely comfortable in the tangled bracken, whose fronds uncurled little brown fists just above their heads.

He discovered that if he kissed May—which he did seldom, and clumsily—it sent a curious thrill to the roots of his being. Vaguely he decided that this had something to do with original sin, concerning which he had been tutored in his youth; and left the brown, scornful face with its berry lips more strictly alone, pretending to be engrossed in the machinations of a pair of fantails, who flirted their tails at him and tinkled like music-boxes among the flat honey-white discs of blossom on the elder trees.

The public rencontres of male and female were less disturbing. Homes—May Simms' home among them, though her parents strongly disapproved of Starkie, taking the view that he was black—opened their doors on Sunday evenings; and the youths stood grouped tall and large-knuckled around the pianos, singing sentimental choruses, the clear little voices of the girls breaking like silver through clouds.

Come back to Erin, mavourneen, mavourneen,
Come back again to the land of thy birth,
Come with the springtime and sunshine, mavourneen,
And it's Killarney shall ring with our mirth. . . .

When Starkie joined in singing 'Come back to Erin', his intentions towards May were all that is most honourable. He tried to catch her eye, to discern some softening of the fine little pattern of her profile and throat. Outside bay windows the world floated blue and vague like an enormous harebell, and the voices of the War generation passed out into this blue straight as the lines of light that slanted through the curtains.

When summer came he began to entertain doubts about marrying May, though he loved her more than ever. May was summer's girl. The brown of her burned proud and fierce; and she was always down on the strip of beach behind the grain-stores on whose cobwebby, warm-smelling floor-space there were sometimes mass assaults with sacks and French chalk in preparation for dances. It was not in those days permissible for girls' bodies, in their red and blue swimming-suits, to come from the sea as fresh as Venus and slide straight into the arms of their dancing-partners. But May's hair never stayed up under her swimming-cap; and when he danced with her afterwards in the grain-store, damp locks of it would tickle his face and tease him with the little tang of sea-salt.

May was as young and self-confident as a cat; and as the summer lamps burned deeper, great stars taking on warmth in their honey-colour, they used to slip away from the dances and escape to the beach. The bathing-sheds were locked after dark, but that didn't matter. They undressed primly behind separate rocks and splashed into the lipping dark water. The moon left a trail like a huge golden snail's across the black water, and they swam and floated directly in line.

At first they huddled into their already wet bathing-suits for the night swims. But then one night he heard a little laugh behind May's covering rock—and out she walked, and stood just for a moment in the moonlight with nothing on. Then, frightened, she raced for the sea and was into the moon-trail like a seal lady. It took Starkie the smaller part of a second to defy his own bathing-suit and leave it a wet husk on the sands. Then he was cautious and flattering and reassuring, out in mid-ocean. Night was made up of laughter and tresses like seaweed, and a new springy freedom which was almost intolerable—like the first draught of mountain air. When they got back to the shallows and sat waist-deep in the foam, he noticed with satisfaction that while the nape of May's neck, her arms, and her slim, tapering legs were nut-brown, the rest of her was white. There was nothing but laughter and sleepiness between them as they walked home.

Perhaps May's face wore for a few days the fineness of the young girl who begins to think herself seriously in love, and who sits with her eyes heavy with dreaming. The gate under the coprosma hedge, in any event, became definitely an enemy strong-point, and Starkie was no longer invited within for draughts and dominoes. Mr Simms appeared in carpet-slippers and spectacles to tell him that he didn't want coloured boys hanging around his house. Starkie retreated, but watched the Simms' gate like a cat at a mouse-hole. He watched in vain. Reason and shame prevailed upon May. Instinctively thoughts of love drew her onward to thoughts of marriage; thoughts of marriage became bound up with the colour question—which had no part at all in the gay, delightful game of being a young Diana worshipped in the moonlight.

With a sore heart, Starkie slunk back to his own lodgings night after night. He went down to the grain-stores very seldom. But one visit was fatal. He saw two people, young and very happy, slip out from the stuffy hall. He heard the girl's tinkling laugh, and watched them head for the flat brown rocks of the beach. Sentiment said unreasoningly, 'May, May, you couldn't!' But he knew perfectly well that for May the charming game had begun all over again on smoother lines. The youth who now partnered her bore the name of Alec, for which Starkie liked him none the better. He brooded over the Alec problem. Then one night he lay in wait behind the grain-stores. Alec and the faithless May hove in sight, and were confronted by a sullen dark figure.

The rest was remonstrance from Alec, squawk from May, straight left from Starkie. Alec, though large, was no boxer. The blow caught him on the point of the chin. It was the end of a brief combat. Starkie departed, feeling avenged, but no more amiable.

In the morning Bob McCauliff warned him that the police were asking questions. He produced a feeble alibi—'I was in bed, sir'—but knew how long that tale would hold water. His brother George was up in the Wyndham Valley cutting flax. Starkie sent him an urgent wire. Within the day the gates of refuge opened for him. George wired:

Job here, young fool, £2 week.

He was through with women for ever. His sole possessions a suit of clothes and a draughts-board, he headed for the Wyndham Valley, flax, and the two Finnegan brothers—of whom Tom Finnegan, was an old bruiser with the cauliflower ear and squash nose of his former profession, and Bob—long and rangy, just as dangerous a customer when crossed. It is a proven fact that the Irish can't argue, nationally or individually, and the brothers Finnegan perfectly exemplified this.

But the life in Wyndham Valley had its tang. Starkie had to walk from Mohawk—for the little train, discouraged, gave up its uphill puffing long before it came to the mountain pockets where the flax stood shiny green, tough, and higher than a man's head. It was cut out from the pockets in huge bundles weighing more than a hundredweight apiece, hooked to thirty feet of trace-chain and hauled by horses to the smoother ground where the waggons for Finnegan's flax-mill could pick it up.

The first ten days were back-breaking nightmares, working

hours spent in envy of the practised ease of the flax-cutters, whose great steel hooks swept the air as evenly as their breath was drawn and exhaled; the nights a matter of crawling stiff and wretched into a bunk in his brother's house. Then he struck the rhythm of flax-cutting, and could do the job on his head. His muscles hardened up, he could let his body take care of the stiff green swathes, and watch the shadows of clouds pass faintly blue over the mountain clefts. It was a wild place, but fresh-smelling, and with a steep beauty. A west-coast bee-farmer had left a score of white hives here, an experimental extension of his domain, and a continual stream of Italian browns and German blacks danced in the air above the hives. The hive-sentinels kept ward; the workers went off to gather the curious dark-brown, pungent-flavoured honey of the brown and white manuka blossoms. The hives were robbed of this, and the dark honey smeared on huge door-steps of bread with which the men filled their bellies at noon.

Finnegan's cook was a Norwegian sailor who had deserted from his ship at the Bluff, and everyone knew that he hadn't had a bath for years. He had worn one suit of clothes, night and day, and they stuck to him. Beard and haircut were of the same grand old minor-prophet style, grey and clotted with grease. For all that, Olaf—if you didn't mind about bodily beauty—was a stout-hearted and good-natured fellow, and nothing was too much trouble for him in the preparation of the awful messes he turned out for the boys. One day he announced plum duff, and the boys scoured the ranges to get him eggs. They came back with eighteen and a packet of sultanas filched from a store at the bottom of the Valley, and Tom Finnegan lent an old white shirt for the boiling of the duff. Starkie stacked the wood, new-chopped red logs of manuka. The duff boiled for three hours, and the rattle of tin plates was a newly invented song of the flax-cutters. Olaf went out in triumph. He returned, blinking tears away from his sparse white lashes, a vast black pot in his hands. The boys looked on the duff.

'I ban forget to tie her oop,' explained Olaf sadly. After that they reverted to eggs and bacon, when they could get the eggs and when the bacon wasn't too much like salted leather.

Tom Finnegan had his off days, and Starkie struck one of them when the flax bundles were being unloaded from the waggons at the mill. Finnegan was on the waggon passing down the bundles. Whether his aim was good or bad Starkie never learned; but one of the hundredweight bundles struck him on the back of the head, almost snapping his neck. Down he went, his face driven into the soggy peat. He staggered to his feet, his mouth full of turf, and the moment he could spit it out told Finnegan what he thought of him. But it would appear that the Irish don't like being called bastards—for Finnegan dragged the back chain across the waggon, and brought it rattling down over Starkie's shoulders. That hurt. Starkie had a clasp-knife that had done for sawing wood, chopping tobacco, and a good many other things. He stuck it out, point upwards. Down came Finnegan's arm with the weight of the chain behind it, and before the Irishman could save himself, that weight dragged the blade of the open knife clean through the muscles of his arm.

There was a fight, but Finnegan was groggy with pain, and forgot for a moment what he had learned in the ring; or luck was against him, as it can be against the toughest. Starkie looked with shock and with the beginning of a scared feeling at Tom's jaw, which stuck out in a very queer way, and wobbled hideously when he tried to speak. The men ran up and carried Tom to the nearest sledge.

'My God, but you're for it!' one of them told Starkie. 'Breaking the boss's jaw won't half get you a sweet time down below. Better clear out while the going's good, kid.'

Starkie cleared. At the flax-mill he drew his pay from Bob Finnegan—£24—and, more in bravado than in lawful spirit, claimed the extra week's notice due to him as a member of the Flaxmillers' Union. He got it. It then became apparent that £26 would profit him very little when the Blue Boys picked him up, and the expediency of getting away from the flax-mill at once presented itself. He walked out of the hut, borrowed Tom Finnegan's tethered horse, and rode into the bush to find his brother George.

George took the news of his brother's new war very philosophically, merely producing a frying-pan and commanding, 'Well, you get into that hut and cook us a feed.' A moment later his head popped round the door once again, and he said with stark ferocity, 'And it better be a good feed, see?' Then he disappeared until evening. Starkie provided his brother with a good feed: corn-cakes, fried vegetables mashed up with tinned salmon, floury scones, and the bacon crisp. George was his idea both of God and of the Devil. The elder Stark's complexion was so much lighter than Starkie's that he might almost have passed for one of his mother's race. But, beside him, James Douglas Stark looked like a schoolboy, and felt like one. George stood six feet seven in his socks, and was broad in proportion. He was a temperate man, had a mind cold and hard as the business edge of a tomahawk, and regarded his brother as a fool kid. Secretly, Starkie worshipped him—but would never have dared to mention or show it. George regarded the thrashing of Starkie as a natural duty, and undertook it at many odd moments. But he had a way of coming to the rescue—in prison, in war, in estaminets. . . .

Next day the Blue Boys were seen coming up the valley. George gave a long cooee of warning from the higher hills. Starkie took the hint and was off again—not entirely discouraged, for he had eggs, bacon, and billy tea in his stomach and £26 in his pocket. When he got to the bottom of Wyndham Valley, wearing dungarees and a woollen shirt, it seemed obvious that dressed as he was he would make no hit in life, and he bought a ready-made suit in a little valley shop. There was no place in the shop where he could try on underclothes, so he went across to a public-house, and there, in front of a fly-specked mirror, admired his fawn shirt, narrow-toed shoes, shoulders square in the new suit. Then it occurred to him that it was a great pity to break into his £26 for vanity, and he departed quietly from the back door of the public-house, carrying one more sin on his conscience and leaving behind him a tailor with shattered faith in human nature.

He jumped the express from the bottom of Wyndham Valley and went straight through to Christchurch, where Alf Byron, living out by the Sydenham workshops, welcomed him as a lodger in his sooty little house with the dejected sunflowers in the front garden.

Alf was a ganger on the wharf at Lyttelton; and his son Arthur, just topping Starkie for age—Starkie was nearing the end of his fifteenth year—worked down among the cranes and wharf-trucks. Father and son were economists.

'Why blow it?' said Alf, of Starkie's £26. 'Keep it in your

stocking, boy, and pay your way on the wharves. There's plenty doing down there for a kid with shoulders on him.'

Shoulder, whatever else he lacked, Starkie could certainly offer. The months of flax-cutting had toughened him to whipcord, and his brown skin shone with health. At fifteen, he could have passed for a youth of twenty, and was careful not to undeceive those blades who took him for one of their mature community. Cloth cap, brilliant ties, shirts of many colours—he imitated the blades in every respect. The work on the Lyttelton wharves was after his own heart, a sociable proposition, the men standing in groups, red-kerchiefed, hard-muscled, rough-tongued, until they were called for by the unloading ships.

He worked for precisely four hours as a dock labourer, unloading from the *Ionic*. Then along came a little man who had not shaved himself, but seemed none the less confident for that.

'Are you a scab?' hissed the little man in Starkie's ear.

'Scab which? I've only come here this morning.'

'Ugh!' said the little man, with profound contempt. 'Green. . . . Well, are you coming out with the rest of the boys, or are you staying on, Scabby?'

Starkie came out; not merely for fear of the one really opprobrious term in the New Zealand worker's vocabulary, but because the delights of loading mutton were not to be compared with the excitement of being involved in the strike. And the strike was no baby. Nineteen-thirteen brought Prime Minister Bill Massey's cockies riding into town—strike-breakers armed with pick-handles and ready to smash any head that came in their way. On the other hand, if one of the 'cocky' specials fell among strangers who didn't like his manner or traditions, he might be wary of the boots that would as soon kick in a strike-breaker's head as not. The strike had spread from one end of New Zealand to the other. The men weren't in it alone. In Christchurch, the strikers' women helped the Unions to win camping-ground in Hagley Park. Here on hundreds of acres of brown grass, ringed in by the stately old English trees planted by the pioneers, tents went up like toadstools. The married men drew rations at Hagley Park and slept at home, but the single lads were fed, bedded, and entertained under the oak trees. Half the city was in sympathy. People from Christchurch gave them cricket bats, women came with concertinas and fiddles and held open-air concerts in the sweet evenings. The youths, with red rosettes in their coats, against whom every newspaper in the country poured forth the vials of its soapy wrath, sang 'Annie Laurie' and 'Swannee' with as much enthusiasm and more tune than the then little-known Internationale.

When the cocky specials landed in Christchurch, riding up the main streets somewhat like John Gilpin, but in sterner frame of mind, the Hagley Park camp was deserted. The young men went down town looking for trouble, which not infrequently they found. Specials never rode alone, and the red rosettes marched in gangs, three or four abreast, ready for the challenge. Men climbed on packing-cases and bridge parapets and made fiery speeches. The specials rode at them and batoned their skulls with pick-handles. The baton wound, a long shallow cut of four inches or so, provides enough gore to look more serious than it really is, and tales of bloody murder were rife in town.

The batoning of Bob Simpson, who had worked on the wharf during Starkie's one lone day as a dock-labourer, provoked a crisis. It wouldn't have been so awkward had not the little party—Simpson, Starkie, and three gentlemen friends—emerged from an hotel laden with bottles of excellent brown ale just as the specials rode by. The specials were young men adroit at taking umbrage. They had a good deal of excuse. Howls of 'Scab', 'Cocky', or the simple combination, 'Cocky Scab', followed them wherever they rode, sometimes adorned with more sinister embellishments. The old lack of understanding between town and country was in full play. The young men used to a clay soil and the smell of cows didn't believe in the muscle or physical courage of the young men used to scrubby patches of garden and a smell of malt. In this they were deluded, as their own frequent downfalls, and later the war years, were to prove. In the meantime, there was between them a mutual hatred and contempt. White arm-bandage and red rosette loved each other as tiger loves jaguar.

Bob Simpson was maybe correct in what he said as to the special's ancestry and personal habits. It was a matter of opinion—and didn't, in Starkie's view, justify the speed with which the special rode straight into the arcade, and brought down his pick-handle over Bob's head. Bob dropped like a log. A moment later the special dropped too—not like a log, but like a wildcat. Starkie dragged him by one leg from his horse, and settled further argument by the fatally handy means of the beer-bottle. Then he ran, and not before it was time. Dodging through the arcade, where the mounted specials could not follow, gave him three minutes' grace, and during that time he espied a bicycle.

The city of Christchurch has only one ambition. It likes to be thought more English than the English. Its pioneers were almost exclusively church settlers, and brought with them English seedling trees, English architecture, English tradition. The results, as applied to the originally flat and dreary expanse where Christchurch was built, are extremely charming and extremely insincere. Stone arches cup a pale sunlight between their uplifted hands. Hagley Park sweeps brown and green over many acres, there is a sad little stream, only deep enough to drown an occasional stray cat and float the canoes of picnickers, which by suffering its smooth banks to be covered with the long green tresses of the weeping willow has become a scenic feature, and is dignified by the soubriquet of the River Avon. If you want to be beloved among the citizens, you produce the more English than the English *cliché*. You can rest assured they will never even suspect that the overdoing of such a thing is an atrocity.

But the sinister truth about Christchurch is that it is predominantly not the City of English trees, but the city of bicycles. People who in any other city would commit *hara-kiri* before mounting one of these ignoble vehicles, in Christchurch cycle and are proud of it. Archbishops cycle, mayors cycle, private detectives cycle, fashionable wantons cycle. When Starkie removed a cycle and thus escaped from the city, he was removing nothing rich and rare, but rather helping in a small way to solve the most inextricable problem of traffic and morbid psychology that has yet arisen in New Zealand.

With the exception of a cigarette, lit between shaking hands and puffed by the wayside, he never halted for refreshments until he reached the Bealey Tunnel. The men on construction work there wouldn't give him a job, but welcomed him for his dramatic news of the strike. He washed shirts for the brawny West Coasters, who decked themselves out for dancing after nightfall, cooked stews with fair success, ran errands to the nearest stores and public-houses. Four West Coast months were free, safe, not unamusing—though he was lonely for the Red Rosettes and the camp in Hagley Park.

The Riccarton races fell at the end of the fourth month, and although this celebrated event takes place on a course within Christchurch boundaries, Starkie felt that the police must by now have enough on their minds to have forgotten an assault and theft of so stale a vintage.

What really cut his pride was that he was drinking lemonade and sarsaparilla at the time of his downfall. Beer, he had determined, was not for him. Beer meant trouble.

'Have a whisky, Starkie!' yelled an exuberant comrade.

A heavy hand fell on his shoulder. A voice said quietly, 'Starkie, is it?'

His heart started to beat very fast. He didn't look round at the face, but at the big square-toed boots. Then he stared around. They were all about him.

'I've been looking for you,' said the voice reproachfully. 'Let's see—just on four months.'

At the Christchurch police-station they must have liked sparrows, for they fed the prisoners on crumbs. Furthermore, the cell boasted three blankets—all lousy. He slept not at all. He had already met fleas and flat, unpleasant bugs; but the louse in New Zealand confines its activities for the most part to prisons or Salvation Army hostels, and its guile was strange to him. He scratched all night, and in the morning when he appeared before a magistrate, at the Christchurch police-court, he was unshaven, crumpled, and disreputable.

'The court is now open.'

Everyone stood up. Starkie was gently urged into the dock. The magistrate peered at him.

'A Maori, is he?'

Sergeant Emerson, of the Mounted Police from Invercargill, spoke up. Starkie heard the complicated facts of his ancestry truthfully explained.

'Red Indian,' said the magistrate, with sad satisfaction. 'A savage.' The charge of assaulting a special constable and making off with a bicycle was droned out. The air in the court smelt fusty.

All the positions of vantage were occupied by thin, grey, unaired-looking lawyers. A small gallery of loafers shuffled uneasily, standing behind a rail which bisected the court. There was no seating accommodation for the public, but reporters lounged in their chairs and drew diagrams with pencil-stubs at one side of the room.

Starkie pleaded guilty. He had no lawyer, and no case. Nevertheless a moment's incredulous and angry surprise shook him when the magistrate said, almost playfully, 'One year's imprisonment with hard labour.'

Somebody laid hold on his arm. He was led out of the dock. He looked back desperately, wondering if George or his father might have slipped in at the back of the little crowd; but Sergeant Emerson's was the only face known to him. The reporters and legal gentlemen all looked studiously unconcerned, like fish in an aquarium. His feet stumbled on the first steps of a shallow stone stair leading downwards from the court-room.

3 Ring and Dummy

When the police escort delivered Starkie from the train at the Invercargill gaol, it was 7.30 at night, and the place, being for the most part invisible, didn't reveal its secrets, pleasant or otherwise. They gave him a basin of cold stew, a plate of bread-and-butter, and a cup of tea. Then a key turned. He was left in his own clothes, and with the Christchurch lock-up's contribution of lice. In the cell he lay quiet and alone, and tried to figure out the number of hours in a year, but gave it up. He could hear nothing but an occasional tramp of footsteps along a stone corridor, and wished they had given him somebody for company, even a drunk.

Next morning, beginning from the reveille hour of six, he said good-bye to civilian life. First he was taken to the store. Here they finger-and-thumb you, get the details of scars or tattoo marks, where you were born, how your father came to marry your mother, the way your great-aunt's hair curls. He was handed a uniform, of which the white trousers and brown coat were less unsightly than the two-peaked cap—which seemed designed to make the convict look like a bus driver going and coming. A warder marched him to a cell, stood in the corridor while Starkie took up position on the other side of the door-way.

'Strip,' ordered the warder.

Starkie removed his clothes, and said good-bye to his cigarettes. When the convict is mother-naked, his clothes are thrown out piece by piece to the warder, and the uniform tossed in. His own suit goes to the stores, where, if the warders don't take a fancy to his cigarettes or such little trifles, the prisoners in charge of the store department get the pickings.

The cell's construction was simple. A hammock provided him with better sleeping accommodation than the stone bench he had vaguely expected. Seven bars criss-crossed the window, and a ventilator in one corner of the roof was the free air's only other channel. The door had a little spy-hole through which the warder on night duty could peer every few minutes. All through the first night he never slept, for one of the walls echoed with the tiny tap-tap-tap of the man in the next cell. Starkie didn't then understand thc Morse code, but he did understand that a convict's first duty is to get the knack of this, and settled down to working it out. The tap-tap-tap—unintelligible, friendly, gentle—went on for hours. In the corridor the warder's boots rang hollow, like some armoured ghost of the Middle Ages plodding by on doom's journey.

Six o'clock, the bell burst inside your head. Get up, make your bed, march along the corridor to empty your latrine tin; march back, get a bowl of porridge, and a cup of sweet black tea. Eight o'clock, another bell—the bells rang all over the prison with a fiendish brassy din—and the convict stands to attention at the door of his cell. A warder comes along. 'Right wheel, march. . . .' They fall in, the prison boots shuffling heavily and dismally along the corridors. In the yard there is roll-call, and the prisoners are dismissed—some to their work, others to the Ring.

Starkie spent some time on the Ring. This is the second-best institution in New Zealand gaols, the best being the Dummy. The Ring is in the prison yard and about thirty feet in diameter. The game is to try to find the end of it; but you never do, although you are marched around it from eleven in the morning until five at night—the close of the convict's long day. Over the dry ground shuffle some great fellows who have known action in their time. In front of the fifteen-year-old savage, gawky in his shapeless white trousers and peaked cap, marched old Jimmy Pearson; Dan Paul the murderer, the grey old badger who battered his wife's head to a bloody pulp when in drink; Archie Sayegh—men for whom prison life held no mystery whatever. Dinner was called at twelve, and wasn't bad—potatoes in their jackets, stew served in tin pannikins and eaten with battered tin spoons. Before the five o'clock meal, each man was searched by a warder, then marched back to the cells and locked in, with two ancient magazines for company. A pound loaf of bread, a plate of swimming oatmeal, and a cup of black tea finished the day's amenities. Then tap-tap-tap again. You could talk in the Ring, your mouth twisted up sideways so that the warders didn't hear. Starkie thought he had got the idea of the Morse code. He pressed his face against the wall, picking up the soft little staccato of taps.

'Bluey' Jameson next morning told him to fall in line with Dave Lester's squad, and he was marched out to the swamps where the prisoners were reclaiming land, shovelling reeds and tons of stinking blue mud. After a mile and a half in line, they were loaded on a funny little black she-devil of a train, puffed along half a mile farther, then dumped out near the swamplands. The mud was no joke. Apart from the fishy reek of it, it clung in great soggy dollops to the shovels, and underfoot the ground gave into pot-holes where the men sank knee-deep. He was wet as a seal before the dinner halt.

The food for the swamp gangs was cooked on the spot—meat boiled up in a foul and corroded old copper which hadn't been cleaned since the day it left the ironmonger's shop. They were out of sight of the gaol's coarse but cleanly amenities. The tins in which the stew, flanked with potatoes in their jackets, was ladled out were foul with grease. Dinner was served in a long shed and eaten standing or sitting on the ground. Talk was allowed at meal-times, and the men had a tobacco issue—an ounce a day of rank black twist. Starkie's lungs craved for the bite of tobacco-smoke. He hadn't yet received his issue, but old Sampson tossed him over a lump of twist. The others lit their little three-inch clay pipes. The flame of a candle-stub was used. Their match ration was one a day, and the stub was a life-saver.

Arney, the warder in charge of the swamp gangs, knocked the twist out of Starkie's hand and trod on it.

'Wait till you get your tobacco issue,' he said curtly.

Starkie saw old Sampson's lip twist, waiting to see him make a fool of himself. He kept his mouth shut and walked away.

Cigarettes weren't allowed either in the gaol or at the swamps, but the men smoked them—the tobacco shredded and rolled in scraps of paper, the cigarettes held in the mouth beside the stem of the empty clay pipes, whose reek was too much for all but the toughest stomachs. When Arney handed them over to 'Bluey' at the gaol, they were searched, man by man, lined up in the Dome—the centre of the great building. Arney stepped out and passed a slate to 'Bluey'. 'Bluey' pondered a moment, then spoke sharply.

'Stark, half rations, insufficient work.'

That night his bread was cut to half a pound. The bowl of porridge had dwindled, but the tea arrived black and strong as usual. He drank it in little steaming sips, then folded his arms over his head and lay on the floor of the cell, too tired to listen for the Morse code.

Arney the warder didn't like Starkie, and Starkie didn't like him. On the next day at the swamps they watched each other, cat and mouse. 'Stark, fall out—no tobacco.' But Hawley, who had known his father before—ten years ago he had disappeared into this secure retreat—slipped him a lump of twist, and the men in the afternoon distracted Arney's attention while Starkie drew the smoke down into his lungs. On Saturday the prison personnel washed its body, and on Sunday sanctified its mind. The men, about a hundred and twenty, were marched in bunches to the shower-room, and stripped to stand under the cold jets, their strong, toughened bodies stretching and turning like an uncouth statue-gallery in the white light. You could tell by their skins and the colour of their eyes what prison had done for them. A man's life in prison depended mainly on his self-control and his stomach. The yellow, uneasy ones were the ex-clerks who couldn't stand up to rough fare. But on a lean diet the labourers had thrived, and the swamps sweated the fat off their bones and the beer out of their blood. They were brown, and trouble had fined the outlines of some of the younger faces. It was a crude, pathetic statue gallery, but not a bestial one. Starkie's bronze carcase was outrivalled by the splendid nugget-black of old Archie Taylor, an American negro with the stature of a giant.

Jim Frenton caught Starkie smoking at the wrong moment, and there was an argument. Starkie, who had begun to develop a constitutional dislike of all warders, told Jim Frenton what he could do. Frenton didn't, but went instead to the Governor. At 2.30 in the afternoon, Starkie was locked up in his cell and that humble abode swept clean of furnishings as though a vacuum cleaner had been over it. Books, blankets, hammock, knife, fork, and spoon were all removed. He was left with the Bible and a latrine tin. After dark the cell was unlocked and his blankets thrown in to him, locked again, and the warder's boots crunched away, leaving him in solitude and darkness. He curled up under the blankets and ignored everything—even the Morse code, which he now understood well enough to deduce his neighbour's ideas on warders. This was not bad as far as it went, but Starkie could have carried it farther. His solitude lasted from Saturday afternoon until Monday morning, when he was taken in front of the Governor and sentenced to three days in the Dummy.

It is always dusk in the Dummy, which lies underground. A vague ghost of daylight slips through from the corridor, but there is no window, no ventilator. At six in the morning the door is unlocked, and the prisoner gets his clothes, all except boots. At nine in the evening he is stripped of everything but his shirt, given a six-foot strip of rubberoid twenty inches wide, and two blankets. With these he makes his bed on the concrete floor. His day's rations are thrown into the cell at the six o'clock awakening—a large tin basin of water, a sixteen-ounce loaf of dry bread. The solitude which is strange and gloomy by day at night becomes unendurable. Lying on the concrete floor in winter-time, the slippery rubberoid clammy under a man's body, the convict finds that big sores break out on hips and knees. At last the lying-down position becomes unbearable.

Starkie invented a game to keep him warm at nights. It was

a very clever game. He pulled a button off his shirt, flicked it as far as he could between finger and thumb, then knelt down in the darkness and groped for it on the concrete floor. Finding it in the pitch-black of the cell took an astonishingly long time, and when he did feel it under his fingers he stood in another corner of the cell and flicked it away again. It was a simple recreation, but it was his challenge to the ponderous four-walled darkness which told him, in that oozy voice of a silence, that he was no longer a man. Flick . . . grope . . . button between your fingers. Somewhere perhaps in the darkness of his cave, starving Neanderthal found a way to take his mind off the sinking flames of his last fire.

It was warmer in the daytime, and then he could sleep, with the Bible for his pillow. He ate his bread-ration at six o'clock, and for the rest of the day went without. At the end of his three days in the Dummy, he was taken up, put in his cell again, and given another bread-ration. Then he was marched out to the swamp again and put on the sand-rake. The bread and water diet hadn't affected him very greatly while he was in the Dummy; but now the rake was too much for him, and the sand, which was loaded on tip-trucks and sent rattling down the line, was a gigantic enemy. He knew he was for it again. Back at the gaol, hc was put on half rations for insufficient work. The next morning, a Saturday, the boys were lined up to parade in the Ring. A little Englishman—Hastings by name—signalled him with crooked finger and wary eyes. Starkie edged close, was slipped half a pound of bread from under the Englishman's shirt. But Starkie was clumsy. Arney saw. Arney snatched the bread and threw it on the ground. Starkie shouted at him, something unintelligible but offensive, was marched off and locked up again. For three more days he lived on bread and water.

The older men among the prisoners didn't like seeing the kid roughly handled, and made things worse by slipping him presents, which he never had guile enough to hide. There was a rumour that Wylde Stark had asked the prison authorities to hand it out tough, saying that it would make or break the cub. This would have been in keeping with the old Indian's character, but he didn't allow for the streak of pride which made Starkie forbear to take things lying down. Anthony, the drill instructor, caught him smoking the cigarette John Cunningham had passed to him in the Ring—smoking it greedily; for almost invariably when the tobacco issue was passed out, came the curt command, 'Stark, fall out.'

Anthony looked through the spy-hole of the cell. 'I'll fix you later,' he promised.

The superintendent was at breakfast. Starkie had heard much prison gossip as to what it felt like to be fixed by a warder or instructor. He got ready. The door opened. Anthony advanced his stout body into the cell.

The most useful piece of furniture in the cell was a three-legged stool. Starkie picked it up, brought it down on the drill-instructor's skull. Anthony went down like a log. Starkie, in a moment's frantic groping, found the gaol keys, burst into the long corridor. For perhaps five seconds he had a wild hope of freedom. Then the bells sounded, fierce, brassy, insistent, all along the grey passages. A fellow-prisoner had given the alarm.

There were six guns pointing at him. He backed slowly into his cell, his eyes mad, every nerve in his body snapping.

'Hold up your hands,' said one of the warders.

'Starkie, for God's sake be good!' urged Frenton; Starkie, seeing the man's brow beaded with little drops of sweat, remembered that they had been at school together, until he was kicked out of that school, as from all the rest. They got one of the handcuffs on him. The touch of steel sent him crazy, and, guns or no guns, he smashed the other handcuff at the face of Goodwin, the warder who was holding his arm. He felt a gun nuzzle into his ribs, and froze. The other handcuff went on. They marched him down to the Dummy.

That night he went before the heads again. Twenty-one days on bread and water in the Dummy. Seven days in 'figure eights'.

Ever since he had heard the bells give warning in the corridor, a queer spasmodic shiver had shaken him every few minutes. He was still shaking when they marched him back to the Dummy.

The 'figure eight' is a mild version of the French Foreign Legion's beloved torture, *le crapaud*. For a period of hours each day, ranging from two to four, the prisoner's arms are doubly handcuffed across the small of his back, wrist and elbows forced together. No leglocks are used. He can sit, stand, or lie, as he pleases. At the end of an hour, the niggling little ache which starts between the shoulder-blades will have forced its way up into the cervical vertebrae. Wriggle or twist as he likes, he can find no position to ease that red thrust through the muscles of shoulder and neck. Then the ache creeps downwards, biting into the ribs and spine.

The new hand makes things worse for himself by tossing about. An hour is enough for most men. When his three hours a day were finished, Starkie's nerves were in pulp. But the stone floor, the shadows, seemed almost friendly. He crept into the back of his kennel like a sick dog, and crouched there, terrified at the thought of another day's passing and the figure eights again.

On the sixth day, Anthony was out of hospital and came down to the Dummy. The door opened and he walked in, a shadow looming among the other shadows.

'You're the one who hit me over the head with a stool, eh?' A fist crashed into the face of the handcuffed boy. Then the door clicked again, footsteps retreated.

In the morning, Starkie complained to the prison superintendent, showing his split lip. He was told that none of the warders would do such a thing.

'You must have fallen down,' said the superintendent, with splendid confidence, and proceeded unperturbed on his way. But Anthony did not come down to the Dummy again.

When the pound loaf of bread was thrown into his cell each morning, the tin pannikin contained plenty of water, yet the curious thing was that he was always thirsty. Lapping the water out of the pannikin didn't seem to ease his throat. The first week he got through the bread ration without overmuch difficulty. Before his sentence in the Dummy was finished, twelve loaves were piled up in a corner of the cell. He would start to eat the bread, gnawing it like a rat. Then the muscles of his throat constricted horribly, salt came into his mouth and nostrils. He swallowed and swallowed, jerkily, but he couldn't get it down. He thrust it aside and lay with arms folded over his face. At least his wrists were free. No more now of the deadly nagging ache which started as a little feeling of nausea, and persisted until it over-rode the world. Seven days' figure eights, and they were all over. . . . He turned his face to the wall of the cell, and the darkness lapped him about.

Overhead sounded the feet of men, hollow on the hollow stone floors.

He began to dream a great deal about water, not only when asleep but in waking hours, when his mind now slid easily and rapidly into daydream. It wasn't that he was ever kept short. He could never complain that the tin pannikin wasn't properly filled. It was just that it never seemed enough, or its water was too flat to alleviate the tightness in his throat. He could see a dark dew-pond in the Canterbury hills, and a hawthorn tree stooped over it, its wizened little berries bright scarlet. In the Dummy, all colour-tones were bleached out into the monotony of black shadow, grey daylight. He could very clearly remember the edge of foam, hissing and pale yellow on the brown sands, where he had bathed with May Simms. Then the innermost waves, translucent, knee-deep, with soft little cold patches which were the half-fluid bodies of transparent jellyfish. Deeper, the sea curled green and laughing against a girl's white breast and shoulders. It was a picture-gallery to him, no longer even the shadow of an emotion. All the strength of his senses seemed to have been sucked out of him. He could turn quietly enough from May to the brownish but very clear waters of the Waihopai stream, and remember the feel of the thick blue-skinned eels between his fingers.

In those nights of his last week in the Dummy, somebody else stood beside him, invisible. He was not aware of this. He only knew that he felt a great deal quieter, and had no desire to eat. The same shadow once stood in the cave-cells of the old hermits who mortified their flesh with fasting, and tore the lusts out of their senses with the chastisements of whips, brambles, and flinty beds. 'They turned to gloomy madness . . .'

A prison doctor—a youthful man named Andretton—came into the Dummy one morning and asked Starkie questions, speaking in a clipped, friendly style. He stood over the boy, who refused to move from the corner in the shadows, ran his hands over the ribs, felt his pulse, felt the movement of the muscles working in his throat. He ordered Starkie up to daylight and full rations three days before his time was up. Starkie never grasped what the doctor was saying until the white beam of the sun pierced into his eyes through a high window as he shambled at the warder's heels back to his cell.

They fed him with porridge, bread, and marmalade, sweetened tea; the black, steaming fluid trickling down his gullet broke the misery of thirst that the dry bread had brought on him, and as he drank, slow tears of thankfulness came into his eyes. There was nobody to see them. When the others were marched out to the swamplands, he stayed behind in his cell still under sentence of solitary confinement.

At eleven o'clock Anthony came along, opened the door, and handed Starkie two pounds of oakum. He made no attempt this time to touch the prisoner, and refrained from the usual rough jeer. Perhaps something in the boy's hollow eyes and silence touched him. The door was shut. Starkie was left with the oakum.

At first glance the prison task of oakum-picking looks like velvet compared with the shovelling of swamp mud. The materials of labour are so small and harmless. One can pick up the twisted ropes in a single hand, and crush the results of a day's work into a coat pocket.

The end of the afternoon found Starkie with every finger-nail on his hands broken, the skin rubbed into raw and bleeding patches, the palms puffing up in great yellow blisters.

The oakum comes in little short rope-lengths, ship-ropes tarsealed, greasy, and hard with perhaps fifty years' wear and hauling on the vessels of the Seven Seas. It is the oakum-picker's task to separate these lengths fibre from fibre. This involves wearing through the tar and grease with the surfaces of the fingers—picking, picking, picking, while the matted hemp resists loosening with all the strength which the hard hands tugging at it on the high seas have given to its compact mass. The amount of fibre to be prised loose from a single rope-length is unbelievable. When Starkie's two pounds were picked, the mass of loose fibre piled up high as an ordinary kitchen table. He stared at it, unable to believe that it had all come from those brutal little tarred ropes. The warder came in, slammed down his rations, departed. He stretched himself out, utterly weary in body and mind.

'Tap-tap-tap, tap-tap-tap,' went the woodpecker in the next cell.

Starkie picked oakum for two days, his broken nails shredding in the tangles of the mass that could be crumpled up to nothing at the end of a day. On the third day they put the oakum in his cell at 8 o'clock. At 4.30 it was still there. 'Bluey' showed his purplish face through the spy-hole.

'What's this, Stark?'

'Take it away. I won't pick it.'

For three days more he went back on bread and water, but not to the Dummy. On the Saturday he was marched into the Ring. Taylor marched before him, his shining black face expressionless as the Rock of Gibraltar. Dan Paul the murderer was three places up in the line.

Starkie heard the whisper, 'Catch hold.' He saw the stubby fingers that had smashed in a woman's skull unclose and pass something along to the next man. The chain, keeping in perfect step, passed the fragments of bread and meat from hand to hand. He could grab at them, and swiftly, with one animal gesture, cram them into his mouth. The warder in charge of the Ring couldn't or wouldn't see. Little Hastings, the weak-chested Englishman, grinned at him. The convict who had given the alarm was somewhere in that moving circle round thirty feet of ground trodden hard by the feet of God knows what naked misery and despair. But for the rest he felt at that moment that not one of them was less than a friend. These men and their Ring, almost as old in their meaning as the circle that is the symbol of infinity, are the stone that the builders of society have rejected. But in this one quality, their queer subterranean loyalty to one another, they are worthy for the most part to be set at the head of the Temple.

That Saturday in the Ring was almost the last time he saw his fellow prisoners. He had started to cough, and instead of being sent back to the swamp gangs was put out to cut and wire tea-tree stacks in the bush, under the eye of a civilian—a tall, brown-skinned man, James Rannock by name. Rannock, on his grey horse, made no more of his authority than to wave a hand as he rode up and down the long roll of the tea-tree slopes. Wind and sunshine beat into Starkie's body with a fierce new delight. Rannock fed his prison labour on honest bush food: fresh meat, billy tea, enormous flat damper scones cooked on the three-legged camp oven. Starkie had no joy in any man's authority, but he would have run at stirrup for 'the Boss'. To be spoken to as a man, to light his cigarette as he pleased, to borrow a match from the Boss if he hadn't one himself . . . his head went back, his chest out, his hands, with their broken nails, handled the slim grey stems of tea-tree like an artist with his paint-brushes. There were no complaints from Rannock to the prison authorities. Yet always Starkie's heart kept the sick dread of going back again—of the shut-in days with the oakum, the Dummy's shadowy hell, the great blue dollops of mud churned up from the stinking swamp.

At nights he went back to the prison and slept in his old cell, with the Morse-tapper for companion next door. One morning, his cell was not unlocked while the rest marched off. He heard the abrupt, sharp orders.... 'Right wheel... forward, march...!' The boots rang along the corridor in that monotonous dreary tread which, with the twisted upper lip, is the stamp of the long-imprisoned man. Starkie's thoughts raced frantically in his mind like mice in a cage. He tried to think what he could have done. He knew he hadn't done anything, nothing really bad; but suppose something should have *looked* bad? He had been free with Rannock lately, suppose the Boss had reported him for cheek? That cringing terror of false appearances is a bogy of the caged life. He resolved not to show them, whatever happened, that he cared what they could do. But his throat tightened again, as it had done when he lay in the Dummy underground.

The door opened. 'Bluey' said, 'March!' He tramped along a corridor, entered the stores. They gave him his suit, crumpled and dishevelled in the twelve months it had lain tossed aside. He was told to strip, took off his white trousers, brown coat, peaked cap; put on, one by one, his old clothes. Queer . . . it was the suit for which he had bilked the little tailor up in the Wyndham Valley. But they had never landed him over that. He was standing in the office, somebody was giving him good advice. He listened in complete silence. Then they handed him twelve shillings and sixpence, his pay for the year's work. He had served every day, though he had long lost count . . . there was nothing but the swamp, the Ring, the Dummy, the fresh air blowing among the grey, rough-barked trees of James Rannock's tea-tree slopes. These things had eaten twelve months out of his youth. Suddenly he remembered that he had celebrated a birthday in gaol, and tried to recall whether he had then been out with the swamp-gangs or down in the Dummy. He couldn't find the place. It didn't matter. . . . He knew, anyhow, that he was now sixteen years old.

He was taken to the gate and told to go. The big building, its prison population poured out of it into mud-holes and punishment cells and the Ring, looked remote and lonely. The street outside the prison was just as quiet. Nobody met him, but none the less he wished that his clothes were not so outrageously crumpled and soiled.

4 Cup for Youth

BETWEEN Briscoe's Corner and the little fish-shop were exactly seventeen lamp-posts. In the fish-shop, sitting on a high stool and swallowing down the sweet little rock oysters from Stewart Island, he felt comparatively safe. But the slatternly girl who thrust the food across the marble-topped counter stared at him, and turned aside to titter. His crumpled clothes. . . . He walked back to Briscoe's Corner. Back to the fish-shop again, to stare in at the window, anxious that nobody passing by should notice him. He stood there until the white pool of the sunlight was gone from the streets, and instead, around each lamp-post, swam the cautious little aureoles of orange.

That night he spent four of his remaining eleven shillings on a bed in a small hotel. He had no sleeping-kit, and crept naked between grey-white sheets. In the morning, passing over the necessity of breakfast for the heavier need of hoarding the money he had left, he went back to Briscoe's Corner. Although he had been born in this town, a door seemed to have closed between him and the intimacies of his childhood. He wasn't going home. Nobody whose face was familiar went past. The passers-by looked harassed, and greatly intent upon their own business; even the mangy stray dogs loped swift and stealthy from one butcher's shop to the next.

But Starkie had one acquaintance in Invercargill who was not likely to disown him—a collective acquaintance, with many slight differences in face and build, but always with the same stolid stare, the same heavy hand on his shoulder, the same heavy, jocose voice. This acquaintance came and stood beside him midway through his second morning at Briscoe's Corner. The big paw dropped on his shoulder. The voice said, 'Where are you working now, Stark?'

'Looking for a job,' he muttered, never looking at the big, bland face.

'Don't be funny, Stark.' The grip on his shoulder tightened. 'I'll give you a job, my lad—two jobs. You can have a job at a ha'penny a day blocking the swamps, or a job at a dollar a day fighting for your King. What's it to be?'

Something inside the mind of the boy who could have two jobs disliked the idea of being run by the police. He had served his time in tomb and mud-hole and irons. He twisted in the policeman's grip.

'I'll give you a job,' he shouted, 'pulling yourself out of this!' Then he took to his heels. The policeman, taken by surprise, floundered on his back in the middle of Briscoe's window-display, splintered glass framing fat body and outraged face. In a minute a whistle shrieked, feet pelted. The running boy was out of sight.

That night Starkie slept in an extremely wet and mouldy haystack down in Roach's Paddock, and found that the fascinating tramps who in his childhood had praised this form of sleeping accommodation were liars like the rest. The hay knotted toughly in his ribs, smelt of mildew, and was full of a tiny red creeping parasite which bit. For two days he spent his time dodging the public. He bought his food, sixpenn'orth at a time, warily over the counters of obscure shops. Always the eyes of those who served him seemed hard and watchful. Always he listened for the sound of the whistle. He made a business of slinking through town on an elaborate, useless system of cross-streets, never proceeding straight in any direction. It was all purposeless, blind and hopeless. He would be picked up, and he knew it. But apart from the game of hare and hounds, he had nothing to do and nowhere to go.

It was on one of these elaborate games that the hare found himself outside the Drill Sheds. He had a feeling that They were on his heels. He edged down to the Zealandia Hall, noticed the flutter of the cotton Union Jack, and the straggling little queue of men in civilian clothes, fell in line with them. He was safe, camouflaged, doing what other men were doing without attracting the notice of the police. He was inside the hall, looking across a desk into the eyes of a clean-shaven man who snapped absent-mindedly as he asked a string of questions, but whose thin mouth had a good-humoured quirk at the corners.

'Ever been in gaol?'

He jumped. But 'No,' he said stolidly.

The eyes of the Captain behind the desk stared with some amusement at his clothes, still bearing the creases of a year in the prison stores.

'Nationality? Age?'

Starkie gave the nationality right, but his age as twenty.

'Had any trouble at *all*?' drawled the Captain.

Starkie shook his head.

'Very well, Stark.' The Captain bent his head, scribbled for a moment on a piece of paper. 'Chit for Dr Bevan, rooms in Speight Street. Hop it, and report here when he's done with you.'

Dr Bevan was easy. Hands that felt the stringy muscles in his lean body, shrewd eyes that stared at him. He went back with the chit to the Zealandia Hall, passed fit for active service.

Captain Grey pored over the chit for a moment, then barked at his recruit:

'Ever been in gaol, Stark?'

'Never, sir,' said Starkie.

The hard face crinkled up in a sudden grin. 'Very well, Starkie. You never were in gaol. Well, there's a contingent leaving in about twenty days' time—you can join up with that. . . .'

Twenty days, and every copper in Invercargill on his tail, ready to box him up until the War was over and done with. For the moment, utterly disheartened, he could only stammer thanks and slink back to the streets again. That night he curled up like a dog and slept in a corner behind the hall. The mere shadow of the arrogant little cotton flag was some ghostly protection to him. In the morning he was inside the office again. For three days he waylaid Captain Grey, joining up with the queues whenever he could edge his way among them, camping behind the hall at nights. On the fourth day, down to his last shilling, he buttonholed Captain Grey as that self-possessed officer strode towards his lair, and begged to be allowed a preview of the War. Captain Grey, who knew precisely as much about Starkie's past and present circumstances as Starkie and the police did themselves, screwed up his mouth, hesitated.

'There's no chance, Stark.'

Starkie broke down. Precisely what he said he could never afterwards remember, but there was a good deal in it about lamp-posts, cops, the Dummy, and a broken window-pane with a police official framed in the middle of it.

Captain Grey looked neither hurt nor surprised. At the end of Starkie's tale, he said curtly, 'A draft leaves for Trentham tomorrow. If anyone falls out sick, you can take his place. The train leaves at six a.m.' He was gone, and Starkie looked after him as never yet had he looked after schoolmaster or ghostly consoler.

The first necessity was money. Starkie thought of the people in Invercargill who might at a crisis lend him money; and the list, when he considered it, was uncommonly small. But in the end he pitched on a friend of his father's—David Kidson, the blacksmith. He caught the smith in his forge, mellow-tempered from the first of a cider brew, and had two pounds in his pocket and a clap on his shoulder almost before he had begun his story. Breathless with this success, he crept around the railway station, bundled himself into a train, and paid the guard for his ticket to the Bluff, where lurked in his memory the wettest little tavern he had ever struck.

When he got there he found that war had cast a gloom over a once companionable pub, and without wasting time came back to the Club Hotel, otherwise Mrs Wooten's. Here he found what he wanted—soldiers of the King drinking His Majesty's health. Nobody minded telling him about the soldiering life, especially when he pulled a crisp note out of his pocket and paid for a round like a man and a brother. By and by Starkie struck what he wanted, a comrade who couldn't hold his liquor. The comrade's name was Alec, for which Starkie liked him none the better; but he looked after Alec like a father after his first-born, presuming that the father wanted the first-born to die of alcoholic poisoning. Six o'clock closing, that most devastating custom of the New Zealander's country, emptied the soldiers out of the bar; but for Alec the fun was only beginning. Starkie purchased two bottles of whisky and took his victim into town to enjoy the martial pleasures of whisky, women, and song. Every step was a risk, but necessary. The bottles did their best—but Alec, though by now in a condition of alcoholic love for all the world, miraculously kept on his feet. Starkie glowered at him, haunted by a dread vision of a six o'clock train and Alec on it. . . . It wouldn't do. His arm around the waist of his erring friend, he steered him gently over the rough-metalled streets to the little house where dwelt an old relative of his, Dick Harris.

Dick Harris had a brew of his own. He didn't uncork it for all the riff-raff in Invercargill, but it wasn't hard for Starkie to whisper his plans while Alec finished the last amber drops of the whisky. A bald head nodded.

'How'll you keep on your own feet, boy?'

'God knows. I haven't had enough to feed a sparrow the last three days, and it won't take much to knock me out. What can I do?'

The old man patted his shoulder.

'Leave it to your uncle, boy,' he chuckled. 'Tea, laddie, tea . . . horrible womanish stuff—but it'll do for you now. Get in there and keep your cobber cheerful.'

At 5.30 in the morning, Alec, with the rug drawn over him, had been sprawling in sleep for three hours. Some subconscious prompting half woke him. He stirred, stretched his arms, groaned, 'Oh, God! . . .'

Old Harris pounced on him like a hawk.

'One more drink, my boy—a toast to all you brave soldiers going away tomorrow.'

Outside the dawn was blue in the tangled trees. Harris had pinned the heavy plush curtains together; there was no light in the room but the splutter of candles, replaced so that their stubs were not too near the warning leap and flutter of death. Alec blinked, reached out his hand, tipped the glass.

'Toas'—brave boys—goin'—' His head dropped. His mouth opened wide in a rattling snore.

'Yes,' said old Harris with satisfaction, 'that one was a knock-out drop.' His horny brown hand caught Starkie a tremendous blow on the shoulder. 'Run, you bloody young cub! Run for it! Half an hour and you're clear.'

One moment to wring that knotted old hand and he was out

in the ice-cold air. It wasn't, thank God! perfectly light. Out of breath, a shadow among a thousand other shadows, he landed on the station, burrowed through the crowd to Captain Grey.

'Beg to report a man sick, sir. He can't leave today.'

For a moment Captain Grey stared in silence at Alec's papers. Then he laughed.

'Give me those tickets.'

Starkie handed them over. Very carefully Captain Grey crossed out Alec's fair name. 'Now,' he ordered, 'get on board that train.'

There were about four hundred men in the draft. To Starkie, still breathless from running, it seemed incredible that tears should be streaking the sunburnt faces of so many among them. Women, patient little ghosts in black, lifted up heavy children in their arms, and the men piled against the carriage windows, or still crowding the station, bent down their heads and kissed again and again the curve of a woman's face, a sleepy child's face. The big feather-laden hats of the women were tilted back at absurd angles by the men's rough embraces; their veils, spotted with big black velvet dots, were torn like cobwebs. A very old man, whose rheumy eyes didn't seem to focus their blank stare on any particular face, went past the window leaning on a heavy ash-stick, and groaning, 'Eee, dear! Eee, dear!' Then a young woman in grey tweeds, healthy as a sheep-dog, dashed up to Starkie, flung her arms around his neck and crushed her fresh lips against his mouth. He was taken by surprise, but the whole impulse of his being suddenly and fiercely wanted her.

Before he could speak or touch her, she thrust into his hand a little hold-all with cards of darning-wool, black and white thread, pins and needles, ran to the next window and repeated the performance. Craning as far from the carriage window as he dared, Starkie saw her breasts taut and her apple-red cheeks streaming with tears as she lifted herself to embrace another man. He felt furiously jealous and contemptuous. It takes a war to get some of them like that about the whole world of men. . . .

Behind the wooden pillars and dingy brown walls of the station, the little he could see of Invercargill was a cup of mist, almost sapphire blue. The minute hand of the station clock jerked itself forward like a cripple on his sticks. A party of men started singing 'Tipperary'. That somehow flicked a spark of enthusiasm into the wet faces of the women on the station. Some of the twisted mouths laughed, others shouted stupid, pathetic words of farewell.

'Take care of yourself!' 'Come back soon!'

The train's whistle shrieked, the crowded blur of faces and waving hands was jolted a pace backwards. Against the dark blue cup of the morning, men and women set their lips and unknowingly pledged one another.

5 The Khaki Place

THE STORESMAN opened his little slit of a mouth and gabbled, without pause for breath: 'Two shirts—two singlets—two underpants—two socks—two boots—knife—fork—spoon—plate—blankets—sign here—*C'rrect?'* Starkie, who had lost count somewhere about the underpants and had not the faintest idea whether his kit was in order or not, nodded speechlessly and signed as he was bid. He was given his tent number—D Lines, Tent Number Eight. 'Hop along and you'll find the rest of Otago there, all boozey,' grumbled the storesman.

Starkie hopped. Finding his way to Number Eight, D Lines, meant negotiating a route through a sea of mud, yellowish brown, like his newly issued khaki. For three days before the arrival of Otago Fourth, rain had pelted down on the flat spaces of the Trentham Camp, and the rabbit-warren trenches were awash. This wasn't Flanders, however, and you could sleep in a bell-tent. Starkie found his, bobbed under the tent-flap, and then cast one despairing glance at the outer world. There were already seven men seated in his tent, and they weren't, strictly speaking, men at all—they were monsters.

An enormous voice bellowed at him, 'Siddown!'

Another enormous voice shouted, 'Take a hand!' and he observed that the giants were playing Rummy. One of them had flaming red hair; another's nose was sunburned and peeling cruelly in a bright red face. The second largest of the giants stuttered horribly and talked more than the rest put together. Their boots, their bodies, their voices, overflowed the tent, and they all looked too large for their uniforms. Even in gaol, man to man, Starkie had been as substantial as the average warder, and better than most. Here he was the baby, and he wasn't surprised when a booming voice elected him mess orderly. Sadly he asked for a list of his duties.

'It means that you go get our tucker, see?'

'And get in good and early, before the cookhouse is rushed.'

'And see there's enough straw in the tent for decent beds.'

'And when there's latrine duty, you're it.'

'And you answer the roll call for two if one of us don't want to play.'

'And you do what you're told, see?'

Starkie saw. He nodded. Then a laugh rumbled from one of the giant's stomachs, a hand like a leg of mutton smote him horribly between the shoulder-blades. He was introduced in turn to the gentleman with the sunburned nose, Jim McLeod—courtesy title, 'Fleshy'; 'Ginger' Sheeth; Silver, whose fifteen stone drew him the pet name 'Goliath'; 'Stuttering Bob' Butts, Jack Frew, and Matthews, who was a sheep-owner and was to be known as 'Farmer Giles'.

'You gotta have a name,' Fleshy told him. 'Let's have a look at you. Yes, you can be Coon.'

After that there was a scrimmage, Starkie disliking the race of Coons and any personal reference to his own dusky complexion from strangers. When the scrimmage was finished, everybody was happy, particularly Fleshy and Bob Butts, who before reaching Trentham had taken the precaution of absorbing a good deal of beer.

Starkie secured their first dinner from the cookhouse, an enormous leg of mutton. This Fleshy undertook to carve, propping it on a truss of straw on the tent floor. In the excitement of the moment he set his foot on it. Into the mud slid the dinner.

'Oh, God!' said Goliath resignedly. 'Come along down to the canteen.'

On tea and little pork pies of a restrained size and parched interior they made their first meal in Trentham.

Getting to bed in the bell-tents wasn't a picnic, unless you were one of the Lilliputians who could really fit the minute trusses of straw doled out by the camp authorities. In Tent Eight this was quite out of the question; Starkie, the lightest of the company, turning the scales at twelve stone.

While the lights still flared in the canteen, Fleshy McLeod tapped him on the shoulder, whispering, 'C'mon.' Tent Eight's mess orderly crept out of the canteen at the heels of his lord and master, and the two made their beds up and turned in while the rest were still putting away pies and tea.

In an hour their tent-mates returned and there was an argument, the upshot of which was that the whole of Starkie's bedding was fairly enough distributed among the others. In the next tent they were audibly drawing lots for their bed-straw, but the results didn't matter, for Starkie, creeping on his stomach to the rear of the tent, cut a slit in the canvas and gently dragged out the straw. All was peace in Tent Eight until after reveille, when it was discovered by the outraged inhabitants of Tent Seven that straw had been dropped between the two tents. In the morning there was a court of inquiry, and Captain Dombey decided that the amount of straw in Tent Eight was against reason and the nature—never very lavish—of the storeman.

Starkie looked round to see which of his mates would spill the beans, but the seven giants remained mute as flitches of bacon, their eyes twinkling in large red faces. Tent Eight got three days' C.B. all round, during which none of his mates chose to reproach their mess orderly. After that Starkie decided that he was going to like the War.

Latrine duty was an undignified aspect of camp life, and affected him more painfully than the incessant barkings of 'Left, right, left, right! . . . About tur-r-r-rn! . . . Quick march! . . . Double march! . . . Forrrm Fourrrs! . . . Forrrm two-deep!' with which a drill sergeant—whose yell was all on the one hysterical note—haunted their hours in the drill ground. The primitive sanitary accommodation of the camp consisted of rows of kerosene tins, neatly set, with as much privacy as could be arranged, between the white rows of tents. Latrine duty entailed a slow and painful 'nightmare' progress among these tins after dusk. Upon the indignities of this Starkie pondered. As his tent-mates had prophesied, the lowest and most untouchable occupations always fell upon him, and he rather suspected that his colouring had something to do with it. The Maoris had marched off in a Pioneer Corps of their own, and Starkie was the only black sheep in the battalion. Nevertheless, he had a mind for higher things than latrine duty, and worried a great deal as to the possible dodging of it. By and by he found a solution, and things were much easier for the next two nights in succession. But his record-breaking performances thereafter did not escape the eye of authority, and he scented the beginning of the end when Sergeant Taine stood affectionately beside a latrine tin for a full half hour, pouring in water and staring with a hypnotized yet incredulous expression as the water miraculously drained away.

Presently Starkie was summoned to Captain Dombey's tent. Here, in serried phalanxes, were sixty-five latrine tins, the bottom of each punctured with four holes. Starkie had employed an unusually large nail, and the effect was ruinous. He was unable satisfactorily to explain this, and got six days' C.B., which was, however, little more uncomfortable than the normal routine of camp duty at Trentham. Exception was also taken to the words 'Rummies' Retreat', which appeared in enormous letters of nugget-black upon Tent Eight: for this a further three days' C.B. was bestowed upon him, and he learned more about drill than some soldiers are perplexed with in a lifetime.

Trainloads of girls came up to the Hutt towns from Wellington every night. In camp the tea bugle sounded at five; the mess orderlies went up for tea, meat, and vegetables; the dishes were washed and returned to the cookhouse, and after that, barring C.B., the bright young night was all your own to play with. The boys used to walk up to the little Upper Hutt towns, where in the big white riverbank houses liquor was to be had; and their clumsy military boots shuffled in the pre-war dances—the old waltz, the schottische, the Maxina, the Valeta, and for the really spry fellow, square dances, the Lancers and the d'Alberts—always called the Dee Alberts. These were danced with the figures all wrong, and a jolly bloke with a concertina shouting, 'Take your partners for the next set! Swing! . . .' Swing they did, the little feet of the girls lifting off the floor, their bodies, with a soldier's arm passed under each arm-pit, flying out dangerously, almost horizontal; their breasts panting in the old-fashioned evening gowns of *crêpe de Chine* and China silk; their faces scarlet.

When they were through with dancing, there was the riverbank outside. The Hutt is only a little river, though its sudden deep pot-holes and odd currents have drowned many a stout swimmer. It creeps, ten yards wide, under silver birch trees and stiff russet-leaved osiers, the kind whose slim, reddish boughs are used in basket-making. Here and there the yellow bank caves in, making niches where among the spangled wild-flowers and tall grass, boy and girl could curl up, arm around each other's waist, tousled poppy-head dropping on khaki shoulder.

The men in camp should, according to regulations, have been between the ages of eighteen and forty-five. In actual fact, the New Zealand ranks from the first held scores of straight-held heads that under their dye would have been white-haired, and still more youngsters who looked the recruiting-agent straight in the eye and lied about their sixteen years.

Some of the khaki-clad who used to make for the Hutt after washing their dishes were shy-babies from the country—kids who had never been kissed. It was easy to kiss a girl in manly style under the tufted willow trees, and to make up unimaginative but sincere little romances in which everything happened 'after the War'. Then they said good-bye, the very shy ones who really were smitten—the not-so-shy who were trying out their manhood for the first time. What did it matter? Under the osiers the upturned faces of the girls were sweet and earnest; and if they were lied to, they need not face the long disillusion of living together. Lie, truth, half-truth, vanished into the black gulf between one world and the next. Some of the men left their mark on the young bodies in *crêpe de Chine* and China silk, and children were born. But that generation of New Zealand girls, and the next, were to learn that there are things worse than babies.

Coming home, there were running fights with the military police, the villains known by their blue hat-bands, their omniscience, and the shamelessness of their behaviour. In camp, during their off-hours, the boys kept themselves warm with fist-bouts among themselves. In Tent Eight, Fleshy suggested a glove fight, and Starkie and Jack Frew took it on. It started off as a pretty little bout, though neither knew much about the leather, but its tempo changed when Starkie's fist slipped and landed too hard in Jack Frew's wind.

As soon as Frew could speak again he called Starkie a black bastard, and after that the fight started in earnest and attracted a large audience, all cheering. Captain Dombey came down and pulled them off one another, stopping the night's leave for both men. Starkie was sore. That night he was the first out of camp, and instead of taking the Hutt trek, caught a train and made straight for the city of Wellington. In the aloof grey streets of the capital he wandered about thinking what a pity it was he hadn't a girl friend. He roamed from Post Office Square to the wharves, where black and mysterious the little waves suck under sea-rotted, weed-twined piles, from the wharves back again to various haunts of publicans and sinners. Somewhere about midnight it was no longer true that Starkie hadn't a girl friend, and he spent the night at her place in Cambridge Terrace, coming back to Trentham at ten in the morning. He was just in time for Captain Dombey's court of inquiry, to which he was taken straight from the guard-room, a military policeman on either side. Jack Frew was the other accused.

Captain Dombey rapped the table and asked for details, and Starkie explained about the Black Bastard allegation. Jack Frew spoke up for himself and made a better job of it than Starkie. Starkie drew three days' C.B., Jack Frew was dismissed, or would have been had not Starkie hit him on the chin as he passed by. This caused a contretemps and *lèse-majesté*. Jack Frew, being hit by Starkie, hit the table, the table hit Captain Dombey, Captain Dombey protested with force, and words passed between judge and accused into which it would be purposeless to inquire. Starkie was put under guard in a tent which stood all by itself in a barbed-wire enclosure, patrolled by a sentry with a fixed bayonet. He had nothing to do but sit, eat, and play solitaire, whilst occasionally his tent-mates, Jack Frew included, came to stare mournfully at him through the barbed wire and slip him cigarettes. By and by the guard conducted him before a major.

'Hat off! . . . One pace forward! . . . Quick march! . . . Enter the guard-room! . . .'

Starkie did as he was bid and pleaded guilty to a charge of assault, and another of using language to Captain Dombey. He was given twenty-one days' barracks.

The barracks, housed in a narrow-faced brick building, stand almost in the heart of Wellington city, on a hill not ten minutes' walk from the main streets. Here they made Starkie a housemaid, and he spent his time polishing brass, scrubbing floors, washing dishes, emptying pots, and going back to shine the brass over again. Beyond making him a brass expert, the Buckle Street authorities treated him with no manner of savagery. The prisoners who got it handed out tough there were the twenty-one Germans brought in from their internment camp on Somes Island because they refused to cart shingle to the top of the hill from the beach. The internment camp spread itself at the base of the green hill-island in the middle of Wellington Harbour, now used for the quarantining of smallpox cases. During the War its life was secret. It came into the lime-light just once, when three prisoners risked their lives in the long swim through freezing waters to the mainland. The seven miles' swim did for one of them, and his comrades left him dead on the rocks. Their own straggling flight didn't get them far. They were caught and taken back, disappearing from New Zealand ken, whilst the old ladies who disapproved of all Germans talked with virtuous indignation of the Hun bestiality which enabled them to leave their dead comrade behind.

The Huns weren't at any time sitting pretty in Buckle Street, and when they struck on their prison task—wheeling barrows of shingle round, world without end—they were put on bread and water. Here Starkie's housemaid chores enabled him to put up a protest against the usages of society. Inside the loaves were clamped nuggets of butter. He wasn't caught out, but the German prisoners got to know which of the men was slipping them extra provisions, and when he left they gave him the only send-off he had in New Zealand. The guard stared suspiciously at the soldier who got cheered by the Huns, but as far as Starkie was concerned Buckle Street's reign was then over.

In Trentham Captain Dombey was in softened mood. He was sorry, he said, that he had had to put a soldier in barracks. On the strength of it Starkie borrowed ten shillings from him and that night went again to Wellington and his girl friend. When he got back, Captain Dombey wanted to know the reason why.

'You gave me the money, sir,' said Starkie.

Captain Dombey shrugged his shoulders. 'Get along. I can't make anything of you.'

It was the parting of the ways. Thereafter Starkie was a soldier and not a soldier. He was useful at times. But they couldn't make anything of him. The final inspection came before they knew it, and involved a trifle of sabotage and rape, for half the men had been giving away items from their kit. Starkie had passed on many of his possessions to the kid brother of his girl, who was short of gear. The Salvation Army saved the situation by giving a final band concert in camp. All the boys went up to listen, for the Army's brassy blare fitted in better than you would have thought with the mud-holes and flag parade. Tent Eight stayed at home and raided the enemy lines.

At kit inspection their gear was all present and correct. Then they got six days' final leave, and Starkie went off to Wellington to be shown the town by Mabel, a dark lass and tall, who, having lived there since her childhood, knew everything from the zoo to the places where the police weren't so quick off the mark if the landlord passed a few sleevers over the counter after six o'clock.

In Wellington there is a far larger Oriental quarter than in any of the other New Zealand cities. This lies four-square over a big block in the lower part of the town—little streets threading and inter-threading over a dusty flatness, where at night the thin, high squeals of the Chinese fiddles are eerie among the dark-crannied shops. With the exception of the white prostitutes who live there, it isn't entirely squalid.

Besides the Chinese, there are scores of Hindoos, with their sparrow legs, enormous eyes, and beautifully cut features. The Hindoo babies look like birds, all eyes and nakedness. The Chinese babies are adorable, pink flushing up through the amber of their skins, their tiny mothers handling them with a delicacy and reserve which the white mother of the slums never knows. You don't see a Chinese woman suckle her baby in public. There is a savour of life in the streets there, life secretive, vivid, tainted with the rotting sweetness of stored fruits, curious with the odour of ginger.

And that isn't all of Wellington. There are the dark, slanting hills, and those enormous crystal-green waves which pour in, translucent hillocks, by the Red Rocks. If you can once be perfectly alone with the hills and sea of Wellington, you have something they can't take away from you, no matter where and why they lock you up. Starkie wasn't alone—he had Mabel, and sometimes her girl friends and their boy friends. But it was a kind good-bye.

The camp, where he arrived a day late, looked already curiously forlorn and empty. Kits were packed, the straw bedding had been taken out of the tents; the sign of a tribe's passing was written in the dust and stir of the khaki place. The mud had dried in a spell of fine weather, but it was all that flat brown; the stockades they had made of wired, dry manuka; and behind the leaning hills, shoulder to shoulder, marching across the sky like ugly futuristic giants. They were lined up and told they were the finest body of men that had ever left New Zealand. This was not a new experience for most of them. On the Invercargill station a fat man had told them the same thing. At Christchurch, where the wet brigade had joined them and turned their progress into the first real grog party, a man yet fatter had repeated it. Once again on the Wellington wharves they were informed of their own fineness; and as with one voice the troops replied:

'Aw, go wipe your chin.'

After the march to Wellington, they were paraded through the streets, bands playing and flags flying. At the wharves they were dismissed. Those who had wives and children were for the most part true, but the rest dived for taverns in the town. Here Starkie got into difficulties with the military police, and arrived at the ship under escort, which prevented him from saying good-bye to Mabel. Paddy Bridgeman, one of the best of the Irish nation, substituted for Starkie, and what he didn't know about blarney with girls was but little, so Mabel wasn't the loser.

The entire shipload of men, brown-clad, red-faced, pressed against the deck-rails and portholes. Starkie, looking down on a crowded wharf in which he had no desire to single out any one person, was suddenly startled by the dreadful expression on the faces of the women. Those faces, ordinary enough in daily life, seemed torn right in two like paper masks. Mouths, wide open, made gashes in them, the eyes, whether staring up at the ships or shut in that deathly exhaustion, were shadowed so that they looked huge as the eye-sockets in skulls. . . . Blackness, blackness, blackness. . . . Those hollow faces, pitted with the dreadful fear of a final parting, the upstretched arms, which looked like roots torn from the flesh of the black-clad bodies, communicated to the men their own foreboding. Sobs began to break out from wharf and ship, a convulsion of sound. All uptorn, the voices, the faces, the straining arms. Time presaged a disaster for them. They had barely known that they were one flesh, but they knew it now. Torn apart, they would never be joined together again, and consequently they were destroyed. The individuality of the women had become fused with that of the men; it wasn't only their partners who were taken from them, it was themselves: their flesh and spirit and their secret, buried thoughts—the thoughts you do bury in a man when you wake in the morning and find him at your side, his sleeping face a profile upturned in the pale light from between drawn window-curtains, one hand helplessly uncurled on the white counterpane. Father, lover, son, all drawn together in the one person, and the receptacle of your secret thoughts—in God's name, how can you lose that and remain the same? How could the men on the ship expect to come back to the same women when, departing, they had destroyed them?

The *Maunganui* sailed at two o'clock. When the ship was several hundred yards away from the wharf, the sobbing of the women could still be plainly heard, a fused wailing sound that outraged nature. Many of the men climbed into the rigging, and at half past three they were still staring back at the place where the wharf had been—where it still was, firmly defined on their inner sight. Half the men of this Fifth Regiment never came back at all, or came back wounded and shattered.

Paddy Bridgeman's Irish wit came to the rescue of the staring men. He produced a note-book, went from one to another of them: 'Can you swim?' he asked gravely.

Presently some of them plucked up life enough to ask him why he wanted to know.

'It's the torpedoes and the mines, darling,' said Paddy. 'A mile out of harbour, and maybe we're liable to be blown up or sunk. They kape a record of the ones that can't swim, and give them a place in the boats, maybe, if there's room enough.' He shook his head pessimistically and went on to the next group. Recollection woke in the staring eyes. Presently there was a shout of laughter as some spark fathomed the truth of Paddy's tale.

New Zealand was cut off from them by a bank of cloud which

lowered itself soundlessly and with great dignity, like the blue curtain of a theatre, between the *Maunganui* and the wild golden gorse on the coastline hills.

6 Conjurer and Pigeon

STARKIE picked up two championships aboard the *Maunganui*, the welter-weight and the C.B., the first after a series of bouts conducted with much joy and few rules among the boys, the second just for things in general. He paid the price of being a good sailor. Not far out of New Zealand waters the ship struck heavy weather, and for eleven days remained miraculously cleared of sergeants, while the mess orderlies—of whom Starkie was one—staggered up galley stairs and down corridors, life just one strawberry-box after another. This heavy fate he combated by eating a little soap, which produced signs enough of seasickness to keep him out of the way for a while.

The ship rolled into the Indian Ocean, and the waves calmed down. Officers appeared as giants refreshed, a drill system which meant sudden alarums and excursions in the dead of night was put under way; and a regular item on the programme was the series of lectures on 'How to stay Healthy in Egypt'. Summed up, these advised the soldier to stay in camp and read a book. A more practical knowledge Starkie got from an Invercargill man among the stokers, who was making his third trip between Egypt and New Zealand, and who had loved not wisely but too well. 'Stay sober', was his slogan. The eight in the rowdiest cabin on the *Maunganui* committed it to memory.

It was barely daybreak when Starkie was awakened by a shout from Paddy Bridgeman: 'Come along up, you old scoundrel, and have a look at your brother Gippos.'

'Come along, Choclit—there's thousands more baboons like you on shore,' grinned Fleshy McLeod, looming huge over Starkie's bunk.

Starkie missed him and hit the mirror, breaking it, the outraged splinters assuring him seven years' bad luck. Dolefully he drew on his trousers, snapped his belt, cocked his hat.

The entire human cargo of the *Maunganui* was crowded at the deck rail; but the ship crowd was nothing to the confusion which bobbed, waved, and shouted alongside. Egypt liked the troopships. Thousands of dinghies, pontoons, dhows, scows, crazy craft with brown matting sails, danced under the *Maunganui's* towering sides, and coffee-coloured men in white robes and black-tasselled scarlet caps like flower-pots or cocktail-shakers kept up one unending scream in praise of their wares. There were huge blood-red oranges—fifty for the piastre—sweet as nectar; watermelons, vast and stripy: long, pale-yellow Egyptian cigarettes which smelt like the floor of a camel-stable, and turned the stomachs of the uninitiated; chocolates, queer fat sweetmeats, pink and pale green, spiked on little wooden skewers. Behind lay a dreamlike silhouette of white buildings black-pitted with window-spaces.

'Oh, boy! Oh, boy! Wait till we get ashore,' murmured Paddy.

The rest improved the shining hour by buying oranges from the Gippo boys and knocking off their scarlet tarbushes with well-aimed shots, hot contests ranging between gangs of soldiers as they scored up their tallies. Starkie lost the show poker game which decided who was to pay for the boys' fruit and cigarettes, and sent down a pound note.

A smiling Egyptian sent back the change in a sugar-bag. Starkie's eyes bulged. The bag was a quarter full.

'Christ!' whispered Jack Frew. 'He's mistaken your note for a tenner, Choclit. Skip below and hide it. Treat's on you when we get ashore.

Ready and willing to spoil the Egyptians, Starkie skipped, and turned over his coin to the Invercargill stoker, who knew Egypt all too well. Stan counted the coin in silence. Then he said pityingly, 'You poor mug.'

'What are you talking about?'

'You're nine and threepence short, soldier. See these here little things?' He held up a copper coin. 'Well there's about twenty of those goes to make up a halfpenny—or maybe now it's forty of the ducks. Anyhow, don't think you'll take in Mother Egypt. Hear them yelling for backsheesh?'

'They yell it all right,' Starkie agreed sadly; 'but what does it mean?'

'It means gimme something for nothing. It's the way they say their prayers out here.'

Up on deck the boys took a stern view of the orange-vendor's crime. Pelting him with fruit was no good, there being hundreds exactly like him, and Starkie's robber lost in the throng, a rich man for a day. With bugles shrilling, the troops marched off the *Maunganui*'s gang-planks. At the bottom of each gangway stood a tall Egyptian with a coin-tray strapped around his waist, shouting monotonously, 'Money changed here, money changed here!'

The old combine from Tent Eight, plus Paddy Bridgeman, landed together.

'Look at all the money he's got,' murmured Paddy.

Somebody's foot slipped. Somebody else flung a sturdy arm round the money-changer's waist, bringing him to the ground. There was a howl of protest. In every direction scattered copper bits, piastres, half-piastres, greasy notes. The line of men from the gangway crowded relentlessly on. An Egyptian, minus his tarbush and with his spotless white raiment ruined, wailed that he had been robbed of a thousand piastres, but those who could hear him didn't believe him, and those who believed him didn't care.

Thus came the Fifth to the land of Egypt.

On the wharves sleight-of-hand men and magicians of every race under the moon had taken up their stance and shouted, 'Half-piastre, me show', to the marching men. Tent Eight stopped to admire one stately Arabian Nights gentleman, his white robe and black scarf garnished with tinsel stars, his tarbush lifting his height proudly above their heads. They surrendered their half-piastres, gaping at him.

The conjurer smiled and produced from a wicker cage a live pigeon. The boys handled it, stroking the sleek feathers, opal and green upon the little creature's trembling breast, hearing its fussy murmurings. The conjurer took the pigeon, popped its head into his gaping red mouth, twisted the bird's body in his two hands, and pulled out the body of a headless bird.

They gasped, feeling a trifle sick. 'Some trick!' one of them shouted, not to be outfaced by an Egyptian knave.

The conjurer smiled again, eyes silky.

'You watch,' he ordered, and put the red stump into his mouth again. Out it came, a whole pigeon, alive and squawking, and fluttered helplessly in his hands.

Starkie paid his half-piastre thrice over to learn the trick, but there wasn't any trick; it just happened. The bird's neck-stump bled; then it was fluttering again, and its little heart beat fast in panic, as though whatever black, fabulous country it had inhabited during that five seconds' death terrified it out of its pigeon senses.

When Starkie left the wharf it was still too pale a morning light for him to see much of Egypt's outline. But Egypt stood bowing behind him, tall, white-robed, wearing a quaint hat and a silky smile. 'Half a piastre, me show.' Of course it was a lie. Egypt never showed anybody anything except sorcery and things that couldn't happen. You were left with a picture of a red, cruel mouth, cruel as wet blood, and wings in their green and opal sheen fluttering with terror. The conjurer, if you dared turn back to look at him, might have grown taller than those white buildings you couldn't see, and the black tassel on his tarbush might curl into a wreath of evil-smelling smoke.

The Fifth was encamped at Zitoun, about three miles from Cairo, thousands on thousands of white tents pricking up among sandy hills. The camp was remarkable for three things: food, lice, and medical lectures. They were handed out round little Dutch cheeses, pink-skinned like apples; beautiful fresh bread, much more palatable than the New Zealand bakings; fresh fruit, tobacco and meat. The butter ran like oil in the March heat. The lice were encountered as soon as the New Zealanders settled down in the tents. Lice are really Egypt's oldest soldiers, with more martial blood in them for their size than any Ajax that ever strutted. These had been reared on soldiers' blood for a hundred generations, and liked it: their descendants would be reared in the same tradition, and when one regiment moved on from their tents to the clutch of the larger leeches, the death-dealers waiting beyond the horizon, Egypt's lice would turn to and prepare a welcome for the next batch.

Officers took a hand in the lectures. A captain who had been with the Otago crowd since the day the train pulled out of Invercargill skimmed the cream of good advice for them.

'Don't do what I do,' he said. 'Do what I tell you to do.'

On the third day, however, the New Zealanders broke camp. They had been restless ever since landing in Zitoun, where the powers-that-were endeavoured to keep them within bounds by holding back their pay. It didn't work. The regiment footed it to Cairo, and those who had money picked up the Gippo gharries as soon as they reached the city—queer little four-wheelers, open like the English royal coaches, but far superior in point of horseflesh. The Gippo steeds were Arabs, and pranced with gay, fine-lady curvetting and flourish of creamy manes and long tails. Mounted on Arabs rode through the streets the Gippo 'Villains', military police who wore white uniforms and carried rifle, sword, revolver, and a knife on each hip. Each man among them bore a forehead tattoo-mark, a little blue ship or a bird with outspread wings, finely traced on the left side of the temple. The Gippo Villains very seldom interfered with white soldiers, but treated their own erring brothers worse than pi-dogs, flogging them through the streets with jagged chunks of wood. All the convicts in Cairo went chained; yet, with the crazy lack of logic which characterized the town, after nightfall most of the gaols turned their prisoners loose, and they could please themselves what they did between sundown and reveille. Abysseia Gaol, where military prisoners—white or coloured—were kept for transgressions that the police really didn't like, was a good place to keep out of.

Starkie's brother George, who had joined up with the Veterinary Corps some months before Starkie emerged from prison, ended a spree in Abysseia, where the Gippo police kicked his ribs in and didn't report a sick man until he was strangling with pneumonia. It was his colour that gave them the guts to tackle a New Zealander. But he pulled through, and had Egypt for a convalescent home during the next six months; which, taking it all in all, was no bad way of winning a war.

When they struck Cairo, most of the men from Zitoun Camp headed straight for the Wazza. There were things to do if you wanted to take the day easily. The chocolate-coloured Gippo drivers set you down from their gharries at cafés where little tables stood in softly curtained alcoves. Stucco and stone, hard white or the colour of ivory, lay in the leaf-gold of March sunlight. The moment the soldiers sat down at table there was a scurry under their feet, and their ankles were firmly grasped by brown urchins, yelling, 'Shoe-shine, saar! Shoe-shine, saar!'

It was no use denying the will of these imps, and if a quarrel arose between them, they settled it in their own fashion. Dan MacKenzie left his boots to their tender care, and arose to find himself with one brilliant tan boot, one lustrous black one. He cuffed the heads of the rivals impartially, and they backed away, crying, 'All right, saar! All right, Mister MacKenzie!'

'How the blazes did those little coots come to know my name?' asked Dan, puzzled.

Three days in Cairo, and the troops knew that every white or near-white man was either Lord Kitchener, saar, or Mister MacKenzie, saar, among the Gippos.

Most of the drinking in cafés was wine, white or red, and cheap enough. In the better sort of place the girls wore costumes, like the pictures of nautch girls—brassière tops, petticoats short as a chemise, and all in bright, fierce primary colours. Their round olive arms were laden with bracelets, clear glass or solid gold. In some of the cafés they danced the *can-can* naked. This was an exhausting performance for dancer and onlooker alike, but the girls showed it less.

The *can-can* took about fifteen minutes, and was something like the Hawaiian *hula*, but a great deal more so—as close an interpretation as possible of the Gippo idea of the sexual act, which is vigorous. Muscles knotted, head tilted back, eyes flashing. When the girls judged that the soldiers were that way, they sat on their knees and twined hot arms around their necks. After that the party as a rule split up and sought privacy, though not always.

There were, during the War years, thirty-four thousand licensed women in Cairo, from little girls twelve years old, to women of twenty-five, their cheeks raddled, their youth used up and done. Those who didn't care what they took, lived in the balconied stucco houses of the Wazza. Three times a week the women were subject to medical inspection, and their health records were on view in little black books like rent-books.

As the soldiers' gharries bowled down the narrow streets women, orange, blue, and scarlet shawls tossing back from their naked breasts, cried, 'Very nice! Very sweet! Only half-piastre!' They had a miraculous knowledge of the paydays in the different divisions of the thousands whose khaki river was stemmed and swirling at Zitoun. When the Australians, in their cocked hats, came in with their pockets great with piastres, a shout of 'Come on, Australia, New Zealand no good!', tossed like a laughing ribbon from one to another of the balconied houses. When the New Zealanders were paid, the impotency of the Australians was shrieked from the Wazza roof-tops. The place was old, old; built of money and dank stone and flesh, and it stank of the animalism which is Lilith's challenge to love.

Paddy and Starkie kept sober in the Wazza. By and by they parted company. Starkie walked up to Rada's sitting-room, which was less of a den than he had expected—a bare little place with cushions of silk, flaring orange like the chemise she wore, and which had caught his eye from the street. Rada was a Spanish girl her hair unbound and waved, her black eyes very big and soft, and a delicate red showing through the gold of her cheeks, as it shows in late summer through the skin of a peach. Her mother was there to watch her business interests, and a lean old hand reached out for five piastres. Starkie couldn't speak Spanish, but he remembered a few broken words and phrases that his mother had taught him, and a Spanish song picked up in the long ago when she had moved so silently about the house preparing food for her Red Indian husband and her three children. It was a nearer link than many of the soldiers had with their girls. In the Wazza the women were Egyptian, Greek, Italian, Maltese, a few of them fine-eyed, deep-breasted and sombre Jewesses. The French girls, known to the troops as the Painted Dolls, had a café of their own and ran it on more reticent lines than the natives. But it all came down to the same gestures in the end.

With the dark drawn down, a silken sheath over the Wazza, the orange room and the orange chemise began the reign of the conjurer and the pigeon. You could see the conjurer, tall and white-robed, smirking behind the high, yellow houses. He puts the pigeon's head into his mouth and bites it off. He shows you the bleeding stump of the neck. Nothing could last out through that. Same in the Wazza. No girl, no thing of flesh and blood, trembling and alive, could stand being swallowed up in the black gut of this street. If you stood still long enough you could see the trick, see where death really shows his claws and teeth. But the conjurer is very clever. Your pigeon, which should by rights be stone dead, comes to fluttering life under your hands. You can feel the beat and tremor of the smooth, silk-plumaged breast. When you draw down the silk, the beat is faster yet, as fast as the rhythm of the girls in their dances. Then the pigeon isn't a pigeon any more, but a falcon or a sword, a narrow thing and dangerous, with flanks of fire. The darkness is damascened with half-lights, half-sounds, like the Arab sheaths that fitted swords carried long ago, the hoods drawn over falcons' eyes. But it was in no good Court that these thing were known. They belong to the evil Court, to the conjurer's palace which, when his silken smile is taken away from it, dwindles down to a rotting pile of fungus and disease, infecting the ancient stones.

Rada was the first expert at the game that Starkie had ever known. Drilling at Zitoun next day, the sergeant said, 'Rada, Rada!', which was odd; but not so queer as it would have been had the sergeant been able to read Starkie's mind and see his meticulous orders transformed into silly phrases, bearing no relation to the arts of war.

Starkie stuck to Rada until after the battle of the Wazza. In this he was luckier than some who wandered farther and fared worse. One of the mates who had gambled and drunk and wrestled with him disappeared ignominiously behind barbed wire. Starkie had one day—visiting the missing friend in hospital—his first glimpse of real pain. He had thought of the figure eights and the Dummy as hard experience, but they, at any rate, came to an end; they weren't unclean and they weren't incredible. He saw men lying in cots of canvas, with nothing but cotton wool sheathing their tortured skins. Faces blotted out by sores; eyes that cried and had no sight in them. . . . Cold panic wormed its way into his heart. But Rada was all right. Rada pretty near loved him. If he liked he could stay with Rada till the end of the War; she and her mother were keen on keeping him. But he wasn't looking for a job in that profession. Nobody but Rada. He went away and drew the shouting and the two-up schools in camp over his mind for protection.

The El Dorado was the French girls' place, and cost twenty piastres.

The officers seldom if ever came to the Wazza, but congregated in one of the hotels. According to the officers, this place was a perfectly respectable restaurant; according to the men, it was the same as all the other houses, but it cost fifty piastres, and didn't admit privates. Its reputation had a mark against it as a nest of international spies, some of them very attractive. But the feature of the place was really Abdul, the chucker-out. Abdul was a huge fellow, reputed to be an eunuch, coal-black, shiny, and with biceps that would have made Jack Dempsey cry. Starkie saw Abdul pick up two of his tent-mates, one under each arm, and carry them to the door of the hotel kicking like two-year-olds. Abdul didn't spank Paddy or Goliath. He deposited them gently in the gutter, wiped his hands on a silken handkerchief, gazed serenely at the sky, sighed, and proceeded indoors, his ponderous legs swinging like tree-trunks.

In the noon heat everything in Cairo slept except the very old women and the male defenders of the prostitutes' quarters, known to the dictionary as *souteneurs*, and to the troops as bludgers. The siesta lasted until four or five in the evening—the girls in their scanty wisps of clothing, limp as rag dolls among their brilliant heaps of cushions. In the streets, under steps, under arches, in the shadow-nooks of old buildings, in the gateways of the mosques, lay curled in sound slumber the Egyptian children. Everywhere on naked or near-naked bodies crawled the great black flies—not hundreds but millions of them.

Once, in Crusading days, there was a place of an evil name, the Tower of Flies. All ill was supposed to spread from there; and Satan, who was stoned, in the East is the Lord of Flies. His satellites, with their scaly wings and big convex ruby eyes, have taken for themselves the flesh of the Egyptian people. They crawled into the eyes of the sleeping children, into mouths and nostrils, where their greedy little suckers drained the moisture from delicate membranes. The children never woke, never cried, never lifted a hand to brush away their persecutors. The Lord of Flies owned them, they raised no dispute with him. Many of them were beautiful children, their limbs lithe and rounded, bronze-skinned, their heads as noble as those graved in the battered statuary of the Cairo Museum. When the sun matured them, the fierce sun, the stink and din of the Egyptian streets, they found their niche in the balconied houses of the Wazza, the little girls as prostitutes, the boys as parasites and thieves.

It was ten o'clock of a brilliantly sunlit morning when the battle of the Wazza began without one word of warning. Starkie was staring at the goldfish in a great marble fountain set in the square. These bore no resemblance whatever to the homely little red fishes to be found in the lakes of his native land. They were exaggerated in size, colour, and shape, marvellously burnished, like creatures from some Arabian tale of Sultans, viziers, and the lopping off of heads. Everything was fantastic in Cairo, and most things were cruel. The red-gold fish, now a foot long if they were an inch, looked as fierce as dragons.

There was a swirl of soldiers across the street. Nobody proffered much explanation as the khaki surged past. 'Come on, boys, it's a battle!' roared a man with the voice of a bull. Then beyond the first row of houses, spreading across the skyline like an enormous blue umbrella, there appeared a writhing column of smoke. The shrieks began, tearing the morning in pieces, and aided by the sounds of splintering glass. In a moment the square where Starkie stood was jammed with the rush of soldiers. A man tipped over into the fountain and was hauled out, dripping, still shouting: 'Come on, this way!'

Aimlessly, yet with the seeming purpose of a mad dog or a Malay running amok, the charge swept on down the streets. Starkie ran with them, yelling as they yelled, without the faintest idea why he ran and yelled. The Wazza began to glare with the pattern of flames against the windows of seven-storeyed houses. There were shrieks and crashes as women and *souteneurs* were thrown down from the upper windows of those tall-balconied rat-holes. Furniture was tossed out and battered into splinters. A soldier reeled into a doorway with a Gippo knife sunk to the haft in his belly, and sat there retching and coughing, a bright red foam on his lips. One hand was pressed against his stomach. Nobody stopped to ease the death that had its fangs in his middle, but there was another roar, 'Murder! Come on!'

Between two high buildings a ladder was run out. From the blazing house on the right a negro *souteneur*, his eyes rolling, his teeth gnashing white, started to crawl along the ladder to safety.

In the left-hand house the bunch of soldiers laughed and cheered him on. When the *souteneur* was in the middle of the swaying ladder they put their weight on the end. The ladder wobbled, tipped up. With one howl the fat man disappeared into space. The sound of his fall was flung up between the gulf of the houses to the soldiers, who did not cease to laugh.

There was one Australian officer who tried to stop the wreckers. He was a brave fool. He set his back against a house towards which the mob were running—a silk-merchant's place. Arms spread out like those of a crucified man, he guarded the silk-merchant's door, shouting something unintelligible to the men as they charged. Starkie saw his brown face, angry, defiant, unafraid. Another moment, and no face was visible at all. The officer was down under the running boots, and men trod on his body as they burst into the store. The Egyptian fire-brigades came shrieking in, to be mobbed by the soldiers. The drivers were dragged off their engines, the hand-pumps smashed and the hoses hacked to pieces. It was so hot that they could no longer stand in the square, but they began to drag barricades of bolts of silk and furniture across the streets and set light to them, repelling the rescue parties who came in at the double from Zitoun Camp. The silk smouldered and then blazed, great piled bolts of it, ruby, China white, green, sky-blue. The flames shot up in a dense and maddening forest, and within that circle the scorpion of the Wazza brandished its sting against its own death. Naked women ran from their balcony-rooms to the damp ooze of their cellars. A soldier among the looters died, crushed under the weight of the grand piano that the prostitutes pushed out of their high window on the heads of the men below. Wherever a house offered resistance, soldiers posted themselves at the door-way and smashed down women and *souteneurs* as the flames drove them out.

With the flames and smoke still streaming into the air, Starkie made his way to Rada's house. During the thick of the looting and burning he had never given her a thought. She was crouching in the cellar of her home, bedraggled and wet as a rat, but with her money in her stocking. He spent the night with her, and crawled back to camp in the morning, red-eyed, unshaven, singed about the eyebrows and hair. As soon as he got into camp he was arrested on principle, as were all the night's absentees. Paraded before Captain Dombey, he swore that he had been hit on the head in the beginning of the battle and rescued by a young lady.

'Young lady!' Dombey's face was as drawn as his own, after a night of frenzied effort steering the defaulters back to camp. 'You look like young lady, you do. Keep it up and you know where you'll end.' He turned away with more crime-sheets on his hands than any officer could hope to deal with unless prepared to decimate his battalion.

Only one explanation was given concerning the Wazza battle, though there was a vague rumour that a soldier had been locked in one of the brothels and had called for a rescue. To this no great authority attaches. The explanation shrieked at a fulminating officer by a man in the ranks of the New Zealanders consisted of only one sentence, but from the psychological point of view it was one of the most remarkable sentences spoken in the history of the War.

'They was better off dead.'

Every civilized race of mankind, and many savage races also, regard with horror the loss of personal identity. Nations with no written history, such as the Maoris, have an elaborate and priestly system of memorizing every twig on the ancestral tree of the individual. In white society, to lose identity is a personal disgrace. One of the penal code's forms of punishment—admitted a barbarous one by most criminals—is to deprive a man of his name and indicate him by a number. Often among the very poorest is witnessed dread of the pauper's grave, the resting-place of which no man knoweth the name any more.

In the Wazza the men who went to appease curiosity or appetite found themselves confronted with the same loss of identity. Women with whom they could exchange no common word of language received them behind doors where, in many cases, they waited in processions for that curious relief. There was no pretence that one soldier's face differed from the rest. The men were used, especially the colonial soldiers whose countries supported no licensed houses, to more regard for their vanity. Even those women who had played the prostitute's part for them in their own lands had, for the most part, woven the little fables of individual romance and liking.

In the Wazza, they were nobody; male embracing heterogeneous female. The first shock of this faded from their consciousness, but it waited in hiding—a resentment that they hardly realized, but that could not be placated except by vengeance. The convict becomes accustomed to the loss of his name and citizenship, but the surface resentment wears down into his deeper hatred of Society. So it was with the soldiers in the Wazza. The place stole their sexual identity from them. They had to revenge themselves. The women who had deprived them, the *souteneurs* who shared the spoils, the houses where they had waited, were—in the phrase of that inspired and hysterical soldier—better off dead.

The Wazza battle was the end of Rada in so far as Starkie was concerned. Warmed by that night of creeping together after the storm, he left most of his gear with her—to find when he went back the next day that she had lavishly bestowed it on an Australian corporal. Black eyes, peach-flushed face, defied him. She was paying him back, maybe, for his share in the battle. Starkie said good-bye to kit and lady, being in affairs of the heart no communist.

The conjurer and the pigeon became of fading importance in Zitoun Camp. In the first week of August, 1915, a curious quiet fell upon the thousands of white tents. The men stayed in camp, the ordinary programme of lectures and drill seemed to slacken. A week later they were entrained for Alexandria. Not even a day's leave was given them to see the city where once Cleopatra's barge flashed its silver oars against the thick Nile waters. Without pause they were shipped to Lemnos.

Hundreds of battleships lay here at anchor, and big merchantmen took shelter among the grey cruisers and destroyers that showed the colours of every allied nation. Until evening the Fifth stayed ashore, drinking red wine at quiet little hostelries, strangely silent after Cairo, where Greek girls with black hair and splendid eyes served them. It was no interlude in a Grecian Wazza. The people of Lemnos seemed little interested in khaki. At sunset the Fifth were taken on board their troopship, the *Redwing*, and with an escort of four destroyers steamed out of the naval base towards Gallipoli. A submarine's shark tooth had torn the side out of one of the transports a few days before, just outside Lemnos Harbour. There was a yell of 'Submarine!' as the *Redwing* slid into open sea, and the soldiers rushed to the side of the boat to take pot-shots with their newly issued rifles at a dark object like a periscope bobbing in the water near by. The splinter, after a lucky shot, proved them to have wasted their bullets on the neck of a cruising bottle; but that took nothing of the fervour of marksmanship away from the soldiers, most of whom were afraid that their heavy ammunition issue would pull them down if the ship were torpedoed.

Between Lemnos and Gallipoli the troops on the *Redwing* saw a strange sight. At midnight the whole of the sky was lighted with a vast aurora. The shimmering, trembling colours—apple-green, rose, tender violet, hazy gold—fringed the horizon with great jester-peaks of radiance. Many of the men on the troopship declared that the aurora was a good omen. The colours danced in the sky until early morning, and the *Redwing* cut through a black-and-silver sea, calm as a pond. The light of early dawn showed them only the vague outlines of cliffs when at four o'clock the *Redwing* lay at anchor off Y Beach, on Gallipoli.

7 Dawn's Angel

WHEN the troops from the *Redwing* were taken off on barges to Y Beach there was no more sound to disturb the morning than an occasional whiplash crack, a rifle spitting far away, or a dull thud which sounded as though a gigantic muffled hammer had been brought down on the earth. They were told in whispers that this was the concussion of a shell; but the front line, six miles distant, was still a legend to them. Everybody talked in whispers; and it was rather amusing to see the giants of Tent Eight—and stouter men than they—walking like cats on hot bricks, afraid of a shuffle of pebbles among the sands. Three miles up from Y Beach they struck Anzac Cove and a standing-up breakfast—boiling water with a pinch of tea-dust thrown in, biscuits, and bully beef.

Against them in the pale rise of the morning was something which for the New Zealanders had especial significance. The

Maori Pioneer Corps, passing this way, had stopped to carve out of the yellow clay face of the Gallipoli cliffs a gigantic Maori Pa. The men now passing quietly by saw carved stockade pillars with their little lizards, ornate whorls, and leaves of carving, top-heavy idols with their huge heads lolling on their shoulders, their eyes squinting, their tongues out. The work was still fresh, and recalled to the New Zealanders their few glimpses of that old world of different fighters—the red-ochred stockades, the wharepunis, the little store-houses standing on their high stilts and daubed with crimson to keep away the night-demons; a world which now and again, behind the bush-veils and the mist-veils of the New Zealand hills, had silenced their childhood with a memory of something that fought to the death. Those native hills pitted with the brown circles of the old Maori trenches, their wounds not yet quite hidden in the green softening of grass, were not unlike the hills of Gallipoli that now slid out of the sheath of the morning mist. But where New Zealand hills hide under the grey-stemmed manuka bushes, with their pungent flower-cups brown and white or delicate peach-colour, the Gallipoli hills were covered with a little shrub of somewhat darker green, its astringent leaves bitter with a flavour of quinine.

A splendid morning sunlight began to break over the cliffs. Paddy Bridgeman and Jack Frew, Fleshy McLeod and Starkie, proceeded together. After breakfast a bugler blew the fall-in, the thin notes thrusting like an arrogant silver spear into the silence of Gallipoli. The troops were lined up above the water-tanks on the beach. Before the men were in their places, the hills above them began to flash and rattle. The fall-in woke up every sniper in the world. Four hundred men stood in line to answer the roll-call. As they stood, a man in the front rank pitched forward.

'Hullo, there's a chap fainted,' whispered Jack Frew.

Somebody turned the man over on his back. Right between his eyes there was a little blue mark, like a dot made with a slate-pencil. Death had given him no time to change the expression on his face—a boy's look of interest and curiosity. He was left lying where he fell.

The men fell into a column and marched four deep up Mule Gully under fire from machine-guns, rifles, and shells. Very few of them were old enough to be veterans of the Boer War. The way up Mule Gully was like the end of the world. Their warning of the shell's coming was a rush of air, a crash, a blinding blue flash amidst the chocolate fountain of the uptorn earth. Shrapnel burst in a dazzling hail of steel—a crash where it struck the ground, then rip—roar—and the fragments tore the sides out of skulls, cut bodies in two, dismembered men as they marched. Captain Dombey was in front of the column as the troops came in plain sight of 971, the entrenched hill of the Turks. In the harbour, British men-of-war, monitors, and destroyers began the barrage, dealing out to the Turks the death which was past the strength of the scanty British artillery. When a battleship fired a broadside at the Turk trenches, the men on shore could see her rock in a trough of smothering foam like a vast grey cradle. Those that lived, crashes and shrieks ringing in their ears as though the echo must last on for centuries, climbed blindly and helplessly up the Gully, and the cliffs pelted down death on them as they ran.

There was a tally of the men landed from the *Redwing* when they reached the top of the hill. Of about four hundred who left the troopship, less than a hundred men had come through unscathed. Some were sent straight to England, others went to the base hospitals at Lemnos and Malta, others rotted on Gallipoli. The survivors climbed into their trenches, and spent the next day chasing Turks out from the holes where an unsuccessful attack the evening before had stranded dozens of them in hostile territory.

The troops had been split up into divisions, and Starkie was properly numbered with Southland Eighth; but Paddy, McLeod, and Jack Frew were all Dunedin men, and Starkie beguiled Captain Dombey—who was half-conscious now after the terrible concussion of the shells—into letting him join up with Otago Fourth.

Silver was the first of Tent Eight's giants to go, shot clean through the head by a Turkish sniper. The sniper is the aristocrat of No Man's Land, the cold killer; and against him Starkie began to develop a murder hate, not decreased by the fact that the Turk snipers were more numerous and better than the British ones. The shell hail, even the death song of the Maxims, gives you warning to keep your head down. But the sniper isn't human. Soldiers are only men. There are times in the trenches when they forget the whole bloody, cruel gambit, stretch their legs and arms, dare to show their fool heads over a mound of earth. That's the sniper's opportunity. When the troops start to relax, from his bush-screened hole in No Man's Land he picks the play-boys off. He won't allow them their decent modicum of rest; and in consequence, where the shell gets a curse and is forgotten except by the men it cuts to pieces, the sniper starts death-feuds. Hunting snipers was a game on Gallipoli, and it wasn't played according to any known rules of sportsmanship.

The Otago trenches turned out to be holes about four feet six inches in depth, with high mud embankments screening them from the hills.

'How in blazes do you see the Turk?' grumbled Starkie.

An old hand passed him a periscope. For one moment Starkie saw the Turk all right. Then the periscope was shot out of his hands, the palms burned where the brass tube had been ripped out of them, and a howl of laughter went up along the trench at sight of the greenhorn's stupefied face. Two minutes later Charlie Saunders wanted to have a look at the Turks. He jumped up, visible above the embankment for just one moment. Then he fell back like a sack into Starkie's arms. There was no blood, just two little blue marks the size of slate-pencils. The body writhed for a moment, as if anxious to express something. Whatever it was, Charlie never got it out. His body was a corpse before his mind had stopped wondering.

In the trenches men lived like rabbits, the mud walls pitted with the little holes where they slept—or tried to sleep. These provided earthen benches, not long enough for a grown man to lie down, but of a size sufficient for him to cram his body into shelter. At night the trenches, from above, would have presented a strange sight, like a grotto illumined by thousands of pale glow-worms. The men improvised candles, half-filling kerosene-tin lids with fat and dirt, and in the middle fashioning wicks of twisted rag soaked in grease. These fluttering little candles, evil-smelling and burning with a spluttering bluish flame, were the only trench lights after dark on Gallipoli.

In the morning the troops were issued a dixie of water to each man—about two-and-a-half cups—from which they could shave, wash, and make themselves a cup of tea. A grimy towel served months long for wiping faces and bodies. It was hot on Gallipoli.

'Aw, hell!' said Fleshy superbly. 'It's only dirty chaps that bloody well need to wash.' And he tilted the dixie to his lips.

'And it's only scrubs go shaving themselves,' added Starkie.

Thereafter, Disraeli's maxim that water is good only for washing with was disregarded in the trenches. The men drank their water issue and let hygiene go where it belongs in wartime. Not that you could call the water drinkable. There were two wells between the trenches and the beach, but both were reputed to be poisoned by the Turks—which left the New Zealand trenches with the chlorinated beach water-tanks to draw upon. The water was carted up in benzine tins, and the men drank shandies of chlorinated lime, benzine, and water. For the rest, they were issued biscuit, bully beef, cheese—they didn't know where the cheese came from, but some of them had a pretty fair idea; jam—instantly covered with swarms of black flies; blocks of black seaweed-like pipe-tobacco known as ''Arf a Mo'', and an amplitude of cigarettes—Red Hussars, Beeswing, Havelock, Gold Flake, Auros, and Woodbines. The boys used to get a real smoke by tying five Woodbines together and puffing them in a bundle.

There were—besides the voices of the guns—two inevitable sounds in the trenches: the yells of the muleteers, driving their stubborn little grey mokes up Mule Gully under cover of darkness; and the long-drawn-out floating cry from the Turkish trenches: 'Allah, Allah, il Allah'. The Turks—all furnished with fine leather equipment from German stores, muffled up in balaclavas, scarves, and mittens pulled over grey uniforms—came over the top with that great cry of 'Allah!' When, after dark, their wounded and dying lay out on the Gallipoli hills, all night long the same cry would rattle up to the British trenches—groans of 'Allah', from lips that would never taste the cup of life again.

On the second morning the survivors from the *Redwing* were taken out into No Man's Land as a burying-party. For this they were stripped of their uniforms, donned khaki shorts and singlets, and went armed with oiled sheets. The purpose of this they saw when they got to No Man's Land, each party breaking off under charge of an officer.

A few men found on No Man's Land were still alive. They were not always lucky. Some were stone blind and crazy with gun-flashes, others crawled near, leg or flesh wounds rotting after a night's exposure.

But the dead who waited in No Man's Land didn't look like dead, as the men who came to them now had thought of death. From a distance of a few yards, the bodies, lying in queer huddled attitudes, appeared to have something monstrously amiss with them. Then the burying-party, white-faced, realized that twenty-four hours of the Gallipoli sun had caused each body to swell enormously—until the great threatening carcases were three times the size of a man, and their skins had the bursting blackness of grapes. It was impossible to recognize features or expression in that hideously puffed and contorted blackness.

And how they had died!—some ripped to pieces by shrapnel—some of them in fragments; others having crept from the place of death to the hollow of some stunted green shrub, their arms crooked round the searching brown roots as though in a passionate, useless plea for the earth's protection against their enemies. Here and there one had found shade enough to escape some part of the disfigurement caused by the pitiless sun; and on these faces such a story was written as nobody on earth will ever dare to tell until the graves give up their dead. The Tommies from the next hill had been over in attack, and some of them lay here like the bodies of dead children, their pinched, sharp-featured little London faces white and beautifully calm. Sometimes the dead man bore only the blue seal of the bullet wound on head or breast, and the boys called that 'the mercy death'. Sometimes a man's tunic was torn open where he had clutched at it with striving hands, and revealed along his swollen body a line like a row of nails driven into his flesh—the mark of the machine-gun's killing.

The burying-party, in squads of four and five, unrolled their oiled sheets and spread them on the ground. Then they lifted or rolled on the sheets the bodies of the slain. Dissolution had overtaken many of them; and as they were lifted their heads fell back in the sunlight, showing blackened mouth and throat, gaping nostrils, as caves for the little crawling life-in-death of ants and maggots. When they were rolled on the sheets the foul air which had gathered in their grotesquely gigantic bodies came out of their throats in one appalling groan, as though in that protest the dead soldier had told all the agony and outrage of his taking-off.

The stench of that deathly gas struck into the senses of the burying-party.

Some of the living and moving men—mere boys of sixteen and seventeen—sweated like horses, and tears ran down their white cheeks.

Starkie heard Paddy Bridgeman groan, 'Ah, blessed Mother of God—fine big men the one day, the next fly-blown and rotten!'

Holes were pitted in the Gallipoli hills, dug with the men's pickaxes. Then the dead were rolled in from the oil-sheets, ten or twelve men to a grave, the faces of some lying against the boots of others in a confusion of death. The living men who dug those common graves stood retching with sickness as they shovelled earth, brown and merciful, over the faces of the dead.

The burying-party were marched back to their trenches and crawled into the dug-outs. An old hand tapped Starkie on the shoulder.

'Cup of tea, mate?'

Starkie looked at the man for a moment. Then he poured the tea into the mud of the trench. He was sick throughout the night.

In less than a month the men thought nothing of the burying-parties, and so little of the corpses on No Man's Land that money-belts were unbuckled as the rotting corpses were rolled into the pits of death.

It was only afterwards—after the War; after that outrageous libel on the normality of the human mind had been, for the time, dragged away—that every twisted limb, every blackened face waiting in those gullies, came back into memory once again, and for ever repeated the protest the tortured body uttered after its death.

In the trenches everyone was dirty and lousy—'five hundred' and louse-catching were the major sports of Gallipoli—but the lice were objected to considerably less than the swarming black flies. Sometimes the fighting between Turk and British trenches was like a dramatic, enthralling, and hideous scene shown in a great green-and-chocolate-coloured amphitheatre. From the apex of their trenches the Otago men saw a party of Turks blown sixty or seventy feet into the air above their fortified hill, grotesque little marionette figures violently jerked skyward by the unseen hands of death.

The Turkish trenches curved in circular formation around their hill. Their aerial torpedoes came flaring over the British lines, looking like big tin canisters with six-foot tails. Little flanges kept these missiles straight, and when they struck earth there was an enormous concussion. The English lyddite shells made more row than any of the other fireworks, and Otago was supplied with Japanese lyddite shells—deadly little blackberries to be fired from the trench-mortars. But the British artillery was a very poor second compared with Johnny Turk's, and barrage was left for the most part to the ghostly grey shapes of the men-of-war riding at anchor along the coast.

They witnessed from their trenches the attack on Suvla Bay, about five miles off, across flat land broken by the cone of Chocolate Hill—a patch of brown in a green land. The Tommies attacked three times, barrage whining and splintering from both sides. The advance and retreat of the little figures was a scene in a melodrama. At the second attack, the Turks, reinforced, chased the Tommies back down the Gully. The third assault drove the Turks out of their position. The attack in all took about twenty-five minutes, and an advance of thirty yards was made by the English troops. When it was over, hundreds of corpses and wounded men—limbless, gashed and slashed and blown to pieces—lay where they had fallen. The blue flashes of the shell-fire continued for a while after the main attack. The concussion rang all night long in the soldiers' ears. In the morning they helped to bury the Tommies. It didn't greatly distress them any more.

Men in the British lines were going down with dysentery; but for the most part it was only known as dysentery in the case of the officers, just as nervous breakdowns were unheard of in the ranks. The ranker got two little white number nines from King, the doctor's assistant. Number nines were used to cure the troops of headache, heartache, stomach-ache, malingering, laziness, cuts, scabies, shell-shock, and dysentery, and on the whole acted fairly well. But the bad cases hadn't a chance, the disease worked in them too quickly. If you were dying of dysentery, you were pulled out after medical parade and got your chance in the Lemnos Hospital. If you weren't dying, it was a long time before the next parade came round. The men crept away into their dug-outs and bled to death. Their mates, coming round with a drop of soup for them, found them stiffened up in the rabbit-holes, just as they had stretched themselves on the cramped earthen benches.

Night-patrol was a queer and furtive prowling in the pit of No Man's Land. Starkie made one of a patrol a little after the Tommies drove back the Turks. With ten others he was taken to a hole in the trench and down into No Man's Land. There was very little barbed wire on Gallipoli. Down in the throttle of the valley lay hundreds of Turks, many of them wounded men who had died after twenty-four hours' exposure—the burning heat of the day, and at night the chill hand of the frosts. Every face on which a light flashed bore the blackness of death upon it. There were bodies piled up in heaps, like logs brought down the waters of a mill-race to lock in some nightmare dam. The ghastliness of this place and its unburied dead became a legend in the lines. The men christened it 'Death Gully'.

By and by there were rumours of an Australian officer lying out in No Man's Land with a whole battalion's money on his back, and so dead that he certainly couldn't use it. Next morning Starkie took up Jack Frew's bet, and crept out from the lines to have a go for it. He had almost reached the little figure pointed out as the late Australian Croesus when the Turk sniper spotted him. Then began a game of cat and mouse, with Starkie for mouse. His lucky star had landed him in a fold of ground behind a rock hummock. Move backwards or forwards, and the sniper splashed dirt into his face. The sniper played marbles round his head, the little jets of soil and pebbles hitting him every now and again just to remind him that he hadn't been forgotten. The men in his own trench watched him through periscopes and yelled encouragement to him; but nobody formed a rescue-party, and Starkie didn't blame them. He lay where he was, stiff as a ramrod, from ten in the morning until after dusk. Then he crawled back to the trenches on his stomach, the vision of the gilded corpse very dim indeed. 'Money-belt? I think the Turks got it, eh?'

Rifles were wrapped in blankets in the front line and inspected every little while by querulous officers who didn't like anything about the troops' kit and appearance. Captain Smythe, after one glance at Starkie's rifle, told him he was a disgrace to Otago, no soldier, and a bloody pest. On this occasion he spoke truer than he knew. Starkie, injured, prepared to clean his rifle. Ten rounds were allowed for, and by mischance eleven had been thrust into the breech.

'Never mind, Starkie; maybe he's missed his bottle from the store-ship,' murmured Paddy encouragingly.

Starkie worked his rifle-lever, chucked out ten cartridges, shut the breech and, thinking it was empty, pulled the trigger to pull the block out. The rifle banged.

Captain Smythe, his face beautifully patterned with gravel-rash, turned again and leapt at the horrified Starkie. 'Did you try to do that? Did you try to do that?'

Starkie swore by all a soldier's gods that he hadn't done it on purpose, and Captain Smythe called him a liar. In this particular instance he was wrong. But to the end of the War, Captain Smythe maintained that Starkie had tried to shoot him.

Men from the Otago lines moved out on burial-party under Captain Hewitt, a tall and rangy disciplinarian who stood no nonsense. Some worked at gathering the dead, some at tipping the contents of the oiled sheets into the open graves. One corpse crumbled in Starkie's arms. Round the decaying body was a money-belt, and in it twenty sovereigns and a half-sovereign, in English gold. Starkie shouted his discovery to Fleshy McLeod. Something cold and round touched him behind the ear. He turned, to find Captain Hewitt's revolver nuzzling against his head.

'Don't you know that I could shoot you for looting?' asked the grim voice of the Captain.

Starkie after that followed instructions. He put the gold back into the money-belt. He got down into the grave, lifted out three of the blackened corpses, laid the soldier with the money-belt face down in the reeking, seeping soil. Then on the four bodies he piled nine more. As the last one rolled over from the oiled sheet into his arms it broke in two. For one hideous second he saw the grave, the dead men, his own body trapped in that cavern of putrefaction, just as they really were. Then Captain Hewitt saved him, shouting to him to tumble out and thank his stars he wasn't in the Imperial Army, where corpse-robbers were shot on sight.

It was tremendously important, on the way back to the trenches, that he should think of the gold in the money-belt and not of the corpses piled up above it. If you start thinking of the expression on a dead man's swollen face, you being stowed away in a rabbit-hole where the next whirling, twisting fire-cracker coming down from heaven may be your own packet, what's going to happen to you? Back in the Otago lines he told the story of the money-belt with a swagger.

'Where's he buried?' demanded Paddy.

'Hi, anyone know where a trumpet is?' Fleshy McLeod chipped in.

'What for a trumpet?'

'I want to play the Angel Gabriel and make him hop up again.'

'That one'll do no more getting up in the morning. Christ, if you'd seen the face—'

'Chuck it, Starkie! One face is the same as all the rest. What's the use of a pile of gold to him? And half of us broke. . . .'

The last was truth. In their rabbit-warren they had nothing to do with their spare time but gamble. The slick hands gathered in every penny that came to the green-horns, and then the soldiers who had made a hit with Gippo girls were left with their last stakes—gold bangles filched from the ladies' arms as 'keepsakes'.

In the evening Fleshy McLeod tapped Starkie on the shoulder.

'Come on. I've got a new game.'

'What's its name?'

'We call it raising the dead,' said Fleshy grimly, and slid out of his corner in the trench. After a moment, Starkie passed a hand across a face dripping with sweat, and crept after him. They raised the dead.

Wherever they put the gold from the dead man's money-belt, on cards, or dice, it couldn't go wrong. Even when chance gave them an hour or two to fleece the Australians, who as gamblers made the New Zealanders look like babes in swaddling-clothes, the twenty sovereigns and the half-sovereign came home bringing little friends with them. One day a Digger asked them where they got the gold, and they were injudicious enough to blab. After that their sovereigns were ruled out of the trench gambling-schools, the boys swearing that it was haunted gold. The Fourth Brigade of Australians barred their gold as well, and from lording it over the rest with their clink of sovereigns they were driven back to the same old sixpenny throws. Between them they had chalked up a profit score of sixty pounds.

The men still used periscopes in the trenches, and it was

squinting through the tube one day that Starkie spotted the Turk sniper camouflaged by the scrub in No Man's Land. None of the New Zealanders loved a sniper; and Starkie, remembering Goliath and a few more—also the way the Turk had dusted the seat of his own pants the day he went hunting the Australian gold-mine—liked him a lot less than most. The Turk sniper had made a mistake this time. He was within easy range of the Otago trench.

Starkie was cat now, and he enjoyed it. His first bullet just clipped the grass in front of the sniper's head; but the second one, before the Turk had time to break for cover, got him in the leg. The man tried to crawl away. Starkie sent little jets of soil up around him. He remembered a story which his father had told to frighten him a long time ago. A story of the Delaware way of killing a man with a small fire. This fire doesn't have to be more than six inches high, just twigs and grasses, but you light it over very close to one side of a man's head. Then you build the pile on the other side. Then lower down. . . .

A man in the trenches cried, 'Stop it, you dirty Hun!' Other voices began to protest. Then a voice Starkie knew said from behind him. 'Give me that gun.' He slewed round to see Captain Dombey, and Captain Dombey wouldn't take no for an answer. He got the gun and stepped up on the parapet to finish off the wounded Turk sniper. Everyone knew he was one of the best rifle-shots in New Zealand.

Before his rifle had time to crack, he put a hand to his throat, said, 'God, I'm hit; get me to the dressing-station!' and tumbled back into the trench like a sack of beans.

Starkie and Captain Dombey alike had forgotten that Turk snipers often went in couples, like snakes. In the scrub of No Man's Land the sniper's mate had been waiting his chance to get a shot in. The bullet had ripped through Captain Dombey's armpit and shoulder muscles, tearing a good big hole, but not low enough to lay him out for good unless gangrene set in.

He was fifteen stone if an ounce; and though Starkie and three others bore the stretcher that took him to the dressing-station on the beach, it was a rough passage, with the bearers stumbling as they scrambled down the scrubby hills, and Captain Dombey groaning about unlimited doses of C.B. The third time the stretcher was dropped he stopped promising rewards and fairies and kept up a thin blue line of curses. Starkie told him, with reminiscent sorrow, that it wasn't as bad as C.B., or latrines, or a job in the prison barracks; but then conversation was held up where the track was blocked with a crowd of Gurkhas and Punjabis, bent on slaughtering a goat. The Gurkhas lived on the other side of Mule Gully, sweet-mannered little brown fiends who kept their faces free from whiskers by pulling every hair out of their chins with tiny tweezers.

The Punjabis were fine, big-bearded fellows, and both the gamest fighters on Gallipoli. You couldn't shove past them while they were killing meat, for if a soldier's shadow fell on their food it became unclean, and on Gallipoli nobody wasted provisions. The stretcher was set down, and the corpse and stretcher-bearers both consoled themselves with a drink and a mess of blazing curry dished up with chupattis. Meanwhile, the goat, a gingery old Nanny bleating forlornly about her home and father, was led in to the circle of black watching faces and sacrificed like Iphigenia, the silver sweep of a Gurkha knife cutting her head off in a single blow.

'Lovely ain't it?' Starkie said to Captain Dombey, his eyes fixed hungrily on the wicked curved blade of the *kukri*.

'You get to hell, and hurry me down to the dressing-station!' querulously responded the gallant captain, and the jolting progress was resumed.

Down at the dressing-station Captain Dombey first cursed them roundly in several different languages, not all known to the secretariat of the League of Nations, then lifted himself up on his good elbow and grinned at them. 'So long, boys; I'll be back in three months—and then look out!' He disappeared from their view, but kept his word. In three months to the day, the hole in his shoulder more or less satisfactorily plastered up, he was back on Gallipoli and seemed to think more of C.B. than ever.

At the water-tanks they lapped up as much as their stomachs could hold of lime, benzine, and greyish water. There was never an adequate water-ration on Gallipoli. They thieved a tin of it and started on their way home.

Captain Smythe met them with a scowl of ungenerous suspicion, Captain Dombey being his especial pal. 'Been long enough, haven't you?' he growled.

'So would you be,' retorted an exasperated bearer, 'if you was carrying an elephant on a stretcher six miles!'

For carrying the elephant they got special rations—Fray Bentos—otherwise bully beef—and Blackwell's marmalade for their bread issue, which was doled out, one loaf to eight men. The marmalade-tins were used everywhere in the trenches for making steps, walls, and floors, and some of the designs in the little earth dug-outs were really clever. Marmalade was more of a success than cheese. Such a thing as cheese that refrained from crawling was unknown in the trenches, like a pacifist louse, but they got used to it . . . used to anything.

8 Bluecoat

REST GULLY was the valley-cup where the men were sent every six months or so for a spell from the front lines. As far as Starkie could see, it was called Rest Gully because while Turk snipers didn't try to pot you there, you were expected to do an amount of pick and shovel work which would have made the average navvy look pretty sick. There were also church parades, presided over by the most popular chaplain with the New Zealand forces—'Tommy' Taylor, who came home shot to bits and crippled with rheumatism after the War, settled down in the slummiest street in Wellington, and carried on his work for the boys.

Tommy had a rough edge to his tongue, and didn't mind taking it with him right into his improvised pulpit; as, for instance, when two soldiers—of whom Starkie was one—stole a parcel which Tommy had brought up from the beach for Captain Smythe. The thieves reasoned that two bottles of Scotch at one go would be altogether wrong for a man of the Captain's temperament, so drank the Scotch and buried the bottles. On Sunday, Tommy Taylor preached a sermon on 'That which was lost, and not yet found again'. 'And,' said he, leaning deliberately from his pulpit, 'some of you hellions know where those bottles got to all right.' Tommy spent a good deal of his time telling the troops the old,

old story about how to take care of themselves in Egypt, but most of them hadn't seen a petticoat for twelve months. Woman was a dream for them—a queer, hot, aching dream; and Tommy's hygiene didn't get much of a hearing. They liked his *mot* about the bacon better. 'Look at it!' he exclaimed derisively, holding out a slab a foot long and of leprous buff and purple colourings. 'All hog-fat—Lance Corporal Bacon.' It stayed lance corporal bacon till the end of the War.

After the Rest Gully spell, Starkie got his first wound of any importance, a chipped posterior having been treated in the lines with a strip of sticking-plaster and the usual pair of number nines. Gentleman the Turk might be in private life, but he had no respect for recreation; and when a score of Otago men lay sun-bathing among the scrub, their sole attire cocked hats made out of old newspapers, Johnny sent over a couple of shells. It was a sweet and salubrious day, and the dull thumping up in the gully wasn't enough to disturb the basking men.

'See who's chucking those duck-eggs around, Starkie,' lazily murmured Fleshy McLeod.

'Ah, they're well up,' Starkie assured him, standing up to see. Then something hit him a violent blow just below the knees. He sat down, and found to his astonishment that he couldn't get up. Still able to curse, though faintly, he saw Fleshy's sunburnt nose poking down at him, bright scarlet, and then woke up to protest as the medical officer down at the dressing-station dug the anti-tetanus serum into an iodine-smeared patch of his flesh.

In the same afternoon, half stupid from a shot of morphine, he was carried aboard the hospital ship *Maheno*, which put out for Malta with a full cargo of badly wounded men. Starkie was one of the minor casualties, and when he had had a look downstairs he dragged himself up to the *Maheno*'s deck and lay crouched on a coil of rope. The ship hadn't bunk accommodation for half her wounded; and the men with holes in their arms, legs, or shoulders crept up from the reek of blood and antiseptics down below to sleep as best they could under the white stars. Starkie's wound wasn't bad for a beginner—in the left leg, a hole through which he could have put three fingers; in the right a pit in which the surgeon's forceps had done some very unpleasant fishing. But his tough young body, hard-trained in prison, camp, and trench, shook off morphine and pain alike.

Nobody paid much heed to the slightly wounded on the *Maheno*, but all night feet creaked solemnly up the companion-ways, and long, awkward shapes were piled together in the stern of the ship. In the early morning he could see them clearly enough—eight men dead overnight roughly stitched in canvas and with fire-irons weighting their feet. The bodies, stitched in their coarse white hiding-places, still kept the vague, lonely outlines of humanity. By and by a sailor came along and spread over them a huge, sprawling, cotton Union Jack. The blue in the sky grew deep and tender, and black from the stern of the *Maheno* stood out a long wooden plank.

The burial rites began. A voice gabbled, 'I commit to the deep . . .' The bodies were dragged one at a time to the plank, covered for an instant with the great flag. Then the colours—scarlet, white, and azure—were snatched back and tossed for a moment in the morning wind. The shrouded bodies tipped downwards as the plank gave under their weight. But the sound when they hit the water wasn't the ordinary splash. Starkie crept to the edge of the boat and saw what happened at the *Maheno* burials. As the corpse shot downwards, weighted by the irons so that the dead man seemed to have stepped of his own free will vertically into the green-and-crystal abyss, the sheath of the water showed the obscene grey shapes crowding beneath. Alongside and behind the ship, the great sharks thrust up the lines of their flat, hustling bodies, and as those canvas sacks took the downward plunge, snouts thrust up from the pale cover of the water. Before the body was out of sight the iron jaws clamped upon it, the rivals fought and tore.

The forbidding doors of the naval hospital in Malta opened and swallowed up the protesting forms of Colonial soldiers, who would rather have gone to hell than join the navy—and didn't want petticoat discipline, anyhow. St. David's was no place for Starkie, being to his mind a good deal worse than the average gaol. You can at least, in gaol, when moved, tell a warder what he may do with himself, but you're hampered when it's a nurse. The whole place was like a battleship, and the nurses were armour-plated too. Everything was done on the sepulchral clang of a bell, and the soldiers found, to their horror, that they were only supposed to talk at specified times. Starkie stayed in bed a week, and then, in the blue coat of the incapacitated soldier, escaped into the old stone flagwork and apricot sunshine of Malta.

It's an old Maltese custom that you can take out any of the girls. When you asked one of the black-haired, black-eyed beauties to come along and see the pictures, she beams on you and agrees volubly. But when you turn up at the rendezvous you will notice with surprise and perhaps with concern that following her are Father—with a beard—Mother—with a bosom encased in black—and unlimited numbers of younger brothers and sisters, all shrieking, and all avid for expensive but low forms of entertainment. The relatives who arrived to show unsuspecting New Zealanders and Australians the town seemed almost unlimited, the Maltese women being unrestrainedly prolific, but within the bounds of lawful wedlock, which was no use at all to the soldiery. It was no worse than the old New England bundling or the Boer damsel's oop-sitting, but the Diggers weren't used to it, and so spent their money on oranges instead, or bought bits of lace and embroidery in the old town of many steps, and sent them home to lawful spouses in lands afar.

The whole of Malta is a huge fort, and on the walls of its buildings and stairways thrust out cannon, wheeled around one at a time to face the main square, while swarthy, taciturn gunners rub up the grey muzzles and gleaming brass mountings.

'Gee,' said Starkie, fondling the snout of a lean grey beauty, 'she'd do me for a rifle! I could make some impression with this over at 971.'

'Yes,' nodded a fellow Bluecoat, 'I could do with a popgun like that myself. How does she work, Starkie?'

'I suppose you pull this little string,' said Starkie, jerking a cord which dangled from the beauty's fittings.

Nobody expected the cannon to make any comment; but instead, she leapt like a stag and roared like a lion, and the Bluecoats noticed, in panic, that large blocks of masonry in the square were playing an inspired round of tiddleywinks.

'My God, she was loaded!' quite superfluously remarked Starkie's comrade.

Starkie, a year's growth frightened out of him and his complexion as near pale green as Red Indian blood will allow, turned to flee, but was instead arrested. Protests, prayers, and eye-witnesses to swear that it was an unfortunate accident got him off with a caution; and in the evening the Bluecoats went round *en masse* to inspect the damage.

Starkie found that he had chipped the edges of four Maltese, none permanently spoiled or injured; he had blown a large hole in the wall of a café where a party of British officers had been breakfasting, but they had escaped without a scratch—thereby proving once again that the Devil looks after his own, and his own are, among others, British officers. The only total loss was a large marble statue of peace—a fat fair woman with an olive branch, a surprised expression, and a fig leaf. She still looked surprised, but her head was now divorced from her body, and she no longer possessed any middle. The Bluecoats averred that it was the proper end for women with fig leaves, and went on their way, rejoicing less than they might have done had not their lodgings for the night been within the dour confines of St. David's.

The Maltese considered, and rightly, that the Anzacs were tough. The Anzacs considered the Maltese respectability too much of a good thing. At the earliest possible moment as many of the Bluecoats as could walk departed for Alexandria.

Starkie got word that his brother George was at Sidi Bish with the Veterinary Corps. How many years since they had seen each other at the flax-mill in the Wyndham hills? George had been gone from New Zealand already when they turned him loose from the Invercargill gaol. There was a queerness in knowing that he was so near again. Starkie applied for leave, got it, and turned up at Sidi Bish to be coldly received by his towering brother.

'What did I tell you when I saw you last?'

'To stop with Mum and Dad,' meekly admitted the youngest of his house.

'And you didn't do it, eh? Thought yourself too clever? What the hell are you doing here?'

'Wounded on Gallipoli.' That ought to make the big tough sit up!

It did. The big tough's Red Indian face hardened like chilled steel. Starkie had seen wardens and sergeant-majors who looked a lot pleasanter. An arm like a piston shot out from a huge shoulder. When Starkie woke up, a military police officer was actually assisting him to rise from a gutter, whilst in the distance considerably more military policemen were attending to the immediate wants of George. These they summed up as a spell in gaol. Starkie next saw his brother when his mate, Smithy—a Vickers machine-gunner—turned up with an urgent message that Starkie should go at once to his brother's skipper and explain that the fracas was his fault.

'Tell him he's about as popular with me as a pork chop in a synagogue,' snarled Starkie. But he went.

George's skipper was a fat man with a grin. 'Tell him to be a nice boy and behave,' he advised.

When George was released from the prison tent, Starkie looked at him, wondering how he could persuade such a one of the expediency of being nice. George stood six feet seven inches in his socks. In khaki his face looked the colour of mahogany, but harder. He weighed fifteen stone to Starkie's twelve.

Starkie, Smithy, and George got Alexandria leave. Starkie understood at the outset that he was tolerated—at a price.

'Got any money?' curtly inquired his brother.

Starkie meekly handed over piastres to the number of four hundred, with four pounds ten shillings in Bradburys. He didn't understand himself. Sadly he trotted at the heels of the lordly two, and when they got to a café George forbade him to drink spirits.

'It's no good to you, kid. I've got to think of the old lady, haven't I?' His massive paw tipped up a glass. He swallowed, gave a sigh presumably of satisfaction, and turned to discuss the day's events with Smithy.

Starkie sat by and watched.

Presently George and Smithy departed on private business of their own, taking with them the four hundred piastres and the Bradburys, and advising Starkie to behave himself. Starkie, having taken the precaution to reserve a few piastres for himself—and retaining as well the whole of his English gold—did the best he could, and thus landed in Sisters Street.

The feature of the tall old stone houses in Sisters Street, craning flat and narrow, one roof pressed against the next, is their internationality, which could teach Geneva a good bit even yet. On one floor you would find Maltese girls, on the next the French lingo would be spoken, and you could climb up and up by furtive twisting stairways through Spain, Germany, England, and the crowded rooms of the coloured women. There wasn't the balcony-waving of the Wazza here. You walked in without knocking, and found your way as best you could to whatever you happened to be looking for—dark, lustrous eyes, scarlet heels, a queer finish to an inadequate costume, a listless girl who spoke your own language but whose English skin had grown etiolated here, with the stifling hours of daytime siesta, the hot, weary nights.

He opened the heavy door which, on the French landing, was standing just slightly ajar, and looked inside. It was a blue room, and kneeling alone on a couch piled with the greenish-blue cushions was a girl in a silk dress, a dress as grey as a dove's wing, and shot with little flares of rose. The girl's eyes looked enormous, hazel in a dead-white face. And she was crying. When she saw Starkie she didn't stop crying, neither did she send him away. Her lips curled upwards in a half-hearted fashion, but all the time they were quivering like the mouth of a child to whom somebody had been inexplicably unkind. The tears went on falling straight down her white cheeks, and her hands twisted a little sodden rope which once upon a time had quite possibly been a white pocket handkerchief.

He shut the door softly behind him, too softly to have disturbed or frightened her. But he didn't go straight up to the weeping girl. Her blue room started to talk to him. He wondered at first just what colour it was—that curious blue-green, like a deep lake—and then remembered a little heart of crushed turquoise which somebody had once given his sister Rose. Turquoise . . . there was a high lamp standing beside her, and a silken shade of the same colour dripped long, delicate fronds of tiny blue and silver beads, like the stalactites of a limestone cave.

The long seat in the window was padded with silk, and there was a blue rug. Its ends were roughly tied as the weavers of camel's hair do tie them in the East; it lay on an otherwise bare floor. Curtains fell down straight behind her—a blue waterfall. If she had been tall and stately, or English, the blue room might have been like a pantomime scene or a chocolate-box picture; but she didn't seem more than a child. Still trying to smile, still twisting her handkerchief, she stood and stared at him, the dark hair taken back in two cool waves from a broad forehead. All the time the tears ran down her face. The room and this particular girl made Starkie feel like a clown. He had talked to so many girls, but not a word he had said to any of them would have fitted in here.

Presently he was sitting beside her, and the smile grew more certain on her damp face. He discovered her name was Yvonne. She could talk English fairly well, though her gentle little voice gave the unmistakable French twist to vowel sounds. How she came there, how her room in a house in Sisters Street should be green and blue like the heart of crushed turquoise, why she was crying—those weren't the things she talked about, and he couldn't have asked her. Instead he found himself telling her a host of things—some true, some false; fables designed to amuse. The night came down, and she touched the lamp under the blue shade into a soft glow of light. They didn't go to bed, but sat talking until very late. Starkie asked Yvonne to marry him. He didn't know why; and he did know pretty well that she belonged to someone or something else—to this street, to a man, or to her destiny. She was nice about it, though. She kissed him in a friendly sort of way, and said, 'After the War, soldier.' But when he kissed her, her warm face was still wet with the tears that kept coming into her eyes; and it seemed so queer to think that it was all real, that they were two people touching each other—and what was likely to happen to each of them soon.

He went away from the turquoise room before morning and didn't stop at any other house in Sisters Street, though the place flared with a naphtha life from dusk to day. Beautiful and sweet and good, as good as anyone he had ever met . . . a girl who wasn't good would never have tried to smile at him when the whole of her heart was taken up in crying for something unseen. But let any man of any race put down five piastres, and he could have Yvonne—as far as that sort of having her went. It hadn't gone far as yet . . . white face, hazel eyes. But life is a damned long time.

When the troopship touched at Lemnos on the way back to Gallipoli, the harbour was still swarming with men-of-war, craft of all shapes and sizes. One, with her five funnels sticking crookedly out of an ancient hull, was christened the *Packet of Woodbines*. Lemnos Harbour offered the ship-lover everything that ever left the slips, barring Chinese junks and coracles. Starkie's first job was digging latrines with half Otago there to help, all swearing that in the next war they would be sanitary inspectors, and damn soldiering! The men's limbs were loosened up by their days in Lemnos—drill broken by trials of prowess between the New Zealanders and the Second, First, and Fourth Australians. The Kiwis took the Kangaroos on at Rugby football, and routed them by 101 points to 3. Then the Australians came over yelling for vengeance at cricket, and cleaned up their national honour, for when the sun set on Lemnos their score was 3000, and the pride of the New Zealand bowlers went home heartbroken, swearing only an earthquake could get the stickers out. There was friendliness enough between them. The New Zealanders reckoned the Australians good gamblers, good soldiers, good pals, and superlatively good liars.

The medical corps were getting a bit fussy about hygiene now, though at a late date for the Gallipoli campaign, and for a day or two the world was full of privates with their pants off stooping down for the anti-typhoid vaccine, after which they did as little sitting down as possible for a week.

They had their first close-up view of a beautiful British general when three thousand of them were playing 'two-up' outside the Lemnos wells.

'What about a spin, Alec?' yelled one hardy trooper.

The General, a superb figure, cantered away. Five minutes later, two dozen mounted police charged the two-up schools, involving a heavy loss of stakes as the men scattered from under the horses' hoofs.

'Not half living up to his reputation,' the men grumbled.

The General was tougher yet when the First Brigade of Australians, aided and abetted by the Third—who, technically speaking, were in quarantine with yellow fever, but who remained surprisingly omnipresent for ghosts—raided the Tommies' beer-canteen and removed four barrels. This served the Tommies right—for when unpaid they would hang around the Anzac encampments with their tongues out, exhibiting painful symptoms of thirst and a hydrophobic horror of mere water; but when their own pay rattled in their pouches they never stood treat for the Colonials. The New Zealanders, being invited by the Australians to join in the festival, did themselves rather well. Came the dawn, and the thin red line of the New Zealanders swayed on its legs, while the air over the Tommy bivouacs was bluer than the ocean wave. Came also the General, thunder in his voice and forked lightning in his eye, a nasty sight altogether. Starkie had the misfortune to wobble somewhat as the General swung past, and was ordered out of line.

'What name?'

'Private J. D. Stark, sir.'

'What battalion?'

'Otago Fourth, sir.'

'I thought so! I thought so!' shouted the General, with a conviction which spoke ill for the fair name of Otago. Somewhat later, Starkie was taken on the mat, charged with being drunk in line and with the theft of fifty-three gallons of beer—a noble feat, but one of which, lone-handed, he had never been capable—and ordered continual drill parade, carried on by a justly indignant sergeant two hours after the others had knocked off forming fours. Lemnos sweltered. It was all too much for Starkie's morale. He did three days, then went for a swim, dipped his shirt in water, and went to bed soaking. Two nights later he was choking with pleurisy, and escaped from the wrath of generals, sergeants, and thirsty Tommies alike in the Lemnos Hospital.

Second General Hospital, Lemnos, was staffed by none but Australian doctors and nurses, and they were about as different from the battle-cruisers of Malta as the buttercup is from the thistle. The girls from Sydney and Melbourne—maybe no models as to discipline, but as game as girls are made—were nice enough to Starkie to make him mend his ways. None of them would at that time have taken a prize in a beauty contest. Some were bits of girls, but all were pale, big-eyed, thinned down. Dysentery had hit the nursing-staff as badly as the men they tended; but they kept on their feet, and spent their pay buying extra comforts for the wards. There wasn't any Lady of the Lamp stuff in Lemnos, nor any clanging of bells. The soldiers talked when they liked—except when the delirious ones babbled themselves into the death-stupor; and pale girls ran about between the beds, cleaning, sponging, dressing wounds, cracking jokes in the dockside argot that the men understood.

Starkie was right again, and somewhat repentant, in time to join his battalion when they left for Gallipoli. There was rumour in the troopship of a big attack pending. The men still wore their first issue of khaki shorts and singlets, frayed with a year or more of active service. A week after their arrival on Gallipoli, the weather went mad, and a burning day was followed by a hailstorm in which nuggets of ice as big as pigeon's eggs pelted down over trenches and gullies. Twelve hours later it was snowing. Great white flakes sailed serenely down, and the underclad men shivered and froze in their earthen houses. But beyond the rim of the trenches, the world held a strange and fairy-like beauty. The little scrub-bushes became crystal Christmas-trees, such as the men remembered from the infinitely remote time of their childhood.

Deep clefts of snow covered the pitiful unsightly dead of No Man's Land. There was no war across that silent and crystal world. The white doves of the snow blotted out sight between the trenches. There might indeed have been an enemy, for British soldier or for Turkish sniper, above the white, woman-breasted hills. But how were they to see one another? Mule Gully was deep in snow, so that even the shouts of the muleteers were absent. They were isolated in a silent and lonely world. The men crept out into the hollows of the hills to gather snow in their tin dixies, and brewed vast quantities of scalding black tea. Until that snowfall, there had never been a day of clean and plentiful water on Gallipoli. For two days afterwards there was another strange difference in their existence. Their eyes, their faces, their rations, as soon as the day heightened, weren't instantly covered and fouled by the swarms of great black flies.

The men in the trenches were told that the Turks were bringing up the heavy artillery brought from Austria. For nine days they burrowed like moles, digging new trenches. Then they were told to pack their kits.

'Slaughter at Suvla Bay, or over on Chocolate Hill,' Fleshy McLeod stated in tones of vast authority.

For an hour they sat in the trenches, their kits packed, nothing but the walls and steps lined with marmalade-tins and the kerosene-tin candles to mark the place of their dwelling. Rifles were tied, guns moved in fixed positions. Then they were marched down to the beach. Lined up above the water-tanks where the first man in the Division had fallen with that little blue slate-pencil dot between his eyes, they were told that they were evacuating Gallipoli.

The place was as quiet as a Sunday in a New Zealand village. The men fell into line, and without laughter, almost without a word of comment, began to move down the beach. Then, as the New Zealanders who came to Gallipoli had first seen carved in the yellow cliffs the great Maori Pa, now crumbling to pieces in the wind and rain, their own country found its voice again, and bade its private good-bye to the hills of Gallipoli. A New Zealand captain, marching at the head of the Maori Pioneer Corps, started them off singing the Maori *waiatas*—the very sweet, very plaintive tribal songs that from one generation to another have been handed down among the people of the Maori race. The Maori girls sing them, weaving lithe arms and bodies in the canoe *pois*, the graceful dance of the womenfolk. The men, a long time ago, played them on little flutes which were carved from polished pieces of human thigh-bone.

Even now, where on the banks of the Wanganui River lie hidden among bank-willows the canoes that were hollowed by the adze from a single log, and with a century's slipping through river-waters are as smooth and shining as tubes of amber, you can hear the *waiatas* sung by the people of the river. The words have been translated, but the songs are not artificial, as is the steel guitar or thrumming ukulele of the South Seas. Where the hills and fern were alone with their own native people, the *waiatas* were first born, the voice of a country.

> Now . . . ees . . . the time
> When I . . . mus' say . . . farewell,
> Soon . . . you'll be sail-eeng
> Far away . . . from me. . . .
> When you're . . . away . . .
> Kindlee . . . remember me. . . .
> When you return, you'll find me
> Wait-eeng here.

The Maori girls sing that, the warm and lovely red flushing up under the brown skin of their young breasts and high-boned delicate faces. Their hair, brushed out, falls below their waists, and although its wavy silk is black, it shows a dusting of light like tiny flecks of gold. They wear, to suit the conventions of civilization, bodices of scarlet cotton above their flaxen skirts. Their names are Rangi, Mere, Puhi-Huia, Hine-I-Arohia, Ritahia, Rata, all pronounced with an even inflexion on each syllable, and with the vowels soft, as in the Spanish tongue.

O, listening dead upon the hillsides of Gallipoli and in the deep gullies of the little bitter-tasting bushes!—it is the voice of your country that is bidding you farewell.

They are going now, with that music on their lips, to slay and to be slain, in other fields. Yet one day, man may truly dwell and act in that loveliness which haunts the hidden places of his mind.

Listening dead, one day a man will come back to you and learn the answer to that song of farewell. He will not stumble away, blind and hopeless, into the deeper pools of blood and filth. For you, speaking out of the knowledge bought by travail, will tell him what paths he must take.

9 Court Martial

In which Starkie speaks for himself

WHEN the boys got down as far as Mudros we started to look around. Very few were what you might call handsome to look at, most having gone in for scabies, which left big sores for the lice to burrow under. At Mudros we met up with the Aussies, and started to buy cake and cigarettes from them, for it looked as if the Aussie women remembered the troops better than the New Zealanders. None of our crowd had got any parcel mail for weeks. Then one of our lot who bought a cake from an Aussie sergeant, opened up the round tin it came in and found his own name on the top, with a note from his mother:

Dear boy,

Many happy returns for your nineteenth birthday.

After that we said we all knew the Aussies were lousy, but we hadn't guessed they were as lousy as that, and Captain Dombey said more fools we.

We had a fortnight at Mudros in which to get back on the thieves, and we did the best we could. Some said we were posted for Salonika next, others were all for Mesopotamia. In the finish we were all shipped to Alexandria, but didn't stop there. We went straight out to Ismailia, which is about ten miles from Cairo, and once there among the sandhills they had got us good and proper. It was drill and nothing but drill. In the morning we were taken out into the desert with full water-bottles and drilled in heat like a stokehold all day long. When we came back, the water in our bottles was measured, and if we'd drunk anything it meant C.B. We all figured this meant desert fighting ahead, and a gentle way of telling us there weren't any beer-canteens where we were headed for next, so the boys did what they could to make up for it in their off hours.

But when you got into Ismailia there was nothing much to spend your pay on. Nearly all the women were Arabs, with big heavy rings like curtain-rings in their ears and nostrils. Nothing in the streets but fat Arabs and big, skinny fowls, running about stark naked among the dung-hills with not a feather to their backs, and the most horrible mottled colour. The women in the Ismailian brothels were worse than the ones you met in the streets, though when the troops first came in from the desert you'd see men lined up in dozens before the doors. There was nothing in town but dirty women and rotten whisky; and most of the boys were glad when we were shifted down to the Ferry Post on the Suez Canal, though here it was hot enough to melt the bars across a furnace; and we still kept on with the pleasant little game of drill.

The big boats kept coming through the Suez Canal, and sometimes the people on them got big-hearted too, and used to chuck tobacco over to the soldiers. Whenever a boat was on her way through, our crowd lined up on the bank and cheered for all they were worth. Sometimes it worked, sometimes not. That was how I nearly got drowned one time. I was in the front line, and cheering too, and the fellows behind pushed me off the edge of the wharf. Then I saw one of those big waterproof tins of tobacco bobbing about a little way ahead of me and swam straight for it. I didn't see another boat coming up behind me until the suction from her wash caught me and pulled me towards her propellers. I was about ready for a sticky death when the boys saw what was happening. Five of them formed a chain from the bank and grabbed me just as I was going under. They pulled me out; and when I got to the bank I shared out the tobacco among them. I'd never let go of the tin.

Next day I was detailed for guard, but I wasn't looking for the honour and glory of any tough jobs, not right then, in the Suez heat. By and by I went along to our M.O., and told him exactly what I felt like. He looked pretty serious, and said, 'You've got the symptoms of sunstroke, old man. You lie down and keep quiet.' He gives me a chit, and when I hand it over to the Colonel I'm excused fourteen days. I didn't mention that I'd read up about sunstroke in a book the night before.

I did the fourteen days in Ismailia. Nothing much happened except the Sugar Cane war. That was when some of the troops—Punjabis, New Zealanders, and Aussies—started a barney in a brothel, and the Arabs got their knives out. We'd been particularly warned we weren't to shoot anyone in Ismailia, and there was nothing else to fight them with but the twelve-foot lengths of sugar-cane, piled up in barrels along the road. The troops got sugar-canes and thrashed the Gippos and Arabs with them. It took a bit of doing to make the Punjabis stop at that, but the war went off all right. After that I was arrested—so were plenty more—and got fourteen days' field punishment.

Then the troops were shifted back to Ismailia from Ferry Post, and stole two jars of rum from headquarters. In the lines everybody spent a quiet night drinking rum, plenty of the officers taking part as well as the men. At 11.30 Colonel Percy came along and told an orderly sergeant to stop the noise. The next thing was Captain Smythe and Captain Dombey came out of their tents and wandered along trying to find out who was making a noise. The boys could have told them. Captain Dombey had his arm around Captain Smythe's waist and was singing, 'I want to be a soldier', and Captain Smythe was singing, 'I want someone to love me'; and I thought, 'A fat chance you've got, either of you, you fat old bastards.' And then Captain Smythe ordered everyone out of my tent, where we were sitting quiet and behaving ourselves. I got up in too much of a hurry, so I fell out instead of walking, and I was put in the clink. I was annoyed at that, so I cursed Colonel Percy a long way back right past his ancestors to their ancestors, and when he came in I threw a tent mallet at him. Then I was locked up in the tent, taken to battalion headquarters next day and court-martialled.

It was eleven days before the big show, the district court martial, came off, and while the rest were all out drilling in the desert, I lay and slept inside the tent, which was as near cool as any spot can be round about Ismailia. Then I was taken up for court martial in front of three officers. I forget their names. They read out the charge—using language to Colonel Percy and trying to brain him with a tent mallet. Colonel Percy said he was sorry but he couldn't repeat the language I used to him, which was funny after what he said himself when I threw the tent mallet. Then they asked me to repeat it, and I said I was sorry, too, but I couldn't remember anything.

I was asked if anyone would speak for me, so I said, 'Yes; send for Captain Dombey.'

Captain Dombey was drilling his men eight miles out in the desert when he got word he was wanted at once at headquarters. So he came in at the double, thinking there was trouble ahead, and turned up at the court so red in the face I thought he was going to have a fit. When he was told he was wanted to speak for me, he didn't say anything, he just stood there with his eyes popping out of his head, getting slowly redder and redder, like one of those penny balloons the kids blow up too high and then they burst.

Presently he opened his mouth and said, 'This man is the biggest, laziest, rottenest, most troublesome—' He stopped dead again, and I could see he was having a lot of trouble to keep his language what they call Parliamentary. 'In times like this he's more trouble than half a battalion put together.'

Colonel Percy looked at me with a pretty cold sort of glint in his eye, nasty as a fixed bayonet, and I began to wish I'd left Captain Dombey in the desert until he'd melted there.

Then he said: 'And in the trenches he's one of the best soldiers I ever had.' He said a lot more after that, which I should blush to repeat, the end of it was that I got off with fourteen days' second field punishment, which meant I had to report myself night and morning, nine o'clock both ways. I did it in Ismailia.

While I was there I used to swim in the Suez Canal, and took it out of the darkies for having such a dirty town you couldn't get any fun out of it. I used to lie in ambush under a big sandbank. Presently a Gippo would come along riding in state on a little donkey, his wife trotting alongside him on foot, carrying a big load on her head. Women are like that in Ismailia. The Gippo donkey-riders always had bags of oranges across their knees to sell to the troops. I used to duck the Gippo and cut the orange-bags open, and when they were bobbing about in the Canal I'd go in after them and fish out as many as the boys needed. Sometimes they came along yelling, 'Choclit! Choclit, gibbit backsheesh!'—and I gave them backsheesh all right, chasing them across the desert. By and by they used to call me 'Le Brigand', and whenever a couple of them saw me there'd be a yell of 'Y'Allah!' and they'd go as fast as their little mokes would take them.

It wasn't long before we all lined up in the desert again, our kits refilled and shortages made up.

At Ismailia we were loaded on cattle-trucks, a few of the luckier ones getting a seat in ancient rattle-bone carriages. We left for Alexandria, everyone cheering, and a fair number pretty full. It was on this trip that a Gippo got shot. The train stopped for water about half-way to Alexandria and the Gippos ran alongside, same as they always did, yelling for backsheesh and offering baskets of oranges. A good many bought the oranges—big blood-red beauties, juicy enough to slake the cinders in our throats. Most of the boys were half canned by now on whisky smuggled aboard the train at Ismailia. One of the soldiers handed a Gippo a note for his oranges, and the Gippo, waiting till the train whistle blew, ducked and ran for it, omitting to remember the change. The soldier he bilked could see him plain from the carriage window, running and dodging like a rabbit. A hundred yards off and he crumpled up and lay face downwards with his white nightgown in the station dust. The rifle-crack hadn't sounded loud enough for the officers to spot where the shot came from, and when they came dashing along, with the Gippos howling bloody murder alongside, none of us would give the show away. So with one dead backsheesh-merchant behind us we left again for Alexandria. Our kits were loaded aboard the troopship, the *Franconia*. Everyone who went aboard the *Franconia* that trip was a Gallipoli veteran, including Otago Fourth's mascot, Jack Briggs's monkey. They wouldn't let the monkey land in France, which was a pity, because she was the best louser in the regiment, and she and Jack cried like a couple of kids when he left her behind. Jack said girls were all right, but he'd never get a girl to sort out the lice like that monkey used to do.

Alexandria was clearer in outline when the *Franconia* left Egypt—it was April, 1916—than Cairo had been when the *Maunganui* had docked there over a year before. Some of the best were left behind, or in hospital at Lemnos and Malta, or behind the barbed wire. One of the chaps had a book about Egypt and read out bits about the different times when foreign troops had landed there before and gone shunting around the old Pyramids and the Sphinx—Julius Caesar, in the Year Dot, and a chap named Anthony that was sweet on that girl they named Cleopatra's Needle after, in London; and old man Moses splitting the Red Sea in two to get his flock away from the land of Sergeants, Scabies and Syphilis. Say 'Land of Three S's' to any New Zealander or Aussie and he'll get you all right.

Way back in the time before the Egyptians settled down to making a steady living on backsheesh and nothing else but, there was a king of their own—I forget his name now—that wanted to turn it into a pacifist show. He wrote a hymn that the soldier with the book read out, and it sounded pretty good with Alexandria growing dim in the east as the *Franconia* pulled out. But the Gippo generals decided after a bit that this king was lousy, and Egypt went back to her old habits. There was too much fighting altogether to be put into one book, but Napoleon Bonaparte got there and was pretty pleased with himself about it; thought of keeping a Gippo harem and ruling the East. Nobody rules the East, unless it's that stone woman with no nose that they keep out in the desert beyond Cairo.

But queer as the old days in Egypt may have been, I can't think of anything queerer than that the troops from New Zealand and Australia should come there on their way to fight. Of all the places that wouldn't be likely to interest a New Zealander, Egypt stands next in line to Greenland's icy mountains and the North Pole.

Most of us had never heard of it, except that it put out a good line of cigarettes, and even that was a lie: those long yellow fags of theirs would turn your stomach. Even now I can't help wondering at times—why, why, why? What did we get out of it, anyhow? It wasn't even a good show. What's Egypt got to do with New Zealanders? Why did Jacko have to stay behind the barbed wire when the rest of us pushed on? He had a girl of his own at home—but oh, hell, when there's nothing to do but plough sand and count the flies and gamble, you can't play saint all the time!

I lost all my gold on the way over to France. The men got over the idea that it was haunted when they reckoned out how much they'd need to spend on a good time in Paris. But there's a lot of exaggeration about Paris. I'll tell you later.

10 The Noah's Ark Country

ON THE grey-quilted satin of Marseilles Harbour black smoke from a destroyer's funnels worked a pattern in cross-stitch. Lean and grey as a badger, she slipped past the *Franconia*, and tied up alongside the wharf they saw the fish she had brought up a day before from the ocean—the biggest Boche submarine caught in French waters since the beginning of the War, and the first to show the ugly snouts of guns mounted on her deck.

Germany, with its blond hair and china-blue eyes, stared up at the *Franconia*'s troops and shouted to them as they marched down the gangways. Big gangs of Prussian prisoners, men from places where life has something of the white savour of newly chopped forest pine, were loading the boats, a sentry with fixed bayonet and a look of intolerable boredom on his face posted behind every squad. The Prussians were giants, every mother's son of them, not one in sight tipping the scales for less than fourteen stone. As the troops marched past they yelled 'Good luck, boys!'—and, with more emphasis, 'It's hell out there!'

Prussia was sportsmanlike, but La Belle France hadn't any

colours flying. There wasn't so much as a cup of coffee, let alone a glass of the bock they'd all heard so much about, to enliven the wait for the troop-trains. This was too much for Paddy Bridgeman's morale, and when he slipped out of the lines, Starkie and two more followed him to take care of him and see he didn't lose his pay-roll shenannigin in his Irish way with the mademoiselles. As it happened, they needn't have worried, for the only inhabitant of the little side-street pub where they took refuge was an old man with an unshaven blue chin, who peered at them suspiciously over his glasses and wanted to see the colour of their money right away. Before they had time to express resentment of this, the French gendarmerie came in, all blue uniform, moustache, and swagger; and when they explained that they had somehow managed to miss their division, they were at once escorted to a train which was starting for Morbecque, and which appeared to be full up with Tommies.

The wheels rattled, a whistle shrieked like a damned soul, and the train bounced its way out of Marseilles on the seven days' trip to Morbecque. All the way the Tommies thieved as the New Zealanders had never suspected that any man could have the initiative, the perseverance, the agility, and the barefacedness to thieve. Everything was fish that came to the Tommies' net—poultry from little farms lying along the railroad tracks, fruit, magazines, stationery, tobacco, and an occasional pocket handkerchief from friendly mademoiselles who brought them cups of coffee at the stations. The discouraging memory of the pub in Marseilles was blotted out for the New Zealanders by the huge stone wine-jars, encased in wickerwork, which were taken aboard at one station and put out, empty, at the next.

The staple diet, apart from wine, was delicious French bread, served in long twisted loaves which seemed always hot and fragrant from the ovens. There were guards on the train, but at a conservative estimate the guards were twice as bad as the Tommies themselves. None the less, when they arrived at Hazebrouck and were escorted to their battalion, which was stationed at Morbecque, they learned that life still maintained a disciplinarian scowl. They were marched into the guard-room and were tried, put on fourteen days' Royal Warrant. The implication of this was that for fourteen days apiece they would fight, drill, loaf, or perform route-marches for their King and Country, free, gratis, and for nothing.

Having something to jingle in their pockets was a strict necessity among the New Zealanders, who had struck a very wet district indeed. Champagne went for five francs a litre; white wine was two francs, and the French would hand you over twelve beers—good beers—for a shilling. Malaga was two and a half francs, and the soldiers' favourite tipple was a frightful brew, half malaga and half champagne, mixed together and carried along in kegs.

In clear July weather the battalion started on route marches to Armentières. A sea voyage and a few weeks in a crisp, cool climate had so transformed the men that nobody would have recognized the yellow-faced, scabies-ridden veterans who had crept into Ismailia three months before. In three months of peace they had had time to forget the worst of it, as far as it could ever be forgotten. Then there was the chief glory of France—freedom from flies. Nobody who hadn't eaten the festering, black-crusted filth of Gallipoli could understand what that meant. Spruce in their uniforms, their new rifles slung jauntily enough at their shoulders, Otago Fourth swung along.

All the way from Morbecque they lost only one man, who got sore feet and threw his pack at a cow, which meant another little problem for the military police. The rest marched, laughing and singing. Every battalion was headed by pipe and brass bands, and the number of Scotties in the Otago crowd meant that its pipes could skirl to some purpose. The Dunedin brass band played under a tall chap named George, and swung along blowing 'Keep the Home Fires Burning' on its trumpets. After them tramped the brawny Scots, with Pat Johnston skirling 'Cock o' the North' on his pipes, and a thousand strong young voices lifted up, in tune and out of tune, keeping him company.

Between the pale hedgerows, brown autumn leaves pricking like goblin ears behind the thickset green, France was a Noah's Ark country, all tiny farms, tiny horses, tiny cows, and barking dogs. Everything was a few centuries old . . . thatched cottages with their slated cow-byres leaning tumbledown and dark against one end of the dwelling-place; fields, chocolate and clear green, ploughed by hand with wooden ploughs and wooden harrows. Along the turned furrows, where birds screamed and fought over tit-bits, walked women in solemn, sombre colours—dark blue and earthen brown, sowing the seed by hand as their mothers had done for hundreds of years.

Little Froggies, too young for blue uniform and swaggers, solemnly milked cows in full sight of the roads, and the soldiers broke ranks to beg for the new milk, steaming hot and sweet, in wooden pails. In dairies of brick, paled almost to apricot-colour, thickset dogs gravely turned the churn handles tied to their shoulders. Dogs, enormous or miniature, but all engrossed in their labours, pattered on the shallow steps of the great water-wheels turned by their running feet. The drops splashed down in little cascades, separate and gleaming. You could whistle and coax the dog, but though a tail might thump in an abstracted kindly way, you couldn't beguile him away from the matter in hand. He was part of the ancient and diminutive sampler of the French country life, into whose pattern of toil everything and every-one—strawberry cows, little girls with flying black plaits, old men in smocks, snorting horses, and friendly dogs—had been stitched.

The route marches covered from twenty to thirty miles a day, the men marching under full packs, with a ten minutes' spell at the end of each hour. Here and there along the country roads they came upon wayside shrines—the Crucifix, white and simple, half hidden in its little grotto of brambles, the Mother holding her Child against a calm breast, with a tiny spring of water bubbling up, dark and limpid, in the worn stone basin set beneath her feet. Soldiers who had ducked the church parades since the beginning of the War fell out of the lines to pray there. There was a notion that it would bring them good luck.

Where they came into contact with the people of Noah's Ark country, they found that the women did all the work: ploughing, milking, sowing, harrowing. Young men, all but the hopelessly crippled, had been swept out of the countryside. The old ones dreamed in the sunshine, rattling imaginary sabres, talking in their incomprehensible patois of Sedan, and of yet older days. The women, their breasts full and firm as winter pears under their blue print gowns, compressed their lips, flashed fierce eyes at the soldiers, had ready-made curses against the Boche, and a shrug of their shoulders for their own position. Half of them, in addition to working their farms and keeping their cottages speckless, worked in little estaminets at nights.

Starkie had known New Zealand women who could rough it; but most of them would have lain down to die before taking on the burden that these square, blue-clad shoulders bore so inflexibly. Yes, the mademoiselles were wonderful—and their mothers too, for that matter. And it was always '*Après la guerre*, soldier'. They had an invincible belief, these women, in the animal nature of the soldiery. Even the heavy-moustached, stout old grandmothers, with behinds the size of a coach and four, patted you on the shoulder, winked at you, and said '*Après la guerre*, soldier', as though when you'd finished cleaning up their Noah's Ark, chucking the animals that didn't belong in it back into the swirling waters of the Flood, you might as a great treat be permitted to seduce them.

Starkie grinned. *Après* several *guerres*, as far as he was concerned.

Nevertheless, you could never forget them—the solid-hipped, red-cheeked women who came into the estaminets, still smelling of the clean faint fragance of soil and cow-byre, and served out the heavy mugs of beer across the little table. Only on the surface their eyes flashed and sparkled. The big arms that girdled a New Zealand soldier's shoulders were casual, really, thinking no more of it than of patting a useful dog who'd done his bit turning the water-wheel. Their eyes, when you really looked into them, were stern and proud. Their hands were strong as a man's hands. Starkie wondered why the Frenchmen always seemed so much smaller than their women. Odd to think of one of these Hecubas surrendering herself to a *gendarme* with a waxed moustache and patent-leather hair.

They started on the last lap of their journey to Armentières. The billeting of the men at night lay with the quartermaster, and they might find themselves in house, barn, stable, deserted theatre, pigsty, or eating peppery little stolen turnips in the lee of a haystack. They passed through the town of Arrantes, marching out at eight in a grey morning after a night when thirty of them had slept on straw in a stable.

At Estaires, after a lap of twenty-five miles, they saw a few wounded being moved back from the front lines, and heard the first mutter of the Big Boys—just a low growl far away on the horizon. Ten of them went to an estaminet here and bought a bottle of whisky, allegedly for the officers' mess. While Froggy dived down to get the liquor, the soldiers sent out a spy to watch where he went. They saw the old man dive down into a little lean-to at the back of the house. Then a raiding-party of five created a diversion, starting a fight in the estaminet, and while the whole staff were busy wringing their hands, shouting and pouncing, Paddy, Starkie, and Fleshy McLeod made away with the shaky old lock on the cellar door and brought up into God's sunshine three cases of whisky and one of *vin rouge*. There was one casualty among the raiders when an old lady knocked a Digger out with her hefty ashplant staff; but the wounded comrade was lugged along with the rest when they joined their battalion, and all were out of earshot before the theft was discovered.

Thereafter the robbers marched in comfort, Tent Eight's old comrades linked up with Tommie McFarlane, Arthur Kelliher from Invercargill, and Andrew Bourse, a Dunedin man, who had done their bit in the raid. They kept the spoils mostly to themselves, claiming that he who would not thieve, neither should he drink. But the men were as contented as sandboys. 'Cock o' the North' floated back to them, and they fell into step, swaggering along the white roads, cursing the French cobblestones when they struck a village.

For more than half the men in Otago Fourth, it was the last trip they ever made.

The country grew deserted as they came near the lines, and they could hear the reason why. A few Froggies stuck on at their little farms, too mean, too dazed, or too penniless to pack their bundles and take the long trail back to safety. They found women in deserted houses, living somehow within three miles of Armentières. The road began to thicken and clot with wheels, as ambulances, forage-waggons, munition-waggons, lumbered past them. Then they saw their first Armentières estaminet standing up as gaunt and forlorn as a scarecrow. It had one wall and one chimney left standing. The rest was an enormous heap of rubble.

The Devil had climbed into the Noah's Ark and tossed all the tiny figures and their trees and houses helter-skelter. At 11.30 and in the blanched moonlight of early autumn they marched into

Armentières town. The buildings lay collapsed in the torn-up streets, piles of broken shards and masonry. One clock-tower thrust up its menacing finger at the sky, its clock-hands stopped at the very hour of their arrival—11.30. The troops christened this place Half-past Eleven Square.

Colonel Chalmers was in charge of the show now, and pretty soon word was passed back along the lines: 'No talking . . . no lights . . . no cigarettes . . . no smoking. . . .' They were nearing the front lines, and for all they had seen on Gallipoli, the spectral black and white rubbish-pile of the moonlit town, the sight of a few mangy cats slinking by, snarling and spitting at the approach of human beings, the terse order to douse their lights, put a clammy finger on a good many mouths not used to silence.

'Huh! The old man's windy, isn't he?' whispered Paddy.

Starkie answered not at all. His own hair was pricking along his scalp.

Quite suddenly there was a terrific din. Ghosts came shouting, singing, and yelling round the corner of an Armentières street. At sight of the silent ranks of the New Zealanders the ghosts stopped, obviously perplexed.

'Strike me pink!' invited an unmistakable Tommy voice. ''Ave you seen a ruddy, muckin' spook, or wot? Ain't the bleedin' 'Uns fourteen miles away?'

The New Zealanders remained quiet for just one moment. Then, from the front ranks to the soldiers who didn't know the joke, one yell of hysterical laughter went from mouth to mouth. Laughing, shouting, singing, damning the Kaiser and the Colonel impartially, the Fourth went through the ghost town, tramping past squares and churches which looked as though an earthquake had hit them. Nothing was spared. Sometimes, as though to cheat strangers with a shadow of its old sturdy dignity, a cathedral or a hall—very proud in the long ago—showed a façade whose stone columns, carved in the Middle Ages with little grey flowers and running animals, remained unperturbed. The moonlight smote once upon the lustrous blue and crimson of a great rose window, its panels of exquisite stained glass unbroken. But the miracle that had spared that lonely beauty had not laid its finger on the buildings behind. Where colonnade and aisle had lifted up their lofty prayer to the heaven in which their builders had placed full faith, there were now blackened grottoes of ruin, their arches broken like stalactites.

The seats had been ripped out of the churches and smashed up for firewood by the troops. Lying on the ground outside one grotesque shell of a church were the great Armentières bells, cast in bronze, many of them now tipped uselessly on their battered sides, as big as the round tables of a council hall. It was possible to discern by moonlight worn inscriptions engraved on some. The boys could make nothing of the thin French script, but little rows of numerals told how the greatest of the bells had been for centuries the voice of the city. Love, death, flood, fire, foreboding of danger—what had they not pealed down through their rich years to the children who knew them as soon as they knew their mothers' voices? And now in the dust and ruins they were dumb, as though the strength that had built up the churches and gifted them with that deep and mellow voice was for ever gone out of the limbs and soul of Armentières. But on the horizon spoke the new voice of the city—the quick, stuttering duet of the machine-guns. The boys called it the Song of Hell.

Very near was the thunder of the shells and vivid blue flashes stabbed into the sky. The nearer flashes showed where the English guns were answering the German entrenchments. Sometimes a hard staccato told where Parapet Joe was playing on his machine-gun. Half dazed and wholly weary, the gay marchers stumbled at last into their billet for the night—an old brewery. Candle-stubs were stuck into brackets. The half-light, pale and furtive, fell upon faces grimed with the sweat of marching and heavy with sleep. A stew of bully-beef was hashed up for them and handed around in tin pannikins. They ate it with their fingers, not bothering to unpack their kits and hunt for spoons or forks. Leaning propped against one another, the men fell asleep just as they sat.

A rattle at the door, and a sergeant—Bob Phayre—poked his red face into the room. 'Buck up and be ready to march in ten minutes,' he shouted, and vanished into darkness.

The men cursed as they dragged themselves out of their half-sleep. 'The dirty, rotten, motherless, lousy, red-tape worms!' Everyone from Generals to Lance-Corporals came in for mention in their commination service. Buttons undone, hair unkempt, they tumbled out into the bleak street, and were trotted away three hundred yards.

Then the storm burst over Armentières. Violent colours, orange, blue, and livid white, gashed the sky. There was a terrific rattling din, and those of the houses that yet stood began to collapse like a pack of cards, sliding inwards together from the handsome castle which some childish hand has raised. The men, staring back, saw the old brewery which they had just left flatten itself out into a heap of bricks and a white, spouting fountain of dust. By ten minutes they had missed being buried alive or blown to pieces.

'Great chaps, those Intelligence Department fellows. They must 'a' knowed it. Great chaps. . . .'

With which mild eulogy the men, half-dead, dragged themselves to the roadside and spent the rest of the night in the open. The air grew bitterly cold towards morning.

When day came they had clear sight of Armentières—and what a sight it was! Masses of broken bricks, whole buildings lying in the street, trees which had been calm and stately snapped in two like tooth-picks, stared at them desolate and accusing. Houses and estaminets, still undamaged, stood just as their owners had left them. The soldiers wandered into these deserted buildings, and the friendly look of kitchen and hearthstone struck them into silence. Most of the French kitchens had tall, scrubbed dressers of white pine, and from shining brass hooks still dangled the thick earthenware of the family—moustache-cups, patterned with roses, for the old men; little mugs with gay and fantastic designs for the children, whose red shoes had been left behind in wardrobes.

The hearths were deep, and lined with broken bricks or tiles of a sunburnt hue. On huge stoves stood shining pots and pans, their tin polished like silver. In the cupboards mildew had raised its bluish crust over provisions which had been left behind. Dead or alive, those struggling exiles who had run down the uptorn road from Armentières? It was so easy to picture—in the great chairs, still dragged comfortably near the hearth-side, a woman somewhat different to those met by the soldiers on their marches—deep-eyed, and with hair like the red corn.

The only estaminet still open in the neighbourhood was a Flemish place, on land which had changed hands twice between German and Allied troops. Here the New Zealanders found themselves about as popular as a bad case of smallpox. The Flemish tavern-keeper and his fat servants grunted at the boys when they tramped in.

'*Très bon,* the *Allemand*—he pay for everything he get. You men pay till drunk, then you rob us.'

The virtues of the German soldier apparently precluded any chance the Colonial might have of making a hit. When the men drifted into the inn-yards to beg for a drink of water, they would find the pumps locked up and a grinning Flemish yokel mounting guard over them. Any one of these stolid gentry would tell the Colonial soldier that the German was all right, the British no bloody good.

In the end the boys became convinced that the Flemish inn-keeper had the right end of the story, and it was up to them to do nothing to disappoint him. So they smashed the pumps and bilked the estaminet for their drinks, drunk or sober. After that they went out and got shot to bits holding the popular Hun back from the disputed patch of ground. Allemand, Tommy, Digger, Aussie, the Flemish inn still stood on, surly, unbreakable, inhospitable. The boys said that, *très bon* or otherwise, the Hun couldn't be worse than the Flemish.

Little vendettas were born in the broken streets. One gang of men found a baby cot crushed to splinters in the ruins under a house, and the floor sticky red with dried blood. 'They want a lot of mercy, and they'll get it,' went the grim promise. But there were compensations. The cellars were still full of wine and beer for the taking—good stuff, some of it fruity vintages from gentlemen's prized and cobwebbed bottles.

Still holding the fort of their brick convent remained a little company of French nuns, women in blue wimples, whose queer little starched white frills crumpled like the paper edgings of chocolates around their serene faces. In their garden, vegetable marrows, scarlet Turks' Cap pumpkins, the bright patches of blue and white flowers where bees droned over their kitchen garden, struggled into life between brown pits where shells had buried themselves in the soil. The convent itself remained unhit, and was used by the New Zealand officers as battalion headquarters. The nuns stayed on, helping the friendless, sheltering the homeless. Before and behind them life splintered into matchwood.

'Waiting for what? Why don't they rat like the rest?' growled Paddy Bridgeman.

True enough, there was something a little indecent in fighting so near to that curious pool of quietude. Nobody believed any more in the hand of Providence. This wasn't a war when people who really wanted to fight marched out into the open, blew a trumpet, flourished a silken banner, and dived for one another's throats. It was a war against droning bees, rows of blue flowers, babies' cots, shining tin pots on a hearth still warm, brick buildings faded to the colour of autumn leaves, sedate women walking to and fro in their garden, their faces framed in starched frill and blue veil. But if the French nuns ever minded, they didn't show it to the soldiers. Their faces bore sedate smiles of greeting. When the troops tramped into the halls of their convent they brought them tea in cups of thin porcelain, and very sweet strawberries—survivors from both starlings and shell-pits in the convent garden. Only the muddy boots of the soldiers terribly distressed the old porteress. She would run after them along the tiled hall, clicking her tongue and scolding, 'Tchk, tchk, tchk, tchk,' like a venerable starling herself.

11 Suicide Club

It was all right in the front-line trenches until some fool of an officer with the Third Australians, who had followed along behind the New Zealanders to Armentières, got ambitious and woke the Germans up with a packet of shells. After that, just when two days of quiet had begun to make the boys fond of their new home, Brother Boche let them have it. The veterans of the Gallipoli campaign found out the difference between German and Turk when the *minenwerfer* shells started to land in the trenches. The concussion alone was enough to knock a man silly, and things were too busy for nervous breakdowns to be permitted round about Armentières. When the ground had stopped rocking you could crawl along and find great holes as big as houses torn out of the earth. If any man had chanced to occupy the spot the *minen-werfers* picked out for their landing-ground it wasn't worth while trying to pick up the bits.

For a solid two hours hand-grenades, shells, and trench-mortar shots smacked into the New Zealand lines, and after that the Germans spent a happy night sending up flares, absinthe green and bright yellow, fifty at a time. Their parachute flares sailed grandly up into the sky and hung aloft, blazing for ten minutes, giving them plenty of time to attend to any of the boys who had happened to be out on No Man's Land with the wiring-parties or on patrol duty.

Tent Eight broke up its old company for good the third day out from Armentières. Farmer Giles went off with a bullet through his shoulder; Ginger Sheeth was carried away writhing and groaning, both hips smashed; and Stuttering Bob Butts went down with a shattered ankle. All Blighty ones, and poor old Goliath dead long ago. Fleshy McLeod and Starkie came through unwounded with Paddy Bridgeman and Arthur Kelliher to keep them cheerful. Then Starkie picked up a new pal, Jackie MacKenzie, who made up in cheek what he lacked in weight.

Jackie was about knee-high to a duck, a thin little shaver with the merriest brown eyes in the lines, and the pertest tongue. He'd enlisted years under age in a false name—Williams, his correct and lawful title was—to get away from fond parents who would have held him back. It wasn't only his youth—he was sixteen, not so much younger than Starkie—but the nerve of him and the speed with which his thin little body wriggled out of the dug-outs at night to join in any fun on No Man's Land that happened to be going on.

Finally Paddy, Fleshy, Starkie, and Arthur Kelliher, who was as good as one of the boys, more especially if the party were headed for a raid on the estaminet, decided that something had to be done about Jackie. He was formally adopted as mascot, and told he'd get the tail lammed off him if he went sticking his nose into danger. Jackie accepted it all with a twinkle in his brown eyes. He had a girl in Dunedin, a little brunette who'd shave you smooth as a new penny or curl your hair for you if you went into her dad's barber-shop. Jackie carried Letty's picture next to his heart in the regular soldier's manner, and behaved as sober as a married man with twins.

The front line hadn't been picked out for its looks, not now with the rain of autumn washing the trenches into heaps of slushy mud. And there was a citizen of No Man's Land that the boys didn't like so much better than the Gallipoli flies. Grey as ghosts and bigger than house-cats, the naked, mangy rats of No Man's Land crawled into the dug-outs, and their sharp teeth gnawed through leather, cloth, and soap with fine impartiality. When the men turned in at night there would be a rustle and scuttle underfoot, and the loathsome grey scavenger, its lean back covered with scabs, its bright eyes inexpressibly hideous in their eagerness, would slide into the shadows. Their rations were shared and fouled by the rats. The bread, doled out in the early mornings, could only be left in the dug-outs. In the evening the rats might have left a crust, but little more. Out on No Man's Land lay the nobler banquets of the trench ghouls—bodies face downwards in the mud, the lobes of their ears eaten away. Where the men could they killed the rats as terriers would have killed them, breaking their backs, shaking them, sticking them with bayonets. It was useless. There were never fewer shadows to slink out from their dug-outs when they threw themselves down in the evenings.

Out of the blue came Starkie's first twig of laurel from his commanding officer. He was told to round up a volunteer squad of bombers. About twenty-one were needed, and they weren't hard to find. Bomber or officer, you got your bullet in the long run, and whether it was Blighty or the rats was a matter of luck. Fleshy McLeod, Arthur Kelliher, and Paddy Bridgeman all joined the Bombers' Suicide Club; and Jackie put his name down, but was only allowed the rank of mascot.

Some of the boys wanted to be bombers because it was one way of winning the V.C., but most of them got wooden crosses instead. Their main job until the raiding-parties were organized in good earnest was to smash the German covering and wiring-parties on No Man's Land at night. They went out fifty yards ahead of the New Zealand wiring-parties, lay down, Mills bombs slung into their bombers' jackets, or carried in their pockets. When the Germans showed up, it was their job to kill as quickly and frequently as possible. The Mills bombs—little iron chaps the size of an apple—exploded exactly four seconds after you drew out the pin, flinging splinters of iron into face and body. It was tough work—but better than sticking in the trenches eating, sleeping, dying in water-holes, reeking mud, and rotting sandbags.

The Second Auckland crowd had been raided and cut to bits in Seventy-Seven Trench, trapped against their own barbed-wire entanglements when the Boche came over. Their main trench led into a little subsidiary one, and it was here that they were caught. Some were killed, some captured, a few scored decent wounds. It was told among the Otago lines that just one man in the trench got off unwounded and scot-free. The Otago bombers shifted up to Seventy-Seven Trench to relieve them, and found an empty hole scattered with bomb-pins. Trapped the Aucklanders might have been, but they had put up a show. Otago was lucky. They waited in the trap all night, but the cat never came back.

Since the company had arrived at Armentières, Starkie's career had been almost too quiet to be natural. It couldn't last, especially not when a couple of Aussie soldiers turned up in town and introduced him to absinthe—which tasted like soap and aniseed, but worked. After that he went back to his billet and had hot words with a sergeant—Taine. Sergeant Taine was short-tempered, and a fight ensued. It ended without dignity—the sergeant departing hotly pursued by Starkie, who just missed him as he dived through the canteen door, his eyes rolling and a naked bayonet gleaming in his hand.

Appeared on the scene Captain Hewitt, who told Starkie his job was to fight for his King and Country and not with his fellow-men. At another time this might have gone well enough, but Starkie was entirely unsophisticated as far as absinthe was concerned. So he told Captain Hewitt what he could do with the King and other members of the British Royal Family, and left in quest of Sergeant Taine—who had taken refuge in a lavatory. Ordinarily the sergeant's lavatory might have been his castle; Starkie locked the door and fired ten rounds, not blank, through the door. Then he opened the door. Sergeant Taine fell out. Two bullet-holes had punctured his clothing, but by some miraculous chance the rest of him was undamaged. Starkie decided to call it a day, and quite peacefully went off to bed.

In the morning he had very little recollection of the stirring events of the day before. Official memory was longer. The men tramped out on parade. Captain Smythe, a sinister gleam in his eye, tapped Starkie on the shoulder.

'Fall out, you! You're under arrest!'

Starkie remembered just enough not to be taken aback by this; but he was surprised when they gave him a guard of twenty-one to march him to the lock-up, which happened to be the pleasant old Armentières nunnery. He spent three weeks of more or less informal captivity here, visited not only by soldiers but by the little nuns—who morning and evening brought him tea and huge leaves filled with the bright-red strawberries from the convent garden. Incurious, bright-eyed, serene, they glided in and out of his days, leaving him staring after them uncomprehending.

The court-martial preliminaries were taken before a solemn-faced Colonel Chalmers. Starkie's charges were read out to him. He found that he stood accused of striking an N.C.O.; half-strangling Captain Hewitt; firing ten rounds at an N.C.O. in a lavatory; blaspheming the King, Queen, and Royal Family, and threatening to give information to the enemy. The grounds for the last charge were perfectly vague in his mind, but he gathered that he had declared he would, at the first possible opportunity, cross to the German lines and tell the other b——s everything of interest that was known to him.

It looked bad. Nobody seemed encouraging—except the little nuns, whose delicate porcelain smiles and sharp-flavoured strawberries were just the same during the two days of his remand before field-general court martial.

Time was up. He was marched under escort to Canterbury Headquarters, and found himself in the presence of a Colonel, a Captain, and a Major. His crime-sheet was read out, and he was asked how he pleaded. Groaning inwardly, Starkie admitted that he was guilty. He was then warned that he was liable to the death penalty, and asked if anyone would speak for him. No Captain Dombey hove in sight across the stormy waters this time; but a sharp-faced camp lawyer, whom he had hardly met, inexplicably came up and told his judges a melting tale, and several soldiers from the ranks put in their word for him.

Starkie was marched out of the court-room under guard. An hour later he was called in, and tried hard to discern in the unbending faces of his judges some sign that they took the affair as a joke.

They read out his sentence. Fifteen years' penal servitude, to be served in England.

When he heard that, all the fight was knocked out of him. He stared round desperately for a moment, looking for the champion who wasn't there. Fifteen years . . . the Ring and Dummy smashed back into his mind; the grey walls of the prison-house rose up and said to him, 'We are stronger than Gallipoli'. He wished he hadn't pleaded guilty, or that Captain Dombey's harvest moon of a face would suddenly glow scarlet among all these grey, precise people and tell them that he was a good soldier in action, one of the Bombers' Suicide Club. It wasn't any use, not even if he passed a resolution that he'd never drink absinthe or back-answer an N.C.O. again. For fifteen years he wouldn't have the chance. When he got out he'd be thirty-two, and maybe the War would be over and done with.

He was taken out—not to the little nunnery, but to the *abattoirs* where military prisoners convicted and sentenced were held in Armentières before the authorities shipped them back to England. The *abattoirs* stood at one end of a long stone bridge. Half-way across you were no longer in France, but in Belgium. A tall old avenue of elms rustled down their russet and orange leaves on a road pitted with shell-fire. It was here that the despatch-riders, racing by on their cycles, were trapped in enemy wires and killed. The Germans used to run the low wires, just eighteen inches off the ground, across the road after dark. If the rider didn't break his neck when his machine somersaulted, a bullet from behind the trees crashed into his spine before he could pull himself to his feet.

In the *abattoirs* prison, Starkie found that the principal brands of suffering were digging all day long, no tobacco, and quarter rations of bread and meat. He had known worse. On the third day he was taken out and told that his sentence was broken down to five years. Colonel Chalmers announced the concessions, staring the prisoner unwinkingly in the eyes. 'Bombers' raid,' thought Starkie. He was right. On the fourth day all that remained of his fifteen years' penal servitude was fifteen days' probation. Starkie was more useful throwing bombs for the next twenty-four hours than eating his King and Country's rations for the next fifteen years.

Starkie was wrong, however, in thinking that if he had stayed in prison he would necessarily have taken two legs and two arms out into the world again. Just before he was sent up the lines, the Germans got the range of the *abattoirs* nicely, and shelled the place.

There was a punishment used in military prisons for soldiers who got too obstreperous. The soldiers called it 'crucifixion', but of course the prison officials could laugh that off. There weren't any nails used, just straps that pegged a man's body tight against the stone wall, his arms spreadeagled with the palms turned out, until he decided to be a good boy. It wasn't what you could call a comfortable position, because after a bit, standing on your toes against a wall makes every vertebra in your spine burn and ache as though red-hot. As it happened, Charlie Dunsterville—one of the boys from the Otago crowd—had been playing up that day, and they brought him along for crucifixion. When they had him neatly stretched out against the wall, standing on tiptoe, they left him there to cool off—as no doubt he would have done sooner or later if the Boche shell hadn't got there first. As it was, they found what was left of Charlie hanging from his wrist-straps still perfectly conscious. One leg was torn clean off at the hip, the other was half severed and hanging, while the blood rained out of him, and Charlie kept saying, 'Mother, Mother, Mother! . . .' Fortunately, before they were able to take him down, Charlie had died on his cross.

Starkie was never so glad of anything as to see his mates again. But there was a snag in this raid. Nobody wanted Jackie MacKenzie in trouble, and the kid wouldn't see it. 'If it's good enough for you, it's good enough for me,' he said languidly. Starkie threatened to punch his head, but the brown eyes only twinkled at him.

The Suicide Club decided it would be bad luck to lose their mascot, so they sent a deputation to Captain Knowles—who, although an officer, was a gentleman. Starkie was the deputation. He explained that Jackie was only a kid and should be left at home. The Captain said he understood, and ten minutes before the raid was on, he called the bombers together and said that any man who didn't feel up to going was to stay in the lines.

Jackie stood his ground like a veteran. There was only one thing to be done, and the boys did it. Starkie and Paddy enticed Jackie into the dug-out for a drink. Then Starkie hit him over the head, and the thin little body crumpled up and went down into the mud. Starkie picked him up very gently and stretched him out on his blankets. He hated to do it, but the kid was best out of mischief. Jackie, though he wouldn't have admitted it to the others, meant more to him than Tent Eight—which had meant a good deal. But Jackie, with his merry, screwed-up face, cheeky as a marmoset, was such a kid, and so dead game.

The men commenced to file out. Every one of the bombers had his face grotesquely blackened with nugget polish, which would save them from confusing their own show with the enemy. When the flares went up, every man with a white face was due to be killed if they could manage it. The night was very calm and not a shot interrupted them as they crept out of the Otago trenches.

'Too quiet,' said Paddy. 'Two minutes to go, and the blighters might all be dead for all the sound they're making.'

Otago Fourth were the driving wedge of the attack, holding the centre position as the company advanced across No Man's Land. Flanking them as covering parties were the Fourteenth and Tenth Companies, one on either side. The centre troops were the killers, the flanks were to stop the Boche from wiping the centre out.

A minute before the order to advance was given, down came the shells. There was a crash, a whistle, and the heavens opened right over No Man's Land. Men who saw one another's blackened faces for one instant in the blue shell-flashes knew desperately that the raid which had been kept so dark was no news to the Germans after all. If it had come as a surprise, the enemy fire would have been directed on the Otago trenches, not on No Man's Land. But they were wise, laughing there beyond the dark and the barbed wire. Crashing straight on No Man's Land came the steel fruits, shells, bombs, trench-mortar, and howitzer.

Behind Otago played the answering fire of the British barrage, tearing into the enemy lines. It was too late to save the raid. The German fire had ripped great holes in the lines drawn up for attack; and No Man's Land found its voice—a voice that rose from a long groan into a sobbing, intermittent shriek; a mindless, sightless voice that howled on and on. No Man's Land was a picture of hell. Wherever the men went the wires caught them—clever little knee-high patches of wire so inoffensive until you stumble into its tearing, clawing cobweb on a black night and wait for the spider to pounce. After the main bombardment the maxims went hunting, a noise like the rattlesnake's coming from their throats. Out of black nowhere the word came for the men to advance. With one great cry, mingled thankfulness and agony, they began to run across No Man's Land.

There was no order in the advance. Starkie heard Paddy Bridgeman yell to the men behind him, 'Come on, you loafers, come on!'

And a young Lieutenant stopped beside him, shouting, 'Take care of yourselves, boys; I'm off for a V.C.!' Then he was gone, and Starkie never saw him again, living or dead, with V.C. or without it. But more than he had disappeared. In the central attacking wedge two hundred and eighty men had crossed the top. Of his own crowd seven got across to the other edge of the pit that was No Man's Land.

After that Starkie's picture grew blurred. He was bleeding at nose and ears from the concussion of the shell-fire, and he saw in the light of the flares other bloody faces, grotesque as the scarlet poured over their blackened mouths and chins. He saw Paddy Bridgeman bearing wounded towards the Otago lines. On his second trip Paddy stumbled and went down, and Starkie groped his way towards him. Out of the darkness came the Irishman's laugh, faint but quite pleased with this strange world. 'Jakeloo, Starkie; she's a little beauty, clean through my arm!' So that one with his big, jolly laugh and his Irish pluck wouldn't lie in the muck of No Man's Land for the great grey rats. Starkie started off again across the cumbered ground. He stumbled on something that moved and moaned a little. When he turned it over he could make out Captain Knowles's features. His hip was blown away.

Starkie hoisted the Captain on his back and started at a staggering trot for the trenches. There was a shriek in the air and a violent blow flung him to his knees. The body held sack-like across his shoulders jerked and was still. Starkie knelt to pick Captain Knowles up again, and to his amazement heard him speak.

A voice whispered, infinitely far away, 'I'm done; get some of the boys.'

Starkie's hand came away wet. Captain Knowles's head was almost split in two. He shivered, then stretched out full length. The darkness had taken him.

The next was little Jimmy Peters, whose ghastly wound, like a blow from some gigantic and brutal battle-axe of the Middle Ages, had shorn down from left shoulder to waist. Starkie picked him up easily enough and carried the boy in his arms to the temporary Red Cross dressing-station set up in the lines. The Red Cross people started to bandage Jimmy; but as Starkie turned to go the boy called out to him, 'Starkie, please take me out; I want to roll on the grass.'

'Let him alone, he's going,' said a medical officer, gently enough.

But Starkie picked Jimmy up and took him out to No Man's Land. There wasn't any grass there, as there might indeed have been on those tawny old Dunedin hills which were little Jimmy Peters's home. But the dying have their own ways of escape from fact; and Jimmy whispered urgently, urgently, 'I want to roll on the grass.' So Starkie laid him down on the thick grey mud, churned up by the feet of a thousand running men. Jimmy said, 'Starkie . . .' and started to tell him something. Then he gave a big sigh and his head dropped on one side like a dead sparrow's. Jimmy lay dead in the deep, heavy-seeded grass of an Otago valley, where the grasses are mingled—cocksfoot, blue Yorkshire mist, tinker-grass on which the New Zealand children tell their fortunes—and in between the grasses the thin pink and blue pennants of wild-flowers. It was a happy ending to Jimmy. The boy who lived went back over No Man's Land.

The next one he found was another Dunedin boy, Alec Payle. His shoulder was blown off, exposing the mass of the lung. He said: 'Curtains for me, Starkie.' Starkie offered him a cigarette, lit it, and put it in his mouth. He couldn't hold it between his lips, but said gently, quietly, 'Stay with me.' Then he said: 'Tell Mum'—and died.

Norman White was next, with both legs smashed—in too much pain to bite back the cries from his throat, 'Take me away from this, take me away from this!' But before they got to the trenches he was dead. Starkie lowered his body down into the trench. There were others, but he didn't know their names. Only a dreadful weariness and blood clotting in mouth, nostrils, and ears as the shell concussion tore in two the delicate fibres of little blood-vessels. The dead in No Man's Land had not even the dignity of death. Their nugget-blacked faces made them look like limp and shattered Christy minstrels. Yet grotesquely he remembered a high room in the Gladstone School, and a school-teacher with blue eyes and fluffy hair leaning over a desk repeating poetry.

Baldur the beautiful is dead, is dead.

When he got back to the trenches in early morning he asked for Jackie MacKenzie. Nobody had seen him. Then Starkie went mad. He ran up and down the trenches shouting, tearing in and out of empty dug-outs. A trench-mortar crew called to him. No, they hadn't seen Jackie. He ran down the trench, then went back to ask them to help him get up a search-party for Jackie. The trench-mortar crew was no longer there. A shell had burst where they were standing. Every man of them was blown to fragments just three minutes after their gruff, weary, friendly voices had called to him as he ran.

Starkie went on No Man's Land again, this time out to get even. A German machine-gun was still getting the wounded as they crawled towards the trenches. Starkie crawled on his stomach through mud and wire until he lay above the gun. Then he drew the pin out of the Mills bomb, pressing his hand down into the mud so that it wouldn't explode too soon. Very gently he rolled the bomb down into the machine-gun nest. There were five men there. He had just a glimpse of startled white faces when the bomb turned the place into a spouting fountain of earth and flesh. He wasn't quite sure about the gun. He dragged it over to the British wires and left it there. The five gunners were dead, so not likely to miss it.

Again he hunted among the wounded, turning over bodies that lay awkwardly face downward in the mud. Then among the corpses with blackened faces he saw one with a white face looking up at the sky. Jackie, and not even the little chance that the blacking might have given him. Starkie searched for his wound and found it under the boy's tunic, the little blue mark over the heart. It was the Mercy Death that got Jackie—and may be best, in this world that groaned for such a long time before it died. But there was nobody else he cared for like little Jackie. Starkie carried the boy back to the trenches and laid him down very carefully, not in the Red Cross dressing-station, but in his own dug-out. He took one wild look round. The kid didn't look any different now from when, just a few hours ago, Starkie had knocked him out and left him wrapped up in the blankets. 'If you'd only stayed here, you poor, game little fool!' he shouted; but the merry brown eyes didn't open to laugh at him. He ran out of the dug-out and blundered across No Man's Land.

There was a German maxim-gun with a crew of three that in the rising dawn made merry across No Man's Land, telling the story of a raid that got cut to pieces before it reached the lines. But as the maxim sang there was a shout overhead and a terrible figure crashed down upon it. The figure wore a tunic torn open at its waist, clotted and dyed and hideous with blood. Blood dripped from its nose and open mouth, blood stained its nightmare club—a great axe-handle with an iron cog nailed to one end. It was neither white man nor black. Under the blacking smeared on face and throat the skin shone red-brown. So much the three German gunners had time to see before the figure uttered a madman's shriek, and with a madman's strength leapt down on them. The axe-handle swung twice, and twice the iron cog came away with hair and blood sticking to it. Then the butt end was thrust into the third gunner's face as he turned to run. The three lay in the pit. The figure groped forward with great brown hands, swung the machine-gun round until its muzzle pointed directly at the gunners. Then the rattle of bullets began. The maxim sang again and its gunners lay on the ground, their bodies impaled by the sharp little tusks of lead.

The terrible figure met an officer from the Otago lines as it dragged the maxim towards the British wire. The officer, a Major, stopped and said: 'Good work, Starkie!' Starkie stared at him, a red world swimming before his eyes. He wasn't the only one. Officers—men gently brought up, trained in decency and self-restraint—were wandering about like madmen, silly from the concussion of shell-fire. Their eyes were bloodshot and dazed, and in their hands they carried naked bayonets, wet with blood. They were still hunting, like animals, with no idea whom they sought or why. Presently they would come to; you would notice nothing unusual about them except in quiet moments, when the thick, glaucous glaze swam over the pupils of their eyes again.

Starkie took Jackie on his shoulders and walked off alone on the wearisome tramp to Armentières. Jackie was very light, and all the way little things seemed to happen that Starkie should have been able to tell him. Even the rich gold of the sunlight on the Armentières road was a thing he shouldn't have missed after the shrieking darkness of last night. But in Armentières Starkie found an old French undertaker, who planed a coffin of beech-boards for Jackie. Then Starkie took him to the public cemetery, and with neither sexton nor priest to aid him, dug a grave in consecrated soil among the weather-worn old French tombs. The graveyard was very full, and he couldn't tell whether the grass and the tangled moon-white daisies he turned over with his pick were the property of some quieter dead—a French girl whose eyes had been startled wide and grey, an old man whose memories of the Crimea had faded away into a rich and peaceful sunset. But how could they mind Jackie, these tranquil dead? It might be natural that the older and harder soldiers should rot in the mire; but surely not a child, who never in his life had done anything worse than laugh, stay clean for the memory of one pretty girl, and fight because at school they had told him that all good lads do fight for their King and Country?

Starkie borrowed a camera from the old undertaker and took a snapshot of Jackie's grave to send his girl. Then he was arrested for taking photographs, taken, still filthy with blood and mire, in front of the provost-marshal, asked his number, name, and battalion. He was sent back to the lines under escort. But this time Colonel Chalmers came along and asked the trouble, and when they told him he said pretty sharply, 'Let that man go!'

Starkie crawled into his dug-out. He was the only one left. On a shelf he saw the letters his mates had written before going out on the raid. It was a standing order that the ones who pulled through posted off the letters for those who didn't, but he never thought he would have to be postman for every one of them. Fleshy was wounded and sent back to Blighty, and old Paddy safe enough. He couldn't help grinning when he saw Paddy's letter.

On top was the pencilled injunction, 'Post this to my old mother in Ireland'—but Paddy hadn't left the address, and where his old mother in Ireland might abide Starkie had no idea. Jackie had left two letters—one for his mother, one for his girl. Starkie buttoned them all into his tunic. Then he stretched himself out on the bench and lay still. The blood from his nose and mouth trickled steadily into his throat.

In the afternoon Colonel Chalmers tramped through the mud and congratulated him. 'You've been recommended for the V.C., Starkie,' he said. 'And whatever comes of it, I don't think you'll hear any more of the other business.'

The other business . . . fifteen years in prison, the *abattoirs*, Charlie Dunsterville. . . . Starkie shut his eyes. For the time he had forgotten all about it.

The raid got into the New Zealand papers, Starkie's V.C. recommendation included. Down south five Invercargill schools, including the Burnham Industrial, proudly and publicly claimed him as an ex-pupil. None of them mentioned the fact that they had all expelled him except the Burnham Industrial, which had shipped him off on the *Kittawa* instead. But the V.C. never got through to him, it not being considered the thing at headquarters for a soldier to win his country's highest honour while on probation for a proud and picturesque crime-sheet. They didn't send Starkie back to the *abattoirs*, neither did they give him his V.C. Upon learning which the Invercargill papers promptly and discreetly forgot all about him, and none of the five Invercargill schools ever again stressed the fact that he was an ex-pupil.

12 Brothers

THE LITTLE estaminet—not the dour Flemish establishment, but an improvised saloon in a caved-in house rather like a cheerful rat-hole—flared now with pale-yellow light. There were no girls present, and almost all the men were drunk. Starkie had passed the black line of sobriety a good hour before. Now he was in a mind to make everybody laugh—even the old Frenchman, dim-eyed as a mole, who peered at him and shook his white head so disapprovingly before once again he turned the tap on his keg and let the liquor splash down, beaded with crisp foam, into the glasses. The company was making noise enough for most, but Starkie wanted more. He was on the table shouting for a song when somebody caught his ankle in a grip like a leglock. Before he had time to turn round, the same person gave him a shove in the small of the back. He crashed to the floor and sat up blinking like an owl.

His brother George, surprisingly in the uniform of an infantryman, said, 'And what the hell do you think you're doing on the drink?'

Starkie hadn't seen George since their last leave in Alexandria. For a long time he had had nobody to talk to except Arthur Kelliher, and Kelliher only cursed and told him to shut up if he said the things that were screaming somewhere in the back of his mind. He didn't bother now to get up, and, anyhow, the floor was pitching like the deck of a ship at sea. He started in a loud, unsteady voice, to tell George all about it. George knew Invercargill and Dunedin like the back of his hand, he'd know the names of most of the boys who had gone over in the raid. Starkie passionately wanted somebody else to know about them. When he had finished, he saw to his amazement that two tears trickled, large and slow, down his brother's face. George passed his arm around Starkie's arm-pits, and pulled him to his feet. Then he dusted his uniform down very carefully with his big hands, as though Starkie had just emerged from one of the many fights of his schooldays and must be made presentable for the eye of classmates and schoolmaster.

'Go along home, kid, and get to bed,' George said gruffly.

Starkie nodded. He was feeling deathly sick, and staggered outside into the draught of the keen air blowing up the long black tunnel which was lit at intervals with the frosty glimmer of stars. But he didn't go home. He slept in a little out-shed, and in the morning, unshaven and dirty, went back to the estaminet again.

Preparations had started for the Somme offensive of 1916. As yet the word Somme meant nothing in this corner of the world. The men were jaded and listless. As far as they were concerned the worst had happened that could be expected to happen. Somme was rumoured to be a big show. They got their kits together, tramped with their bands still playing for the marching feet of ghosts past the great fallen bells of the city and the Flemish estaminet that locked up its pumps when the British soldiers were near. *Très bon*, the Allemand! Starkie couldn't bear to look aside at the weedgrown patch where Jackie lay. He had a wild idea of telling the nuns about it, and then drew back from the black robes and serene faces. So many dead . . . where would women be if they started noticing which was which?

The route march put the men into better spirits. Twenty miles out from Armentières and they were singing again. The brass throats of the trumpets, the bagpipes, yelled their defiance to the level French sky. 'We're still alive, still alive.' Morval in the lower Somme area was their first stop. Nothing there but manoeuvres piled on manoeuvres and Generals looking picturesque in red tabs and smart leather gaiters. The troops were entrained or pushed on by foot from here.

They arrived in Fricourt and couldn't see the place for mud. The rains had started here in good earnest—not the violent, brief rains or silvery drizzle to which the New Zealanders were accustomed, but hour after hour of level, steady, slow-pattering rain, which bogged them in misery. In the middle of the rainstorm, their boots clogged with the khaki-coloured mud, they manoeuvred, formed fours, wove and interwove in circles, staged mock rushes and cursed. N.C.O.s yapped like sheep-dogs on their flanks. It was nothing but dazed eyes, clogged running boots, and the sea of mud, dirty yellow, around them as wide and formidable as another flood, shutting them off from any imagining of peace and security. They slept in rough billets at night, and in a short while marched in as supports elsewhere where they heard again the crack of the guns.

Somme became like an enormous picnic, and at first sheer weight of numbers and the daily arrival of fresh troops—New Zealanders, Australians, Scottish, and Welsh—kept the men good-humoured. Arthur Kelliher came back from leave and joined forces with Starkie. They stuck together on the way to the trenches. Kelliher was a fine figure of an Irishman, two inches taller than Starkie, broad-shouldered, broad-tongued. All the way from Fricourt he told dirty stories. When they were in sight of the trenches he still showed no signs of running out.

The men knew they were near home two hundred yards from the trenches. On the air hung the deathly stench of a battlefield. When they reached the lines where they must live until they were killed or relieved, they found them full of rotting corpses. The German attack had failed here, and the bodies in their sodden field-grey lay unburied, the reek of their decay crying out the horrible and unheard protest of Abel. Young and old men, Bavarians with their big square heads, youths crumpled up with their arms drawn over their faces as if asleep, until a hand touched them and their flesh fell apart. . . . The dead welcomed the living into their homes on the Somme.

There was church parade on the following Sunday. The lines attended in full force, and a good many of the men found some childish comfort in an hour of quiet and droning words. But this day the chaplain read out the Decalogue. The steady voice said, 'Thou shalt not . . . thou shalt not . . .' And at last, 'Thou shalt do no murder.'

Starkie got up and walked off.

A sergeant followed him and clapped a hand on his shoulder, swearing under his breath, 'You come along back, and quick about it.'

Starkie marched back.

The man with the steady voice asked him what the trouble was. He stared at them—officers with expressionless faces, men shuffling their feet, uneasy, their eyes fastened on their boots. Then he spoke, and to his surprise his voice sounded high and squeaky. 'What's the use of praying not to kill one moment and sending us out murdering the next?'

They let him go, and he never attended church parade again—though for a long time going into action, like many of the soldiers, he carried his own cross on his back—two light pieces of wood nailed together and carved with his name, strapped under his tunic. There was a horror of the unnamed graves of No Man's Land.

All leave was in Fricourt—not a bad little spot, though you'd have to be hard of hearing if you wanted to miss the constant stutter and rumble of the guns. He got two days clear at the same time as his brother's final leave, before the mass attack. They were good days. George and Starkie hunted together, Starkie trotting at his immense brother's heels as he swung along the roads, tramping for exercise—a heresy of which very few of the troops would have been guilty while there was a pub handy. Since their meeting in Armentières, George had grown less formidable to his brother. The gap in age and height wasn't so alarming. Starkie began to see how they could have been friends . . . how George had always been a friend really in his tough, not too talkative way. Only, being younger, Starkie was the kid brother to George. As a matter of policy and duty he had to have his head smacked now and again, to have the starch taken out of him, to be shouldered off the primrose path. It was funny, really, considering all he'd seen and done since they threw him into the Dummy. But he could see George's point of view now as he couldn't before. He had felt something like that with Jackie MacKenzie. Not to have punched Jackie's head on the night of the raid would have seemed like a crime. If Jackie had tried to get tight in the estaminets, Starkie had yanked him out by the collar. The feeling one has for a younger man. . . .

Starkie was glad of it, tramping after George. He was dreadfully tired, with a weariness which had nothing to do with a fine-trained, springy body. In the evenings they did hit the estaminets, and filled up together. But if he carried it over the edge, George's voice boomed reproachfully, 'Now, kid . . . Now, kid . . .' He couldn't hold his liquor as well as he had done before the Armentières raid. It wasn't that he pigged it like some of them, but he got excited. A few drinks and something like a brilliant blue electric spark flashed, crackled, and snapped inside his head. The snap was a horrible moment, because after it happened—just for a minute or so—he wouldn't be able to move either arms or legs. He found himself waiting for it. Sometimes it was a long time coming. Then the brilliant blue spark, visible to some inner eye, lighted up again inside his brain, and he had an insane impulse to start yelling and never stop. Snap . . . his body was a log, nothing more, dumb and motionless. Nobody ever seemed to notice.

When it was over, in sheer relief, he found himself talking sixteen to the dozen, sending up words like sky-rockets. Like the spark inside his brain, the words flashed and crackled. But they made other people uncomfortable. He saw them stare. That was why, after a while, it was very good to be pulled out of the room by George, urged gently like a sheep up the black crevasse of the staircase, put to bed. George pulled his boots off, dented the pillow under his head with his great fist. Then he lifted Starkie on to the bed and pulled the covers over him. Himself, he seemed not to feel the need of sleep.

He sat beside the bed, a vaguely outlined figure in the grey light, head propped upon his hands, straight black hair falling down over his eyes. It was a weary, patient attitude: that of a thinker rather than that of a fighter. It suddenly occurred to Starkie that his brother George really didn't like fighting. That must be why he originally joined up with the Donkey Mob. Not afraid . . . there had certainly never been a man in Invercargill that George couldn't lick . . . he just didn't *like* it. Then why had he transferred here? To be near Starkie. That conclusion safely arrived at, Starkie turned over and went to sleep. For a ridiculous moment, on the edge of that warm tide, it seemed to him that in spite of his great height and his hatchet face, George was very like their mother, not in the least like their father.

At the last minute Starkie asked for permission to join up with George's crowd, but it was a busy time and he was refused. They said good-bye, shaking hands gravely, on the way to the trenches. Then George said, 'Best of luck, kid', and strode away, his huge strides seeming to carry him over the edge of the world.

The dead men in the trenches had been buried, they and the unanswered argument of their decomposition. But now a drizzling grey rain broke and made a long daybreak for the troops. It was the early morning of September 15th, and at six in the morning the guns started, the first warning of the Somme offensive.

First the tanks went across. In the grey morning their huge bulks, lumbering and yet gifted with an uncanny swiftness, were weird enough to Starkie, who had never seen them in action before. But at night, when nothing was to be seen but the flaring orange eyes of their headlights and a shadow behind, they were like prowling monsters from the first slime of the world. The Otago Second Battalion crowd, George with them, went over the top in advance of the rest. It was impossible to follow their straggling run very far. The smoke from bursting shells, and a yellow cloud that might be gas, hid them from sight. Heavy bombardment started to hit the British lines, and the men, fidgeting in their places, shouted when they got the order to advance fifteen minutes after the Second Battalion had left their trenches. A whistle shrieked; then they were over the top and running across broken country, hideously pitted with the great torn-up gaps of the shellholes.

Face blackened with smoke, Starkie was halted in his run by a wounded man from the Second Battalion who hadn't been badly hit, but seemed to have gone crazy. A splinter of steel had torn part of the calf from one leg, so that he limped grotesquely, like a shot rabbit trying to run. To Starkie's surprise the wounded man seemed to know him. The wide-open mouth in his vacant face shouted, and his hands gesticulated. He shouted, 'Do you know who that is?'

Starkie stared at the object the wounded man indicated with his circling hands. It lay on the ground, but at first he couldn't see why the wounded man had asked him *who* it was. *What* would have been the right word. It was dark and bloody and messy. A horrible foreboding curiosity tore at him. He fell on his knees beside the thing and turned it over. There wasn't much of it, only a head and shoulders. The legs that should have belonged to it sprawled fifty yards away, and there wasn't any middle at all—the shell had ripped it in half.

But the head and shoulders belonged to his brother George. The wounded soldier stared at him, vacant eyes quite mad, but he never knew. There should have been some terrible, vital argument between him and the grim mouth of this thing lying on the ground. *Where had George gone to?* The eyes, open and agonized, couldn't tell him. But the thing might have been important to George, so Starkie scooped it up and carried it over to the fragmentary trunk. Then he started to dig a shallow pit in No Man's Land, tearing at the soil like a dog, sometimes with his bayonet, sometimes with naked hands. When it was about three feet deep he put the awful contorted bits of George into the pit, but he couldn't make them look like a body. So he tore off his tunic and hid what he could with that; and then, denting the pillow of the earth as George a night before had dented his own pillow for him, found that the head, lying back in the brown soil, looked comparatively peaceful.

He shovelled the soil back over his brother, sobbing as he worked—great noisy sobs like a child's. Presently the mound was high enough. He stuck George's rifle above, with his pay-book in the breech. He couldn't wait any longer, the shells were shrieking like eagles gathering for the feast. One desperate glance he cast around him. The wounded man was squatting on his haunches, his body rocking slowly backwards and forwards. Starkie was sure that he had gone mad. He left them together, madman and fragmentary body of George. Then he took to his heels, sobs tearing at him in hiccoughing gusts. In half an hour he had rejoined his own battalion, but the men didn't know him. When he tried to talk he stammered. An officer pulled out a flask and poured out a tin pannikin of rum, filling it to the brim. Starkie drank it down and started out to kill. It wasn't so much vengeance as a desire to find George. Somewhere at the back of the sodden field, straining before him, George might be. He wanted to slash his way through.

The Somme attack was going well on the British side. The German prisoners were already pouring in, squads of a dozen at a time. The officer who had given Starkie the rum told him to stop where he was. Starkie smiled up at him.

'I'm all right, just mad,' he said, and started to run once more.

A little line of prisoners came in sight shepherded by their guard, a New Zealand officer. Starkie emptied his revolver into the field-grey. The guard yelled at him, and he swung his revolver round at the angry man in khaki and told him to shut his mouth or he'd put five rounds into it. Then that group was gone. He was stumbling over a dug-out, a big cave filled with wounded and exhausted Germans. A face stared up, white and young. He asked, 'How many down there?' and the German answered something—it sounded like sixty. Then Starkie drew the pin out of a Mills bomb and flung it into the dug-out. He didn't wait to see what might crawl out of the cascade of mud and brushwood. Fragments of men . . . fragments of George. . . .

He came to a wire blockade. Some of Otago's survivors lay there on their bellies, waiting for the tanks to plough through.

At last they came, leviathans heaving through the terrible red-and-yellow mud, and ploughed through the barbed wire as though the entanglements were a row of pea-sticks. Starkie recognized Arthur Kelliher suddenly at his side. The big Irishman was panting like a dog. Like Starkie, he didn't seem cold or hungry, as most of the others were by now. The rain had never ceased to fall since the beginning of the attack. Starkie and Kelliher joined forces and came on to Flers. Here the German dug-outs were full of wine, schnapps, cigars, and chocolates—an officers' line. A row of dug-outs had to be cleared of Germans before the New Zealanders could get to the liquor and tobacco. It was done, and all that night men crept up from No Man's Land and burned the freezing death out of their veins with spirits.

They stayed for a few hours at the little ruined village of Flers, and next morning attacked again at eleven o'clock. The survivors of the New Zealand battalions moved up on the left of the Black Watch, who in company with the Royal Irish had attacked the night before. The Irishmen were driven back, leaving the Black Watch sandwiched between the two German flanks, a little spear-head of men pricking into the groin of a roaring enemy. Half the Scotsmen had been cut to pieces by enemy fire in their captured trenches, and word was passed along to the Otago bombers—recruited anew after the Armentières raid—to relieve the trapped men.

Starkie and Kelliher were among the bombers who crawled along the lines to relieve the Black Watch. When they got there they found it wasn't so easy. The Scotties, game to the death, were down to a very few men, and their wounded lay helplessly exposed to fire on clay banks which could not be protected from the steel hail of the German grenades. Doggedly the Scotties stuck it out, the stick-bombs falling right among them—queer-shaped missiles like jam-tins stuck through with skewers of wood. Wounded men would start to crawl away. Then helplessly they would see that no part of the death-pit was under cover. Like snakes with broken backs, they would still contrive to hitch themselves along, looking for the corner of retreat that was not to be found. Then into the daze of the wounded man's mind the crash of another stick-bomb. If he were lucky, the splinters struck a vital part.

The Scottish and Otago bombers were using Mills bombs, and the New Zealanders had brought up a large supply. The cockpit held by the Black Watch became so deadly a place that again and again the Germans were driven back. The earthen wall was low between attackers and attacked, and from their trench the defenders could see German officers driving their men along, red-faced and blind with fury. At four o'clock in the afternoon the thrust of German soldiers, whipped forward by the officers, came against them and was met with the fire of captured German machine-guns turned straight into the mass of field-grey.

Starkie had one machine-gun and clung to it as to a sweetheart. The machine-gun fire was unexpected; and the men, herded onward, seemed bewildered beyond the intiative of retreat. Still in the rear, those unable to see the sweep of the guns shouted and stormed. The Germans broke, like a mob of sheep driven to the *abattoirs*. Half of them made a desperate, gallant attempt to stamp down on the bombers' post, and then the reaping of death began. The machine-guns swung their grey snouts, and bodies toppled over clumsily—corn whisked from the earth by an unseen scythe. By this time men of the Black Watch and the Otago reinforcements—those of them that were left—were standing on the parapets, red-eyed, watching the harvest. The desperate German stampede swirled backward, the men trampled over their officers in retreat. It was the final repulse. Not enough of the attacking party lived to come again.

A Colonel of the Black Watch walked into the cockpit, a trickle of blood running from his temple. In other parts of the line his regiment had suffered heavy losses. Here the Scotties had been twenty-one when Otago sent bombers to their relief. Now there were two of them left alive; and the wounded, unable to find a refuge, had died many deaths, hit again and again on the floor that was an evil porridge of blood and mud. About forty dead men lay there. The Colonel never spoke of them, but stood for a moment, the tears running down his face. Then he took the names of the survivors, among them Stark and Kelliher. 'You won't be forgotten, men,' he said, and walked away. The next day they heard that he had been shot through the head on his way down the lines.

Under cover of night the Otago men went back to their own

battalion, known now as the Otago First under the necessary reorganization. They had little enough rest. The first Somme offensive took up twenty-four days of fighting, twenty-four circles in an Inferno that no Dante ever dared to dream. On September 25th, at ten in the morning, orders were run up on the boards along the New Zealanders' trenches. All money-belts were to be worn outside the men's shirts. 'Handy for the vultures,' said Starkie. Then the battalion went into attack again, running on a steady grade downhill. The German fire was too hot, and in an all-day attack about three-quarters of a mile was the sum total of the advance.

There were about twelve thousand men all told in the attack. But at sunset a disorganized rabble wandered about in the field in little groups. Starkie and Kelliher found themselves in a shell-crater with Bill Howard, a young Lieutenant from Invercargill and a good boy. They were lost, and had no idea where to go or what to do. All night they lay in the shell-hole, drinking the brackish and filthy rain-water which had to be lapped from little hollows, and which dried the throat like brine. In the morning they managed to collect about sixteen men, wanderers like themselves, stunned with the concussion of a heavy bombardment, but none of them badly wounded. About a hundred yards on lay a little German trench.

'Come on, boys,' cried Lieutenant Howard, seizing on the first job he could find, 'we'll take that trench for our side!'

They started on the advance, and odd scarecrow figures in khaki, seeing them appear, popped out of shell-craters and from behind banks, and ran towards them, shouting and waving. The attack numbered about fifty strong; but they had woken up the enemy, and from their trench the Germans opened fire. Suddenly there was a shout, and Starkie saw that Lieutenant Howard's left eye had been shot out of its socket and hung hideously against his cheek. With one magnificent and terrible gesture, the young officer tore off the hanging eyeball and flung it on the ground. He shouted, 'Come on!'—and a second later dropped on all fours, shot through the stomach.

Sergeant Mason, an old gold-miner from Kaitangata, took the lead and got the men out of the line of fire. They set to work and dug a strongpoint for themselves, a half-circle on the plains of the dead. They filled it with German machine-guns, dragged in under cover of night from the black gulf where no power but death held any sway. For two days they held the strongpoint, without officers and with nothing to eat but their iron rations. On the second night a New Zealand Colonel appeared from nowhere and ordered them to dig a communication trench back to their nearest lines. The men, still unfed, growled, sweated, and dug. The rabble had won another patch of French ground. The Colonel received a Military Cross. Big Sergeant Mason, wrestler, fighter, who had brought the men out of the enemy fire and held them together in their improvised strongpoint foodless and leaderless, never got a mention.

For two days the rabble from the Somme valley held their new trench. Then they were relieved and marched back to Mametz Wood.

For a while the wood was their home—a deathly place, its beech-stumps rising in thousands along the gentle swell of the road. On the roadside not a tree was left standing in its old grace and beauty. Hidden away among the stumps, that rose like decayed and blackened teeth against the brown curve of earth, were thousands of German bodies, carrion which not all the scavengers of earth and sky could bear off from the glades their insulted and mangled flesh now defiled. But if you came through the wood to the far side there was the strange sight of a little row of young larches still standing. In this darkness of winter they were stripped of their leafage and stood white, slender, and gleaming, tree-Phrynes, exquisite in their delicate nakedness.

Along twigs black and madder-rose depended the slight and softly tinted drops of dew, necklaces of clear moonstone. After a shower of rain the larches were in full regalia of jewels, swaying and trembling spider-patterns of drops, nature's gift to her shyest and most secret trees. Occasionally sitting at their roots could be seen the brown little person of a rabbit—contemplative, perhaps, but apparently not worried at the strange change which had overtaken the edges of its private world. A step nearer, and the white scut would flick out of sight among the brown pools of the fallen leaves, which had become skimmed over with the frosts of last autumn, now frozen hard into mirror-patches of blue-grey translucent ice. At moments there was a fragile loveliness here. Then the wind would stir again, like some cowled leper creeping out of his ancient and accursed hiding-place among the trees; and to the soldier who lay in the woods would come the stench of the rotting corpses.

Besides the sodden shapes in their field-grey, there were dead Australians and Tommies to stumble on. 'Any kangaroo feathers where youse come from, soldier?' Strange and pitiful friendliness between armies from the ends of the earth; a laugh and a jest, by a sudden match-flare of light in some ruined town, and then the feet tramped on again, each keeping to their own leadership. At the last they were given grace to rot together; and the German corpses, as though no division could be for ever strong enough to hold apart the different kinds of flesh that had perished in the wood, might rot lying above or beneath them, hand touching the near skeleton of alien face. What did it matter? It was Death who had captured this wood, no other King or Kaiser was supreme there for any length of time.

Starkie's company was moved back to Fricourt, and explored new territory. One day they were taken up and shown the hill where, according to legend, King George V had stood and watched his soldiers of many nations fight. Some ardent spirit had filled in the King's alleged footprints with concrete, and there they remained sempiternal, a source of mingled curiosity and scoffing among the hard-boiled Colonial soldiers.

The two big hills had for a year been the centre of heavy fighting, and now that action was suspended for a while everyone went souvenir hunting. The only casualties for weeks were the boys who lit a fire in the woods, hanging their dixie of tea on an iron bar between two dud shells. The shells woke up, and the boys—their smoky tea still untasted in their tin mugs—were blown to glory.

One of the hills behind Fricourt had been mined and re-mined by German and British sappers, the British burrowing lower than the Germans. The soldiers used to explore in little parties, or prowling about, lone wolves on the hunt for Iron Crosses. One day Starkie crawled into the black gut of a deserted hillside tunnel, the grass already growing green and ragged over its raw-lipped gash in the clay. It was a long way down to the end of the tunnel, and there he saw a sight he never forgot.

From the other side of the hill the Germans had worked through by tunnels to make an underground field hospital. Timbers propped up its high roof, its walls were heavily stayed, it was better equipped and apparently safer than a great many of the field stations on the surface of the earth. Only the great cracks in the earthen floor showed how the safety of this place had been betrayed. From the mines the British sappers had exploded, the dense fumes of choking gases had poured upwards, splitting the earth in two. Perhaps in a few seconds the underground hospital had been filled with poison. And there on their stretchers and cots lay the German wounded, stifled in their narrow little white beds.

Beside them lay several crumpled bodies, and the death-trap held four men in white coats—surgeons whose knowledge had not availed them, or who had stayed at their posts with the dying until flight was impossible. Not a scratch on the bodies or faces of those men in white coats, nothing but the cracks in the floor to show how they had died.

He gathered up a few souvenirs and crept out of the place. Its silence seemed to stretch a long hand after him as he groped his way down the tunnel. He reported the hall of the dead to headquarters, and the entrance to the tunnel was filled in, boarded up, and then hidden under soil by a party of New Zealanders. There all of them lay, until the white coats of the surgeons were a long time dust, and the wounded men had ceased to show in their staring faces any surprise that the choking in their lungs should have distracted their attention from the torture of mangled flesh and splintered bone.

13 Passport to Hell

ANYHOW, that Canterbury corporal needn't have saved up a grudge for ten months over a punch on the jaw. Starkie didn't sock him with malice aforethought. Huie Goodyear had come by a jar of rum, and called the boys over to drink the health of his crowd, Second Otago. And it was easier to get drunk now than it was at the beginning of the War. At Sailly Sector, where they were pushed off from the Somme to relieve the Australians, there was nothing to think about but baby raids, fatigue duties, rats, lice, and colds. Trench boredom is something that gets into your bones, a deadly grey ache, and makes you feel you'd rather whoop it up with lemonade at a spinsters' tea-party than sit at home and do nothing.

The boys hit on a pretty good way of getting liquor out of the estaminet when their pay was running low. Two or three of the big chaps who could keep their faces straight would tie puggarees round their hats, the distinguishing mark of the Military Police. Then they'd stalk into the estaminets and fine the frightened old Frenchmen for selling grog to soldiers after hours—which was a thing no estaminet-keeper in France ever refrained from doing. After that they'd go on to the next pub and spend the 'fine' on more liquor. Maybe that was the way Huie came by his jar of rum, maybe it wasn't; but at all events he acted like a Christian about it and handed it out among the rest.

It was just luck that on the way back to the lines, Otago should mix it with the Canterbury crowd, and hard words lead on to a little trial of strength. Then again, when Starkie hit the Canterbury corporal, he hadn't even noticed that the road was lined with those queer Froggy dykes—asphalt slopes stuck with pieces of broken glass and running down into ditches three feet deep, full of green slime that didn't look as though sanitary inspectors ever made much headway round about here. The corporal didn't suffocate in the ditch, because two of his mates grabbed him by the ankles and pulled him out, but his face was as full of broken glass as a porcupine of quills, and the language he used warned Starkie that this was no place for a good woman's son. So he took to his heels, and next morning, with Arthur Kelliher to keep him company, joined the volunteer squad who went off from the Otago lines to help the Canadians mine Messines Ridge.

Canadians are a queer crowd, and it seems they don't mind living in dank green pools of water, working day long in the slimy tunnels where, listening through the ear-phones, you can hear the little tap-tap-tap of the frantic German picks, racing to finish their countermines. That tap-tap-tap isn't so bad when you hear it on the wall of a prison cell. It means 'I'm with you, boy, and to hell with the police!' But when you hear it under the earth, tunnelling below Messines Ridge, it means, 'I'll get you, I'll get you, I'll get you!'—and it isn't even just a threat—it's a sort of crazy, clicking panic in case the other chap should touch off his mine first. All along the tunnel sentries with fixed bayonets were posted at a distance of four yards. For months and months it was nothing but yanking rotten sand-bags and clay out of the bowels of the earth, loading them along to the tunnel-mouths, where the huge spoil-dumps were camouflaged with green boughs and scrim so that the German fliers wouldn't bomb the sappers in their tombs.

The food here was rotten, nine men to a loaf of stale bread, four men to a tin of sardines. When you started handing in the boxes of explosives, that little far-away tap-tap-tap became something like the way a man's heart throbs and bursts when he struggles to wake himself from a nightmare. You didn't need to hear it unless you put on the ear-phones, but the temptation and fascination of putting them on again was too much. After that, you wanted to bang your head up against the mud walls and have done with it. The tunnels narrowed and pressed in on the men as they worked, and the stifling air tightened their throats up with inconceivable thirst.

Then kneel down and lap up the water from the cave-pools. It stinks, but what's that between friends? All the seepage of No Man's Land has oozed down into those little patches of water. The Canadians, with their shadowy hatchet-faces and steady swinging arms, take life in the tunnels better than the New Zealanders, but everyone knows they're bloody amphibians and keep beaver-tails stowed away in the seats of their breeches.

The luxury—the wine-aired, wind-cooled luxury—of sleeping at night in a pigsty. The billet's at Neuve Eglise, and kings couldn't ask for better. Planks nailed across the feeding-troughs, and there you are with a dining-table. In the stalls the men spread straw and sleep as quietly as the swine did before the exigencies of war made their pampered bodies into bacon. No common swine, those weren't. The pigsties appertain to the florid château of the Hennessy's Three Star Brandy king, who has gone away forgetting to leave any of his popular medicine in his cellars for the troops. If you wander in the gardens of the château, with its background of slim black boughs and belated leaves swaying like orange fans, you will find the lawns straggling with clear springing grass, pale green and unkempt. Through the black mould of long garden beds, crocuses push the little flame-blue ellipses of their pointed buds. There is a delicious smell in the air of lemon-scented verbena, and in the avenues shuffle russet-coloured horse chestnuts, piled up high in the gutters. Once upon a time, maybe, peacocks with white breasts or sapphire strutted up and down on terrace and lawn. But the pigs were more important. To live as well as the Hennessy pigs used to do is a pretty fair achievement in times like these.

Then it's a shift to Green Camp, so called because everything about it is painted green to hide from German sky-riding bombers the hangars where fifty or more British war-planes drone in and out like enormous wasps. Queer game, that fighting in the air. It makes men look so little. When a German 'plane broke its back in a cow-paddock overnight, the pilot and his mechanic, scampering away in their leather helmets from the pursuing British, looked like toy figures on a great green playing-field. They were caught and marched to the compound, of course; war all over for the two of them.

At a little Y.M.C.A. near Green Camp you could get cups of cocoa and penny packets of biscuit, not bad when you came dripping out of the tunnels. If your taste didn't run to Y.M.C.A.s, there was a tramp of some few miles to Bailleul and Val's little estaminet. The old man and his wife still nodded on, folded hands, white head, shiny pale-blue eyes; but grand-daughter Val ran the place, with her flyaway golden pigtails and her jolly laugh. Starkie got on well with Val, but on strictly respectable lines. She wasn't the sort of girl who took you upstairs to bed afterwards. There were two little sisters, very prim, very solemn, and never allowed inside the warm room where the soldiers drank. But if you liked kids you could slip into the parlour where they practised on an ancient piano—just as bad as New Zealand kiddies: nothing but thump, thump, thump, the loud pedal on half the time; and then a brown goblin face peering over one shoulder to see how you liked the effect. Starkie and Kelliher helped about the place and garden whenever they could dodge away from the tunnels and from Green Camp, and, as far as Val was concerned, they could have stopped at the estaminet till the end of the War. Unlike many of the French girls, Val wasn't tight-fisted. When they came in late there were always huge door-step sandwiches of fresh French bread, with slices of ham and sweet pickles in them, just like the old counter-lunches you could once get in any New Zealand pub by putting down sixpence for a handle of beer.

One evening at eight o'clock the boys went back to Val's estaminet again, singing about what Shang said to Patsie, which was the pet song with Otago, and had begun to spread among the Canadians too. What Shang said to Patsie was pretty good in spots, but it can't be printed, so let it go at that. Anyhow, it kept their feet moving until they got to the gate and turned down the garden patch again. It was too dark to see until they got right up to it, that the estaminet wasn't there.

Not even part of it—a wall of the room where they used to drink, or the wreck of the kids' piano. The bomb from up in the sky had registered a direct hit, and—well, that jagged hole in the ground was all. The old French couple, gran'*père* and gran'*mère*, Val's golden plaits and the two kid sisters, hadn't even fragmentary existence. Saved burial expenses, the Hun flier did; and blotted out at one shot all the fun, the gentleness, and the laughter that had waited for the men when they climbed out of the stinking pits of the tunnels.

Maybe it's hard for those who haven't seen it to imagine what if feels like to be blown up. A few days after Val's estaminet was hit the Otago's men got a pretty fair idea. The morning after their last tramp up the road to the estaminet, their work with the Canadians was finished.

They were lined up and drafted back to their own battalions, and glad to go. You lose a friend, one among many, but somehow individual for her white teeth and her merry eyes. After that the place is like death to you. And it isn't likely, after that, you'd remember that ten months before you knocked an N.C.O. into a ditch. What's a tumble into the mud, with friends to hoist you out again? Maybe the estaminet people were sound asleep when it happened. Or maybe the kids woke up and saw the bedroom roof cave in on them.

But the Messines business was done on the grand scale, and with dress-circle seats for the troops, all in broad daylight. At 3.10 a.m. on June 7th, 1917, promptly, it all began. There was a hill that had stood rooted in the earth for many ages. Its people, hare and grass and cloud, had never thought of any change. Then it was lifted in its entirety from its pedestal, and a hundred feet in the air it disintegrated into rock-masses and crumbling torrents of mud. A village which had clung to the gentle slope of one side became instantly a mass of rubble and broken bricks. In the air was one long, high, continuous scream. A mere ghost of agony, as though the earth itself cried out. In imagination one saw clear against the sky several little figures of men, jerked high on their invisible wires against the curtains of this ghastly puppet show. When they descended again to earth their bodies seemed to vanish: the force of the fall drove them head first, feet first, into the ground, and the British troops, running over that wreckage a few minutes later, came upon arms, legs, and heads protruding from the tomb of clay, just as though some god had seized on a vast tent-mallet and hammered them like pegs into the earth. Those bodies which remained on the surface of the ground had one peculiarity: they could be rolled up like pieces of paper. Every smallest bone in them had been smashed. Pipe-spills made of twisted flesh. . . .

Birthday Farm is where Sam Frickleton got his V.C., leading his platoon straight through enemy barrage to take a German trench with rifle and bayonet, turn on the captured machine-guns, and play the 'Song of Hell'. Nobody knows whose birthday the farm was named for, unless it was Sam's. It was a place deader than death. Otago was ordered to hold a trench, and stuck it under heavy fire. In the morning the troops advanced, capturing three field-guns, nineteen machine-guns, and three hundred prisoners, several officers among them. The Dinks—the New Zealand Rifle Brigade—had been getting it in the neck here with every sort of music the opposition could turn on. Then the bombers got the order to clean out a row of German dug-outs.

Cleaning out dug-outs is quick work, and not without its thrill, as you never know who's laying for you down under in the mud and brushwood. The padded jackets of the bombers are filled with the iron apples, which give four seconds' notice before an explosion. The job is done in three movements—jump down into the trench, pull out the bomb-pin, and throw it straight into the dug-out. The rest can safely be left to nature; and one thing about it is you very seldom know how many were inside the dug-out when the bomb arrived.

In the last dug-out there was an unnatural absence of sound or movement. No bullet whipped out as the New Zealanders ran along the parapet. They broke in the door.

For six days the German wounded hadn't been able to get down the lines, and no medical officer had contrived to fight his way through and bandage their wounds. Those who lived were all badly wounded men. The dead lay twisted on the dug-out floor, and their companions, unable to escape from the contamination of their putrefaction, lay beside them, or propped up on earthen benches, huge-eyed, starving, with ghostly, unshaven faces. Not a man among them spoke as the bombing party burst in. Every man's eyes had the dreadful and quiet patience of the dreamer who has drifted almost across the black, forgetful river. Every man's wound showed the white, moving crust of maggots. It was as though dead and living, silent in their tomb, cried out with one terrible whisper, 'Leave us in peace!' The river of death crawled between living and living over the dug-out floor. And on the other side British soldiers stood cursing and weeping.

After that, Otago was relieved and sent back to town billets at Nieppe. The dwindling companies were reinforced and swung out again on route marches southwards.

You wouldn't think a corporal would remember that nearly twelve months before he'd been hit on the nose. He couldn't have been inside a dug-out like that last one. . . . Starkie was spotted before he had gone twenty miles on the route march. There wasn't any alibi, for all the other coloured soldiers among the New Zealanders were in the Maori Pioneer Corps, and Starkie couldn't pretend that the corporal's nose had been hit by a horse of another colour. The Villains picked him up and he spent a night in the lock-up with George Moran and George Cummings, also in line for trouble. Next day Colonel Chalmers prescribed a field-general court martial for him. This time nobody appeared to speak for him. He got ten years' penal servitude, and, by the gleam in his Colonel's eye, somehow he felt that this time he was for it.

The prison billet where he was locked up that night was an informal sort of half-way house to Hell—otherwise Le Havre, where the toughest military prison in France was situated—and right next door were Otago headquarters. When the heavy German bombardment began at eleven o'clock next morning, everyone promptly left the neighbourhood, taking with them Moran, who must have been a good boy to one of the guards, and leaving Cummings and Starkie to do what they liked about it. The doors were locked on them, but Starkie picked the lock and got into headquarters, where a careless person had left an automatic lying about. He removed it for safe keeping and strolled outside, to find that Colonel Chalmers, returning quite alone, was staring up anxiously at the sky.

Something was going on up there. German and British warbirds were mixing it in an aerial free-for-all. A scarlet 'plane, like a dragonfly suddenly hysterical, darted again and again past the British fliers. Suddenly it described a graceful arc and nose-dived straight for the ground, trailing behind it a plume of thick black smoke. As the 'plane hit the earth its body opened into a towering sheaf of flames. Two little figures struggled and screamed in the cockpit. Colonel Chalmers and Starkie started to run towards the burning 'plane across the field, but it was too late. Either the pilot and his mechanic were disabled, or their bodies were jammed in the cockpit. They dropped back into the incandescent heat of the red 'plane like two chestnuts fallen from the bars of a fire-grate into the heart of the flames.

Colonel Chalmers looked for a moment like an out-of-breath old man. He said, 'Poor devils, poor devils! What a death to die!'

Starkie had had every intention of shooting his Colonel. But for the moment he felt almost soft towards him. As they went back, quite slowly and without loss of face on either side, in the direction of the lock-up, he dropped the automatic into the grass. Whether it was found or not he never knew, but the next day they told him that his ten years' sentence had been broken down to two years, and that was final. Colonel Chalmers seemed not to realize that two years is a long time, and Le Havre a place with a very unsavoury name. Starkie longed for his automatic, but it was too late. They handcuffed him between Moran and Cummings. The three men were stripped of all arms and badges of their soldierhood. Then they were started at a jog-trot to cattle-trucks, and sat in irons, jolted to bits on the crawling journey to the French coast, the train stopping every now and again to pick up Tommies and Australians.

In the prison-yard at Le Havre they were lined up in a concrete square and their handcuffs removed. A tall English Major read out the charges one after another. When he came to Starkie's—assault on an N.C.O.—he nodded amiably and said, 'We'll fix you up.' The prisoners were ordered to stand to attention. Starkie didn't like the tone adopted by officials in this place, and gradually his feet wandered apart; but not for long. In a moment a sergeant-major's cane—a thin and wicked little jade—flicked out and slashed him across the legs.

Somewhere back in the memories of Starkie's childhood there stirred the phantom of a face he had always bitterly disliked, though he could hardly have said why. Then it wasn't one face, but many . . . a rapid and flickering succession, a portrait gallery. All the faces had in common their tight lips and hard eyes.

The sergeant-major had also a very determined chin. Starkie hit him hard on the end of it, and then became a little confused about events. He was lying on the concrete, heavy boots were crashing into his ribs with a certain mathematical precision. When he woke up he first became conscious of an appalling pain that split him in two between his shoulder-blades. He had known something of the sort before, but never to such an excruciating degree. . . . Figure Eights . . . no use trying to wriggle your numbed arms free of that iron grip. At least he could pass his tongue over his lips, which were split and felt enormously swollen. When he did so he felt the bleeding gap where three of his front teeth had been knocked out.

He was lying face downwards on the concrete floor of a box-like apartment with galvanized iron roof and walls. Dimly he guessed that this was the state-room in the most unpleasant place as yet known to him, either as old lag or as soldier.

14 Le Havre

First the barbed wire, not little eighteen-inch cobwebs such as were spun over No Man's Land, but sprawling entanglements of a considerable height; then the tents where the military prisoners lived, except when under special punishment, which meant indoors attention in the galvanized iron boxes. All around the compound, which covered about an acre and a half, were little sentry-towers like the pill-boxes of No Man's Land. Separated from the military prisoners only by the barbed-wire entanglements, German prisoners sang, worked, and tramped stolidly up and down their own little cage in full view of the three hundred British soldiers—Tommies, Australians, New Zealanders, Canadians, men from every corner of the Empire—who were the especial charge of the English Major and N.C.O.s who ran the gaol. These were all Imperial Army men, and tougher than their own boots, or even than the meat they served out to the prisoners.

Starkie's first three days were in the cell. He was kept in irons, and lived on the daily ration of a pound loaf of bread, thrown into his little box every morning. They gave him as much water as he could drink, but no tobacco and no society, for which, at the end of his spell in solitary confinement, he was beginning to pine. There wasn't even the tramp of a sentry passing by. He was as alone as though the blazing crumps had really finished the world once and for all, as so often in the trenches they had threatened to do.

On his fourth day in Le Havre he was put into a tent with Ginger Crombie, of the Royal Irish Rifles, doing a stretch of five years, and the two new-comers who had arrived with him—George Moran and George Cummings. Moran seemed dazed and stupid; but as soon as Starkie had time to settle in his tent, he knew that part of it was all right. Each one of his tent-mates passed him over a little parcel, bread and meat saved up from their own rations. It was law in the military prison that the prisoners stood together, and infinitely closer to them than the officers were the round-eyed, square-headed giants whose vacant faces stared through the barbed-wire entanglements from the German compound.

But when the prisoners were put to work next morning, Starkie knew that this was no place for him. The basic idea of discipline for the refractory was 'breaking them in'. This was best done by endless, purposeless tasks, with no reason and no completion: no moment when the satisfaction of a job finished and done with might make a man's eyes light up. The individualist was dealt with by being treated as the ox under the goad. Early in the morning they started to roll heavy bridge timbers, fourteen feet in length, across the prison-yard, building them up in tiers of an equal height. When this was finished, they tore the timber-stacks down, rolled them on to handcarts and trundled them off to be stacked up again in another corner. Over and over again the same movements, the wrenching, back-breaking tugging at the great timber-piles, were made, and made for nothing. The rain poured down, but in no way infringed on their occupation. At noon they were marched back to the gaol, given potatoes and a tin of fat and water glorified by the name of bully beef, taken back to the yards, and put to precisely the same toil. At four o'clock they were marched back to the gaol and locked up.

There is another excellent means of taming the rebellious, and it was used at Le Havre. Hunger. After a few days Starkie was used to seeing military prisoners hunt like pariah dogs for scraps of food. They grubbed in the mud for pieces of banana and orange peel, and the days which took them down to the beach to hammer stakes into the sand were welcomed for the chance they brought of picking up potatoes washed in from the boats. Cigarette butts were treasured like gold. French soldiers walked past the prisoners on the beach, chewing tobacco, and when they spat the cuds from their mouths, these were picked up, taken back to the compound and dried out, to be rolled in bits of bark for cigarettes. Tobacco was the worst craving, and gaunt British soldiers handed bread over the wires to the German prisoners, who would trade cigarettes for food. No gift packages, however belated, ever got through to the military prisoners, whereas the Germans did occasionally get the parcels made up for them by mothers and sweethearts in little towns behind the Black Forest. Hunger and cold weren't as formidable as the craving for tobacco. Soldiers hung about by the compound wire, dodged the guards, and threw the shirts from their backs to the Germans, in the hope—usually vain—that a cigarette might be tossed back.

The four o'clock march back to the prison tents didn't mean any cessation of their duties. Each man was given a prison task of burnishing up old iron—stirrups, spurs, and chains, left lying about on the battlefields. It came into the prison with the red rust of its months on No Man's Land eating into it; the prisoners, with rags and sandpaper, had the duty of burnishing it like silver. Failure at this meant shot drill.

Starkie got three days' shot drill at an early date. The prisoners were marched out into an exercise yard under Sergeant Jackson. Each man was given a forty-pound block of concrete. He had to hold this straight out from his body, keeping his arms rigid, march four paces, bend his knees, and lower the concrete block to the ground, his arms still held straight; then rise, lift the block back to its first position again, march another four paces, and go through the same performance. It had the same happy logic possessed by the treadmill and the crank in the vilest of the early Victorian gaols.

When Starkie had lifted and lowered the concrete block twenty times, Sergeant Jackson still didn't like the way he held his arms. 'I'll show you how to hold that thing,' he snapped, and did so. 'Hold it like this.' Starkie received the block thrust into his arms again, but only for a moment. Then he dropped it on the sergeant's toes, and a howl of fury showed that even the Imperial Army self-control may be flawed in certain emergencies.

After that he was given seven days on bread and water in the punishment cell, with 'figure eights' for four hours each day. When the bread was thrown in, early in the morning, his arms were locked behind him at wrist and elbow. A wise man would have waited for freedom, but his body was crying out for food. He would creep across the stone floor of the cell, and kneeling or lying on the ground eat the bread exactly as a dog gnaws a bone. The contortions involved by this amused his guard, and he usually had an audience of grinning faces and voices barking encouragement. The ghost of a chance, and he would have murdered at least one of those men—it wouldn't have mattered which, they were all the same, shadows of the face he had loathed since his childhood. He could dream at night of bringing down his handcuffs on their heads, waiting behind the wood-stack with a club. The chance never came.

The men were woken at six o'clock, in the bitter black twilight of the winter mornings, with a faint rime of sea-salt on the wind. They stripped to their trousers and were marched out to the square. Half the company drilled while the others crowded into the wash-house to scrub faces and heads under a tap. A watch was kept on them in the latrines, and if they didn't tumble out quickly enough to suit their guards they were dragged out. After half an hour's drill they were marched into line and received their breakfast dole—bread, a bowl of porridge without either milk or sugar, and water in lieu of tea. A new prison task was set for them after the first few weeks. They were put to making duckboards for the trenches.

Every man was expected to make thirty duckboards a day, and it couldn't be done. A little yellow-faced devil of an ex-carpenter curried favour by setting a crack pace, and grinned over his shoulder as the inexperienced, with their butter-fingers, cursed in trying to keep up with him. They hurried, blundered, smashed their fingers and thumbs with the hammers, and were always behind in the end. Starkie knocked off work for a moment to pick up what looked like a heaven-sent cigarette butt from the mud. Sergeant Jackson's little cane played its tattoo on the back of his knuckles.

This time Starkie didn't hit the sergeant or anyone else. He grew as pale as is possible for a man of his colour, and stared at him.

'Well, Butterfingers, what about it?' invited Sergeant Jackson.

'I'm going to get out of here, I'm going to escape.'

'Mad, are you? Well, try escaping from the clink for a start.'

Door locked, walls of iron, floors of stone, no sky, no voice. Then the tall Major stood over him.

'What's this about escape, Stark?'

Unconcerned, colourless tones, that sounded somehow hollow and thin.

Starkie had known a murderer with more of a man's voice than that. He said, 'I'm going to get out of here.'

The colourless voice spoke over his head.

'White men have tried to escape from this prison, Stark, and they didn't bring it off. We're not afraid of a black man getting away.'

Footsteps retreated. Black man! Black man! . . . Somehow the words held a significance he found hard to grasp. Was it because he was a black man that he found the civilized world his enemy?

'I'm going to get out of here. I'm going to get out of here.'

On the following night, white men managed to break the prison camp from the German compound, but they couldn't have done it without the help of the Major's black man. Among the scrap-iron brought in from No Man's Land were rusty wire-cutters. Starkie and his tent-mates, when the iron was handed out to them for burnishing, went around and helped themselves besides at the pile from which the other men could withdraw their task-materials. Their own wire-cutters they kept safely in their pockets. The spares they threw over the entanglements to the German compound.

The Germans weren't having as rough a passage as the British military prisoners, but you could read in their big, fair-skinned faces and hollow eyes what the French call *le cafard*. That dreadful homesickness, when the whole of life is one unending procession of laborious little pictures—pictures of cottages and firelight and women and public-houses, pictures of the irretrievably lost. A man in civilian life and apparently in normal circumstances can become affected by this same complaint. Nothing exists but the dead past; he can't get to it, yet he must, even if it means crashing his way out of life over a high bridge or under the wheels of a train. The Germans, with that look in their eyes, weren't getting much flavour out of their tobacco. The night the prisoners passed them over the wire-cutters seventeen of them made a run for it.

Starkie never knew whether any man of the seventeen got away for keeps. Four escaped all right, but not down the roads. The sentries' bullets got them between the shoulders as they ran.

There was hell to pay over the wire-cutters, but nobody could prove anything. Starkie and his mates could produce their wire-cutters on demand. If any of the other prisoners had seen who helped themselves to the spare scrap-iron they weren't saying so.

Three mornings later they were making duckboards in the outer yard. On one side lay the prison tents, on the other, in full view, the German prison compound behind the barbed wire. Through the yard gate at one end messengers and officers passed to and fro. An N.C.O., his rifle on his shoulder, kept guard there. The other gate was a mass of barbed wire.

Riley was Sergeant Jackson's pet hate next to Starkie. Starkie tried to create a diversion by getting Riley to tell Sergeant Jackson he was wanted at the other gate, but Sergeant Jackson said, 'Mind your own business and get back on the job'; so Riley was outed as a means of support. Inspiration came to Starkie as he saw a soldier land his hammer on his hand, instead of the duckboard, and curse profusely.

Starkie's hammer, brought down with the full weight of his body behind it, smashed the thumb on his left hand into a bleeding pulp. There was no acting about the yell he gave, nor the pain-twisted face with which he staggered towards Sergeant Jackson.

'My hand's done for, Sergeant. Look at it!'

The blood trickling down his wrist put Sergeant Jackson off his guard for just the one necessary moment. It was enough. Sergeant Jackson fell like a sack among the duckboards, and Starkie, expecting the crack of a bullet behind his ear, dived for the gate. As he ran the prisoners in the German compound watched him and raised a wild, strange cheer. He saw a military policeman on one of the sentry-towers lift his rifle. The gun snapped like a whiplash, but the shot was a clean miss, and he was running as he had never run before, down the three-miles ribbon of road between the prison camp and the seaport of Le Havre.

At a bend in the road he ran straight into the arms of a big *gendarme*, but he had one advantage: he was expecting trouble; the *gendarme* was not. He hit low, and the man doubled up on the ground, writhing and speechless. A side lane opened its cool tunnel and he flung himself into the shelter of its long brick walls. He had been seen, and he heard a guard shout, 'Halt, or I fire!' Starkie set his teeth and ran on. A bullet might, with luck, mean hospital. Going back meant hell.

For a moment his heart stopped, and the sweat poured off his face and chest as he stood still. The lane whose curve now hid him from sight was a blind alley. He had missed, a few yards up, the turning that would have taken him to sea-beach and railway station. In the five seconds it would take him to retrace his steps, the military police would have him. There was no way out. High and blind, a twelve-foot wall rose before him, its top garnished with spikes and broken glass.

He heard them shout, and knew that in a moment they would be round the corner and upon him. Then came an interlude that was nothing afterwards in his memory but an incredible scramble. Starkie was climbing like a cat, toes in a crack of the wall. As he flung himself over the top the broken glass caught his hands and cut deeply into them, marking his flesh in scores and scores of vertical slashes which in twenty years' time still showed their record of the day's events. He missed by inches the sharpened iron spike that would have impaled him. Holding by bleeding hands to the top of the wall, he dropped, and was lying in the grass of an old orchard. His left ankle began to throb in a curious way which sent spasms of nausea shuddering through his stomach, and he knew that he had sprained it. The place was a wild tangle of trees, high, ancient, and deserted. He flung himself into the lowest boughs of a great quince tree, and started to climb. By the time he heard voices and tramping feet on the other side of the wall he was lying overhead, stretched out like a cat along one of the highest boughs. The beautiful wild neglect of the unpruned trees hid him from sight.

He heard a voice say, 'No man ever jumped that wall.' Another voice answered discontentedly, 'Better look what's on the other side,' and they tramped off. He knew they were hunting for a gate.

It seemed incredible that they shouldn't hear the steady pumping of his heart. The Villains were in the garden, hunting among a thick, waist-high growth of blackberries. Yes, not a bad place to hide, but the quince tree was better. One man was talking almost affectionately to a dog-track among the blackberry bushes, 'You'd better come out of there, Stark. I don't want to fire into the bushes and kill you. This is your last chance, Stark.'

Another man scoffed at the beguiler. 'Hell, a fine time he'd be having lying there on his belly waiting for us to pump lead in him. That chap never stopped running. He took the turn higher up and beat it for the railway station. I tell you he's under cover in a cattle-truck and laughing at us. There'll be some of you mugs for the front lines over this. I'm getting fed up.'

Blessed, blessed rain . . . darkening the sky with its sudden veil, swishing in big drops among the quince-leaves, parting the long wild hair of the grasses below. It started to stream down, after the first heavy patter among the branches. The men below stared round them uneasily.

'Come on,' said the man who had insisted that Starkie was hiding in a cattle-truck, 'I'm getting out of this. Leave a guard if you like, or empty your gun into those bloody nettles. It's just waste of time; the bastard isn't here.'

Even then he wasn't sure they had really gone. He lay perfectly still, listening on his bough for the slightest sound. There was nothing but the swish of the rain, and in a far tree a blackbird's voice lifted, a wild little peal of sheer gaiety, as silken blue-black feathers made themselves seemly in the shining fall of big, steady drops. Starkie dared to make himself comfortable in the top of the tree. He was dry with thirst, and hard little unripened quinces were pleasantly tart in his mouth when he reached out to pluck them.

Presently it was night. He slipped down from the quince tree in heavy rain, limped over to the wall and climbed another tree, whose sturdy branches leaned horizontally across the top. As he had expected, a sentry was posted beneath, not fifty feet away. He didn't look very big for one of the Villains. Starkie waited until the Villain was directly underneath; then he dropped, and so did his prey. There wasn't any fight. The weight of his body knocked the smaller man unconscious. To make sure, Starkie half-strangled the guard and then turned the limp body over to see who it might be. To his joy he recognized one of the men who had worked on him in the prison, a little terrier who had once filled his eyes up when he couldn't hit back. Starkie did the same for him, robbed his pockets of eighteen francs, walked away. Fifteen yards distant he remembered something. He limped back and drove his sound foot into the man's side. 'That's for my mates left behind, you dirty little bastard.'

Starkie kept away from the railway station. They seemed to be expecting him over there. He struck the American base camp, and remembered it was the glorious Fourth of July, his own birthday, and the big night with all the George Washingtons, when he saw what was going on in the American lines. The big mess-room's windows flashed with light. All you could see inside was Stars and Stripes, for which Starkie didn't care so much, and poultry and fruit, for which, his stomach concave under his belt, he would have given his very dim hopes of heaven.

Two white-coated men, mess orderlies by the cut of their jib, came flying out of a side door, and hastened to a hut. Those white coats bulged too much to be natural. Starkie waited till they had returned to their post of duty, then crept into the hut; and in ten seconds was putting himself outside of two delicious little roasted squabs and two bottles of ice-chilled lager beer. The sheer ecstasy of eating good food, food that tasted, took away half the heavy poison from his mind. He wasn't so much afraid now. The friendly hut offered a way out of another big difficulty. Starkie decided to become a Yankee.

In a short time he was surveying himself with curiosity and admiration. He was a U.S.A. soldier down to the brass letters on his shoulders, and what was more, he had more stripes, flags, and crossed guns on his tunic than a British Field-Marshal. The Yanks kept themselves warm that way. The little white spats that went with his fancy dress were a good deal of a social problem. He put them on at least a dozen times, and each time they looked somehow queerer than before. Finally he decided it was his legs that were wrong and not the spats, and left them on. He didn't help himself to his Yankee friend's automatic, but he took all the tobacco he could lay hands on. Then he went straight into Le Havre. It was dark enough to hide his bronze skin unless he stood directly under a street lamp and whistled up the police. Besides, Starkie was leaving town that night, preferably for another and a better land where the sergeants ceased from troubling and the Villains were at rest.

He went to town and spent two of his eighteen francs on beer, after which he felt like a man again. Down on the wharf things weren't any too promising. At the gangways of the big boat now in port he could see the stalwart bodies of the Military Police; and he knew just what they were waiting for. Up and down the hold gangways passed an endless chain of men, all carrying bags.

They went up from the wharf with their loads, set them down, and filed straight off down the next gangway. Starkie's heart nearly stopped once again when he came near enough to see the sweaty faces, lifting, wide-mouthed and grinning, into the lamplight. The Negro Labour Corps were working on the wharves at Le Havre. Providence had taken him by the buttonhole of his handsome new Yankee uniform, and was now whispering gently, 'Get rid of these duds.' Starkie went down to the latrines on the wharf. Here he picked up one of the labour corps' three-cornered bags and sacrificed his all, down to his trousers and singlet. With the bag on his shoulder, bending almost double, he dropped into line and went up the gangway, brown face, brown shoulders and arms inconspicuous among others that ranged from the sickly mulatto yellows to the glossy black of the full-blooded, thick-lipped African negro.

He was on board. The ship swayed just a little under his feet, very gently, reminding him that land is one kingdom, sea another. On the sea a ship's captain is king. Ship's captains are funny birds; some of them sour as mildewed mustard pickle, others with clipped speech, frosty blue eyes, and nerve enough to tell the King of Hell what he could do with himself sooner than pass over a refugee. Starkie wasn't taking any chances. He hung about in the shadows until a whistle blew for the negroes' smoke-oh. Then he asked a big buck nigger what time the boat sailed. His throat stiffened again with disappointment when the nigger said, 'Day after tomorrow.'

Two days—give the Villains two days, and there'd be no exit for Starkie. It had to be tonight or never.

Fifty yards out to sea, her sharp bows a darker line against the grey mist of the sea, stood another ship. Starkie learned from one of the lounging negroes who were beginning now to stare at him with curious eyes, that she was due to sail at midnight. It was the one chance left. Quietly he slipped to the far side of the boat, hung by his two hands a moment from the deck-rail, then dropped.

Starkie lived for a hundred years on the ocean floor, only sensible of two things—his bursting lungs and the terrible, steel-toothed cold that ate into his spine. Gasping and labouring, he fought to escape from the dense green water-blankets that enfolded him. He knew he was never going to make it, and the salt water in his lungs turned him limp. Just as he felt that his troubles were all over, his head shot up violently into air as cold as an ice-chamber's. He couldn't swim for a few minutes, but lay on his back, dog-paddling with both hands. When at last he had shaken the water out of his eyes and ears he couldn't see the ship for which he had started. The mist was thicker than he had thought, and from water-level she was invisible.

Then a dreadful panic overtook him, and for a time he floundered about in the water like a goldfish in its bowl, swimming in circles. He had never been a first-class swimmer, and his injured ankle, together with the numbing cold of the water, were too much for him. He would have opened his mouth to yell for help, but already the outgoing tide had swept him a good twenty yards from the black ship which had been his refuge for five minutes. Nobody was going after a deserter into water as bitter as this. He let the tide do what it liked with him, splashing just enough with hands and one foot to keep himself above water for a little longer yet. It was breathless surprise when something tall and solid loomed out of the mist before him. He heard the stiff rattle of the ship's anchor chain, and hung there a minute, completely exhausted. Then he paddled his way round the side of the ship until he found what he wanted—a rope-ladder.

Anything was better than the soft, freezing death under the waters. At the top of the ladder Starkie met a man in a jersey and a funny little round hat, who opened his mouth like a codfish and said, 'Christ, if we ain't picked up a—mermaid!'

'Le Havre—the cooler.' It was all Starkie could get out.

The man in the little round hat said 'Christ!' again. He added, 'One of the chaps down in the stoke'old 'as a brother up there. You wait 'ere. No, come over among them winches, where you won't be seen.'

Starkie crouched dripping among the winches. In two minutes his friend came back again, finger on his lips. A china jug-handle was thrust into his hand. He tilted it, and down his throat—stiffened with cold so that he could hardly breathe or speak—poured the steaming, muddy coffee. Life began to stir in his veins, and for a moment was exquisitely painful. His hurt ankle, which he had barely remembered since he had left the quince tree, now began to throb as though its bruised flesh would burst.

''Ere, take this. Not much, it ain't. Dry 'ash.' The little man's voice was so mournful that Starkie could have laughed.

Dry hash, sailor? Ever see a man hang about on the sands till a Froggy spits the tobacco out of his mouth, then take it away and dry out the spittle and say, 'Thank you, gentle Jesus'?

When he had eaten the hash he was taken down into the stokehold. There wasn't any time for introduction to the demons down there. Stokers and trimmers didn't mind a runaway, but there was no telling what the first mate would have to say about it. In five minutes nothing of Starkie was visible to the world but his mouth and nose. They buried him in slack coal.

About 11.30 the violent ringing of bells woke him out of a half-stupor. The ship pulsed under them, a creature come alive. Starkie in his coal bin smiled as best the slack and coal-dust would let him. 'Black man, Major—too bloody right, I'm a black man. If you could only see me at the moment, you'd notice I'm a lot blacker than you thought. But you and I aren't seeing each other from now on. The black man's gone and broke your gaol.'

His eyes, the lashes clogged with a mixture of salt and coal-dust, screwed up for a moment, trying to picture the expression of rage and disgust on the composite face that he hated. It was no use. The weight of sleep was too much for both pain and excitement in his strong young body. Still buried in the coal, he fell sound asleep.

15 Runaway's Odyssey

THOSE chaps down in the stokehold were pretty good to me. In the morning a hand shook me up, and I heard a voice say, 'Come along, now, Darkness, it's time for you to hop out of bed.' When I looked up there were men standing grinning all along the little black passages between the boilers. So they unburied me, and a trimmer nips in with a towel and a basin of hot, soapy water. The chap who got me on board told me to strip, and after a lot of burnishing they had me pretty near clean again. We were a day and a half at sea on the way to Boulogne, and before we got to port I felt I was among friends. We spent the night swapping war yarns, and I wasn't too worried about what was going to happen when we got on shore again. I'd already decided to strike out for No Man's Land, yell '*Kamerad!*' when I saw a Hun with the right sort of face come along, and try what the German prisons were like. There was no place for me in France but Le Havre—and maybe Dartmoor or Broadmoor if I got to England—so I figured Germany where they'd treat me as a regular soldier, couldn't be any worse.

When we reached Boulogne the military police guarded every gangway, but the boys in the stokehold had a way of getting me out. Every man of them, stokers, firemen, and trimmers blackened their faces and arms with coal-dust, until they were so filthy there was no telling any difference between us. I was blacked up to the eyebrows as well, and we went down the gangway, chipping the Villains as we passed them. I did my share. One of the boys said, very loud, 'How'd you like to be a military policeman, Doug?' 'Better be a stinking, rat-eaten corpse out on No Man's Land,' I told him, and the Villain looked sore, but he was stood there on business looking out for a dangerous criminal, and hadn't any time to take notice of what two ignorant ship's trimmers had to say to each other.

In a Boulogne estaminet I struck some Aussies who hadn't too much of the discipline look about them. Aussies, same as the New Zealanders, were apt to kick up their heels sometimes, and by this stage of the War you could have found a good many of them in gaols and lunatic asylums here and there in France and England. The bunch in the estaminet didn't make any secret of the fact that they were all A.W.O.L. Some had been missing from their lines for two years, some just for two months, living by their wits. Wherever they went they hung together, and when you asked them the name of their battalion they'd round on you. I was in good company, so I told them where I came from myself, and within ten minutes I was an Australian Light Horse Trooper, down to my new shiny spurs, and liked it a lot better than being a Yankee, because this time I hadn't got to wear any dinky little white spats.

All six Aussies were up against military law, and each man

among them carried a gun. After a bit we left the estaminet and went along to the Green Lamp district to get some sympathy. The girls in the Green Lamp houses were just the ordinary French girls: dark skins, plump, and with the beginnings of moustaches along their upper lips. Their dresses were pretty, what there was of them. After a while we went back to the estaminet and decided we'd had enough of Boulogne, so we went down to the railway station and stowed away for Paris in a cattle-truck.

In Paris we couldn't go out in the daytime. The streets were rank with the military police of all nations, mounted on everything from horses to elephants—or pretty near it. That city was a pickpocket's nightmare. We'd heard a lot about the Apaches, but though we went up their part of the town we never struck anything, and we figured they were like ourselves—waiting till God did something about the superfluous cop problem.

There were some Yankees at the estaminet, too, and though they were a bit inclined to lord it over the rest, having plenty of cash in their pockets, they fraternized with the Aussies. Finally one Yankee tried to drink as much as one of our crowd, but he collapsed and the Aussies carried him upstairs and put him to bed. In the morning he wasn't grateful, claiming that he had been robbed of three thousand francs and his wrist-watch. When I got downstairs I knew at once that something was in the wind, for the Yankees, instead of breakfasting with us as they had done in the past week, sat by themselves at another table and looked as sour as lemon-peel. I asked the Aussies what was wrong, and they told me all Yankees were liars; which we knew before—so why take exception to it then? Then, after two or three drinks, I strolled over to the Yankee table and asked *them* what was wrong; and what they said about the Aussies couldn't be repeated, but it meant they were thieves and robbers and Judases, every man of them.

They also told me they were going to get even. So, being in an awkward position if the military police should arrive—as they were bound to do the moment the Yankees and Aussies started to mix it—I decided I'd leave for the trenches. I called my girl friend, who came down in her dressing-gown, and after a bit of fooling we pretended we were going upstairs for something we'd forgot. When we got outside the main room I kissed her good-bye and ran for it. No, it wasn't I that got the Yankee's three thousand francs and his wrist-watch. I didn't even know he had it on him. The Aussies were good sorts on the whole, but they didn't divvy up with the spoils like our crowd would have done. Just as I left the estaminet I heard the war begin, and I knew the front lines would be nothing to it. So I never stopped until I got to the railway station and, hunting around the trucks, found a row labelled 'Bapaume'.

There were little sliding windows on the side of each truck. I climbed in and made myself comfortable among bags of oats. After a wait of hours I found she was moving. I thought, 'It won't be long now'; but for two days she kept on going, and during that time I hadn't a drop of water. Try eating the husks of oats with a dry throat. On the third day from Paris we stopped to shunt at a wayside station, and looking out I saw a pool of water gleaming in an old tarpaulin. So I opened my porthole, climbed out, lay down and drank. A brakesman saw me as I was climbing into the truck again, caught me by both legs, and tried to drag me out. The train started moving, and I kicked. He fell away, and we were off again; but I knew that would mean trouble soon, so at the next stop I got off and hunted for another truck. I found one full of frozen beef, and for the next twelve hours lived on strips of blackened meat peeled away from the edges of the carcases. That night the train backed into Bapaume station, but I couldn't see any New Zealanders about. I met a traffic cop and asked him, and, by God, for a cop of any sort he wasn't bad. He took me into his hut and fed me on bully beef and boiling tea, and told me the New Zealanders were out at the front line.

Early in the morning I jumped a munition train for the line, and got as far as the supports, where I was told the New Zealanders were all hundreds of miles away at Ypres. That nearly finished me. I knew that at any time I was liable to be picked up and sent back to Le Havre, but I thought that if I could get back to my own mates again they'd take me in if they could. I was lost and worried. I saw the light train chuck off its load and take on field-guns, so I thought there must be something in this story of a wholesale shift to Ypres.

That was the time when Fritzie broke through at Bapaume and captured, I believe, a large number of prisoners. Headquarters left Bapaume on the same train as I did, but not in the trucks, like me. We went back to a place called Steenwerck. The heads were all vanishing in their cars into a beautiful moonlit night when I heard the high drone of a Boche flier right above. That was enough for me. I dived straight into a four-foot ditch of stinking green slime, and stayed right there till the war in the railway station was over, where the 'plane dropped a bomb dead centre. I didn't know whether he hit any Generals, but I hoped so.

At daybreak I crawled out of the ditch and met some Tommie soldiers. I heard about Otago from them. The Tommies left for Morbecque by train, and I travelled with them. When I got there Otago Fourth, my old lot, were quartered there. I could hardly believe it was true, and could have howled like a kid when I saw a face here and there that I knew. I was still in the Aussie Light Horse Trooper's uniform, barring the hat, which I had lost. So I waited till I saw two boys I knew: Dick Simmonds, a quarter-master-sergeant, and Bob McCullogh. They had me into their billet in five minutes, and gave me tucker and a New Zealand uniform. I hadn't any pay-book, any regular rations, any number, any official place in the world at all. In a fortnight they called for guards from the munition dump and works at Reninghelst from the Fourth, and I thought I might as well go there as anywhere else, so I moved on. Twenty men were chosen from the company, but there were twenty-one who shifted with the Otago crowd, and the heads none the wiser. The men just passed me the word when officers or N.C.O.s were coming, and I ducked till further orders.

At Reninghelst there was nothing much to do but drink beer in the estaminets. The German 'planes had been over the place several times and dropped bombs, missing the ammunition dumps, but each time hitting the Chinese Labour Compound. The little Chinks hated the Boche like hell, and you couldn't blame them. About a hundred and fifty of them had been slaughtered in the last air raid, and never a chance to hit back. The French, to my mind, treated the Chinks like dogs, for all they came ready and willing to help. They were kept behind barbed wire in compounds like the V.D. men, and marched to and fro under guard to their work every morning. Some said it was because they made things too hot with the French women, and there'd been no end of a row when inspection revealed that some of the Chink Labour Corps were women, come all the way from their own country to stick it out with their men. Can you imagine it? I'd always heard the little yellow girls had their feet tied up—'golden lilies' they used to call it—but these women had marched from the seaports same as the men, and worked as hard, like the women coolies do in China. Not all the Chinks were coolies either. Some of them were young student chaps who could talk English pretty near as good as I do. But you've got to own it looked pretty odd when Chinese babies kept on getting themselves born in the compound. One night the Chinks broke out of the barbed wire, and we had the job of chasing them half over France. I brought home seven, but not in too much of a hurry. Live and let live. Anyhow, they'd come a good long way to do their bit for La Belle France, and prettily she thanked them for it.

Next day I was at the munition dump, looking at salvage bombs: picking them up, trying their detonators, tightening them up. A good many duds had been brought in, but a huge pile was in perfect order. First thing I knew, three little Chinks stood over me waving their hands and pointing. I could see they wanted something, but didn't know what. By and by I had an audience of about twenty, all in their cardigan jackets, khaki trousers, and little stocking caps. I looked around to see nobody was watching who would take too much interest, and then exploded a couple of grenades for them just as a treat. Believe it or not, while the men of every other country bit their finger-nails when the bombs went off, the little Chinks used to brighten up and take a real pleasure in life. It seems they've got the idea that the air is full of devils, and noise scares 'em away. When in the evenings they were marched back in droves to their compound, they used to light little bunches of stolen cordite and throw it up in the air, devil-chasing. You'd know the Chinks were coming by that little crackle and red sparkle, like the beginning of a gorse fire.

My two bombs must have just about finished off some of their leading devils, or scared ten years' growth out of them, anyway, for when I looked up the circle of little yellow men were as pleased as kids at a Punch-and-Judy show, clapping their hands and pointing. From the signs they made I could see they wanted bad to learn how to use the bombs. So I made signs of my own with a twenty-franc piece, and they fished in their cardigan pockets—Chinks always have money—and parted with twenty francs each for bombing instruction. I felt as if I were back in the old days at Armentières when we formed the Bombers' Suicide Club, and I don't mind saying I never had smarter pupils than those Chinks. It wasn't long before they could pull the pin out, put a detonator in, let the spring go, and away she goes, inside of four seconds. There was a lot of noise, but they were used to it round about the munition dumps. In the finish I reckoned the Chinks were the best bombers I'd ever had through my hands, and I couldn't see why they didn't get more encouragement in France.

I found out one reason that night. Chinks are supposed to be phlegmatic, but don't you believe it. They're subject to funny impulses, and there's absolutely no holding them. Also, they were born with weird ideas, like hating devils, and when they hate, they hate hard. The Chinese hated the Germans for wiping out their men—maybe some of their smuggled womenfolk, too—from the air. In their shoes, I'd have hated the French worse, as an ungrateful set of bastards with a bossy manner. But it didn't work out like that. We'd had three boxes of bombs open, and before they knocked off for the march home that night each Chink helped himself to four, and hid them under his cardigan jacket.

That part of it I saw, and smiled to myself, thinking, 'Well, Old Man Devil's going to get the fright of his life tonight if those little yellow boys have anything to do with it.'

But there I failed to understand the heathen. Instead of going home in the ordinary way, when they came to the German prisoners' compound they split into two files and marched around it. It was all done in such apple-pie order that the dumb guards thought new commands had been sent from up top, and nobody had the sense to halt them. Along they went, solemn as yellow images, until their two ranks closed like a letter O around the compound. Then the men with the bombs chucked them straight over the barbed wire in amongst the prisoners, with not so much as a 'By your leave' to their guards. Straight on they marched, while guards yelled at them; and from behind the barbed wire came the shrieks and groans of German prisoners, caught unawares, some wounded, others blown to glory, and those who got off with their skins undamaged half crazy with terror.

British headquarters was madder than the Germans; and though the little Chinks were locked up, they never took the grins off their tight mouths. I suppose that was the one time during the War they ever had a chance to hit back at the enemy who wiped out hundreds of them. All the same, one day I'd like to see a French Labour Corps sitting in a barbed-wire compound somewhere in the middle of China, playing tiddleywinks. Then it would be evens.

There was some pretty stiff questioning as to where the Chinks learned to throw bombs, and though there was nothing actually known against me, I had the feeling that they were looking for me again. So I faded away to Bac St. Maur, and there ran into Colonel Hardy. Either he didn't know I was supposed to be in Le Havre doing shot drill, or he'd forgotten. As soon as he saw me, he said, 'Stark, isn't it? Thirty men wanted for a raid tomorrow night, Stark.' It was the first order I'd had in the ranks since the time they told me to forget about escape from the gaol.

This time I saluted and said, 'I'll be with you, sir.' So I was. I went back to the estaminet in town, first letting the boys know I wanted to join them when they went over. That night a young private dropped in at the estaminet and told me the time they were going over next evening. I sent back a message to my mates to say I'd be there when they wanted me. Next morning I went down to a little farm to visit two girls I'd met—Val and Blanche, their names were—and stopped there all day: milking cows, stooking oats, and turning a churn-handle with them like a farm boy, bossed about by their little old grandmother. Val and Blanche were just about the nicest girls I'd ever met, sweet and rose-cheeked as pippins. They fed me on new milk and dairy butter in pats and black bread in twisted loaves about a yard long. The French black bread looks pretty bad, but it's got a nutty taste the boys took to once they were used to it.

In the evening I said good-bye to the people at the farm and went along to the boys, keeping well out of the way of anyone with stripes on his sleeve. They handed me out white rags, same as they were wearing themselves to distinguish one another. All the others wore brass disks on their wrists, numbered from one to thirty. I hadn't any disk, I was the orphan. At twenty minutes to twelve they started to file out of the trenches into No Man's

Land. The bombardment was on, and our side had been throwing trench-mortar shells at a tank and pillbox. The pillbox was what we had to raid. I was over in No Man's Land before the thirty were out of the trench, because I didn't know who was taking the lead with the raiding party—somebody, maybe, who'd tap me on the shoulder and say, 'Back to the cooler for you, Stark.'

When they got to the pillbox that part of it was all over: but Sergeant-Major Stevens grabbed me by the arm and said, 'You son of a bitch, I'm going to send you up for killing a man in cold blood.' I'd seen men killed myself in plenty dirtier ways than being knocked on the head with a rifle-butt as they came out of the pillbox. But I was trembling all over like a dog, and my head snapping, so I told him to dry up or I'd give give him the barrel. Then I saw a man start to crawl away over No Man's Land. I didn't know or care who he was, he was just somebody else to kill. Charlie Frane sings out, 'Chuck it, he's wounded', and the same minute I harpooned him with my bayonet.

Then I found myself walking along a trench with a little Hun, one of the seven prisoners. He wasn't any more than up to my shoulder, and he kept wringing his hands and saying, 'My poor brother! Oh, my poor brother!'—like those Bovril advertisements. It turned out his brother was the last man I'd hit on the head when he came out of the pillbox—and I knew he'd never get up again. The little chap pulled photographs out of his pocket and showed them to me when we got into the trench—howling all the time—pictures of a nice-looking young fellow sitting in front of his house quiet as anyone else, with two fat kiddies on his knees and a tall girl standing behind him looking proud as Punch.

Oh God, of course I was sorry; wouldn't anyone be sorry? But what was the use of it all by that time? Being sorry don't bring people back to life. We were sent out there to kill; what in hell's the use of pretending anything else? It turns my stomach when people bleat about cold-blooded killing. When did the Zepps stop slinging down their bombs because women and children weren't expecting them? When did the poison-gas merchants act as warm-blooded as frogs? If you start you've got to go on with it.

At Bac St. Maur I reported to Colonel Hardy. He wouldn't take me back into the troops, but he gave me twenty francs and told me to go and get myself a uniform. I did that, and looked like a decent New Zealander again when I left the stores. By now it was after three in the morning, but I had a promise to keep, and I kept it. I went straight down to the little farm where I'd worked the day before. It was 3.30 when I got there, but the old lady was sitting up for me, as she'd told me she would. She had supper spread out on the kitchen table: a loaf of bread, thick-buttered, a funny sort of salad swimming in olive oil, those fat, pink sausages with bits of ham in them that the French use, and a bottle of *vin blanc*, which was a big touch for a lady old enough to be my grandmother. But I guess she knew what soldiers like.

Val and Blanche were in bed, where they ought to be; but they heard Grannie talking to me in the kitchen, and by and by I saw their heads pop round the corner of the door, their eyes sleepy and their hair done up in braids. They wanted to hear about the raid, but I didn't tell them anything much, especially not about 'My poor brother, my poor brother!' What's the use? Then, when their blasted little ginger farm cockerels had begun to crow loud enough to bring the Boche fliers down on us, the old lady put me to bed. It was still dark, and she lighted me upstairs with her candle, walking in front of me and nodding as she counted the stairs. The passages upstairs were low and uneven, and I was sleepy enough to have broken my neck without her. She put me in a room with a pointed roof, the eaves sloping down so that there was just room enough to squeeze my bed in beneath them, and a diamond-shaped window was just opposite my nose. On the bed was one those quilts made out of scores and scores of coloured patches, and stuffed with goose-feathers. I guess lying in that bed was the same thing as lying on a cloud.

The old lady acted as if I were about six; she just turned her back and hustled about while I got my things off, and when I was in bed, ready to sleep for a hundred years if I got the chance, she kissed me and said, '*Bonne nuit, mon enfant*', which is 'Good night, little one' in the Froggy talk. From the smile on her withered old face as she lifted up the candle and went out you'd never have thought there was a war on a few miles away, or that I'd just come in dripping from it, as you might say . . . though my new clothes hid that.

But the funniest thing about that peak-roofed room was the chamber—with great big pink roses around it in wreaths—which stood on top of the wash-stand as if they were terribly proud of it. At first when I saw that I just laughed, but then, as I was getting off to sleep, it began to look sort of familiar, and I remembered where I'd met nearly the same thing before. It was right back in the old Governor Grey Hotel days, when I was a kid. . . . I remembered they used to have some of those fancy devices in the best rooms for the guests, under wash-stands with marble tops. I used to think they were Christmas decorations, George and me being stuck with an old enamel jerry, and chipped at that. And I remember one day I sneaked into a guest-room and used one of those flowery affairs, and a maid we'd got—a Maori girl—saw me coming out and peached to my father . . . and how he lammed me. It was queer coming across the same thing here.

The shells got too thick around that district, and the old lady and her grand-daughters packed up a little while later and went to Paris. I never saw them again.

16 Rum for His Corpse

LEFT, right, left, right, you motherless foals, you peelings off the muck-heap, you blooming fag-ends of soldiers! Lost your battalion, have you? Well, march along at the heels of your betters; men who've still got regiments. See that long white bridge ahead of you? Keep on going till you get to the other end. Halt! Get out your little pop-guns and fire 'em off till we've got the bridge mined and you're told to come back again. What's that moving white cloud of dust on the road? Yes, that's the Huns, all right—the Uhlans leading the infantry; thousands of them coming up to make it hot for you. Oh yes, and they've got machine-guns for you, too! Want to get back to your own battalions? Should have thought of that before you left 'em. Got lost at the cross-roads and came on to Albert, while the rest of New Zealand tramped by to Mailly-Malet, ten miles ahead! Well, there isn't any cross-roads over that bridge, and now you've got to hold it till you're told different, waifs and strays, as you are; otherwise the Hun'll take Albert, that used to be a nice little town once upon a time, even if nowadays there's nothing but starved pigs and fowls running loose about the streets, and not a bit o' skirt to be seen within miles. Halt where you are. Eyes right! Now watch for the Hun coming. Yes, that's him all right.

Half-way over the bridge the wounded begin to drop in little bunches, knocked over by the machine-gun fire. They lay on the white planking, staring at the huge drop beneath through cracks in the sunbaked, worm-eaten wood. The word is given for the strays to retire—the bridge is mined. Those of the wounded who are still conscious know what is going to happen next. They writhe into sitting or kneeling positions, their eyes voice the old, speechless cry of the battlefields, 'Don't leave me behind, fellows! Hell, you can't leave me here! They're coming now!' One minute before the mine explodes. The machine-guns play on the bridge as the Germans advance on Albert, and the men who live stumble over the bodies of the wounded and dying in their flight back to safety. Some of them are still on the bridge when its timbers thrust upwards in a great brown V, then snap in two, like pipe-stems. The Uhlans are blocked for the moment; the wounded men on the bridge—out of it, anyway.

There's a dead man in kilts lying on the outskirts of Albert Town. A big chap, he was, and dandy in his tartan and sporran and funny little forage cap. Wouldn't look too bad on you, Starkie, and he don't want it for himself any more. It's all yours; help yourself. Maybe provost-marshals and military police won't chivvy a man from place to place if he's wearing the Scottie's get-up. Got a big reputation, the Scotties have. Never heard of a Scottie with your sort of skin? Aw, hell! In times like these, who's going to look at a man's face? We're moving back to the Somme, and they say this time it's going to be a bigger show than the first. Just fancy that!

The strays who can't march with their battalions hang at the heels of the others as best they can, and feed on an army's leavings. Three weeks, then, with the Black Watch and the Argyll and Sutherland Highlanders to keep the half-dozen strays company—a great crowd, and tough as their own granite, with raw-boned, high-coloured faces and grey eyes deeply sunken under their brows. They're tough with a different kind of toughness from the New Zealand brand—talk less, move faster. The New Zealanders curse and spend a lot of time in the estaminets, so the Red Tabs say they haven't any discipline; but when it comes to dying they're as good as the rest.

What's wrong with the Scotties and a quiet life, anyhow? There's usually bread, hash, black tea, and chocolate to be had if you hang about long enough. The height of Highland hospitality, except there aren't any girls around here. Nothing much wrong with the Scotties, except that they aren't my own crowd and I'm homesick. I want to get back. Say, soldier, where are the New Zealanders? Still at Mailly-Malet, camping in dug-outs by a shell dump and waiting for the Hun to register a direct hit and blow them all to Kingdom Come? Good enough. Now we know where we're going. Come on, boys, nobody don't want us round these parts, we're going to Mailly-Malet. Wait till you meet up with the New Zealanders. They're a great crowd, they are. Better than these stiff-necks, with their porridge faces. Thank you, Mr Provost-Marshal. A letter to headquarters in wayside towns telling them for God's sake to pass us along, all six of us, if they can't break our necks in transit.

It's strange how all brewers turn out to be fat. But we get the better of them sometimes. When they had to run from the old brewery near Mailly-Malet, six miles off from the New Zealanders—who camp between a sugar refinery and a shell dump in musky, muddy dug-outs—they forgot to take their liquor along with them, or maybe they ran that fast from the Huns they just couldn't carry the baby. Think of it, boys, a brewery for a billet. This is better than those pretty little sties at Neuve Eglise where Mr Something Something used to keep his pet porkers.

The Yankees at Boulogne who used to turn up their noses at good beer and sing out for those pesky little thimblefuls of red-hot liqueurs, never imagined anything like this. No, sir, that they didn't! If they'd imagined anything like this we'd have had the American Army right down on our tail this minute—instead of sitting here snug and comfortable, just the six of us, and as many mates as we care to call in. We can be the big men around here. Wouldn't do to let the Yankees know we could bathe ourselves in champagne and chartreuse if we wanted to here; those Yanks don't take so much interest in winning the War, anyhow. They're disappointed in the French Maries. They say we've taken the bloom off them.

Taps turn on from the great wine-vats, flooding the cellars that you reach by little twisting passages whose cold flagstones ring deep and hollow under your feet. The wine drips ruby out of its soaked red-brown wood. In some of the cellars where new wine has been stored you can hear the song of the bubbles by putting your ear to the cask—a little hissing, fizzing song that says: 'Let me get inside your veins, soldier; I'll soon brighten things up.' But that new stuff isn't worth drinking. What you want is the old wine that's been rocked to sleep these fifty years or more and runs now, deep and slow, thick as blood, inches deep, feet deep, into the stone floors of the cellars. Roll up your pants, bend down, and you can drink like a dog from a stream. There used to be a Roman girl called Poppy something that took her bath in she-asses' milk, and Nero kicked her to death for it. Quite right too. Milk never was any good; but wine's a different matter, especially if you mix the red and the white. The air in the cellars is heavy as poppies. It smells as if all the grapes in the world, and all the sunshine, had curdled together here in the darkness.

There's one cellar at the far end that'd been flooded before we ever got to it; and by the stone corridors you reach a shallow bank of floor sloping down to the steps where the tide of red wine is slow, luscious, and thick against the edges. Pretty good bath-room for the troops, this one—and no law against drinking your bath-water, either. Say, who was it went and turned the bath-water into wine? Come along to the edge, boys! . . . God, there's something pretty dark over there! Fetch a torch, one of you. That's right. . . . Now hold it over the middle of the pool. Lend us your bayonet, Shorty. God, I can't even begin to touch bottom in this place! I'm going mad, maybe. Whoever heard of wine six feet deep in a cellar? This place gives me the bloody creeps! Hold that torch higher! Wait . . . now I've got it! Hang on to me at the rear and I'll fish it to the edge.

God, you'd think he was leaning back in an arm-chair, wouldn't you, floating in all that red, his head tipped backwards, his hands stretched out, so comfy and peaceable? He's been here ten days or more, or he wouldn't have floated up to us like that. He's a Maori, poor devil; can't you see his brown face pickled in the wine? I dare say he'll stay like this till the end of the War! No, I'm not going to take him out and bury him. I don't like corpses in my drink. This place gives me the creeps!

Can't you see what's happened? He found this place by himself, and he wasn't letting on. He got drunk in one of the higher cellars, maybe. Then he came down here without a light and turned the tap of the wine-vat on. It began to leak out, red and thick and heavy-scented, and presently he felt it splashing around him. He must have thought: 'Lovely, that is. . . . Oh, Mother, home was never like this!' So he drank some more—and more after that; and then he felt kind of queer, and went round in the darkness turning the taps on, pressing his ear against the wood to hear the song of the wine. But he never heard it, because the wine is old and sleepy and deadly, like a cobra.

It waited for him till it was beginning to get deep. Then: 'You son of a bitch,' it says, 'I'll teach you to come wading in here with your muddy boots and your pants not even rolled up! Do you think I was put to sleep for the likes of you?' He began to get stupid, and the air was a soft, dainty reek, hundreds of years old and wicked. He groped for the steps, missed them, pitched down on his face. Maybe he went to sleep then, with his face just out of the bath-water, or maybe he struggled and couldn't find the way out. The wine went on running and running, emptying itself over him, over the whole War. . . . I'll bet wine doesn't like the War, it likes to be sipped in little fiddling drops, just like small rubies set in old crystal glasses. So it got back on him, covering him up. He looks peaceful enough, anyhow. Come along out of this and leave it alone with him. This place's haunted.

Living in a brewery with a corpse pickled down below and most of the good stuff drunk isn't so good after a bit. Better to camp out on No Man's Land and keep near the boys. That young Captain Frere, he's a pretty good sort. He'd take a man back if he could. The strays need never go short of rations while they're near the Otago dug-outs. One good turn deserves another. See that hillock out in No Man's Land, Captain? I was lying on my stomach near there last night, and I've got pretty good reason to think it's a Hun strongpoint. Very good, Stark. That's a job for the bombers. Half a dozen to train at bombing, downstairs in a dug-out.

But, oh God, these boys are dumb! If they'd seen the way the little Chinks picked up the knack of it, went ahead and cleaned up the enemy without a word of argument or a mother to guide them, these slowbellies down in the dug-out would blush yellow for shame. *Not* that way! Look, this!—look—see?

Who was to know that Alec Suter, just as they were getting ready to file out, would say again: 'Where do I go, Starkie?' That was the twentieth time, and the boys all keyed up. Well, there was only one word said in reply to Alec; and if an automatic did happen to go off and leave a souvenir in the fleshy part of his thigh, it was only what the big gaby was looking for. But now there's hell to pay. Captain Frere is white with rage—you'd think he actually loved that big mutt; and the raid's all off.

'Get along where you belong, if you belong anywhere.'

Very well, Captain, I'll go out hunting by myself.

A little flare dipped in grease and tied to the end of a long stick. After that, when they're potting at the Jack o' Lantern from the strongpoint, creep round flat on your stomach from a different direction and roll the bomb down above them. Five tin hats to bring home and one Hun prisoner, and Captain Frere gets forgiving and says, 'You won't be forgotten, Starkie'—but I've heard that tale before.

A hand of poker down in the trenches, sitting in the bombers' dug-out. Every now and again they hear the little whiplash crack from No Man's Land, and there's no use pretending it doesn't take everyone's mind off the game. Out there the Germans have turned on a sniper who knows his job. His tally for the one morning is six British soldiers, each potted clean through the head. A message is shouted down the lines: 'Colonel Chalmers says ten days' leave in Paris or England for any man who'll kill the sniper over there.' The men tell Colonel Chalmers what he can do with his Paris or England leave. Broad daylight and a fine morning on No Man's Land, and yourself for the sniper's Aunt Sally. At home they told us suicide was the coward's way out. Go tell the Colonel to pot his own sniper.

Months and months of back pay, all tucked away where you can't get at it. The face at Le Havre, waiting and grinning. Nobody's soldier. Odd jobs, running wine from the corpse-pool for the men; tagging along at the heels of the battalion; getting the boots of the Provost-Marshals and the Military Police in your face; moving along till further orders. A little raid now and again, but nobody takes any notice of that. Nobody except the men. Hanger-on till the end of the War—and after that, God knows what. One thing's certain. If a chap doesn't belong to their war any more they aren't going to pay to ship him back to New Zealand. If he went anywhere at Government expense, it would be Le Havre, or Dartmoor, or Broadmoor.

'Tell Colonel Chalmers I'll kill the sniper for a cup of rum.'

Five minutes later. 'Tell Stark to report at once in my dug-out.'

Into the dug-out, grinning, abashed, a little defiant. Colonel Chalmers never said a word, not so much as: 'Good chap, Starkie!' or: 'Don't bother any more about that little business of socking the corporal, Stark; and they're full up now at Le Havre.' He broke the red seal on a jar of rum, poured it out, filling a tin mug to the brim. One thing to be said for the Colonel. Whatever he gives you, there's an awful lot of it—rum, trouble, or hell.

The rum's overproof, too, and the full mug sends little wisps of fire flicking through your body. That's the stuff to bring a man's courage back. Easy to cock your head on one side and grin impudently at the Colonel.

'Well, good-bye, Stark.'

Just that. The Colonel thinks the sniper is going to get you. Get you in the neck this time, and a good job too. Better out of the road . . . nobody's soldier.

But it's easier to die at midnight, when you need never know what hit you . . . like poor little Val, in her old estaminet. Gran'*père*, what's that? I am Death, my child. . . . In the middle of a fine morning, with the sky a tent of pale-blue triumphant silk above you, it's not so simple.

'Cup of rum, you bloody black lamb for the slaughter, you! Can't you see he only wants you out of the way? Let him do his own killing.' Then a stretcher goes past, and on it young Jackie Kearney, with the bullet between his wide-open eyes. That makes seven up for the Hun sniper in one morning. Well, so long, boys. I'm off now!

Three thousand watching from the trenches, enough to give the show away. First shot in the duel, a clean miss on both sides. No one to say whether the sniper's hiding in a shell-crater or in the old German strongpoint where he picked up the five tin helmets. They only used that at nights, but you couldn't tell what a new sniper might get up to.

Down into an old communication trench. Double back again, and sling a shot into the strongpoint. Was that a stifled groan? Better luck, maybe. Five hundred yards from the British trench the grass is high enough to reach over a man's head if he lies very flat. Rank grass, keen with the smell of winter. Inch by inch now. My father was a Delaware Indian, and I'm playing at snake in the grass. Safely under the wire, and there's the old strongpoint straight ahead. The point is, where's the sniper? In there, or waiting in the shell-crater to pot a man in the back?

Once upon a time in the Invercargill hills there used to be a tunnel that burrowed straight into the earth; disused, its black mouth hung with a green fringe of fern, its walls dripping with the cold sweat of porous rock. One of the kids, an imaginative little beast, swore black and blue he had seen a horrible creature go in there. There weren't any such things; everyone knew it. Someone dared Starkie to go in. Round the first corner of the tunnel the light was blotted out, the air smelt fetid. For a minute the beast was quite real. The tunnel's wall was icy and dripped rank water. Looking into the old strongpoint was just like that, but this time death was at home.

At a range of six yards, crack, through the right lung. The shock lifted him clean off his feet, but when he went down he was still perfectly conscious. He pulled the Mills bomb out of his pocket, pressed it into the mud so that it would explode two seconds after he threw it into the strongpoint. Mustn't give the beast time to run away.

The bomb rolled gently into the strongpoint. There was a flash, and the solid earth quivered like a quicksand. The roof of the strongpoint was torn away; and the sniper, almost cut in two, lay under the rubble-heap of its walls.

From the British trenches a long roar, which meant the three thousand Jack-in-the-box heads were pleased. But all the blood ever spilt in the War can pour up through the lungs into one man's throat, mouth, and nose. It's like old Pharaoh being drowned in the Red Sea. Dirty trick that, Moses always sucking up to God so that the other fellow never had a fighting chance. The Maori in the wine-cellar had a red death too. Stumbling, falling, clambering to a crawling position again. Then collapse, but he couldn't lose consciousness. Peter Macy, Mick McGrath, Tim O'Dorman, came running from the trench. He was picked up, and then lay on a blanket in the bottom of a dug-out, while Captain Dryer, the doctor for the Otago crowd, cut away his shirt and looked him over.

'It's curtains, Starkie.'

All those officials' faces, hated so long, not hostile any more; just stern, set, saying good-bye with indifference to something that wouldn't be missed much. Oddly, you knew they'd say good-bye to life themselves in the same manner when their turn came round. I have a rendezvous with death. . . . No, no, not yet to die. When you can't speak, you can still form the shapes of words with your bleeding lips.

Colonel Drury bent down. 'It's an outer, Starkie.' That was the official answer to his question; but Starkie wasn't going to die.

Morphine starts from the prick in the arm and works upwards in waves of drowsy, heavy gold. First the crushing, tearing pain in back and lungs was beaten down and numbed, then his eyelids were weighted with a sweet drowsiness that made him want to cry. His breath laboured a little less painfully. Colonel Drury's face became long, vague, and blurred. Of the friendlier faces that had bent over his stretcher when he was carried into the dressing-station, he could no longer distinguish which was which. He was drifting out fast on a tide of sleep, and made a great effort as he went to remember things, things that would be a rope in the swift water. Things dying men said, patient, submissive things. . . . 'Tell Mum . . . .' 'Don't leave me here.' 'Leave me, I'm done; go and get some of the boys . . . .' 'Take me outside and let me roll on the grass . . . .' All whispered. That showed they were ready to die.

With the last ounce of strength in body and brain he dragged himself out of the morphine and sat up. With the movement, the blood gushed anew from his lungs in great clots, and someone ran towards him. He spoke thickly through the blood, 'I'm — if I die!'

17 Sunshine

'DON'T leave me, Nurse! Please don't leave me, Nurse! Please hold on to me, Nurse!'

'Hush! . . . Go to sleep again. I won't leave you.'

> Rest, rest on Mother's breast,
> Father will come to thee soon.

The dream again; and the young chap's face lying on the pillows of the next bed, whiter than marble and graven with such a strange, sweet look. Unfair—unfair that youth, meant to sin and battle, and break itself against the rocks of the world, should cease from its striving and look so unearthly sweet. Eyelids deep sunken as if in mortal weariness, black lashes a shadow beneath them. The corners of the mouth faintly turned down, not quite enough to express disappointment or bitterness, but surely yet a little sorry for somebody. . . .

'Hush! Go to sleep again. I won't leave you.'

Little stiff rattle of wheels as the white trolley comes along bearing trays with white surgical dressings, gauze, cotton-wool, needles plunged into jars of hot water, forceps wrapped in sterile gauze, pots marked with red and blue poison labels. What's yours, Digger? What about a couple of good old number nines? What's the name of that blinking little coffin on wheels, anyhow? You'll find out soldier. That's the agony-waggon.

Ah, Christ, Sister, what're they doing to me now? Doctor—ah, Nurse, Nurse, don't leave me! Three great hulking orderlies sitting on my legs holding me down, bending my body back—God, it's set all stiff and crooked, stiff like a corpse! Yes, soldier, it's set stiff, that's why we've got to bend you up again. Nearly breaks a man in two, that does. Aa-aah . . . ! What's that? Knife stuck into a man's back? That's the glass needle, soldier. Got to pump the blood off those lungs of yours. Hold him still, Nurse, it'll be over in a minute.

Ah, Nurse, don't leave me!

Keep still. You'll go to sleep again in just a minute.

There, that's done! Give him a quarter, Sister.

Dab of iodine, a little tiny prick where the steel needle secretes its drop of morphine in the veins. Sleep, welling out of the unutterable depths of a man's weariness . . . sleep, drawn up in buckets from the pit of death, and dropped into you through the hollow fang of a tiny needle. On the white pillow the man in the next bed sleeps for ever and for ever. Don't leave me, Nurse.

'Hush! Go to sleep. I won't leave you.'

Better now. The great yellowish globes of light in the X-ray department are all ready and waiting for you. The oiled sheet on your bed can be cautiously, gingerly lifted, inch by inch. With scarcely a jerk you're aboard the trolley. See those humped shapes in the beds you're passing now? They often hear the trolley rattle by, and mostly they turn over again and say: 'Well, poor blighter, it's a little hole in the ground for him.' But this time you've got the laugh on them. We're only going to take X-ray plates, we'd like to see just what that bullet's done with your inside. Can't go swallowing lead like you did, soldier, and not expect to have a stomach-ache. There's the big, solemn lights, waiting to fizz and crackle with the power that can see through to your bones. It's all dark except for the white-coated men with the shades on their eyes. Straighten him up there, Sister. Get those sandbags along beside his arms, I want him perfectly still. Now on your left side. . . . Right, Sister; that'll do for now. Take him away again. . . .

Say 'good morning' to Dr Paget, Stark. That lean, lined face is familiar, out of the looming depths of a hundred years or so. Well, Stark, you don't know how lucky you are—and you never will. You always were tough. You've got a heart of stone, and that bullet's ricocheted off it.

Going to live, do you hear that? Beat them all at the post—Colonel Chalmers, Colonel Drury, the doctors, the Hun sniper. And what's that gnawing feeling down in the pit of your stomach? God, that's not a bullet, that's hunger. Sister, Sister, I'm starving. Don't they give you any tucker in this shop?

See that little girl moving about among the beds? Just a shine of brown hair peeping out from under her nurse's cap. . . . That girl isn't like the rest of them. I've watched her for a month, and I ought to know. You never catch her out when she isn't laughing or smiling—not rough, just a plucky little kid who'd try to make a chap see the funny side of things even if she died for it. The others are all right—good girls; but that little smiling one's different.

I've seen men brought in here with the most frightful wounds you can imagine—men nearly torn to bits, and the gangrene spreading up their bodies as they lie. And I've seen others with the death-sweat dripping off their faces in big clammy drops, and there wasn't one of them that didn't try to smile back at that plucky kid. The dying tried to die easier so they wouldn't hurt her; I'd try myself if I were dying. I've got a name for that little girl. I call her Sunshine. It's all over the hospital now—she gets 'Sunshine' whenever she comes into the ward, and I'll bet she doesn't know who started it. Maybe she does, though.

Anyhow, last night she came up to my bed and laughed in that friendly way of hers, and she said: 'Well, I'm going to call you the Chocolate Soldier.' So there's me with a nickname and a pair of crutches, leaning over this rotten little gas-ring and trying to make toast for the nurses' supper. I've cut the fingers as pretty as you please; but how can I make it fit for the poor kids to eat when we haven't got any butter, only that slimy, grubby margarine? God, girls like Sunshine oughtn't to hang about in a country like England where there's nothing fit to eat and Zeppelin *strafes* every third night or so! Sunshine ought to live out in New Zealand, where the cows are something like, and we can mind our own business and live happy.

There's only two things worrying me. There's that church parade stuff, the moment you can hobble they get you along to church on Sundays. I told Sunshine and Sister Froude—she's a nice woman, she comes from Taranaki—that I'd got claustrophobia, that I was a Mahommedan, and that I jolly well didn't believe in it. It's no use. They did get me along, but the whole time I was in church I kept thinking of that 'Thou shalt not kill' stuff. When it was over I had a long talk with the padre, and he seemed to understand. He's the first padre that ever did. He just looked old and sorry, and said some kind of a mumbo-jumbo prayer when I went out. But I'm not going back again. I can't stand it.

And there's the way they all chip me about what I said when I was delirious, and won't tell me straight out what I did say. And when I ask Sunshine she gets as red as a poppy and tells me to go to sleep. It's not fair chipping a fellow about what he says when he's off his nut. And it might have been such a lot of things. Oh, God, I hope it wasn't that! Not to Sunshine. I'd never be able to look her straight in the face again. God, a little kid like Sunshine oughtn't to be hanging about hearing things like that, and knocking round with a lot of soldiers who've been out where we came from! But she did say she'd tell me tonight what I said, because she knows it's worrying me. She doesn't want to, though. God, if it was that I'll clear out, and I'll never see her again!

Flowers, flowers—won't anyone bring me some flowers? How can I be expected to keep all you boys looking nice if nobody gives me any flowers for the ward?

All right, Sunshine, we'll go and get you some flowers. Come on, Jim. Come on, Fitz. We've got to go get some flowers for the ward. Sunshine says so. Hell, the way they polish up these floors you'd think it was done specially so we poor helpless cripples could slip and break our useless necks! Ever think you'd go skating on crutches, Big Fitz?

. . .

Big Fitz the tunneller, and Jim Turner—who came from Invercargill—thought the place was sure to be pretty posh because you could see peacocks strewing their blue-and-green tails over a strip of terraced lawn. There wasn't anybody in sight, though to be on the safe side they'd crept very cautiously up the long, beech-leaf-coloured drive. Flowers, scanty but beautiful, with the sparse purity of an English spring, nodded at them from various dark-soiled plots and borders, but there weren't enough of them for Starkie.

So they roamed about in the grounds until they found a nest of glasshouses, ten of them in a row. Here the flowers were as brilliant and manifold as humming-birds in a tropical forest, and soon they had a load for the wards—Chinese white, saffron, and all the tints shading through from apricot to rich pink, from pink to cerise, from cerise to the proud velvet heads of crimson and purple. There were also eccentric flowers with freckled faces, light green and brown—flowers which oddly reminded Starkie of rushes by a frog-pond and the garments of fine ladies. He brought some of them along too.

When Sunshine saw the flowers she behaved in the silly manner of very young girls contemplating delight and beauty—she clapped her hands; she danced several steps of a *pas seul*; she made little exclamations of incredulity, astonishment, hope, and finally rapture. Then she said reproachfully, 'Oh, boys, boys, you must have spent a fortune on these! Cattleyas. . . .' And a delicate pinkish spray curled its elfin blossoms in a place of honour against the round of her cheek.

'Ah, rats, Sunshine; them didn't cost us anything! Them was give to us,' semi-truthfully protested Big Fitz.

'Not too good for any of you.' And, with a swish of her skirts, Sunshine disappeared.

Some hours later—when the ward looked like Christmas—it was penetrated by policemen, detectives, gardeners, and a member of the English peerage. The last was a grand old gentleman with a monocle in his eye and a wail on his tongue. Full in the centre of the ward he stood, and lectured all New Zealand. From the beds arose a simultaneous cry of 'Hot air!' The men who could get about well enough to fall under the doctor's suspicion were lined up as for a firing-party, and treated to a discourse on orchids. Starkie gathered, rather appalled, that some of the stolen blossoms were worth ten pounds a spray and a wholly impossible sum per plant.

The worth of orchids was above the heads of the simple-minded New Zealanders. 'Surely you don't grudge a man a few of your flowers?' growled a one-legged soldier.

The noble lord drew himself up to his full height, uttering one despairing cry: 'Ignorance—ignorance—ignorance—!' and dashed from the ward, followed by an indignant howl of 'Ignorant yourself!'—in which both parties were perfectly correct. In the ward beyond, the wounded sang, 'God Save the King' as the orchidaceous peer fled by. After which the three robbers confessed, and were dragged before his Lordship to make their sheepish apologies. These the peer accepted, though sadly, and departed from the scene of the outrage with but an occasional groan.

There had been a war on for some time, but never before had he actually gone so far as to notice it.

There was some corner in his greenhouses that had been for ever England—impregnable, comfortable, valuable, overheated, and as densely ignorant in its own impenetrable self-conceit as any Jackie Abo who ever knocked his block-head up against the rising walls of a civilization, but without Jackie Abo's excuse.

That corner was now, beyond prayer or pardon, hopelessly colonialized.

O si sic omnes. . . .

'Now,' said Sunshine, not without dramatic effect, 'you've gone and done it.'

'Sunshine,' whispered her Chocolate Soldier, 'I wish I could 'a' had that little glass window-pane out of his eye. For church parades, Sunshine. I wouldn't mind church parades if I could 'a' had that little glass window.'

Sunshine upset a cup of cocoa over him, scolded him, tucked him up again and fled, kissing her fingers as she ran past the robbers. He kept her to her promise that night. Speaking very low, as the time came for the lights over the men's beds to be lowered.

'Sunshine, what *did* I say when I was off my head?'

'You came out of your sleep six times, Choc'lit. And now do you want to know what saved your life?'

'Please, Sunshine.'

'Very well. This is what you said.' And she told him. Starkie dived under the blankets and stayed there. He felt her hand on his shoulder gripping it quite hard through the white coverlets. Her voice was as near hard, too, as Sunshine's voice could ever be.

'Don't you think we'd rather you said things like that and stayed alive? Do you think we like seeing them go out? Do you think I like it when they try to hold my hand, and say, "Good-bye, Mum"?'

He heard her footsteps retreating down the ward, but he stayed hidden under the blankets. Somehow what he had said to her pricked into the blue-skyed bubble of this new world. *All* filth outside . . . loneliness, beastliness, tooth and claw. He couldn't have hoped to get away from that. But it hadn't seemed very real when he was stooping over the gas-ring, making toast for supper.

In the morning the man in the next bed said, 'Let's have a look at Choc'lit, what colour is he now?'

He sulked like Ajax in the tent of his bedclothes, only muttering: 'I'm bloody sorry you nurses ever had to put up with me, anyhow!' until the day was saved by the arrival of a new convoy of wounded. Helping to carry the stretchers, he came on Sunshine again, just as she came back to the ward from the operating-theatre. A tired, rather wan Sunshine that day, with the smell of iodoform heavy about her.

'Sunshine, I am sorry. I didn't mean to say anything like that to you. Truly I didn't.'

And all she said was: 'God bless you, old Choc'lit!' Then absently: 'How old are you, Choc'lit?'

'Getting on for nineteen. I'm an old man, Sunshine.'

'Ah . . . !'—softly, and with infinite passion. 'War . . .'

The French girls said that often. '*Ah, quelle guerre . . . ah, quelle guerre . . .*' But with more resignation. Sunshine as if she spat on the very name of war. She ran back to her wounded, and Starkie limped out into the clear morning air.

He could spend hours now in the green and level stretches of English parks, and became a chocolate lion among the children—who hopped about near him, fearless as sparrows. Soon, whenever he appeared in the park, there was a shriek of, 'How's your penny-pocket, Choc'lit Soldier?'—and he scattered coppers among them with all the dignity of Haroun-al-Raschid. The English children were the first he had known since his own outlaw childhood, and their red-cheeked faces and blue eyes were like pictures out of a nursery-rhyme book. They wore short socks, buttoned gaiters, brown stubby-toed sandals, straight fawn coats and fur muffs in which their paws curled up as neatly as the red baby squirrels—who, to Starkie's enchantment, tore up trees in the park and chattered at him *molto con agitato*.

A little maiden of two summers would wander up to him and demand attention, slavery, and creature comforts as engagingly as Titania making free with the excellent Bottom. Sometimes nurses or even parents—magnificent, self-possessed creatures—would pass by with their children. But it was war-time; he wore a blue coat, and his crutches sprawled beside him on the park bench. Nobody ever struck him with word or look.

Old gentlemen handed him cigarettes, and seeing the crutches, peered at him mistily, looking for the stumps of limbs. 'Poor young fellow! Terrible business, all this.' The mothers, their close-buttoned, fur-trimmed splendour fawn-coloured as the English trees in early autumn, nodded and smiled at him. In this little circlet of England, with a white and delicate sunshine brittle as frost-spears among short grass and brown trees, and with Sunshine to supervise his time in the hospital ward, Starkie was happier than he had ever been before.

Now that a ghost of his old strength was beginning to come back to him, he was worried at having no pay-book. But the men of his own battalion didn't let him wander about broke. Padre Spearman walked into the ward one day after the final examination which set him free to go on leave, shouted his name, and produced a letter which contained a fair packet of money from the boys in France. They all knew he hadn't owned a pay-book for well over a year.

Two days later he got a wire commanding him to report at Headquarters, London. Headquarters still gave an uneasy little twist of fear in his memory. He didn't intend to go at first, but he had a long talk with Sunshine, and she was very wise and dictatorial about it. 'Of course you'll go, Choc'lit.'

'Don't suppose you'd ever write to a fellow, Sunshine? You girls haven't the time.'

'You know perfectly well I'll write to you.'

'Then we are friends, Sunshine?'

'Yes—friends.'

The clear pity in her eyes made her look older than she was. He would remember her for ever like that—her white uniform against the buff walls of the hospital, the brown hair just showing under her cap. She kept her word, too. Months afterwards, she was still sending him cigarettes and little letters.

In the doctor's office Starkie got a lot of good advice about what not to do in London, and the two little packets of preventives handed over to every soldier discharged on leave from the English hospitals. So it had all begun again. He said good-bye to them —nurses, doctors, sick men lying under their monstrous iron cradles, and Sunshine. Then he stumped away down the hospital drive.

18 London and Laurels

SOME city, and some fog. Everything draped in black, as if you were perched up on the old hearse already. Everything at a standstill except the pubs—where you can still get a drink, thank God, before going on to Headquarters! Well, what do you expect to find roosting around the Brass Hats' chicken-coop but the Villains, dozens of 'em, great big chaps scared of nothing except having to go and do a spell in the trenches? Can't come in here, my man; you're drunk, you are. Say, Captain, I've an appointment here with the General, he *told* me to come here; if you don't let me in he'll wreck this show, see? Stunned, is he, Captain? Well, Stark, still fighting, I see. Yes, General, still fighting. Well, remember you're not in the trenches now. You're in London. Come back here at two o'clock sharp and report at my room. And see that you're sober.

Better than the Villains, the General is. Got a funny look in his eye, all the same. Wouldn't trust any of them farther than I can see them. Russell Square; bed and breakfast, five shillings. Beg pardon, ma'am, can I get a bath right away? I've got to see a General at two o'clock, and I don't look much of an oil-painting coming in out of that fog of yours.

Say, if the father of that lance-corporal had known what he was going to act like when he grew up, he'd have had to get himself created, not begotten. Nobody in his right senses would go and beget a lance-corporal that acted like the Grand Cham, and his buttons not properly shined, either. Ever heard of Lance-Corporal Bacon, you little runt? On Gallipoli we used to carve your sort up with our bayonets, we did, and eat you off the end, but we gave up the practice because our padre said you was altogether too hog-fat for the insides of decent men, and, by Christ, he was right! Now you get out of the road, I've got to see the Colonel.

Let that man alone, he's dangerous. Knock on the door. All clear ahead.

God, one General at a time isn't bad, even if he has got an eye like the point on a jack-knife; but what about six all lined up in a row? Maybe they're going to do their own arresting for a treat. It's not fair—six Brass Hats, all solemn as images and staring at me; nowhere to look, either, but the hole in the carpet. Sit down and smoke if you like. Thank God for a fag, anyhow! Full war record.

Three hours. Iron lips moving in a stiff sort of smile. That's right, all your papers are here. At least you've been telling the truth; now go outside and wait till you're sent for.

Come in, Stark. Sit down again. You've been a good soldier, and we want to do what we can about you. Back crimes washed out, all fines refunded, back pay restored, and the Major at Le Havre has agreed to drop his case against you. Now we want you to return to New Zealand. You've done your bit here.

I want to go back to the trenches. I want to see my mates.

Disability . . . the Captain up in the board-room will tell you the same thing. All right, go and let him take a look at you. Breathe in . . . yes, that chest of yours hurts, doesn't it? Now mark time at the double. Well, soldier, you can't call that much of an effort; you'd look pretty silly after the first ten miles on a route march, wouldn't you? Trenches nothing. There's your chit. Take it down again to the General.

Doctor's report is final, Stark. It's New Zealand for you, and you can be a recruiting agent if you like when you get there. God, I'm not going back home in the middle of this war and leave my mates thousands of miles away. General, I can't go back to New Zealand. I'll get five years straight on end if I do. They're looking out for me. What for? Something over a woman, sir. Now they'll think I've raped a bit of skirt or committed bigamy, but it can't be helped. Well, fourteen days' leave, Stark; but take care what you get up to. You're a very sick man still. After that you can go back to camp. What do you know most about? Bombs? Well, fourteen days' leave in London, then you're appointed a bombing instructor at Sling Camp.

Ever been kissed by a General? That was the Froggy one in blue clothes. The rest just shook hands hard and proper; but the Froggies put their hands on your shoulders, and before you know what's struck you—whack, there she goes, first on one cheek, then on the other! Guess that's what the Froggies do when they turn the other cheek, and they're that quick off the mark you haven't any time to nip in and stop them. Well, that's the first time ever I was kissed by an Army officer, and I'm content to let it stay at that. Makes a chap come out red in the face, and gives that lance-corporal cause to snigger behind his fat hand.

A brand new pay-book, though, with a big credit balance. First thing, money sent back to the boys in the trenches. Then there's four of the boys want to take their girl friends along to see the *Rosary*—and Flo's not a bad little kid, either, when you meet her for the first time and she swings those long black-stockinged legs of hers. How much do you think the seats at the *Rosary* break you for? Five shillings? Don't laugh. Fourteen bob a time, and when we sold a horse to see who'd pay for the lot of us, I was the one. Cost me about four pounds ten to get us into the *Rosary*.

I never had any luck gambling since I lost that gold we took out of the dead man's money-belt on Gallipoli; while I kept that I couldn't go wrong over a bet. And now we're here, everybody's crying. It's a story about a blind chap. . . . God, you'll find plenty of them trying to pick their way around hospital. They fit you out with a little white cane, and then everybody knows they've got to be nice to you unless they're in an awful hurry. Let's get out of this and take a look at the river, Flo. I hate sad plays.

Dirty Dick's is down in the East End, and you never saw anything like it before—not outside London. The tale is that a man and his wife poisoned each other at their own wedding-breakfast down here, and when you get down into the room where they did it—it's a cellar sort of place underground—everything's left just as it was when they smiled across the wedding-table. There's plates and spoons and forks—gone rusty—and things that might have been fruit and wedding-cake lying about, only they're all blue-mouldy, like the food we found in the cupboards near Armentières after the Boche shells had wrecked the place. The breakfast-room in Dirty Dick's is all bunches of grey, silky cobweb, and people pay a penny a time to have a look down there. In the next room you can get something to drink. Juniper berries is what these old London girls go for, and beer or whisky for the soldiers.

If there's one thing calculated to ruin a soldier when he's had a few to drink it's that moving staircase affair down in the

Underground—the Tube, they call it. You go down a long sort of passage, all lit up, and you'd think it only takes a minute to get out again, but there's where the Tube people get the better of you. Want to know how long I was down in that spooky hole? Seven hours! First the little electric trams dashed past so quick that I couldn't get on 'em before they were tearing off again; and then, when I did catch one and hopped off at the other end, I see this moving staircase in front of me and try to walk up it and get to the outer air, where it's Christian in spite of the fog, and you can get something new to drink. Well, I bit the dust about a hundred times. Every time I started to walk up the staircase it rose up and knocked me down, and by the time I was half-way up my shins were bleeding and I had all the skin off my forehead. Finally a soldier gives me his arm and holds me still while that rotten little staircase takes me up by itself. Everybody's laughing at me. No more Underground for Starkie, I'll tell you that much!

Aren't you going to stand a girl a drink, soldier? The London girls are pretty too, and good sports—with their big curly feathers, their quick tongues, and their bright eyes. Little Florrie Courtney's as nice a girl as you could want to meet. I did meet her in a pub, but all the same she and me would have been married if the parson hadn't kept us waiting so long in the church. We got right into the church, we did, down in Holborn. Florrie had a new hat which I bought for her, and she looked like one of those old Gibson Girl posters we used to see at home.

But I guess both of us were a bit restless—me in particular; and the parson didn't come and didn't come. So then the boys got talking. 'Come along out of it, Doug.' 'You'll think better of it when you're sober again, old man.' 'What's the good of a girl marrying a soldier, anyhow? If the girl's fit to be married, it's a moral the soldier ain't.' So I picked up my hat and fled, with Florrie's girl friends all pointing the finger of scorn at me and shooting out their lip like the Bible says, and when we got to the open air I found the boys were perfectly right. I felt a lot better knowing I wasn't married after all. It wasn't that I didn't like Florrie, she was the gamest little sport you could wish to meet, and pretty; but I dare say a soldier's life is too full of ups and downs for matrimony, especially mine.

Hear that far-away sound right up in the clouds? No use giving yourself a stiff neck, you won't see anything until the searchlights go on, and maybe not then. That's the hell messengers. That's what all the soldiers call the Zepps here in England. They wait for dark nights like this, and then they're up above you with their bombs. August, 1917, and they're well into their stride. Seem to know what part of London they want to hit. It's weird in the blackness, with the sirens shrieking like mad and the searchlights beginning to clamber up the sky like those beanstalks in the fairy-story, pale and long and moving across one another.

The sound of the bombs falling is an awful shriek like a fire engine's, and when they register a hit the walls are splintered and the roads torn up. They use worse stuff over England than over the French towns. They hate England more than all the rest put together. Everybody runs for shelter, but I keep out in the open, because that's the way we're trained in New Zealand in case an earthquake happens. Out in the open's dangerous, but it's the best chance you've got, we think. For one that gets killed in the open there's twenty buried in a wrecked building or caught in the flames.

When it's over you see people creep out again, and they're very cheerful. It's always: 'Well, that dirty Hun didn't do so much damage, after all.' In the mornings you always read in the newspapers that the raid was unsuccessful. I never knew about a successful air-raid in England yet—not from the newspapers. All men are liars—but they aren't all such liars as those newspaper fellows. In town we live on saccharine tablets instead of sugar, but wounded men on leave get extra, and I always send mine back to Sunshine at hospital. The idea of going to Sling Camp isn't any too popular with me—I hate the thought of taking orders from N.C.O.s. I don't know why it is, but there's something about an N.C.O. which gets me fair on the chin; and what's more, from the way they look at me, I don't believe they like me either.

Thousands and thousands of bosses, all living in huts at Sling Camp. The bosses are new as the verdant grass, some of them, but don't let that worry you, they'll stop you just the same and tell you how to clean your rifle; nothing's too much trouble for the little dears. Great lads, brought up on a strict diet of mothers' milk. Reveille at six a.m. Have a wash, tumble out of your hut, get ready for breakfast, polish your buttons, parade, march past the saluting base, salute the flag, drill till twelve o'clock. Then you fall out for dinner. After that, drill and lectures from one to four-thirty. Tell me the old, old story, Sergeant. I will, my lad, here it is again. Dismissed, have tea, hop away to the beer canteen, 'cos there's no other place to go. Canteen closes at eight, and at nine o'clock you've got to have your lights out and your head under the bedclothes. Wholesome, that is.

> Oh, we love the Colonel,
> And the Major just as well.
> And we love the Sergeant—hell,
> We don't think!

There's one quiet place in Sling Camp, and that's the clink, where there aren't any N.C.O.s and no roll-call either. And there's the best place for me. I haven't got any crimes on the list, but the chaps in the clink aren't objecting to that, especially as I can figure out a way to get them beer. You can't bring it in at the front door, see, because the Major mightn't like it, but the wall at the back is cut out in little squares like rabbit-hutch doors, so that the latrine tins can be passed in and out easy, see? Well, you take away a latrine tin and pass through a petrol tin of beer in its place; and after that, when you go into the clink, there's a sort of beautifully calm and happy look about everyone, like the well-known smile on the face of the tiger. But they get very hostile in the lines—the N.C.O.s I mean—because I'm instructing some of the greenhorns in Two-up, which they ought to know if they aren't going to have the pants fleeced off them the moment they get to France.

However, leave isn't hard to get, because there's a chap in the office who'll plank the rubber-stamp down on faked leave-papers with a good one on top. The signature of the Captain who is in charge here is the sort a blind schoolboy could forge with a rusty nail. So I got some London leave, unexpected by all, and went off. I was stopped by the Villains before I got out of Sling Camp —military police are like lice, if you didn't have them about you you'd never know you were alive—but I showed them my pass, and there I was, off by the railway for London again.

In London I went straight to headquarters to draw some pay. I was standing talking to the paymaster when the General came up.

'Hullo, Stark. Haven't you been to camp yet?'

'Yes, sir. Fourteen days' special sick leave, sir.'

Seems to me he took a lot of interest looking over that pass of mine. Then his eyes twinkled. 'You're a lucky man, Stark. Well, how much of your pay do you want? Twenty pounds? Nonsense. Give him ten pounds and chase him out of here, Sergeant.'

Honest, Florrie, I didn't mean to insult you. Yes, I know it was rotten, leaving you in church like that; but the boys all started to chip me, and the parson didn't come, so I didn't properly know what I was doing. Besides, you've got no idea what a let-off it was for you. I'm no good to a pretty girl like you. I'm only the shell of a man, with bits of lead sticking in me, and a wheezy chest. Oh, all right, I'll clear out if you say so. But if you'll meet me at the Black Swan tomorrow, I'll have a little surprise for you, something nice, Florrie. You wait and see. Well, there's no need to slam the door on my nose. I wasn't going to make a nuisance of myself.

Good day, soldier. Rotten, this fog, isn't it? God, if it's like this all the time in England, it's no wonder the girls have all got frozen faces and cold hearts. Doing what? Oh, just looking for more company. Come and sit down. The drinks are on me.

Right-o, girlie. Just one more drink and we'll go home. This beer they serve seems muddy stuff to me as a general rule, but they've put something in it tonight. The floors are going up and down like a ship at sea. What's your name, anyhow, girlie? What did you call her, mate? The Red-Headed Wonder? Well, it sounds all right to me. Come along, kid. Once in New Zealand I had a girl with red hair, but she wasn't a patch on you. I can tell you she was a nice girl, all the same.

Well, you might have looked all right in the pub, but I don't like the look of you now, though I can't say that to a lady, can I? How did we get here last night, anyhow? What's that you say? You half walked, half carried me? Oh, God, I must have looked pretty silly over that beer or I'd never have let a woman carry me to a place like this. And she's taken out her teeth and she's got the paint off her face, and she's getting on for sixty if a day, I'll bet on that. Red-Headed Wonder, all right. Wonder why that lousy soldier in the pub called her that? Hold on, what's this? Six pounds short in me cash! No sense in making a row about it, though; her sort always has two or three chaps with blackjacks waiting down in the hall. Look here, sweetheart, you nip down and make me a cup of tea, see? I've got a head on me like a punching-ball. You'll get your money for it all right, only get a move on.

Now Florrie always keeps her money under the linoleum. We'll have to have a look into it, and quick. I'd have been sold for keeps if she'd kept it tucked down her stockings, that Red-Headed Wonder, but luckily her sort don't wear stockings inside the house, and nothing else much except that grubby kimono. Not in that dresser . . . not in the chest of drawers . . . three corners of the lino, and I can hear her coming back. Struck it on Poverty Flat. My six quid and five more besides. She got that off some other mug, I'll bet. That's why they call her the Red-Headed Wonder. Well, this time she'll do the wondering herself.

Hullo, sweetheart, thank you for your cup of tea. I'm going to get dressed now; you turn your back like a good girl. Rotten tea, sweetheart. I'm an ungrateful bastard, am I? All right, I'm going now; you won't have to put up with me any longer.

What about yer bed, eh? I'm not going to be robbed by the likes of you. Thirty shillings, yus, that's for yer bed and me. All right, sweetheart, that's cheap at the price. Now good-bye. So it was cheap. I'm still showing a clear profit of three pound ten, but she won't know that for a little while. However, I won't go near New Zealand House today. Somewhere in London a hard-faced dame is looking for me, but she hasn't got a hope. Hullo, Florrie, so you did turn up after all? Shut your eyes, now open them again. I told you you wouldn't be sorry if you came. Yes, it's real white fox, that fur is; as soon as I saw it I said to myself. That's white and soft, and it isn't going round the neck of any other girl in London but little Florrie Courtney, because she's the whitest and softest. . . . So you do forgive me now, don't you? I want you to do me a favour, Florrie. I'm not feeling too well. Let's go home and stop up in your room all day. As a matter of fact I'm expecting a call from a chap I don't want to see. He's always singing out for loans, and I don't like to turn the poor blighter down. Let's turn on the old gramophone and listen to those Pink Lady records. It's like home now, with the fire lit; and that's good beer, Florrie. This is the best little place in London; but you ought to see New Zealand.

Thirty-nine days adrift in London, which was getting on for an A.W.O.L. record with the New Zealanders. He roved around to Russell Square, more out of curiosity than anything else, and was promptly set upon by a band of Villains.

'That pass is a month overdue. You come along.'

'I was always rotten at dates,' admitted Starkie, and seizing the pass, stuffed it into his mouth and ate it. Nobody wanted faked passes spotted.

Starkie decided that the day was young and he wasn't going quietly. He had no weapon but a billiards jigger, and with this he smote a Villain amidships and made good his escape, hotly pursued. On the fortieth day of his absence from the paths of duty he landed in the little White Swan Hotel. The circular bar was peopled by large old ladies with massive beer jugs, gossiping in their age-old and inimitable manner, with an occasional scowl for the soldiers. Enter the Villains. Starkie flung himself bodily over the circular bar, amid a thunderous crashing of beer jugs and screeching of female voices. After that he was very glad to escape, not so much from the Villains as from the Harpies. Behind him male voices were raised in lament as the stout bodies and broken beer jugs were hurled upon them. Starkie had awakened the latent feminism of English womanhood. The ladies with the beer jugs were doing their best to ruin the Villains, simply because they were men and matter out of place.

He boarded the first train he could see, and to his own confusion found himself promenading up and down the river-banks at Walton-on-Thames, a girl friend named Alice leaning on his arm. Walton-on-Thames strongly reminded him of Christchurch and its little River Avon: the same misty green of weeping willows in their last leafage, the same level stream sliding between green banks. The girl friend asked him to marry her, but he told her he was a bomber and couldn't do it. Then she wept a little, which was more than Starkie could bear, so he told her the soldier's tale, promised to marry her on Tuesday and turn over all his pay to her besides. He could say no fairer. He intended on Sunday to take her to Hampstead Heath, but found himself instead in Trafalgar Square, gazing with interest at a stone lion which had been flippantly crowned with a tin hat brought back from France. With equal interest, all around the Villains gazed on Starkie. He suddenly saw trouble in every direction, and so flung his arms around Sweet Alice, hugged her as never in her comparatively virginal young life she had been hugged before, then fled. Twenty yards down the street he was playing ring-a-rosy with the Villains, who grasped him stoutly by either arm. Starkie tugged till both sleeves suddenly parted from his tunic, was off again, and headed for Russell Square, climbing fleetly up the narrow flight of stairs that led to the closed pay-offices.

Here he got his back to the pay-office door, and for a time was not unhappy. Very soon there were not less than two thousand spectators, and on the road reposed five Villains. Along came a Tommy Captain. He hesitated, looked at Starkie not without sympathy.

'Come down in the name of the King,' he ordered.

'Not for him, Ned Kelly, or Harry Lauder,' was the reply.

After that the Tommy Captain returned with two London bobbies, large and gentle creatures with motherly hips, who spoke quite kindly, but whose batons were heavier than had been dreamed of in Starkie's philosophy. His right arm paralysed by a blow from the abominable black truncheon, he got meekly into a car between the elephants. The meekness didn't last. When the car was opened in Chester Square, some were limping, some hopping, whilst Starkie's nose was bleeding, his face scratched, and no buttons remained on his tunic or trousers.

'Scratch-cats,' he hissed, and was dragged before a large and serious Provost-Marshal.

'This is Stark.'

'Um! Know your charge, Stark?'

'Forty-two days' A.W.O.L., and God knows what else.'

'Right. Take him away for the present. Lock him up and keep him handy.'

In the lock-up Starkie met Old Joe. After the War he met Old Joe again, as barman of the most conservative club in Auckland; but at the time of their first meeting this would not have been prophesied. Old Joe had been for six months a floating island in London and a danger to navigation. The lock-up was a peculiarly Arcadian little gaol, the sort that begs to be broken, and five minutes after their meeting Starkie and Old Joe were discussing plans for escape. He was interrupted by policemen who took him before the military authorities, answered their questionnaire, and to his disgust found himself parted from Old Joe for the night, taken to a civilian police station, and in the undignified Black Maria, 'just for safety', grinned an enormous policeman, swinging his truncheon.

In the morning he rejoined Old Joe in the lock-up, and received visits of condolence from Provost-Marshals and Villains. Early in the afternoon he was produced from his cell and marched in front of Major Withers, after which things went with more of a swing: Take your hat off in the orderly room! March! Halt! Charged with A.W.O.L. forty-two days and resisting arrest. How do you plead? Guilty! Fourteen days' second field punishment. Dismissed.

Field punishment in England was a trivial but boring affair of constant drill and fatigues. But before Starkie issued forth from his charnel-house he was taken before a Canterbury doctor, prodded, stripped, made to hop. Finally the Canterbury doctor asked, with a stern eye, 'What's wrong with you?'

'Fourteen days' field punishment,' replied Starkie practically.

'What for?'

'Absent without leave forty-two days.'

'How long adrift?'

'Forty-two days, Doctor.'

'Hell—! All O.K. elsewhere?'

'O.K., Doctor.'

'What's that red on your shoulder for?'

'Shot through the lung, Doctor.'

'Very well. Now breathe in.' The doctor's stony eye was slightly veiled by the merest hint of a wink. He scribbled hastily. 'Here's your chit, Stark: J. D. Stark not fit for any form of field punishment, with or without labour. Now get out.'

Starkie's face grew long. The clink was the only place at Sling Camp where he felt comfortable. Major Withers' face grew longer. Irritably he suggested that Starkie should get out and do what he bloody well liked. So Starkie returned quietly to Sling Camp and sought refuge among the prisoners.

Sergeant James used to slip the prisoners whisky from the Sergeants' Mess. He was a good chap, but he'd been through too much in France. Whenever they talked of going back, his face would go grey and his mouth began to twitch.

Fights, beer canteen, shouting N.C.O.s, drill, salute the flag, revels and riots with the Royal Irish, Shang, Boozey Bill, Jimmy Daws, Bill Turner, Dick Hunter, the tall half-Gurkha, banded together with Starkie against the rest of the world. Crown-and-Anchor schools going on all over Sling Camp, half of them run by Art Butter, who kept the little barber-shop over against the camp, and was Crown-and-Anchor king of this end of England.

Tussle with a long Irishman who ran amok through the lines, shouting, 'D'you know who I am?' and then announcing with immense satisfaction that he was the middleweight champion of some God-forsaken little spot in Ireland. All the same, Starkie knocked him out in the third round of a bout, and since he'd drunk too much to come round easily, they carried him home to their own hut and tucked him up in bed. When they saw what the hut looked like next morning they voted the Irishman no gentleman. So they stripped him of everything but his trousers and threw him out on the road, offering up a little prayer that a General in his nice fat car might run over him.

Constant guerilla warfare with Major Withers. Stark, fall out. . . . Stark, are you blind, deaf, dumb, mad, or just silly? I'm not any of that, Major, I'm just honest. Are you? Then you trot along to the guard-room. We've had about enough of your nonsense. It's time you were sent home.

The travelling medical board came round to Sling Camp while Starkie was still in the guard-room. Something had to be done, and he did it. He begged the guard to let him cross over to his hut and get his razor.

'Come along, then.'

They crossed the compound. The razor was found; it's cold edge caressed the guard's neck.

'Hey, you savage, what the hell's all this about? What did I ever do to you?'

'Nothing. Only you didn't take me to the Medical Board, and that's where I want to go, see?'

Straight to headquarters, into the board-room. Before a wooden-faced row of medical officers he begged to be Boarded, got his wish. In the morning they took him out on the road, made him strip to his pants and run up and down for ten minutes. In the office stethoscopes waved over him like tentacles of octopi.

Half the Board seemed to think he'd do; the rest said 'No good for active service.'

He did double mark times for them until his chest was ready to burst. He could see they weren't impressed.

'Why do you want to go back, anyhow?'

Starkie decided to lie. He did it well. He told them about the way his mates called to him at nights, asking him to come back again, asking why he'd run away and left everything for them to do, living and dead. By the time he'd finished his forehead was beaded with sweat. He wasn't quite sure whether what he had told them was a lie after all. He stood with head hanging and waited for their verdict.

'Very well, Stark, you can go back. Passed A. There's a draft going tomorrow. Maybe you'll be in it. You can go now.'

It wasn't till eight that he knew for sure he had been picked up in the draft. Major Withers brought him the news. He walked in, stretched out his hand, grinned the first honest-to-goodness grin that Starkie had ever seen on his face, and said, 'Well, Christ be thanked, Stark, you're leaving us.'

So now it's good-bye, England, the queerest, cussedest, most contradictory spot on earth, the one place where you haven't a dog's chance of telling what's going to happen to you next. Froggies are Froggies, and act according. The Gippo girls worked to schedule, too; but what can you make of a place that grows girls like Sunshine and tarts like the Red-Headed Wonder? And you can't ever make up your mind if England's terribly old or terribly young. Parts of London, with the stone lions folding up their paws, quiet as the Rock of Ages, and Dirty Dick's just the same as it was years and years ago; and the old women with their beer jugs just as big and grim and funny as their great-grannies used to be—you feel it's like the beginning of Time. It's no place for a New Zealander, then; he has to whistle to make sure he's alive at all. Then he turns a corner and finds himself in a round sort of little green, not much bigger than a bowler hat, and if he sits down here to reflect on his sins, he'll wake up and notice that things seem to be happening around him for the first time in history. Bright green wash of buds over thin sticks of black trees; squirrels carrying their dandy tails over one shoulder and making faces at you; kids sailing boats on a bit of pond, their cheeks red as pippins. And everything around them: trees, pond, squirrels, deer, clouds, nurses, Bobbies, toffee-sellers, designed specially as a background to fit the London kids. There's no way of explaining it. It's a good place for a soldier to think about, but I don't suppose he'd get on any too happy living there. If he didn't turn out to be a million years too old, he'd be a thousand years too young.

This little Lark Hill, where the draft got held up overnight on their way from Sling Camp, just over four miles from the thousands and thousands of huts where soldiers from all over the Empire are parked, waiting their turn for a go at the Huns—it looks as if nothing much had ever happened there. Maybe one morning a lark got up and sang extra special, and that's the big event it was named for. Might be worse at that. Anyhow, there never was a lark like the lark of Lark Hill that the New Zealanders gave birth to, stopping on their way from the camp.

It wasn't that we didn't intend to go quietly, having had about enough in England of Villains and Bobbies of every sort whatsoever. But what could the draft do, when half Sling Camp came along after them howling like mad dervishes, 'Hey, soldiers, aren't you going to give us no send-off nor nothing?'

So the send-off started at a hotel near Lark Hill; but all the same the window-frames and the blinds stayed whole, though eventually there wasn't a single bottle in that pub that didn't pass out of life by means of a broken neck. The boys were mad but sober. Presently bottles seemed too fiddling for them, so we got nine great hog's-heads out of the cellar and smashed them in with axes. After that the boys drank out of hats, boots, anything else they could grab hold of. A roll-call wasn't possible that night, the Fourth Company being so mixed with the Eighth that no soldier would have presumed to call his soul or his pants his own.

In the morning when the company marched to Southampton they were still mad drunk and singing all the way: songs I never suppose old England will hear the likes of any more. When they met the motor-transports they held them up and smashed all the head-lamps with their rifle butts. But when we landed in Southampton, one of England's slow grey drizzles was there to dampen the boys' spirits, as though the country was crying just a little because we were leaving her, but not very much.

We were shipped for Boulogne on Troopship 17; first to One

Blanket Hill, near Boulogne—famous for snow, blizzards, hail, wind, sleet, frostbites, one blanket per man, and a Green Lamp district where you could get a lot of sympathy from long-haired friends if you wanted it. Then on to the New Zealand base camp at Etaples. It's queer, but once you were back on French soil the rest all seemed like a dream. I couldn't believe it had happened—Florrie Courtney, Sweet Alice, the Red-Headed Wonder, and the forty-two days' A.W.O.L. Only Sunshine used to keep on sending me fifties of cigarettes, so I knew she'd really existed. We were going to Bapaume now for the second time—after that, maybe Ypres, maybe the Somme again. It was sure to be merry hell whatever else they called it.

19 Last Reveille

THE LINE of the second Somme could be told by the black smoke and towering flares of munition dumps, as the German army, rolling back in thousands, destroyed its munitions along the road of its retreat. The hunters that followed marched straight into death—death from the futile, blind, exasperated defiance of a terribly broken army; death that came billowing over them in the sickly green and yellow clouds of poison gas, in the stand made by hidden snipers and machine-gunners guarding the retreat of their main bodies, in the flesh-eating horror of the *flammenwerfers*. Sometimes the German line held, and the forces locked. Since the beginning of the world man had never of his own powers staged a drama of such destructive magnificence. Here was the very climax of hate and defiance turned into steel, flame, and powdery vapours, or marching on, flesh disguised from its humanity in uniforms of sodden khaki and field-grey.

Jack Benshaw was always talking to the other men about the girl he left behind him in London, and from what he said she must have been some girl. He had her photograph always with him. She was just a kid, her head tilted back from a long, slender throat, and a mist of chiffon hiding the sweet cleft of her breasts.

The eyes laughed at you, and the frame of light hair about her little face was as misty as the chiffon.

'She's such a kid, it seems a shame she had to fall for a tough soldier,' Jack Benshaw said; 'but I'm marrying that kid as soon as we get back to England. I'd have done it before we left, but I didn't want to turn a little kid who never knew a thing before I met her into a common soldier's widow. Sometimes when I think of her I feel a dog for ever having come near her. She's pretty enough to marry a duke if she felt like it, and now she's nothing but a soldier's sweetheart.'

About nine days after they got back to France, Jack Benshaw said, 'Come along with me and bring your rifles', to half a dozen of the boys.

'Can't you take it easy, Jack? Let a fellow rest till he has to go out and pot at the Huns.'

'Come along and bring your rifles,' repeated Jack.

They went with him over the top of a little hill, and there, nailed to a tree, was his much-prized photograph of the girl who didn't know anything till Jack Benshaw met her. He'd nailed it up very carefully, so that the nails didn't damage the young throat, laughing eyes, soft hair.

'Get to a range of fifty yards,' he ordered, 'and shoot the —— to bits.'

Then the rifles cracked, one after another, and when they'd finished Jack Benshaw's girl was nothing but a black, grinning hole against the tree. After that Jack went and gave himself up, but he might have done better to keep a bullet for himself, for he wasn't one of those that got better.

Seventeen days before the Armistice they were marching in the German line of retreat through the battle area. The bombers were together, and Starkie had just landed his Iron Cross, having shot down the German who wouldn't hand it over quietly. Then a shell landed beside the bombers, and only one man of them was left standing. He was Peter Macey, and for a little while, when he saw what had happened, he ran up and down tearing his hair and saying, 'What'll I do, Starkie, what'll I do now?'

'Go and win the bloody war yourself,' advised Starkie, who was perfectly conscious, but tight-lipped with pain.

Four German prisoners jolted and bumped his stretcher back

to the Second Otago lines. They dropped him as they reached the dressing-station, and from his stretcher he put a bullet through one man's arm. Then his active service was all over for the time being.

At the casualty clearing station thousands of wounded men lay on their stretchers waiting their turn. It was just luck whether or no they bled to death before the M.O. could reach them. Somme was going down in a red sunset. Blood soaking through clumsy, inadequate bandages, Starkie lost himself in the vast conglomeration of groans, jolting ambulances, disinfectant reeks, that was Somme's harvest, gathered and ripe for England.

When Starkie got to hospital he didn't feel like a man any more. In some odd way his wounds, which had gone septic on the way over and blackened his clothes with poison, seemed to him a kind of disgrace. He couldn't reason, he only knew that no woman was going to look at those wounds. The hospital was staffed with woman nurses. The doctors didn't come, and it was no wonder, for the whole hospital was an insane kaleidoscope of men torn up and broken like trees in a storm—writhing limbs, terrified faces, open mouths and open eyes like great black caves in the surface of their flesh. He couldn't stay there and let the women lay hands on him. He crept to a door at one end of the long room, caught a pair of crutches that had been abandoned by some cripple, and swung himself down the steps and into the beating blackness that was London. As he went laboriously, the blood from neglected wounds in arms and legs ran down his clothing. A blur of swimming lights, clanging street-sounds, and enormously high stone buildings, London led him to the one little alley. Like a dying dog, he crawled up the stairs into Florrie Courtney's room. He could hear the gramophone playing the music of the Pink Lady Waltz. Lying in the hall outside, he thrust one end of a crutch against her door, and heard the gramophone needle run down as she listened—perhaps frightened—there inside her warm little room.

The door opened, and Florrie stood before him, her eyes wide and startled, her hair loose over a fleecy pink dressing-gown. There wasn't any other man with her, as he might have feared if he'd had reason enough to be afraid of anything but the touch of strangers.

'It's me, Florrie,' he whispered.

She stared down at him, and he could tell she didn't know who he was. Then suddenly she did know. She clapped her hands to her mouth and started shrieking, the abrupt, horrible little shrieks of a woman in hysterics. As abruptly she stopped and fell on her knees beside him, sobbing. 'Oh, you poor old thing, you poor old thing!' she moaned, pulling his head over so that it lay against her breast.

Very vaguely he remembered that strangers did get him after all. He heard Florrie's voice, high and far away, crying, 'For God's sake, go easy with him on those stairs!' He was lying on a flat, white bed, an ambulance stretcher. After that it became a matter of dreading the times for his dressings—thrice daily. The little tubes dug into his flesh, groin, right arm, right leg, draining the poison away and still the doctor shook his head whenever he came round. Outside his window, though he could not know it, stretched the green fields and little grey river of Walton-on-Thames.

Everyone was in league against him. They wanted to take his arm off and turn him out a cripple. Six times they operated on it, chipping off little bits of rotten bone, leaving new bluish-red slivers on his flesh where the surgeon's knife opened it up.

There was a New Zealand doctor in the hospital, a Major from Taranaki. Starkie told him one day what the others were trying to do to him. At first the Major pursed up his mouth and shook his head like the rest. Then he said, 'Well, we'll have one more go at it, Starkie.' And Starkie woke up to find himself lying in a very queer position, his arm and leg slung up so that they pointed at the ceiling. They still persecuted him with the fiendish little tubes, but the pain began to grow less. The Major said, 'I think you'll do now, Starkie.' He was the inventor of 'Bipp', an intolerable stuff with a smell that was used all through the war hospitals. And everyone knew the Major was proud as a kid of his awful 'Bipp'. You had only to say, 'Great stuff, that ointment, Doc!' to get a smile out of him.

Nine days after he came to the Walton-on-Thames hospital, the outside world went mad. Whistles and sirens shrieked in the distance. Near at hand a factory hooter kept up an enormous, incessant toot. The voices, the laughing, crying, crazy voices, hurled themselves by outside, out in the rain and the wind of an England suddenly lit up with delight, a black November cavern where they'd flicked on the electric button and everything went golden.

Nurses, doctors, all the patients who could hobble, they all deserted the ship and ran outside to cheer. 'Back in a minute, soldiers, be good.' Laughing faces, with the tears running down them. Clumsy hands, waving anything they could get hold of for a flag. You could imagine London's face uplifted, that grim, blackened old face which has seen so many hard centuries; and into London's stone eyes, into London's stone tresses, into London's stern-lipped stone mouth, floating and falling the rosy cloud of the confetti. All the young voices wreathing round and round London, a glorious branch of flowers twined round an old altar. Soldiers: the blind walking straight as if they saw, the lame standing erect, their faces shining, their wan eyes proud. Somebody patting the stone lions in Trafalgar Square. For another hundred years, maybe, old lions, for another hundred years. All's well, Admiral.

Send him victorious,
Happy and glorious,
Long to reign over us,
God save our King.

Nothing florid about it, nothing to set the blood dancing in the veins, as does the air of the Marseillaise. But now, with millions on millions of faces lifted to sing it, faces with wet eyes and open, singing mouths, it has majesty. It is like a great wave booming against a rock, the rock of London. Still stand, rock, and the wave of a people's soul pours over you. Send him victorious. . . .

'Oh, God, Paddy, we've got to do something about this. We can't lie here like fishy-eyed, clammy-faced corpses in the bloody morgue.'

'Well, you and I'll celebrate too, Starkie.'

Paddy Mahoney, a Wellington soldier with one foot amputated, tore off his splints. In the ward the cripples ripped up their pillows, dug the flock out of mattresses, and had the air flying like a snowstorm with the only confetti their thwarted patriotism could lay claws on.

'Ah, Mother of God, the throat on me dry as a politician's heart!' groaned Paddy. 'Where would the little sisters be keeping the medical supplies of liquor, now, do you think?'

They found the medical supplies of liquor, including two bottles of Three Star brandy and one of stout. When the doctors and nurses returned the cripples were sleeping the sleep of the unjust. The only sequel was that in the morning Paddy woke up with the wrong sort of head on him, quarrelled bitterly with Starkie over the proportioning of the brandy, and tried to drown him in the bath.

On Christmas Eve they sailed from Southampton. Starkie was down in the hold with the Maori Pioneers, getting by as one of them and joining in their songs until somebody recognized him and dragged him aloft again. Nine out of ten among the Maoris had contracted Bright's Disease, and their eyes were badly affected, but they sang better and laughed more than the rest of the hospital ship put together. Christmas Day broke in storm. The men were served out a beer ration at dinner, but with one tremendous roll the ship voted prohibition, sending beer-bottles and men crashing in heaps under their tables. The ship was loaded with unopened boxes of gifts for the wounded, travelling back to New Zealand. The men tricked the keys out of a sister, got into the store-room, rifled the boxes and strutted about in knitted socks, mufflers, and with pockets full of cigarettes and chocolates for the rest of the trip.

The Yankee authorities turned out a banquet for the hospital ship at Panama, and those able to get ashore found it very fruity. Replete with meat and drink, they lolled back in their chairs, gazing with brotherly love at America's lean and hungry look. 'Didn't we win the War?' demanded a Yankee. 'Too bloody right you won the War,' cooed a one-legged soldier. 'Come over and win the next one for us too. We like it.'

The Yankees drank mostly a stuff called White Mule because it had the biggest kick in the United States. Some of the troops had a hang-over till they landed again at Colon, and there they got more White Mule from more Yankees. Then a fight developed between the Colon darkies and the wounded men, and four cripples—of whom Starkie was one—kept the pass by wielding their crutches like battle-axes till the Spanish police and a salvage party dashed down, cursing, to rescue them. Starkie landed back in New Zealand still wearing a black eye.

Last port out, one of the boys who'd lived like a hermit right through the War—he had a girl of his own in New Zealand—went on shore and celebrated on White Mule like the rest. He was late back, and everybody laughed at him, until three days later, when the ship was getting near port. Land was in sight, just a faint blue line along the horizon, above it floating the band of silver which made the old Maori canoe-explorers call New Zealand *Aotearoa* Land of the Long White Cloud.

St. Anthony stood at the deck-rail, watching till land was clear. Then he looked over his shoulder and smiled at the boys. 'Well, good-bye,' he said, and was over the rail before anyone could reach him. He must have weighted his pockets, too, for he sank like a stone.

There was a lot of cheering when the ship docked at Auckland, but what the men wanted for the most part, even the ones who were dying, was beer. The hospitals were full up. From Wellington some of them were sent down to the Dunedin hospital, and just five, an overflow, went back to the queer, desolate loneliness of old Trentham camp, its long burrows of trenches and little canteens still showing, but alive no longer with crowding men and shouted laughter.

Queer . . . queer . . . . Even big Jim McLeod, 'Fleshy', they used to call him, didn't come back to New Zealand. He got right through Armentières and the Somme, with nothing but a comfortable Blighty wound. Then when he was wearing his blue coat, he went to a football game in England, and that wet climate of theirs slid like a snake into his shirt and coiled itself round his lungs. He was dead in twenty-four hours of pneumonia, which, when you come to think of it, seems a damn' silly way for a big man like Fleshy McLeod to die. Where was Tent Eight in that empty row where the moonlight scarcely showed how the ground had been scarred by tent-pegs, broken up into trenches, drill compounds, and little barbed-wire enclosures for the prisoners, so short a time ago? It seemed impossible to Starkie, looking down from the hospital window, that nobody was going to come along with a fixed bayonet and march him off behind the barbed wire of the clink. Dirty job, a guard's. He'd been a guard just once himself at Trentham, and the day was hot, so when the poor beggars began to complain, 'Ah, have a heart, Starkie! Can't we just go over to the barber's and get a smoke, under guard?' he had done his best for them. Marched them all down to Wellington, and of course they'd come back soused, which meant field punishment for Starkie. ('Come on, Starkie, be a good sport.') But he didn't worry a lot about that. Everything . . . life even . . . is field punishment, except for those rare moments when you're in love with a nice girl, or having fun with the boys, and no shell-fire to interrupt you.

You get back into peace, and the little chaps, the civvies—grown suddenly important—stick out their chests and their pocket-books, and hustle you worse than the Huns ever did. You have your mates, girl or boy. In time they forget you, or die, or are changed before your eyes, so that going to them isn't going home anymore. But apart from your mates, the world just speaks to you in a series of orders: 'Present arms!' it shouts. 'You black bastard, your rifle's muddy and I don't like the look of you, anyhow! Right about face! Mark time! Hats off in the orderly-room! Halt! Do you know your charge?'

'Charged with being Starkie, sir; and God knows what else.'

Notes

THE MAIN sources quoted in the notes are:

Manuscripts

Typescript of *Passport to Hell* titled 'Bronze Outlaw: A New Zealand Soldier's Story' by Robin Hyde. Held by the University of Auckland Library. *MS B-10.*
Two handwritten exercise books containing notes made by Robin Hyde while Stark told his story. Titled 'Bronze Outlaw' and in the possession of Robin Hyde's son, Mr Derek Challis. *MS Notes.*

Printed Sources

Alexander Aitken, *Gallipoli to the Somme*, Recollections of a New Zealand Infantryman, Oxford 1963.
O. E. Burton, *The Silent Division*, Angus & Robertson 1935.
A. E. Byrne, *Official History of the Otago Regiment, N.Z.E.F. in the Great War 1914–18*. 2nd ed. Dunedin 1921.
H. Stewart, *The New Zealand Division 1916–1919* (Official War History), Whitcombe & Tombs 1921.
Fred Waite, *The New Zealanders at Gallipoli*, Whitcombe & Tombs 1919.
Denis Winter, *Death's Men: Soldiers of the Great War*, Lane 1978.

As Robin Hyde observes, she kept a few names and invented the rest. Both *MS B-10* and the *MS Notes* have the original names as given by Stark. His memory was not entirely reliable and Hyde occasionally had difficulty with his accent (she seems to have heard Hargest as Harcus for example). Identifications of the more frequently used names are: Captain Dombey (Captain W. Domigan), Captain Smythe (Captain D. White), Captain Hewitt (Captain J. P. Hewat), Colonel Percy (Lt. Col. A. H. Herbert), Colonel Chalmers (Colonel A. B. Charters), Captain Knowles (Captain W. D. Jolly), Lieutenant Bill Howard (Lieutenant Bill Howden), Captain Frere (Lieutenant E. V. Freed), Captain Dryer (Captain N. H. Pryor), Colonel Drury (Lt. Col. D. N. W. Murray), Dr Paget (Captain C. V. A. Baigent), Padre Spearman (Rev. R. S. Watson).

Page 3

'I first heard of Stark'. Hyde seems to have first heard of Starkie from the Reverend George Moreton in 1932 prior to her article of 13 October in the *New Zealand Observer*: 'Landlords Lock their Doors Against the Friend of Down and Outs', where she retells Starkie stories related by Moreton—later repeated by him in the biography by Melville Harcourt, *A Parson in Prison*, 1942, pp.222–7.

'his Colonel . . . remarked "Curtains, Starkie."' Dr Pryor examined him and simply said, 'Good bye Starkie' (*MS Notes*). Hyde, of course, preferred her phrase and also used it in her *N.Z. Observer* article on Stark, 4 April 1935. In the text (p.184) it is Captain Dryer [Pryor], not 'Colonel'.

Page 4

pakapoo. A Chinese gambling game not unlike Bingo. Hyde wrote an article on the game in the *N.Z. Observer*, 5 May 1932.

Page 5

'my childhood'. Hyde's youth was spent in Wellington, not Auckland.

Page 6

Ronald Fraser. Sir Arthur Ronald Fraser (1888–1974), soldier, diplomat, novelist, and one of Hyde's favourite writers. Her review of *The Flying Draper*, *N.Z. Observer*, 3 September 1931 notes, 'Ronald Fraser and Stella Benson are the only two modern novelists whose books have a quaint delicious sense of having been written in the fourth dimension, where, more can be seen and experienced than in the ordinary world.'

Lionel Britton. Britton's book, *Hunger and Love* (1931), is a powerful attack on 'bourgeois' manipulation of society. 'Next to belly hunger sex hunger is the most imperious of all our needs. Unless these two are satisfied the race does not go on . . .', p.55. On the book page of the *N.Z. Observer*, 28 January 1932, Hyde notes that *Hunger and Love* had been banned in Australia.

Page 8

'his V.C. recommendation'. See note below for p.133. Starkie was not recommended for the V.C. according to other commentators.

impi. A group of armed men (Zulu).

Page 9

'third Stark baby'. According to obituaries (*Southland Times* and *Southland Daily News*, 5 November 1910) Wyald Stark married twice and left a daughter by his first wife and three sons by his second. Starkie was the third son.

Wylde Stark. Wyald Stark died on 3 November 1910 aged 78 years. As his obituary notices (see Introduction, page xiii) reveal, he seems to have been a more interesting figure than the one provided by Starkie for Hyde. His parents' names were George and Amelia and his mother's maiden name was Soldier. When his father died on active service he went from Florida, U.S.A., to England and joined the gold rush to Victoria; he followed gold to New Zealand and made his way to Invercargill. 'He first built a wooden store in Avenal, and part of his business was to cart stores to Mataura to supply the gold diggers there. He next started in the hotel business, his house being the first of its kind in Avenal; it was subsequently known as the Governor Grey . . . . When in 1881 the wooden building was burnt down he erected the substantial brick premises which still bear the title of the Governor Grey buildings.' He sold out and entered into private life in about 1890. (Information from obituaries and the Registrar of Births, Deaths and Marriages, Invercargill.) Starkie could not have been born in the old Governor Grey Hotel then and this is consistent with the fact that Wyald Stark (Wyld in the Registrar's information) is listed as a labourer in the birth registration. He was probably born in the house in Lowe St, Avenal, that Wyald Stark is noted as occupying in Stone's *Southland Directory* of 1895.

'Invercargill may be a dry district'. Invercargill did not become dry until 1906, following the election of 1905 (M. H. Holcroft, *Old Invercargill*, 1976, p.109) so that Starkie's birth could certainly have been celebrated in a hotel.

James Douglas Stark. His birth registration lists him as John Douglas Stark.

Page 10

'Delaware Indian from . . . Great Bear Lake'. The obituaries note his darkness but refer to him as of 'Spanish blood'. 'Delaware' was the English name for the Leni or Lenape, a tribe of North American Indians of Algonquian stock settled on the banks of the Delaware; they were pushed west by Europeans and in 1789 were placed on a reservation in Ohio—a great distance both from Florida and from Great Bear Lake which is a large lake in Canada's remote North West Territories.

'shooting of Higgins the outlaw'. In the obituaries he is noted as capturing, not shooting Higgins: 'Many would rather be inclined to boast of such an achievement, but Mr. Stark was not that way disposed and never mentioned it even to his nearest friends, who became acquainted with the fact from one who was in Victoria at the time.' *Southland Daily News*, 5 November 1910.

Page 11

'girl born in Madrid'. Hyde's notes from Stark are unclear as to which of the parents was born in Madrid: 'North America—had north American blood—great Bear Lake—Wylde Stark—Born in Madrid. Father 6 foot 4½—Mother 5/9—old man straight as a gun—came to Australia on a cattle boat . . .', *MS Notes*.

'white whiskers'. Wyald Stark must have been about sixty-two when his son was born.

Page 12

Green Mansions. One of the writer-naturalist W. H. Hudson's accounts of his youth in South America, published in 1904.

Rose Stark. 'Sister Rose—Beautiful girl—all dead', *MS Notes*. Rose seems to have been Starkie's invention, his step-sister (identified as 'Mrs Adcock of North End' in the obituaries) was presumably much older since Wyald Stark remarried in 1884 after the death of his first wife in 1881 and at his death left nine grand-children and eight great grand-children.

'July 4th, 1898'. The Registry of Births, Deaths, and Marriages, Invercargill gives his birth date as 17 July 1894. Hyde deliberately makes Starkie younger to emphasize the effect of environment on him and make his more brutal acts seem less his responsibility (see Introduction), though Starkie always insisted that he was born in 1898. Letter to Downie Stewart of 10/9/26, General Assembly Library.

Anita Stark. Her name was Florence and she must have re-married after

Wyald's death and gone to Australia. In the N.Z.E.F. Rolls she is listed as Starkie's mother and next-of-kin: Mrs Florence King, Footscray, Melbourne.

Page 13

'the racehorses'. 'Mr Stark was a keen follower of racing years ago, and was the owner of horses which captured many of the chief stakes in Southland, his better known winners including Kate Kelly, Lady Avenal, Selina, Island Lass, and Brunette.' *Southland Times*, 5 November 1910.

'Nothing was too good for the Stark game-cocks'. 'He was a breeder of game birds, and to the last he treasured the remains of a champion bird, the hero of many fights, which after death was stuffed' (*Southland Times*, 5 November 1910). I have not been able to trace Dunedin Museum's ownership of the game-cock.

Page 14–16

Starkie's truancy. In the first edition through to the sixth impression of July 1936 these lines were taken up with an incident which Hyde expanded from Starkie: 'Father took him took chain and padlock and fastened round waist—In the Gladstone School—Fifteen lb chain padlocked nailed to stairs—McNeil was school master' (*MS Notes*). For the New Edition of 1937 she rewrote the passage removing reference to Mr McNeil and the Gladstone School. She also wrote publicly retracting the passage, to the *Southland Times*, 17 October 1936 (Introduction, p.xiv).

Page 15

'a new sort of harpoon'. In Starkie's account, Gladstone School: 'Rubber harpoon fired pen at Gladstone School teachers', *MS Notes*.

Pages 15–16

'an arrogant Irishman'. Starkie simply mentions a priest. 'Went fishing down Waipoi [*sic*] in Thompson's Bush—eels and circuses—In the bush—went with Chris McCarthy and Pete McCarthy—a priest caught him with cane across two hands—Chris McCarthy serious—Ran away' (*MS Notes*). The Marist Brothers' School opened in 1897. Peter and Christopher McCarthy are listed as entering the school in 1901 which would coincide with Starkie's brief attendance. The masters in 1901 were Br. Dunstan, Br. Walstan and Br. David. See J. O. P. Watt, *Invercargill Marist 75th Jubilee 1897–1972*, 1972.

Page 17

Sentry. 'hauled up before Mr. Cruickshank—white beavers and side whiskers' (*MS Notes*). Mr G. Cruickshank S.M.

Pages 20–22

Victimization by 'first mate' incident. 'Mate appointed from A.B. dirty work frowned on—smudging brass—next day getting into port—Starkie washing shirts and hanging them on Derrick—mate chipped him—Hit and fell on deck—sent to dock—Pennington warns him of police—Swings off by rope—got lost in Port Hills', *MS Notes*.

Pages 23–26

Canterbury sheep-station incident. 'followed fence down to Station—met dark little girl called Rita—daughter of Station owner—got out with horses—finished up by putting his name in Rita's birthday book—walked back to Christchurch', *MS Notes.*

Page 26

'Dalgety's wool store . . . . George Lord'. Forty-four lines omitted from the typescript *MS B-10* concern a brief stint in the wool store. New characters are brought in and there are a couple of incidents involving 'tickets in Tatts' and one of Starkie's fights. The section adds nothing to Starkie's character and little to the novel, unless the mention of Dalgety's, 'Tatts', Sir Joseph Ward's Arawarua Estate, and domestic violence are necessary to the New Zealand background.

George Lord. George Law, *MS Notes.*

Pages 26–27

May and Fanny Simms. May and Fanny Gibbs, *MS Notes.*

Page 28

'"Come back to Erin"'. The third line of the version that I have (*Grandad's Songs*, Allan, Melbourne N.D.) reads 'Come with the shamrocks and springtime, Mavourneen'. In *MS B-10* the song is 'The Bells of Saint Mary's'.

Page 30

Tom Finnegan. Finnety, *MS Notes.*

Page 31

Olaf. Andy. *MS Notes.*

Page 33

'one more sin on his conscience'. 'Bought ready tailormade suit—arrived in dungarees, and shirt—Bought shirt, sox, shoes—went to little pub and tried it on—Jumped the express' (*MS Notes*). Hyde's vision of the growing Starkie required that he steal it.

'his fifteenth year'. Starkie was in his nineteenth year. In *MS B-10* it is 'fourteenth'. See note for p.12.

Page 36

'the Bealey Tunnel'. Bealey is the early name for Arthur's Pass, eighty-eight miles from Christchurch. The reference is presumably to the eastern entrance to the Otira tunnel.

Page 37

'lemonade and sarsaparilla'. 'sarsaparilla and raspberry', *MS Notes.*

'They were all about him.' Not police, but: 'Hemmed in with drunken miners', *MS Notes.*

'"Red Indian" . . . "A savage."' Not in *MS Notes.*

Page 38 ff.

Starkie in Invercargill gaol. Hyde follows Starkie in the account of prison but she already knew most of the details from her investigation for the *N.Z. Observer* article of 5 March 1931. The detail of the latrine tin is from the article, not Starkie.

Page 40

'Jimmy Pearson, Dan Paul the murderer, . . . Archie Sayegh'. 'Jimmy Dee, Archie Taylor, Dan Swan the murderer, Dan grey old badger for battering his wife—Archie Taylor American black. Bob Cunningham International black', *MS Notes.*

'Bluey' Jameson; Dave Lester. Bluey Dickenson; Dave Dunlop, *MS Notes.*

'old Sampson'. Bob Cunningham, *MS Notes.*

Page 41

'Arney, the warder'. Romrey, *MS Notes.*

Hawley. Hawkins, *MS Notes.*

Page 42

Jim Frenton. Percy Challis, *MS Notes.*

'taken in front of the Governor'. 'Taken up in front of Cruickshank the magistrate', *MS Notes.*

Page 43

'Hastings by name'. Hazel, *MS Notes.*

'Wylde Stark had asked the prison authorities'. Not in *MS Notes*; Wyald Stark had been dead some three years.

'Anthony, the drill instructor'. Mr Douglas, *MS Notes.*

Page 44

John Cunningham. Bob, *MS Notes.*

'A fellow-prisoner had given the alarm.' 'Fellow prisoner Schuter rang the bell out in the corridor—He was cleaner', *MS Notes.*

'Goodwin, the warder'. Balwin, *MS Notes*; Baldwin, *MS B-10.*

Page 45

'twelve loaves were piled up'. 'About 14 loaves in the corner couldn't eat. Dr Fullerton ordered him out. "I'll never give in" Put back on rations that morning . . .', *MS Notes.*

Page 48

James Rannock. Tannick, *MS Notes.*

Page 50

'little fish-shop'. 'Joe Bascoe's fish shop', *MS Notes.*

'rock oysters from Stewart Island'. The Stewart Island oyster is not a rock oyster.

Page 52
'the Captain'. Capt. Black, *MS Notes.*

Dr Bevan. Dr Crawford, *MS Notes.*

Captain Grey. Black, *MS Notes.*

Page 53
David Kidson. Kidd, *MS Notes.*

'Bluff . . . the wettest little tavern'. The *closest* pub was in Bluff, Invercargill being 'dry'.

'Mrs Wooten's'. Walker's, *MS Notes.*

'Six o'clock closing'. Six o'clock closing was not introduced until 1917.

'into town'. 'took victim to Invercargill', *MS Notes.*

Page 54
'old relative . . . Dick Harris'. Uncle, *MS Notes.*

Page 55
'young woman in grey tweeds'. Starkie simply noted that a hold-all was pushed into his hand 'by old lady', *MS Notes.*

Page 59
Sergeant Taine. Bain, *MS Notes.*

Page 61
'he hadn't a girl friend'. 'went to Wellington—stopped all night at a girl friend's place', *MS Notes.*

'a major'. Major Cattow, *MS Notes.*

Page 63
sleevers. A sleever of beer: about three-quarters of a pint. (*O.E.D.*) Six o'clock closing had not been introduced.

Page 64
'dreadful expression'. 'The dreadful expression on the faces down on the wharf—The sobs could be heard a hundred yards from wharf', *MS Notes.*

Page 65
'Fifth Regiment'. Fifth *Reinforcements.*

Page 67
'Invercargill stoker'. Dan Brewer, *MS Notes.*

Page 68
The conjurer incident. An embellishment conveying, evidently, Hyde's view of Egypt.

Page 69

'A captain'. Captain Domigan.

Page 71

'nautch girls'. Professional dancing girls.

'not always . . . . There were'. Thirteen lines cut from *MS B-10*, concern prostitution in New Zealand.

'"Very nice! Very sweet!"' 'Girls come along—Houses with little balconies—"Come on New Zealand, very nice, very sweet, very clean"', *MS Notes.*

Page 73

'One of the mates'. Frew, *MS Notes.*

Page 74

'one of the hotels'. 'Shepherds'—international nest of spies—one part burned down—An officers' brothel—Same as the Waaza—Army rendezvous', *MS Notes.*

Pages 75–78

'the battle of the Wazza'. Wazza—a street of brothels and bars. As John Tait pointed out (see Introduction), the first 'battle of the Wazza' took place on Good Friday 1915 when Starkie was in New Zealand. 'On Good Friday of 1915, immediately after hearing their orders to leave for the front, a few Australian and New Zealand soldiers determined to exact some sort of punishment for certain injuries which they believed themselves to have incurred at some of the brothels in the street known to them as "The Wozzer"—the Haret el Wasser, near Shepheard's Hotel in Cairo. While they were ransacking the house, a story started, no-one knew where, that a Maori had been stabbed there. The bad drink sold in the neighbourhood led this demonstration to greater lengths than were intended—beds, mattresses and clothing from several houses were thrown out of the windows and piled in a bonfire in the street. Accounts vary as to whether Australians or New Zealanders predominated—both were involved. The British military police, always a red rag to the Australian soldier, were summoned. A number came on their horses and found the Haret el Wasser crowded with Australians and New Zealanders, nine-tenths of whom were spectators. The native Egyptian fire brigade which was rather pluckily trying to put out the bonfire was being roughly handled . . . . A Greek drinking shop was accidentally burnt in the *mêlée*.' There was, however, a second battle of the Wazza which Starkie may well have been part of. 'Men of the 2nd Australian Division some months later tried to emulate this scene in the "Second Battle of the Wozzer".' (Both quotations from C. E. W. Bean, *The Story of Anzac*, 1933, p.130, n.12.) Starkie gives the date of his skirmish as 'About August 4th 1915', *MS Notes.*

Page 79

'Three miles up from Y Beach'. Another of the factual errors for which Tait chides Hyde; she was simply following Starkie here and his memory was wrong. Y Beach was near Gurkha Beach, quite a long way from Anzac Cove: closer to twelve miles (map in A. E. Byrne, *Official History of the Otago Regiment, N.Z.E.F. in the Great War 1914–18*, 2nd ed., Wilkie & Co., Dunedin 1921, p.25). In fact, Starkie had all his distances wrong: from No 2 post in the North to Chatham's post in the South—the southern extent of Anzac—was 2 miles, while Quinn's post in the East was approximately 1,000 yards from the sea (Major Fred Waite, *The New Zealanders at Gallipoli*, Whitcombe & Tombs, 1919, p.136). Presumably the Fifth Reinforcements came ashore at Anzac Cove, where the piers were, then moved along the 'Big Sap', a large communication trench leading to the outposts. The Sap ended at No 2 Post on the far side of Sazli Beit Dere. The Maori contingent had worked on the Sap and left a carved figure labelled 'Pah' on its wall (Waite, p.194). The Reinforcements arrived at No 2 post on 8 August in the middle of the most savage battle of the Gallipoli Campaign, the fight for Chunuk Bair.

Page 80

Mule Gully. A gully running up towards the 'Sphinx' just north of Walker's Pier and parallel with the trenches of Walker's Ridge. Mules were stabled in the cliffs of the Gully (photograph in Waite, p.164). It is about 1,000 yards from No 2 outpost where the 5th Reinforcements were thrown into battle so Starkie may be confused in his memory.

Page 81

'971, the entrenched hill'. 'Immediately south of Suvla was the loftiest and wildest mass of hill country at this end of the Peninsula. Its name was Koja Chemen Tepe (Hill of the Great Pasture) but it was known to the army by its height in feet . . . 971', Bean, p.206.

'four hundred'. 'The Regiment . . . receiving an added strength of approximately 300 all ranks. Without any preliminaries this new force was thrown into the violent struggle then raging' (Byrne, p.66). On 16 August, eight days after arrival: 'The recorded total strength of the Battalion . . . was 360 all ranks . . . including the additional strength derived from the 5th Reinforcements', Byrne, p.67.

Page 82

Charlie Saunders. Rattray, *MS Notes*.

Page 83

'two wells'. 'Wells were sunk in all likely places . . . . The wells, however, did not last long . . . . Greek tank steamers brought the bulk of the water from Egypt . . . . Two quarts a day was often the ration—this had to be used for all purposes. Mostly it was drunk in the form of tea. Any tea left over was not wasted, but used for shaving!' Waite, pp.160–1.

Page 85

'the apex'. Not just an apex but *The* Apex—the most easterly point of Anzac penetration with reinforced trenches. It lay at the head of two gullies—Chailak Dere and Sazli Beit Dere—directly below the ridge of Chunuk Bair (Waite, p.202). The drive up the Deres to capture Table Top and Rhododendron Spur was made on the night of 6 August. The Turkish counter-attack on 10 August after the terrible battle for Chunuk Bair was held up at the Apex and the defence consolidated. On 20 August the Otago Battalion returned (having been relieved on the 15th) to hold the Apex. Byrne, pp.66,67.

Page 86

'the attack on Suvla Bay'. Part of the overall strategy of the attack on Chunuk was a surprise landing on Suvla Bay, five miles or so north of Anzac Cove. But it is more likely that Starkie was remembering the attack of 21 August (just after Otago's return to the Apex) by the British 29th Division and the 2nd Mounted Division of British Yeomanry from Chocolate Hill against Scimitar Hill (Waite, p.246).

'an advance of thirty yards'. '300 yards' (*MS Notes*), which is more accurate.

'number nines'. 'a standardized purgative pill known as Number 9. . . . The Number nine pill was said to counteract the constipating nature of much of the only food available up the line', Brophy and Partridge, *The Long Trail*, Deutsch 1965, p.180.

King. 'Kingie the doctor's orderly', *MS Notes*.

Page 87

'Death Gully'. Valley, *MS Notes*.

Page 90

'a story which his father had told'. The story is Hyde's.

'"Stop it, you dirty Hun!"' 'Boys go crook', *MS Notes*.

Page 91

'slaughtering a goat'. The details are provided by Hyde.

'than ever . . . . At the water-tanks'. Eighteen lines cut from *MS B-10* concern the relative danger of bathing off Gallipoli—sharks against bullets.

Page 92

'Fray Bentos'. The name of a particular brand of bully-beef, often used for all bully-beef. Also used facetiously as an approximation for *très bien*, especially in reply to an enquiry about one's health.

'used to it . . . used to anything'. Thirty-six lines omitted from *MS B-10* concern the terrible conditioning effect of violence and the lack of understanding by those who control it from afar.

'Rest Gully'. '"Otago Gully"' (Alexander Aitken, *Gallipoli to the Somme: Recollections of a New Zealand Infantryman*, Oxford 1963, p.23). 'This rest consisted in going up to the line by night, as before, to dig in four-hour shifts, or by day to the beach to carry back the tins of bully-beef and biscuits, the '3-by-2' or '4-by-2' wooden beams, the bags of rice, or the sheets of corrugated iron, past the mouth of the Chailak Dere and the dangerous corners' (Aitken, p.28). 'Yet still today men remember the unfairness of using rest for hard manual labour, back-breaking labour with doses of that crippling fear in burial fatigues and wiring parties, which men thought they had been rested from for the time', Denis Winter, *Death's Men*, Lane 1978, p.159.

'Tommy' Taylor. Thomas Fielden Taylor (1880–1937). Born and educated in England, he came to Nelson, worked in the diocese and became Canon of

Nelson Cathedral. In 1914 he became a chaplain with the N.Z.E.F. and in 1919, Wellington City Missioner. 'Mr Taylor had served with distinction as a chaplain at Gallipoli. His war injuries necessitated his discharge from active service. He took up his residence in typical Taranaki Street quarters and with a genius for appealing to boys and men, he soon made friends with many down and outs. He established clubs, a night school and Bible classes. On Sunday evenings he held a Mission Service. . . . The Mission came into its own during the slump years', H. W. Monaghan, *From Age to Age*, 1957, p.111.

'of whom Starkie was one'. 'stolen by youths' (*MS Notes*); another instance of Hyde's deliberately darkening the portrait.

Page 93

'usual pair of number nines'. Starkie is more amusing: 'Private got 2 no. nines. Headache, heartache, toothache, piles, laziness, malingering, cuts', *MS Notes*.

Page 94

'the rivals fought and tore. . . . The forbidding'. Twenty-two lines cut from *MS B-10* concern the shipboard wounded, the beauties of the aurora, and the horrors of Gallipoli and after.

Page 95

'old stone flagwork'. Is 'flagstone work' intended?

Page 97

'piastres . . . four hundred'. '300 piastres', *MS Notes*.

'Bradburys'. Pound notes: from John Swanick Bradbury, Secretary to the British Treasury 1913–19.

Sisters Street. 'Sisters Street was the brothel street of Alexandria' (*MS Notes*). This is evidently the extent of Starkie's contribution to the following passage.

Page 100

'superlatively good liars'. Hyde's addition.

'a beautiful British general'. General Alec Godley (*MS Notes*). Major General Sir Alex Godley, K.C.M.G., C.B., General Officer Commanding N.Z.E.F.

'"Not half living up to his reputation."' 'Living up to his name' (*MS Notes*). Suppressing Godley's name has ruined the joke.

The raiding of the Tommies' beer canteen. Hyde has this story slightly wrong: 'Tommies used to come for beer. N.Z. beer ran out. Tommies wouldn't stand any. Night came. Tommy canteen raided, four barrels taken. 4th Brigade Aussies helped/1st Brigade in quarantine with yellow jack', *MS Notes*.

Page 101

'Came also the General'. In the *MS Notes* he is accompanied by Lady Godley. Aitken (p.19), notes that the Otagos were reviewed by General Godley at Lemnos on 7 November 1915.

'Otago Fourth'. '1st Battalion Otago', *MS Notes*.

'continual drill parade'. '14 days second field' (*MS Notes*). '. . . pay forfeit, sleeping under guard and the performance of such fatigues and pack drills as could be crammed into the day. . . . a diet of water and biscuit. Worse, he would not be allowed to smoke during any of the twenty-eight days' punishment', Winter, p. 43.

Page 102

'the weather went mad'. The 'famous November blizzard, which must have hastened the date of Evacuation by proving that it was impossible to live on Gallipoli during the winter months. It fell on the night of 26th November', Aitken, p.29.

'heavy artillery . . . from Austria'. 'a report went about that the Turks were bringing up 10-inch howitzers to drop shells at a steep angle into our trenches and gullies. . . . We were set to work constructing deep dug-outs, large square vaults described as H. E. Shelters (but promptly named "funk holes")', Aitken, p.33.

Pages 102–04

Evacuation of Gallipoli. It took two tries to get Otago evacuated. After spending most of the night moving down to North Beach, the Battalion had to turn back and await the evening of 14 December. 'This second attempt ran without a hitch. We filed down without casualties, and along the beach by Fisherman's Hut to the pier' (Aitken, p.38). It seems unlikely that the Maori Pioneer Corps sang '*waiatas*' since silence was crucial and one of the Otagos was killed in the first attempt and a number of men sustained slight wounds. It is true however that the Maori contingent moved out with the Otago Battalion, Waite, p.280.

Page 103

'A New Zealand captain'. Captain Broughton (*MS Notes*). Capt. E. R. M. Broughton.

Page 105

Ismailia. They camped half way between Ismailia and the small village of Nefisha, a site that later became Moaskar Camp.

Ferry Post. 'north of Ismailia and on the eastern side of the Suez Canal, where it debouches into Lake Timsah', Aitken, pp.51–52.

'game of drill . . . . The big boats'. Thirty lines cut from *MS B-10* concern the response from the Australian and the New Zealand guard when not apparently noticed during inspection by the Prince of Wales.

Page 106

'our M.O.'. Dr Paigent (*MS Notes*); probably a mishearing for Dr Baigent. Captain C. V. A. Baigent, Otago Medical Officer.

Page 108

'shortages made up . . . . At Ismailia'. Nineteen lines cut from *MS B-10* concern an inspection by Sir Alexander Godley and his wife who appears rather foolish. This was presumably the occasion noted by Aitken (p.54) when Godley announced that they were going to France.

Page 109

'Everyone . . . was a Gallipoli veteran'. The greater part of the First Battalion Otago went aboard the *Franconia* on 6 April (Byrne, p.81). 'By no means all who went aboard were Gallipoli veterans' (Downie Stewart, review of *Passport to Hell*, *Otago Daily Times*, 4 July, 1936). Starkie had not said so—it was Hyde's phrase. They had been joined by the 7th Reinforcements, Byrne, p.78.

'a king of their own'. Presumably a reference to Amenhotep IV (or Iknaten) who ascended the throne of Egypt c. 1375 B.C., put aside the warlike aspects of his rule and devoted himself to changing the balance of Egypt's religion from polytheism to monotheism. There was a violent reaction to his policies after his death. All of these comments are Hyde's, not Starkie's.

Page 110

'Boche submarine'. Submarines were active in the Mediterranean at this time and Aitken (p.55) records a scare on the voyage but does not mention a submarine in harbour.

'fourteen stone'. 'fifteen', *MS Notes*.

Page 111

Morbecque. Moerbeke in the text, which was in the middle of Belgium, half way between Antwerp and Ghent in German occupied territory. Hyde may have looked it up and found Moerbeke and since it was in Flanders assumed it would do. Morbecque was in France, half way between Hazebrouck and Steenbecque (H. Stewart, *The New Zealand Division, 1916–19*, 1921, p.20). The journey has been expanded by Hyde and certainly did not take seven days but Starkie may have broken it up with stops.

Page 112

'for nothing . . . . Having something'. Thirteen lines omitted from *MS B-10* concern Downie Stewart—how he paid the Battalion out of his own pocket when pay was stopped, and his parliamentary career after the War.

'along in kegs . . . . In clear July'. Fifteen lines cut from *MS B-10* on the difficulties of fraternizing with the 'mademoiselles' because of their seriousness and domesticity.

July 'route marches to Armentières'. The 1st Battalion moved from Morbecque to Estaires on 9 May. The march took four and a half hours, the distance was thirteen and a half miles and no one fell out (Aitken, p.63). Stark has misled Hyde; he makes it into a journey of fifty miles in two days.

Pat Johnston. Thompson, *MS Notes*.

Page 113

'talking . . . of Sedan'. Hyde is no doubt referring to the terrible battle around Sedan, August–September 1870, in which the French Army was defeated by a much larger German force and Sedan capitulated.

Page 114

Arrantes. There is no Arrantes between Morbecque and Estaires; Starkie does not seem to have remembered this journey well.

Page 115

'At 11.30 . . . early autumn'. Aitken (p.66) notes arriving at 'dusk'; and it was spring—13 May, Byrne, p.88.

Page 116

'fourteen miles away'. An exaggeration: the front line was two to two and a half miles from Armentières, Aitken, p.60.

Page 117

'Parapet Joe'. 'This enemy machine-gunner, with his fine judgement of elevation, went by the nickname of "Parapet Joe"; in the front line he had the height of the parapet to an inch and was able to cut the bags along an arc of 200 or 300 yards; sometimes he would make his spray of bullets switch suddenly back, to catch any unwary head', Aitken, p.71.

Bob Phayre. Fife, *MS Notes*.

Pages 119–20

'brick convent'. Probably 'the Hospice Mahieu, an almost deserted charitable institution which still sheltered a few old men and several devoted Soêurs de Charité, one being Irish and thus able to interpret' (Aitken, p.67). It does not seem to have been used as 'battalion headquarters'.

Page 120

'fool of an officer . . . woke the Germans'. Starkie mentions an officer and, separately, the Third Australians (presumably the 3rd Brigade of the Australian forces). Hyde has conflated them. The First Battalion Otago went into the front line for the first time on 21 May 1916, Byrne, p.93.

minenwerfer. 'The German "Minenwerfer" was a heavy trench mortar which flung projectiles of the size of a small oil drum', O. E. Burton, *The Silent Division*, 1935, p.149.

Page 121

'all Blighty ones'. A 'blighty one' was a wound sufficiently serious to take the sufferer back to England.

Page 122

'in the evenings . . . . Out of the blue'. Sixteen lines omitted from *MS B-10* concern the capture of a German prisoner by Starkie's group 'the Wet Party'. The implication is that Colonel Charters sent them out to get rid of them.

'commanding officer'. Colonel Charters, *MS Notes*.

Page 123

'The Second Auckland crowd . . . cut to bits in Seventy-Seven Trench'. It was the 1st Auckland Battalion and the attack occurred in the trench systems of 74, 75, and 76 on 3 July (Burton, p.150–1). Otago 1st was to have relieved the Auckland Battalion on the night of 3–4 July, but because the relief was postponed twenty-four hours, Otago avoided the fate of Auckland (Byrne, pp.100–01). Aitken describes coming in after the attack, pp.90–91.

'never came back . . . . Since the company'. Twelve lines omitted from *MS B-10* concern the training of a raiding party and the calling off of the raid.

Page 125

'fifteen days' probation'. '21 days', *MS Notes*.

Pages 125–6

'next fifteen years . . . . Starkie was wrong'. Twelve lines omitted from *MS B-10* are concerned with a letter Starkie endeavoured to smuggle out saying that he would 'have two legs and two arms . . . while some of those bastards are pushing up the daisies'. The letter was intercepted. In Starkie's account the death of Charlie Dunsterville (Duncan) occurs before the writing of the letter and is presumably the reason for it, *MS Notes*.

Page 126

'crucifixion'. Field punishment number one: 'A man here might be exposed in public, handcuffed to a waggon wheel and spreadeagled for two hours daily', Winter, p.43.

Page 127

Knocking Jackie MacKenzie out incident. Jackie is not knocked out but told 'he'd get a b-good hiding', *MS Notes*.

'Otago Fourth were the driving wedge'. 'Under the prearranged plan scouts and parapet party were to move out from the sally-port 45 minutes before zero hour and the flanking parties fifteen minutes before that time, and take up their positions in shell-holes with the object of protecting the flanks in the event of a counter-raid. The scouts were then to return and lead out the remainder of the raiding party to a concealed position in front of and distant 150 yards from the line to be assaulted. Our artillery was to open with a slow rate of fire 10 minutes before zero, at which moment artillery and trench mortars were to open with full intensity over the enemy's trenches and wire entanglements. Twenty minutes later the trench mortars were to direct their fire against the flanking trenches, while that of the artillery was to be lifted, thereby forming a semi-circular barrage round the area to be assaulted. Scouts and parapet party were then to rush forward, the scouts' duty being to ascertain the condition of the wire, return and lead the raiders through the gaps. The parapet party was to cross the enemy's trench and bomb suspected shelters in rear, while the assaulting parties were to work along the trench itself in four different sections. . . . The 8th (Southland) Company was to provide a patrol to cover the right flank of the raiding party, the 10th (North Otago) Company acting similarly in respect of the left flank', Byrne, pp.101–02.

Page 128

'two hundred and eighty men'. 'The personnel of the raiding party, all told, comprised six officers and 175 other ranks' (Byrne, p.101). The casualties were:-

killed: 4 officers and 31 other ranks; wounded: 4 officers and 118 other ranks; reported missing: 6 other ranks, Byrne, p.103.

Page 129

Jimmy Peters. Petrie, *MS Notes*.

Alec Payle. Bayley, *MS Notes*.

Norman White. Black, *MS Notes*.

Page 130

'Baldur the beautiful is dead'. The closest I can find to this line is from Sydney Dobell's poem on Balder: 'My Beautiful, my Beautiful/Thou art slain, Thou art slain', *Poetical Works*, 1875, vol.II, p.278.

Pages 130–1

Death of Jackie MacKenzie. 'saw a white face looking at the sky. Found his little pal, Jackie. Searching for his wound, find he has a bullet through the heart—dead. Carried him back & left him in his dugout. Another maxim took up the song—got it for Jackie [. . .] Took Jackie on shoulder & walked the seven miles to Armentières to an old French undertaker. Had him put in a coffin, taken to the public cemetery & buried. Borrowed camera & took photograph of grave. Arrested for being in possession of camera . . . ', *MS Notes*.

Pages 130–3

Starkie's part in raid after disappearance of Jackie. Aitken had also been part of the raid—in 10th Company—and had observed Starkie: 'Private S——, a more or less permanent inmate of the clink (not for moral faults but from a congenital recalcitrance to discipline), had asked to be given some remission of punishment by taking part in the raid. He was wounded, but went back over the parapet at least a dozen times, bringing in a wounded man each time, and at dawn had to be restrained by main force—a hot-tempered and impulsive man—from going out again. His sentence was remitted; a decoration, in the circumstances, would hardly have been appropriate, but he received mention in Divisional Orders' (Aitken, p.104). Starkie remembered bringing in 16 (*MS Notes*). Another account put it at 11: 'Then came the high-light of the raid. As we entered the trench midst a hail of bullets came Jack Stark with a badly wounded man on his shoulder. He laid him at the doctor's feet as gently as a kitten. Backward and forward he continued carrying them so easily. We were too busy at the time to note how many he brought in, but later we ascertained that it was eleven. Jack did not return to us that night but cleaned up a machine gun crew that had caused a lot of casualties', 'J.H.', Ranui (letter cited by Moreton in *A Parson in Prison*, by Melville Harcourt, p. 227). Downie Stewart also remembered the raid: 'The events recorded as having happened in the trenches in front of Armentières are substantially correct, and the present writer can testify to the signal bravery displayed by Stark in carrying in the wounded under heavy fire on the occasion of a disastrous raid. But Stark has evidently merged together in one chapter events of different dates, as he was not on this occasion recommended for the V.C., but only notified that his bravery had wiped out a prospective imprisonment of five years, which he had at that time been sentenced to serve after the War', Review of *Passport to Hell*, *Otago Daily Times*, 4 July 1936.

Page 131

'a Major'. Major Carew (*MS Notes*). Can this be Major D. Colquhoun, commanding 14th (South Otago) Company? I cannot find Major Carew.

Page 133

'In the afternoon Colonel Chalmers tramped'. '8 a.m.', *MS Notes*.

Mention of the raid in N.Z. papers and reactions of Starkie's schools. The raid did get into the papers, with some of Starkie's actions, but no mention of his name or V.C. recommendation: 'A private under suspended sentence of five years' penal servitude, behaved with great heroism. He was seen boldly standing up under heavy fire, and repeatedly lifting wounded men over the parapet. His sentence was remitted' (*Otago Daily Times*, 20 July 1916; *Southland Times*, 21 July 1916). Starkie only mentions four schools, not five: 'Claimed by Gladstone School, Park School, Waikiwi and Marist Brothers all claimed him—Belonged to none', *MS Notes*.

Page 134

'back to the estaminet again . . . . Preparations had started'. Ten lines cut from *MS B-10* depict Starkie continuing to drink and Colonel Charters telling him to forget about the V.C.

'Preparations had started'. The British launched the Somme offensive on 1 July 1916. The activities of the New Zealanders and other troops of the Second Army were to keep the Germans occupied and prevent them from withdrawing troops to strengthen the line in the Somme.

Page 135

'They got their kits together'. The Second Battalion Otago was relieved by the Black Watch on 17 August and the Regiment was clear of the line after a three-month occupation of the Armentières sector. On 2 September after a period of training, the Regiment moved off toward the Somme.

'Morval in the lower Somme'. Starkie's memory is at fault. Morval, at this stage, was in the hands of the enemy and indeed was the object of a proposed Fourth Army attack (leaving Armentières and moving to the Somme the New Zealand Division had passed from the Second Army under General Plumer to the Fourth Army under General Rawlinson).

'the crack of the guns . . . . Somme became'. Seventeen lines cut from *MS B-10* deal with the meeting between the 'Tommies' and the New Zealanders, an inspection by General Godley resulting in three days' C.B. for Starkie for being unshaven, and an addition by Hyde where Starkie asks to join the Maori pioneers and is refused by Colonel Charters who wishes to retain his 'black sheep'.

Page 136

'rotting corpses'. Aitken does not mention rotting corpses.

'carried his own cross'. No mention of this in *MS Notes*.

Pages 136–8
Time spent with George. 'saw George for the last time. . . . Couple of days together . . . All right untill leaving. Broken up when going away', *MS Notes*.

Page 138
'the Donkey Mob'. Veterinary Corps.

'the first warning of the Somme offensive'. 'On September 16th a dirty grey dawn. Drizzling rain—Trenches full of thousands of men. At 6 a.m. the guns break out in the first stages of Somme' (*MS Notes*). As Hyde corrected it, it was 15 September, but it was fine (Byrne, p.118). It was certainly not the 'first warning of the Somme offensive'; that had commenced in July, but it was the beginning of the 'second phase', marked by technical innovations like the tank (John Buchan, *The Battle of the Somme: Second Phase*, Nelson, N. D. pp.10–11). The tanks were not 'gifted with uncanny swiftness': 'Their pace was not more than on average 33 yards per minute, or 15 yards per minute over badly shelled ground' (Stewart, p.72). The men themselves endowed the tanks with mysterious powers: 'About noon [13th September] a curious rumour began to circulate, of armoured cars with caterpillar wheels; such marvellous powers were attributed to these that at first the matter was dismissed without consideration. Scepticism was shaken when a few officers, N.C.O.s, and men were given permits to visit a group of these "tanks"', Aitken, p.130.

Page 139
'advance fifteen minutes after'. Starkie does not provide this detail. 'The 8 companies moved abreast in 4 waves about 50 yards behind each other. Each wave was made up of 8 platoons in single rank, some 3 yards separating man from man. The advance was marked by admirable direction pace and alignment. . . . Trudging up the hill, the men hugged the barrage which lifted 50 yards a minute. They twice knelt down in the shellholes to let it precede, firing as they knelt at the machine guns in Crest Trench', Stewart, p.73.

Pages 139–40
Discovery of George's body. 'Worked and cried at the same time. Had him buried. Closed paybook in the breech of his rifle stood rifle at grave' (*MS Notes*). Starkie could have had a shovel: 'Fastened down the centre of every other man's back was a shovel or pick', Stewart, p.72.

Page 140
'Starkie emptied his revolver'. Starkie does not mention a revolver and as a private he would not normally have possessed one.

Pages 141–2
'the Otago bombers'. 'The work accomplished on this morning by our bombers . . . was of a very gallant order. The enemy resorted to volley firing, and in addition to being more liberally supplied with bombs, had the advantage of position on the high ground. However, our party succeeded in accomplishing its task of establishing and maintaining a block, notwithstanding the fact that every bomber of the Battalion who had been engaged had become a casualty' (Byrne, p.125). It is no doubt the struggle of 20 September in which the Black

Watch were involved that Starkie remembered: 'The handful of Black Watch bombers, who had not yet been reinforced, were driven back down Drop Alley, and the enemy swarmed round and in rear of our left flank. . . . In this soldiers' battle many gallant deeds were done of which no record survives', Stewart, p.94.

Page 142
'the Scotties had been twenty-one '. It is clear that the 'twenty-one' are Otago reinforcements: '21 went along—Started to bomb the Hun . . . Scotties down to a very few men' (*MS Notes*). Starkie wrote out another account of this incident for Hyde, which is slightly different: 'along Comes a Black Watch Colonel. he looks at us. and says. Good work men. for 7 long Hours we had been Holding Him: we started with 14 Bombers of our own. and 12. Black watch we finished with 4 men. Charles Frew, *the Drone* or *Sleepy Charlie* was His Handle amongst the Boys. & 1 Black Watch Bomber. The Colonel now takes are names & Regiments. A Kelleher. C. Frew, A McGregor, BW. & my own. and tells us we will be Releaved Right away as we need Food & Rest. & He is going to see we get. it He Had not gone far. when we all Ducked and Whish Bang He got the Colonel. that one Screaming Shell. and killed Him. He said you will all be Recomended & Some one Sang *Tell me the Old Old Story*', Stark MS with *MS Notes*.

Page 143
'first Somme took up twenty-four days'. Not the first Somme offensive. 'On 3 and 4 October the New Zealanders were relieved and went back. They had been fighting for twenty-three consecutive days', Burton, p.179.

The attack of September 25. The attack of the 25th went smoothly and successfully (Byrne, p.129). Starkie seems to be remembering the disastrous attack of 27 September.

'three quarters of a mile advance'. A map (Aitken, p.150) indicates an advance of about 700 yards. Three-quarters of a mile would have been a considerable advance.

Death of 'Bill Howard'. Lieutenant Bill Howden (Stark MS), died of wounds, mentioned in despatches (Byrne, p.406). This was also the attack (27 September) in which Aitken received the wound that took him out of the War. His comments on the horror as he crawled back show the difficulty in writing of war: 'The road here and the ground to either side were strewn with bodies, some motionless, some not. Cries and groans, prayers, imprecations, reached me. I leave it to the sensitive imagination; I once wrote it all down, only to discover that horror, truthfully described, weakens to the merely clinical' (Aitken, p.171). 'The 1st Battalion's attack against the Gird system of trenches and along Goose Alley on September 27th unquestionably represented the Regiment's most bitter and costly experience on the Somme. When the Battalion marched out of the line on the night of the 28th it was reduced to a strength of 113, which was considerably below that of a company', Byrne, pp.132–3.

Sergeant Mason. The gold-mining detail is Hyde's. Sergeant James Mason, Sixth Reinforcements, Otago Infantry Battalion.

Page 144
'a New Zealand Colonel'. Presumably Captain James Hargest who commanded

the 10th Company and assumed command of the remnant of the four shattered Otago Companies. He was awarded the M.C. 'Harcus got a military cross. Mason about 6 foot 1—good athlete, wrestler, never got a mention', *MS Notes*.

'marched back to Mametz Wood'. The first Battalion of Otago was moved to Mametz Wood on 29 September. 'Forest blown to pieces—not a decent tree standing up . . . In the wood thousands of dead, Germans, Australians, Tommies of all brigades. Death had taken the wood', *MS Notes*.

'Mametz Wood . . . . For a while'. Thirteen lines cut from *MS B-10* concern a lecture from Colonel Charters to the few survivors on the Otago tradition of bravery. There is a cynical suggestion that calling for cheers for the Colonel earned a sergeant the military medal.

Page 145

'Starkie's company was moved'. The Otago Regiment marched out of the Somme Battlefield on 3 October 1916, the 1st Battalion moving to Pommiers Redoubt and the 2nd Battalion to Base Camp at Fricourt. After a few days the 1st Battalion and the 2nd Battalion were both moved on by stages, the 1st to billets near Bac St Maur and the 2nd to Armentières, Byrne, pp.142–3.

Pages 145–6

Discovery of the underground field hospital. 'Everyone dead—Red Cross nurses, doctors, sitting & lying, just as if asleep—all dead—all dead, all dead, all dead, all dead'. *MS Notes*.

Page 146

'how they had died. . . . He gathered up'. Nine lines cut from *MS B-10* has Hyde describing a dead German nurse and her luxuriant hair, a piece of gratuitous horror.

Huie Goodyear. Goodlet, *MS Notes*.

Page 147 ff.

Incident of hitting Canterbury corporal. 'Starkie punched corporal returned to billets', *MS Notes*.

Page 148

'tunnelling below Messines Ridge'. It had been decided by the Allies that the capture of the Messines-Wytschaete Ridge was necessary for the overall strategy of the Western Front in the early part of 1917. 'Along the original Second Army front there were 24 mines, which had involved the driving of 8,000 yards of galleries' (Byrne, p.170). 'So far did individuals become removed from their own units that it is related that on more than one occasion, a Canadian tunneller emerging after a relief had taken place on the surface, was suspected by the relieving troops of being a deserter', G. W. L. Nicholson, *Canadian Expeditionary Force 1914–1919*, Ottawa, 1962, p.501.

Page 149

'Y.M.C.A. near Green Camp'. I have been unable to trace Green Camp as an aerodrome. Starkie's account to Murphy calls it 'the Canadian Headquarters', but I have no evidence of this. Perhaps Starkie confused it with

'Green Dump' a large supply dump in the rear of the Longueval-Bazentin road, Stewart, p.89.

Page 150
'a handle of beer . . . . One evening'. Eight lines cut from *MS B-10* deal with the man in charge of the tunnelling job, Captain Bevis, and the advantages of Bailleul for relaxation.

Page 151
'twisted flesh . . . . Birthday farm'. Eighteen lines cut from *MS B-10* deal with Starkie's account of the capture of a large German prisoner and the destruction of the man using him as a screen to snipe from.

'Birthday Farm . . . where Sam Frickleton got his V.C.' About 700 yards ahead of the British lines towards the Messines-Wytschaete road (map, Byrne, p.161). 'The "London Gazette" of August 2 announces the award of the Victoria Cross to 6/2133 L.Cpl. Samuel Frickleton, NZ Infy. Although slightly wounded Frickleton dashed forward at the head of his section, pushed into our barrage and personally destroyed with bombs a machine gun and crew which was causing heavy casualties. He then attacked a second gun, killing the whole of the crew of twelve . . . Lance Cpl. Frickleton who is a miner in civil life, gained his V.C. at the capture of Messines on June 7 last', *Chronicles of the N.Z.E.F.*, vol.II, no.24, 8 August 1917, p.277.

Page 152
'ten years' penal servitude'. The acount Starkie gave to Murphy has only 'two years Hard Labour'.

Page 153
'automatic lying about'. Not in the account to Murphy.

'aerial free-for-all'. 'At this period enemy night-flying aeroplanes were active and frequently dropped bombs over the billeting area', Byrne, p.249.

Page 155
Ginger Crombie. Riley, *MS B-10.*

Page 157
'shot drill'. 'An obsolete form of military punishment in which the soldier punished had to carry a cannon-ball', *O.E.D.*

Sergeant Jackson. Johnson, *MS B-10.*

'early Victorian gaols . . . . When Starkie'. Ten lines cut from *MS B-10* deal with the fact that the treadmill and the crank were used on the dregs of London while the men oppressed here were fine soldiers.

Page 158
'The chance never came . . . . The men'. Eight lines omitted from *MS B-10* concern a visiting General who, when he learns Starkie is a New Zealander orders that he be taken from solitary confinement and put back with his fellow prisoners.

Page 159

'world his enemy . . . . "I'm going"'. Nineteen lines cut from *MS B-10* concern colour prejudice, which exists in New Zealand in spite of not being supposed to, the Maoris being treated as domestic pets, and whites' continuing oppression of blacks.

Page 160

Starkie smashing thumb with hammer. In the Murphy version Starkie slashes his hand with a piece of glass.

Page 161

'twelve-foot wall'. '8 ft wall' in Murphy.

'sprained ankle'. He twists his ankle prior to climbing the wall in Murphy.

Page 162

'eighteen francs'. '10 francs', *MS Notes*.

Page 163

'helped himself to . . . automatic'. 'never took automatic pistol or money but took tobacco' (*MS Notes*). Took 'A big automatic fully loaded', Murphy account.

Page 164

'The Negro Labour Corps'. 'African Labour Corps', *MS Notes*.

Pages 164–5

Escape by swimming incident. 'Frozen & frightened—Lay on back, took a blind guess at boat's direction. Swam there for ½ hour—finally struck the other boat', *MS Notes*.

Page 168

'Apaches'. 'a band of robbers and assassins in and around Paris and other European cities' (*O.E.D.*). Not in *MS Notes*.

'superfluous cop problem . . . . There were some Yankees'. Ten lines cut from *MS B-10* deal with living in Paris on the run.

Page 169

'Fritzie broke through at Bapaume'. The German break-through at Bapaume occurred on 21 March 1918 (Stewart, pp.336ff.), but Starkie had already returned to the Otago Battalion in February; see note below for p.174.

Page 170

Dick Simmonds. Hunt, *MS Notes*.

Bob McCullogh. Duncan McKechnie, *MS Notes*.

'kept in . . . compounds like the V.D. men'. This is a detail added by Hyde and touches on General Richardson's belated effort to control the disease among the members of the N.Z. Division in England. 'He had every available officer preaching incessantly at the men. "Irrigation huts" were established in each camp. An early set of Routine Orders laid down that all who had been exposed to infection must present themselves within 24 hours for treatment either in camp or at certain hospitals in London. To become infected after failing to do this was to be guilty of disobedience. Those convalescents who persisted in breaking out of hospital were "enclosed in a high barbed wire fence"' (P. S. O'Connor, 'Venus and the Lonely Kiwi: The War Effort of Miss Ettie A. Rout', *New Zealand Journal of History*, vol.1, no.1, 1967, p.24). The Australians had issued 'preventives' to men going on leave from 1916, but General Richardson, O'Connor writes, 'shared the official New Zealand horror of this—it "would be tantamount to encouraging immorality"—and thereby bears his portion of responsibility for thousands of cases of infection which, as he later came to realise, could have been avoided'.

Page 171
'brought home seven'. 'They broke out one night—given job of chasing them' (*MS Notes*). Hyde has written 'given' so that it looks like 'seven'.

Page 173
Colonel Hardy. Harcus (*MS Notes*); presumably Hargest.

Page 174
Sergeant Major Stevens and 'killing a man in cold blood'. Stevenson (*MS Notes*). No doubt this is the incident reported by Byrne: 'During the night of the 19th–20th [February 1918] a successful raiding operation was accomplished by the 1st Battalion. The party committed to the task comprised 30 other ranks from 4th Company, under the command of 2nd-Lieut. W. O'Connell . . . . The objective was a portion of the enemy's line at the northern edge of Juniper Wood, including the derelict tank and "pill-box" previously referred to . . . . The derelict tank was reached and surrounded, and five of the enemy secured as prisoners, but one of them was immediately shot by Pte. Stark, who was not officially one of the raiding party'. Byrne, pp.269–70.

'Charlie Frane sings out'. 'Charlie Frame points out wounded man crawling away—Starkie harpooned him with bayonet'. *MS Notes*.

'When did the poison gas . . . . go on with it'. These two sentences replace thirty-three lines from *MS B-10* concerning Starkie's reception back in the trenches by Lieutenant Freed and Colonel Charters—astonishment with grudging admiration.

Pages 175–6
Episode with Val and Blanche. 'Got uniform went straight down to see Val and Blanche. Arrived there 3.30 a.m. Stopped there all night—Shortly afterwards they went to Paris and he never saw them again', *MS Notes*.

Page 178
'It's strange . . . brewers turn out . . . fat.' This sentence replaces ten lines in *MS B-10* of unnecessary jocular explanation of why God made brewers fat.

Page 180
'This place's haunted . . . . Living in a brewery'. Twenty-six lines cut from

MS B-10 deal with Starkie taking some bottles of wine back to his mates, having it confiscated, then returning for a kerosene tin of the wine the Maori had drowned in.

Page 181

Alec Suter. Soper, *MS Notes*.

'heard that tale before . . . . A hand of poker'. Twelve lines cut from *MS B-10* deal with the effort to stop a fire spreading in the ammunition dump and an officer recognizing Starkie.

'"Colonel Chalmers says ten days' leave"'. Colonel Charters had been evacuated suffering from the effects of gas poisoning on 7 March 1918 (Byrne, p.271) and had not returned when this incident took place.

Page 182

'"I'll kill the sniper"'. 'Two mins after sent Peter Race after him to tell Freed Starkie will kill him for a cup of rum', *MS Notes*.

'nobody's soldier . . . . But it's easier'. Fifteen lines cut from *MS B-10* include eleven lines from Alan Seeger's poem 'Rendezvous'—see note 3 for p.184.

Jackie Kearney. Jack McGregor, *MS Notes*.

'I'm off now! . . . Three thousand'. Six lines omitted from *MS B-10* describe Starkie's dash back to the trenches to write letters to mother and girlfriend.

Pages 182–4

Duel with the sniper. The incident occurred in early June 1918. On 1 June, 1st Battalion Otago relieved 2nd Battalion Canterbury in the La Signy Farm sector. 'The opening days of the 1st Battalion's tour in the line were quiet and the weather perfect. Frequent daylight reconnaissances of the enemy's lines were being carried out by Pte. Stark, until when single-handed he rushed an enemy post near La Signy Farm and was grievously wounded; his adventurous career thus abruptly terminating for a time at least' (Byrne, p.298). 'He shot Starkie at range of 6 yards clean through chest—He got Starkie, lifted right off feet with the blow, as Starkie fell he threw the bomb into the hole with him. Both won—Sniper blown out of hole', *MS Notes*.

Page 184

Peter Macy, Mick McGrath, Tim . . . O'Dorman. Peter Race, Mick McGrath, Tim O'Gorman, *MS Notes*.

'"It's curtains, Starkie."' 'Captain (Dr) Pryor—Looked him over, said three words. Good bye Starkie' (*MS Notes*). Seven lines cut from *MS B-10* following this sentence deal with the responses as he is carried in: 'Is that the Outlaw? Isn't he dead yet?'

'I have a rendezvous with death'. The opening line of a famous World War I poem that begins 'I have a rendezvous with Death / At some disputed barricade . . .' by Alan Seeger, killed in action in 1916, *Up The Line to Death: The War Poets 1914–1918*, ed. Gardner, 1964, p.32.

Page 185

'Rest, rest on Mother's breast . . .'. From the lullaby 'Sweet and Low' from Tennyson's *The Princess*, II, 456–71, *Poems*, ed. Buckley, 1958, p.141.

Page 187

Sister Froude. Roode, *MS Notes*.

Page 188

'Big Fitz the tunneller, and Jim Turner'. 'Fitzpatrick . . . Turnbull', *MS Notes*.

Page 189

'"Cattleyas" . . . a delicate pinkish spray'. 'Cattle-eyes' in the text; Hyde did not correct it though she wrote to John A. Lee: 'By the way I tried to be luscious and lavish with the nicest girl in the book so gave her a spray of very expensive orchids—cattleyas—trailing misty pink over her shoulder. Somebody once gave me a spray, and I never quite got over it, so passed the idea on. But the publishers settled any tendency to be lavish, once for all, by spelling it cattle-eyes with a hyphen', Letter of 29 May 1936, held by Auckland Public Library.

Page 190

'"This is what you said."' 'I'm a — if I will die', *MS Notes*.

Page 191

'sulked like Ajax'. Hyde seems confused; it was Achilles who, after he surrendered Briseis to Agamemnon, retired to his tent and refused to take any further part in the war against Troy.

'"Getting on for nineteen."' He was 24.

Haroun-al-Raschid. A favourite literary figure for Hyde, see the letters to J. H. E. Schroder, Turnbull Library.

Page 192

End of Chapter 17. The final three pages—some sixty-six lines—of this chapter have been cut from *MS B-10*. They are an attempt to bring Hyde herself into the narrative and relate how four years earlier when very sick she had been told that she must have a night nurse. The woman was faded, unattractive and inadequate—unable to keep awake—Hyde disliked her. She had nursed at Brockenhurst during the war and been called Sunshine. Why, wondered Hyde had she been brought to New Zealand 'already overflowing with unemployed and sexually unemployed, female as well as male'. Surely, she thought, she couldn't be Starkie's Sunshine, who, like all the women who nursed in those long wards deserved happiness and beauty.

Page 193

'the General'. General Richardson (*MS Notes*). Brig.-General G. S. Richardson, Commandant New Zealand Troops in England.

Page 194

Sling Camp. The New Zealand Training Depot on the Salisbury Plain in England, Byrne, pp.393ff.

Page 195
'see the *Rosary*'. The most likely play seems to be E. E. Rose's *The Rosary*, first produced 30/6/1913. See Allardyce Nicoll's Handlist of plays 1900–1930 in his *English Drama 1900–1930*, 1973.

'Juniper berries is what these old London girls go for'. Juniper berries are used in making gin.

Page 197
'August, 1917'. Starkie's chronology is confused; if this leave is after Le Havre and the wounding, it is well into 1918.

Page 198
'there's a chap in the office'. 'MacKenzie used to give stamp', *MS Notes*.

'The signature of the Captain'. 'Capt. Bevis's signature forged', *MS Notes*.

'the General came up'. General Richardson, *MS Notes*.

Page 200
'but you ought to see New Zealand'. This phrase replaces two pages—about fifty-three lines—in *MS B-10* of fragmentary further adventures while absent without leave, dodging the 'Red-Headed Wonder' and the Military Police.

Page 202
Incident with the Provost-Marshal. 'Arrive, some limping, some hopping,—Starkie nose bleeding no buttons on tunic & face scratched. Met Provost Marshal', *MS Notes*.

'most conservative club in Auckland'. 'Pacific Club', *MS Notes*.

Page 203
Major Withers. McClymont (*MS Notes*). Major, later Lt.-Col. J. B. McClymont, originally 2nd in Command Otago Battalion, in Command Otago Reserve Battalion at Sling Camp 1916–March 1917 and again August–December 1918.

'"Hell—! All O.K. elsewhere?"' 'Jesus. O.K. down below?' *MS Notes*.

Sergeant James. Ned Jean, *MS Notes*.

Page 204
'Royal Irish'. Royal Irish Rifles, *MS Notes*.

'Shang, Boozey Bill, Jimmy Daws, Bill Turner, Dick Hunter'. 'Shang Watson, Boozy Bill Goodlet, Jim Doyle, Bill Turnbull, Dick Hunt', *MS Notes*.

Art Butter. Arthur Butts, *MS Notes*.

'some God-forsaken little spot'. Ballyhooley, *MS Notes*.

Page 206
Lark Hill. Larkhill was another military camp nearby, between Bulford and Bustard Camp, formerly used by the Canadians (Nicholson, p.36) and in 1917 by the Otago Reinforcements, Byrne, p.396.

'grab hold of . . . . A roll-call'. Twenty-nine lines removed from *MS B-10* show Starkie in a different light—defusing an attempt to loot the camp store run by an old Jew and his two daughters. Starkie's account of this is in the *MS Notes.*

Page 207

Beginning of Chapter 19. Eighteen introductory lines omitted from *MS B-10* concern the fact that Jack Johnson the great boxer had had his training camp at Etaples, and that a ruined cathedral where the New Zealanders were billeted was supposed to have stored £17,000 of gold which the French removed.

'sodden khaki and field-grey . . . . Jack Benshaw'. Twenty-two lines cut from *MS B-10* concern the use of gas masks and the horrible fate of a young soldier who did not take a gas warning seriously and didn't put on his mask.

Pages 207–08

Jack Benshaw incident. Hyde has expanded on just one line: 'Firing party for photographs of girls who knew nothing', *MS Notes.*

Page 208

'Seventeen days before the Armistice'. At 11 a.m. on 11 November 1918 hostilities on the Western Front were suspended under terms dictated by the Allies. Starkie is probably referring to the operations of 23 and 24 October. 'The two Armies, the Third and Fourth, were simultaneously to continue the great sweep east and north-eastwards on the 23rd . . . . The 1st Battalion of Otago and the 2nd Battalion of Canterbury, disposed from right to left, were selected to open the Brigade's attack' (Byrne, p.365). There was strong opposition and Starkie may have been one of those casualties in 8th Company caused by shellfire (Byrne, p.366). Overall, in a very successful and important operation, the Battalion lost: 'Killed one officer and seven other ranks; wounded—two officers and 54 other ranks', and captured: '204 prisoners, 14 machine guns, and one 77mm. field gun' (Byrne, p.369).

'Starkie . . . landed his Iron Cross'. 'Hun with Iron Cross dived [?] under his coat—Starkie shot him', *MS Notes.*

Pages 208–09

'Four German prisoners jolted . . . his stretcher'. Curiously, the section in Byrne describing the events of 23–24 October has a photograph of 'German Prisoners carrying out Wounded', opposite p.368. See front cover of this edition.

Page 210

Walton-on-Thames. No. 2 New Zealand General Hospital was situated at Walton-on-Thames.

'a Major from Taranaki'. Major Holmes (*MS Notes*). This must be Lt.-Col. G. Home C.B.E., O i/c Surgical Div. No. 2 N.Z. General Hospital.

Page 211

Paddy Mahoney. Maloney, *MS Notes.*

Page 212

'two bottles . . . brandy and one of stout'. 'two bottles Three Star & Four of Stout', *MS Notes*.

'On Christmas Eve they sailed'. The *Marama* left London 19/12/18, Stüdholme, *N.Z.E.F. Record*, 1928, p.378.

'Maoris had contracted Bright's Disease'. It is very difficult to ascertain from the *MS Notes* whether Bright's Disease refers to the Maoris or the natives at Colon; the latter appears more likely: 'Four men with crutches fought back howling mob—Rescued by Spanish police, keeping white mule all the while—nine out of ten had Bright's disease, eyes all affected—Put down among the Maoris because they took him for one.' Colon was 'notoriously unhealthful', *Encyclopedia Britannica*, 11th ed., 1910, vol.VI.

Passage through Panama. Starkie seems to have reversed the direction of travel. The city of Panama is on the Pacific, while Colon is at the Atlantic entrance to the Panama Canal. The Canal was opened to commercial traffic on 14 August 1914, but not declared formally completed and opened until 12 July 1920.

Page 213

Episode of suicidal soldier. 'Man belonging to medical Corps, 3 days from Auckland, went ashore, for first time had love affair with woman—"goodbye, boys"—went over the side—', *MS Notes*.

Page 214

The last two chapters of *MS B-10*, 'Apres La Guerre' and 'Home was Home Then', thirty-three pages of typescript, were omitted from the final version. In 'Apres La Guerre', Hyde brings the narrative back to her own experience of the War and notes the inadequacy of the country's response to the returning soldiers and the bond the War had created between them. Then we follow Starkie on his almost inevitable drift to prison. In 'Home was Home Then' he marries a Maori and Hyde describes some of their difficulties as well as those of Maoris in general in their own country. After his wife's death Stark appears headed for prison yet again and the work ends where it began with both Hyde and Stark despairing.

Robin Hyde's Published Volumes

FICTION

Passport to Hell; the Story of James Douglas Stark, Bomber, Fifth Regiment, New Zealand Expeditionary Forces, London, Hurst & Blackett 1936, 288pp. Six impressions between April and July 1936. Cheap edition, May 1937.

——, new edition [with revisions], London, Hurst & Blackett, July 1937, 256pp.

Check to Your King; the Life History of Charles, Baron de Thierry, King of Nukahiva, Sovereign Chief of New Zealand, London, Hurst & Blackett 1936. Reprinted 1936, 1937.

——, with an introduction by Joan Stevens, Wellington, Reed 1960.

——, Auckland, Golden Press 1975. Photographic reprint of the 1936 edition.

Wednesday's Children, London, Hurst & Blackett 1937.

Nor the Years Condemn, London, Hurst & Blackett 1938.

——, [photographic reprint] with an introduction by Phillida Bunkle, Linda Hardy, and Jacqueline Matthews, Auckland, New Women's Press 1986.

The Godwits Fly, London, Hurst & Blackett 1938.

——, edited with an introduction by Gloria Rawlinson, Auckland University Press 1970. Reprinted 1974, 1980, 1984, 1985.

OTHER PROSE

Journalese, Auckland, The National Printing Co., 1934.

Dragon Rampant, London, Hurst & Blackett 1939.

——, [photographic reprint] with an introduction by Derek Challis and a critical note by Linda Hardy, Auckland, New Women's Press 1984.

A Home in this World, with an introduction by Derek Challis, Auckland, Longman Paul 1984.

POETRY

The Desolate Star and other poems, Christchurch, Whitcombe & Tombs 1929.

The Conquerors and other poems, London, Macmillan 1935.

Persephone in Winter; poems, London, Hurst & Blackett 1937.

Houses by the Sea and the later poems of Robin Hyde, with an introduction by Gloria Rawlinson, Christchurch, Caxton Press 1952.
Selected Poems, selected and edited [with an introduction] by Lydia Wevers, Auckland, Oxford University Press 1984.

Commentary, Bibliography, and Interpretation (not included above)

James Bertram, 'Robin Hyde, a Reassessment', *Landfall*, September 1953. Reprinted with a Note in *Flight of the Phoenix, Critical Notes on New Zealand Writers*, Wellington, Victoria University Press 1985.
Jennifer Walls, comp., 'A Bibliography of Robin Hyde (Iris Wilkinson) 1906–39', typescript, Wellington, Library School 1960.
Margaret Scott, comp., 'A Supplementary Bibliography of Robin Hyde (Iris Wilkinson) 1906–39', typescript, Wellington, Library School 1966.
Joan Stevens, *The New Zealand Novel, 1860–1965*, 2nd edition, revised, Wellington, Reed 1966.
Gloria Rawlinson, 'Robin Hyde and *The Godwits Fly*', in *Critical Essays on the New Zealand Novel*, ed. Cherry Hankin, Auckland, Heinemann 1976.
Frank Birbalsingh, 'Robin Hyde', *Landfall*, December 1977.
A script for solo performance on Robin Hyde's life, *The Flight of the Godwit*, was written by Bridget Armstrong and performed by her in 1982.
Patrick Sandbrook, 'Robin Hyde: a writer at work', Ph.D. thesis, Massey University, 1985. Includes a descriptive inventory of some of Hyde's manuscripts.
A full-scale biography of Robin Hyde by Gloria Rawlinson is in preparation.

The New Zealand Fiction Series

GEORGE CHAMIER
A South-Sea Siren

ROBIN HYDE
The Godwits Fly

WILLIAM SATCHELL
The Land of the Lost

JANE MANDER
Allen Adair

SYGURD WIŚNIOWSKI
Tikera

MARGARET ESCOTT
Show Down

RODERICK FINLAYSON
Brown Man's Burden
and later stories

FRANK SARGESON
I Saw in my Dream

FRANK S. ANTHONY
Follow the Call

DAN DAVIN
Roads from Home

FRANK S. ANTHONY
Gus Tomlins

A. P. GASKELL
All Part of the Game
stories

JOHN REECE COLE
It Was So Late
and other stories

RODERICK FINLAYSON
Tidal Creek

JEAN DEVANNY
The Butcher Shop

MAURICE DUGGAN
Collected Stories

WILLIAM SATCHELL
The Toll of the Bush

ROBIN HYDE
Passport to Hell

EDITH SEARLE GROSSMANN
The Heart of the Bush
(in preparation)